THE TOWER OF BEOWULF

THE TOWER

OF

BEOWULF

PARKE GODWIN

WILLIAM MORROW AND COMPANY, INC.

New York

It is the policy of William Morrow and Company, Inc.,
and its imprints and affiliates, recognizing the importance of preserving what has been written, to print the
books we publish on acid-free paper, and we exert our
best efforts to that end.

Library of Congress Cataloging-in-Publication Data

Godwin, Parke.
The tower of Beowulf / Parke Godwin.
p.   cm.
ISBN 0-688-12738-X
1. Beowulf—Adaptations.   2. Epic poetry, English
(Old)—Adaptations.   3. Northmen—Fiction.
4. Monsters—Fiction.
I. Title.
PS3557.O316T68   1995
813'.54—dc20   95-20130
                                                    CIP

Printed in the United States of America

2 3 4 5 6 7 8 9 10

BOOK DESIGN BY

JUDITH STAGNITTO-ABBATE

GODS, HALFLINGS, KINGS, THANES, MEN, AND WOMEN OF THE STORY

IN FRISIA:

Father Eligius—a Christian priest, Beowulf's first true friend

OF ASGARD AND THE GODS:

Loki—part god, part giant, all trickster
SIGYN—his halfling daughter
GRENDEL—halfling son of Sigyn and Shild Scefing
Freyr—Vanir, god of fertility
Gerda—of the Utgard race of giants, Freyr's wife
Shild Scefing—their son, later god-king of the Scyldings

OF THE SCYLDINGS AT LEJRE IN DENMARK:

Hrothgar—king of Danes
Weltheow—his queen
Hrethric—their older son and heir
Hrothmund—their younger son
Hrothulf—their nephew, desirous of the crown
Esher—thane and close friend to Hrothgar all his life
Unferth—an exile at Hrothgar's court

OF THE GEATS AT HELSINGBORG IN SOUTHERN SWEDEN:

Hygelac—king of Geats, uncle to Beowulf
Hygd—his queen
Herdred—their son and heir
BEOWULF—son to Edgetho, later king of Geats

Edgetho—brother-in-law to Hygelac

Hondshew—Beowulf's closest companion

Gorm, Ulf, Canute—young boat companions to Beowulf, later of his
    council

INA—wife to Hondshew, later hand-fasted to Beowulf

FATHER JUSTIN—Christian missionary to the Geats, Beowulf's friend

Wiglaf—young cousin to Beowulf, his royal successor

Yan—a Wylfing slave

THE DRAGON

The sixth century. Before men reasoned such things could not be, when all men knew they could.

IF LIGHTNING HAD NOT STRUCK Father Eligius' roof and set the thatch afire, the monk would never have seen the longboat sliding westward through the first light of morning.

The thunderstorm began in the early morning darkness, a few minutes after Eligius rose sleepily for Matins. At the monastery of St. Martin where he first consecrated himself to God, Eligius could count on the subprior's handbell to wake him. Here on this Frisian island, he relied on his garrulous rooster. If his offices must depend on the humors of a chicken, surely God would allow some latitude.

"Know thyself," Christ said. Nothing salted that lesson into an honest man so well as time. After thirty years in Gaul, observing the fortunes of Childeric and Clovis, Eligius admitted to his abbot and himself that he wanted to be alone. Never deluded about an exalted calling, Eligius had always been happier in the fields than the cloister. He yearned for some remote, serene place where one could come face-to-face with the mystery of God and perhaps know some small part of it. Of the ancient Gaulish blood with a Roman consciousness, Eligius found the Franks coarse and more opportunistic than sincere in their conversion to the Church. Besides, the notion of solitude appealed: a hut, a goat, and a few chickens, bees perhaps, and a few rows of beans to tend as his father had. The honest smell of wood smoke in the morning blended with that of the byre, and in the warmth of the day, Eligius could weed and hoe his rows, collect his eggs, and talk with God like a friend at his elbow without waiting for the offices.

Here on this coastal fringe of islands trailing west to east like drops of wine spilled from a goblet, the people were a mixture of native Frise and westward-moving Saxons. Small difference in language or customs between them: fisherfolk mostly, but taking considerable profit and goods from the seagoing traders who put in for fresh water and food. The local chieftain was wary of Eligius at first, then indifferent. He might live among them and preach of the White Christ to those who wished to listen, but must never practice any magic that would incur the displeasure of Odin or Freyr. The chief was a tolerant man, Eligius must appreciate, and not ignorant of the monk's incomprehensible religion, but there were his own priests and the people's welfare to consider.

There had been Frankish novices at St. Martin's. From them Eligius learned something of their pagan beliefs, though the converts, glossy with new holiness, spoke of them with contempt. Here *his* beliefs were alien while Odin, Freyr, and Thor held sway. They lived far to the north in Asgard, powerful entities guarding their splendid halls against the giants from Utgard, but knowing they would ultimately be defeated in the way of things.

Defeated? "Tell me how you can call them gods," Eligius put to one of the island's warriors, "when they seem fallible and vulnerable as men?"

The thane only shrugged and refilled his mead horn. "Everything passes, old man. Everything dies. While I live, the Norn-Fates help me if I have stomach enough to help myself. For honorable men there is Valhalla, but death is certain. If you can leave nothing but reputation, let men remember your name and sing it."

Eligius was allowed a hut near the marshy northern shore, but apart from the nearest village. He husbanded his goat and fowl, planted his garden, and in time made a few converts. Most of these he persuaded while assisting them with a weed hook, manuring their vegetable patches or helping to deliver a calf, work he had known from birth. The Frisian peasants read more of Eligius in his earth-wise hands than in his talk of heaven or the odd way he wore his whitening fringe of hair in a circle around the shaved pate.

Devout or not, a man past fifty learns more of the world than prayer and the duties of his calling. Eligius came to like the taciturn island folk, though true comprehension was difficult. He lived on the outskirts of a northern world vast and alien to him. Sometimes when the thick North Sea fog drifted toward his shore, he saw it as a veil hiding that world from him. He thought sometimes that if he were younger and still burning with the zeal of God, he might have asked for a mission beyond that mist—to the Jutes or Angles or even farther, among the Danes and Geats. The desire was not wholly religious. Eligius was curious about these huge people and their gods. Could the halls of the Aesir really be found in the northern fastnesses beyond that mist? Were there really giants lurking just outside the precincts of such gods? Did the trickster-chimera Loki actually exist, or was he, as Odin to God, simply a crude pagan parody of Satan?

No, incredible. Blasphemy even to ponder . . . and yet Eligius often peered into that fog like dull white wool and wondered.

Once a fine longboat had come from the north and he was allowed to stand with the chief and island notables to receive the visitors when they put in for fresh water before making for the mouth of the Rhine. A royal retinue, a Jutish princess and her escort, bound for a treaty marriage with some prince of the Heathobards. That was some winters past. The weather had been biting cold. The princess had made the journey from north Jutland in an open boat with no more than a lean-to shelter, but she stood straight amid her guard. The men were helmed and mailed, with long spatha swords slung from shoulders bunched with muscle. The cold had reddened and cracked their skin, and rain had frozen to ice on the enormous golden cruciform brooches fastening their cloaks. The frost seemed to glint in their very eyes. The woman's lips were blue and cracked from the wind. Her clothes, though thick-woven and heavy with ornaments, were soaked through. She must have been miserable, yet neither she nor a single man of her guard would let themselves slump with fatigue or even shiver.

No more than sixteen, she was going to marry a man she had never met in the slim hope of an alliance between her Jutish king-father and the Heathobards. As these people went, she would not prevent war forever nor would her place likely be a happy one, but the thing was to be done.

Eligius tried to grasp their essence but found them elusive as the fog itself. One came to God with humility, opened to mercy. Where in their stoic, fatalistic souls would such people find room for Christ? Where their mere comprehension of Him when their own gods were arbitrary and irresponsible, even treacherous? Like the Jutish princess, frozen and miserable but defying her body to surrender to it, did they expect themselves to be as hardy as their deities?

Last night when the cock woke him to Matins, Eligius stirred on his sheepskin and sighed with the queasy sounds of waking. The night air was sultry and thunder growled over the sea. Beyond his door the dark went blue-white with sheet lightning. He was just swinging his legs to the earthen floor when the lightning struck again, too crack-of-doom close. His body jerked, and in the byre end of his hut, the goat bleated plaintively and the chickens squawked, flapping about in their brainless way. Eligius smelled the flat, heavy taint in the charged air, then heard the crackling of flame.

He thrust his feet into sandals, crossed himself with a hurried prayer, and crept outside to see the little tongues of flame licking through his roof thatching. By the time he'd stumbled about to find his ladder and clamber up with a bucket of sand, the rain was coming down—a pattering, then a hiss turning into a roar as the heavens tore asunder, inundating the low island.

Already soaked, Eligius tossed his sand onto the thatch for good measure and left the rain to finish the task. Inside, kneeling before the cross at his Matins, he reflected how even his converts would be cowering in their huts, supplicating Christ to protect them but believing far more surely in Thor's great hammer, Mjollnir, hurled across the sky to bring the thunder.

When the sun came up, Eligius climbed the ladder once again to see how much of the reed thatch must be replaced—so, as he perched with one leg over the ridgepole, he saw the longship sliding westward in the first light of morning. He counted fourteen pairs of rowers who bent, pulled, and stroked as one. Thirty men in all, everyone mailed under his short cloak, braided hair falling below the helmets, and a strange banner curling from the boat's high stern board.

A war band bent on raiding. Perhaps they would pass by toward the westward islands, but even as Eligius considered the possibility, he heard the clang of iron from the village where other watchful men had seen the keel and beat out a furious alarm.

In such a craft without even a sail to power it, they could only be coming for quick loot. They would be disappointed here, finding little treasure but enough fighting men to protect that little. The longship slipped beyond view, hidden by tall reeds as it worked inshore. For an hour then Eligius heard the braying horns, a din of distant battle, shouting and crash of iron on bossed shields. Many of the villagers fled eastward along the shore, collecting about Eligius' hut for safety, the farmers and fishermen worried and silent, mothers clutching children to them and warning sharply when a toddler strayed too far from reach or out of sight.

Then the clamor ceased. Before the clouded sun climbed high, one of the chief's war thanes, shield slung over his back, spear resting on his shoulder, came to tell the frightened folk that the danger was past.

"Who were they?" Eligius plied him. "Will they come again?"

The warrior appeared quite certain. "No."

He set his spearbutt on the ground and pulled at one of his long mustaches. A tried man with many years of service, gift-rings of gold on his fingers and one attached to the pommel of his sword as signal of reward from a grateful lord. He looked at his feet and spoke with distaste.

"Not men but boys. Not a beard in the lot."

Well armed but not that skilled with weapons. "Some of them ran away when we charged. Boys . . ."

Eligius heard sadness in the way the words trailed off, and a kind of baffled disgust. The thane hefted his spear again. "We caught the ones who ran away. They're all dead."

He turned and stalked off toward the chief's hall. Eligius watched him with sympathy, knowing the man's kind better now. To defend their home against proven thanes would have been honor, but an hour's work against thirty foolish boys . . .

The thane halted and turned, as if he had to ask the question of someone. "I don't understand. If they came for treasure, there is none here. If it was for honor, they never had a chance. Why?"

The rain had beaten down some of his beanstalks and caked the mud thick about their roots. Delicately, as he would splint the broken wing of a small bird, Eligius collected twigs of the right size and tied the plants upright. After Vespers, he took up his hoe and worked down the rows, loosening the black soil before it could dry and cake, aware of how still the island was at this evening hour after a day of such violence, with only the whisper of ebb tide along the shore.

Eligius straightened to rest his back, glancing toward his hut raised up on its terp-mound of seashells and packed midden. He caught a hint of movement just inside the open door.

No mistake: Someone had slipped into his hut, probably one of his converts wanting confession. They barely understood what he taught them but liked the notion of paradise after a lifetime of hard work and the cleansing novelty of confession, especially the women, who were content just to have someone sympathetic to listen to them. Eligius climbed the log steps, set his hoe by the low entrance, and ducked inside. In the moment needed to accustom sight to the gloom, he saw nothing except that his fire wanted more fuel. He turned toward the wood basket slung from the ceiling—and caught his breath.

In the far corner, the man facing him was huge, bigger than any warrior on the island. Of middling height himself, Eligius would barely come up to the mailed chest. In that moment, he could well perceive why giants peopled the tales of these folk. A giant faced him—silent, sword drawn, shield in hand. In three long paces, the warrior stepped across the space between them and Eligius saw him clearly: one of the luckless raiders, still a callow boy for all his height. The iron helmet was decorated with workings of copper, the expensive ring mail quite new. The long legs were encased in good linen trousers tied at the ankle, shoes of soft leather and barely worn. The round bright-painted shield evidenced no mark of fight, the sword the boy gripped as new as the rest of his gear. No peasant this, Eligius deduced, but very fortunate to have survived.

All the war fierceness was in the boy's gear. His face had the same wintry set that Eligius read in the Jutish princess and her men, framed by the same dull yellow hair gathered in tight braids and wound with silver wire. But none of their bearing. The sword drooped, the shield hung at arm's length. The youth's whole body, barely begun to fill out its leviathan frame, sagged with exhaustion he obviously labored to hide.

"Welcome," Eligius greeted him in the Saxon tongue. "May I know who shares my fire?"

"Be so good," the boy husked. "Something to eat."

Though heavily accented and rather singsong, Eligius understood the dialect. The boy stumbled toward the low table of roughhewn plank and collapsed on an upended stump that served as one of the stools. Eligius lit a candle and set it on the table. In the new light, he saw the sparse, barely visible blond beard starting along the boy's jawline.

The stranger gestured toward Eligius' cross. "Thor?"

"What? No, that is the sign of my God."

The boy's eyes were of the color of periwinkles. Unclouded by weariness, they might glow with intelligence and vitality someday, perhaps with a strength not yet attained. Now they reflected only suspicion and fear. He made a queer sign in front of him, lacing his fingers together. Eligius interpreted it as a warding sign, protecting himself against the magic of an alien god.

"Come, we will eat," the monk invited, filling a clay mug from his skin of beer. "I am Father Eligius. What is your name?"

The boy drank greedily, draining the mug which Eligius refilled, pouring a smaller measure for himself in a glass beaker. The youth stared wonderingly at the painted glass.

"Roman?"

"Yes. From the works at Cologne."

"They said you had many treasures here. Roman gold, as much as a man could carry. Treasures like this. We never had time to find any before they were on us. All that way from Helsingborg."

"Where is that?"

"In the land of the Geats. I must get away somehow." The youth drew his longsword and laid it on the table. "If you try to tell them about me or work magic against me, I will kill you."

"I will not," Eligius vowed sincerely. "There has been enough killing. What are you called?"

The question seemed to pain the boy like an unseen wound. He picked up the glass beaker, studying the bright-green bird exquisitely detailed on one side, the red bull on the other. Or perhaps some indefinable shape beyond the glass in his own suffering. The immature mouth trembled.

"When there was honor, I was called Beowulf."

Beowulf he had been only days ago when there was honor, or at least a chance of it: son to Edgetho and nephew to Hygelac, king of the Geats. Vanished now, all hope of honor or even escape from shame, dead as the rest of his boat companions. Better to be in the underworld with Hel. Perhaps, Beowulf reflected with a boy's bitterness, this rank peasant hut was part of Hel. The very drabness of the monk's miserable hovel—the goat and squabbling chickens in the byre half, the bed shelves and fire pit where oatcakes cooked now on an iron plate, the worn saddle quern for grinding grain—seemed to mock him with their poverty. Not even gold for profit. *What did you expect?*

He tried to look this shaman in the eye and show no fear. That was difficult when he was so tired, tensing his body and arms to control their trembling. This harmless-appearing old man must be a magician of the Romans. *Monk* he called himself, and *Father*, though there were no women or sons about. A magician who might easily work evil against him. Beowulf had heard from coasting traders how these Romans feasted on their god's flesh and drank his blood in their rituals. When he first slipped into the hut after hiding in the reeds all day, Beowulf saw the cross and at first thought it the familiar sign of Thor's hammer such as he wore under his mail, but the crosspiece was higher up, and he guessed where he had come.

He drank beer and ate the boiled eggs and oatcakes in silence, avoiding the monk's questions out of shame, for truly he was no one now and deserved to die. The tallow candle should not burn so brightly; its glow betrayed his fear to the Roman who would know him for a coward who had deserted his comrades in battle.

Could any of them have foreseen this when they drank in the hall at Helsingborg? A special feast for the sons of Hathcyn, King Hygelac's brother. All the untried youngling sons of thanes came to the feast, and there the notion of a voyage for fame took fire among them. One boat, thirty swords, the fame and treasure to be shared equally among them. A few days' pull on the oars around Jutland, south to the islands where Roman gold lay piled high in Frisian treasure houses, guarded by only a few who hardly expected a surprise raid. Gold for the taking: coins stamped with the likeness of Caesars, gold ingots the weight of a man's sword and scabbard, skins of Frankish wine. More than all this and brighter with each horn of mead downed as some already rolled drunk under the board, the bright noon-blaze of fame and repute for thanes' sons who had never raided or even fought before, untried but eager for testing.

Too eager. The mead had sung in Beowulf's fuddled head. This raid and its booty would be recounted until its echoes reached Heorot in

Sjaelland where his father Edgetho lived in exile at the hall of Hrothgar. Edgetho was forbidden his homeland and Hygelac's court not from shame but from his royal brother-in-law's cautious present policy. He killed a man in single combat—but the wrong man at the inconvenient time. Such doom sometimes fell on a thane when personal feuds ran athwart a king's treaties. But Edgetho would hear how his son traveled the sea road to plunder and returned with booty and fame. The Scylding king Hrothgar who settled Edgetho's feud with gold would be repaid, the exile comforted and warmed with pride.

The boat companions made their pledge at the board. No man would shirk or desert in the face of battle, come what may, and all existing quarrels would be laid aside for the duration of the voyage. Drunk as they were and thrilled at their own daring, they were the blood of kings and tried thanes, assuring each other in drunken solemnity that they were well aware promises made over mead must be fulfilled in action. Mead boasters were always more plentiful than heroes, fierce at the board but nowhere else. Scops sang of deeds, not pledges. None dropped away from the venture when the boat was readied and provisioned, though all of them would have been wiser to do so. They did not store enough food and had to put in at a Jutish village on the north coast to replenish. They might have raided and taken what they needed but none of them were used to such long stretches of rowing. Exhausted, they simply paid the exorbitant prices demanded by the Jute villagers. They were virtually spent when the island hove in view at morning light.

Time was wasted in finding where to go, and by then some sharp-eyed sentry had sounded the alarm. On empty stomachs they lifted shield and sword in hands still raw and bleeding from the oars, and tried to fight. Pitiful. After the first rush, they saw the difference between boys and hardened fighting men. When too many died in that first clash, the rest, already dispirited, turned in terror and ran. Beowulf fled with the rest, running for his life. They were already cut off from their beached keel. He had thrown one fear-frozen glance over his shoulder. Some of them had stood fast around Erming, nephew to Hathcyn, a forlorn last ring of defenders vanishing even now in the Frisian attack. Beowulf ran on and lost himself in the marsh reeds.

The Frisians caught and killed all the others, stripping the bodies of their fine new mail, shields, and swords. Though Beowulf was only one of the majority who broke and ran, the others at least had the mercy of oblivion. He must live with his shame or outlive it with twice the deeds expected of a Geat warrior. Only let none discover; if Odin granted him that one mercy, he promised such restitution in deeds and repute as would ensure him a place by kings while he lived and in Valhalla afterward.

By Odin I swear this, Beowulf vowed in the sick shame of his sixteen years. *By Edgetho's ancient sword I swear I will have my name again, thrice enlarged with honor.*

Easily said, he realized with bitter self-scorn. For now, he must find a boat and steal away tonight, make east for the Angle coast. That would mean two days and more of rowing. Part of payment. If his blistered hands tortured him, that was no more than deserts for such as he. The Angle tribes were tributary to Hrothgar and would pass him across to Sjaelland where he would tell Edgetho of the raid, that though outnumbered they fought well, Beowulf alone *wyrd*-spared to fight again. A pitiful lie, *nithings vaerke,* and let it be the last stain on him. Let him get home and he would be, at whatever cost, a model of what the harpers sang in Hygelac's hall—valiant and an honor to his royal family.

Dusk deepened into the long twilight of northern summer night. Eligius offered more food, which the boy wrapped in green leaves for traveling. The sword still lay ready and the youth watched Eligius' every move with frightened, wary eyes.

"Where will you go?" Eligius asked. Though this was an enemy, he supposed, he couldn't help a large sympathy for the fugitive. All half-grown boys, the thane said. God alone knew why they had come or what they expected to find. Useless . . . and yet Eligius read the boy's fear and exhaustion and the touching vulnerability of the large-framed body shot so tall at puberty like a quick-growing reed, no bulk yet in the shoulders, no solid strength in the gangling limbs.

"I will go home," the boy mumbled. "Need a boat. If you have one, I will pay for it."

Eligius leaned his elbows on the table, considering. He had a craft—not much more than a hollowed tree trunk with a single-plank seat and oars, but he needed the boat for fishing more than the price of it. On the other hand, the boy would surely be seen and killed in the morning, and of what use one more death? More to the point, he fully believed this young Geat would kill him if need be, terrified enough to do anything to survive.

"My boat is in the reeds by the shore," Eligius told him. "A long pull for one man."

And one so barely grown into his ridiculously large man frame that the boy of him yet rattled loose in it. The youth called Beowulf only drained the last of his beer and attempted an arrogant smirk that did not quite convince the monk.

"I am Geat."

"I see." So much for bravado, as if that chance of birth guaranteed the impossible as a matter of course.

"Beowulf," Eligius repeated the foreign name. The sound seemed to echo with the crackling of northern ice. One thought of blue shadow on snow that never melted high in the mountain fastnesses beyond the farthest villages.

"Tell your scops they will hear my name again, and with such honor as will task their art to describe."

Beowulf fumbled at his sunburned neck and drew off the gold chain from under his mail. The attached amulet, as long and thick as a man's forefinger, appeared to be an inverted cross with a shortened crosspiece. Chain and symbol were pure gold by their weight in the monk's grasp. A corrupted symbol of God? Had someone already carried Christ into that darkness beyond sea and fog? Eligius pointed to his own cross on its pedestal, then to the amulet.

"Christ?"

"No." The boy shook his head in vigorous contempt; the yellow braids whipped about his shoulders. "You are stupid, old man. That is Thor's hammer, Mjollnir. It is strong, one of the greatest charms against evil. I wore it and I am alive where all the others died. It is yours for the boat and the food. Call on Thor when you have need, and perhaps he will answer."

Eligius took the offering in trade, tactfully declining comment. The amulet would be melted down to buy whatever his flock of converts needed in the coming winter.

The tall boy got clumsily to his feet, sheathing the longsword. "I have given you my last protection. From here to the Angle coast I have only my prayers to Njord for help. Swear you will work no magic against me."

Eligius protested. "I have no magic, only a faith."

"Do you not eat your god and drink his blood?"

Eligius failed to understand at first; when he did, the laugh was involuntary. "It is only a point of faith, Beowulf. Bread and wine that become the Body and Blood of our Lord."

"That is magic." The youth glowered. His suspicious glance slid to the cross. "Swear."

"By my faith," Eligius mouthed, feeling utterly foolish, "I will not harm you."

"Now the boat."

The shore would be deserted now. All the same, Eligius decided against carrying a lantern. "Follow close behind me."

The marshy path was familiar enough to his own step, but the Geaṭish boy stumbled repeatedly and fell once with a rattle of mail and sword, cursing fretfully. Then Eligius parted the tall reeds to one side of the path. Just beyond, pale moonlight silvered the incoming tide. He untied the small boat from its mooring stake and helped the boy push it out through the reeds until the bottom floated free. The boy clambered over the side, gathering up the oars.

"Remember me," his voice floated back to Eligius over the swash of oars. "I am Beowulf of the Geats. One day your scops will sing of me."

"Go in peace," Eligius returned softly. "I know you pray for courage and why. Remember: There is never courage without fear."

No answer but the creaking of the rowlocks and the soft rush of oars through water. For a little time, the boat and the rower bending to his stroke were a dark shape against the water, then part of it and gone.

The amulet and chain clinked in Eligius' hand. Once again he felt himself standing on the very edge of the known, sane world. One step more and he would topple over the brink into that vast darkness, the opposite of all he knew, where this boy's gods lived on a mountain at the end of a fiery rainbow, beyond them an unending wasteland of ice where, in their concept of hell, one did not burn but froze; where a huge serpent girdled the world and a monstrous wolf waited to devour the gods and all their works. . . .

BOOK I

GRENDEL,

PRINCE

OF

DANES

1

OF ALL THE AESIR GOD-FOLK dwelling amid the gleaming halls of Asgard, the least reliable was Loki. No one, least of all Loki himself, knew where his true loyalties lay. He was a creature of moods, and no humor claimed Loki that did not rule all of him while it endured. The gods tolerated him in Asgard, but never quite accepted the halfling son of an Utgard giantess. In the matter of Loki's father, a prudent silence was maintained in Asgard, since utterance might point more closely to Odin than the All-Father would appreciate. Odin had only one eye, but that one was known to wander. And what honorable father would acknowledge Loki? Trickster, shape-changer, friend one day and foe the next, subtle in malice or clumsy as a child, taking most often the human shape of man after that race he most admired, while irresponsibly fathering monsters and occasional beauty.

From Loki sprang the serpent who coils at the bottom of the World Ocean, and Fenrir the wolf that ever threatened to devour that world. By his loyal wife, Sigyn, he sired the daughter Hel after whom was named the underworld of death she came to rule. As his loins, so his nature: One never knew what would come from Loki. In man-shape he was umbered and scorched from a hundred fiery mishaps, scarred from as many ill-conceived misadventures. Still, some women of Asgard like Odin's respectable wife, Frigga, would have thought Loki handsome were it not for an indefinable something in his expression quite alien to the honest countenances of god-folk. To look on his face was to see one who had, perhaps, found too many bushels of beans weighted with pebbles or as many goddesses whose attractions too soon palled. Loki wore dissatisfaction like an unbecoming garment that yet fitted him better than any other. Where Odin could look on Valaskjalf, his magnificent hall, or the hammered gold roofs of Gimli where the wise and righteous feasted, and call them perfect, some perverse atom in Loki would raise an eyebrow, curl his lip, and inspire a yawn. When Odin's son Balder was paraded before the warriors in Valhalla and his beauty acknowledged by all, Loki's applause was faint and his smile forced. In truth, though sometimes he could agree with Odin on the overall majesty of Asgard, or with Frigga on the undeniable virtues of her son, more often, he would grumble to his wife Sigyn—

"It is all so perfect, so . . . balanced and *boring.*"

Want of that balance was the key to Loki's mutable character: easily bored, quickly restless to be gone, to be doing, to put things in motion no matter the consequence, to steal fire from the sun even if the mischief seared him, or to paint a comic face on the moon. And it was lamented among the noble Aesir that Loki had influenced far too many of the humans in Midgard. He could never control his moods or desires. Sometimes in a desperate need to escape perfection, he stole away to the vast, gloomy caves of Utgard and there amused himself among the giants. If they were misshapen, Loki found them refreshing after Balder; if their dwellings were ever shadowed in chilly gloom, the darkness was respite from the glitter of Asgard. Not wholly of the gods, Loki tired of splendor.

Volla the giantess could not be called splendid unless for her size. She towered three times the height of a human woman, twice that of an Aesir or Vanir goddess, and in all drinking contests among her cave-dwelling kind, Volla always won. She was of a remarkable ugliness which Loki found picturesque, and powerful. Her jaws could crunch a whole ox in two, her skin more like blackened iron than flesh, and one swipe of her talons could take an iron-fastened door off its hinges. Very much a woman despite these startling attributes, her eye lighted on Loki and stayed there. She would have no other company and, when they were wearied of coupling, joined Loki in his wildest adventures. They would creep up on the bridge Bi-frost from the Utgard side and taunt the sentry Heimdall, try to steal the trumpet Gjallerhorn or create alarums to make him sound the horn and signal Ragnarok, the approach of doom. Heimdall was infuriated by the distorted intruders but never guessed one of them was Loki. No one in Asgard, least of all his wife, Sigyn, suspected Loki's alliance with Volla, though it was common knowledge among the giants, none of whom were surprised when wild Volla quickened and eventually brought forth a daughter.

When Loki saw his child, he was secretly gratified that the dark infant had so much human in her, though she resembled Volla much more than himself.

"Take her to be raised in Asgard," Volla sued to her lover, a new ambition sprung up with the birth of her child. While lacking remorse,

Loki was not incapable of simple prudence. For his own well-being at home, he could not take the child to Sigyn. He would raise for her the fairest hall in Midgard, among men, yet safe from their reach. That resolve posed its own difficulty. Men were spreading everywhere over the earth, building halls of their own in crude imitation of Gimli and Valaskjalf. Loki searched for some remote island, but what spot so secluded that the prows of men's questing craft did not touch there? He spent days flashing to and fro over the earth like sunlight through cloud shadow, trying to find a haven to build his infant daughter the hall he promised and she deserved.

At length, finding no suitable place, Loki grew tired of the search, weary with the weight of the child in his arms, and rested on the shore of a dismal mere. He caught a hare for his child to eat. She tore it apart with claws nearly hard and sharp as her mother's, drank the blood, chewed the meat and picked the bones with sharp teeth.

"Truly, you are a giantess and all will know you for one," Loki sympathized. "What am I to do with you?"

If she could never claim a place in Asgard, the child would be honorably named: Sigyn, after his wife. As Loki gazed out over the mere and his child's future, his glance registered the dreary landscape. He could not remember even in Utgard a more forbidding view. The waters of the lake hissed and foamed, teeming with huge creatures that knew nothing but hunger and the hunt. As he watched, three times hovering gulls glided too near the surface and thrice a saw-toothed maw thrust up, caught, and dragged it below. Other creatures floundered about on the black, bird-limed rocks of the opposite shore.

"Nowhere else will Sigyn be so safe," Loki decided. Were she fair as Freyja of the Vanir or even the giantess Gerda for whom, it was said in Asgard, Freyr himself longed, no man in Midgard would dare this mere or its inhabitants to harm her.

No sooner thought than done. Loki gathered up Sigyn and leaped into the seething waters. Sensing his presence, the hungry mere-dwellers turned in their ceaseless search for prey and converged on god and halfling. Descending toward the deep bottom, Loki fended them off with one arm while his daughter only laughed at the prospect of more to eat. Until her father fed her the hare, she had nourished only at Volla's horny breast, the milk stronger than any brew among gods or men—but with meat and blood coursing through her, the babe knew

her natural sustenance. When one great sea beast wrapped a thick ten-
tacle about her neck and tried to drag Sigyn from Loki's grip toward its
snapping parrot beak, Sigyn only snarled and shredded the entrapping
coils with talons and teeth. The wounded creature fell away as others
drove in to tear it apart. More of them surrounded the swimmers, but
none could best Loki, and those that attacked Sigyn were gutted, snapping at each other in their mindless greed, devouring even as they were
devoured, until Loki's feet touched the hard bottom, so far below the
roiling surface that the strongest shaft of light died out far above.

"My daughter will have air!" Loki decreed, sweeping his scarred
arms out before him. As he did, the mere's waters fell back beyond the
pale carved by his movement.

"Sigyn will have light!" her father vowed, drawing all the aug-
mented qualities from the feeble sunlight struggling down through the
murky waters. Illumination for his daughter streamed into the space
Loki marked out for her, streaked and shimmered through the water
walls rising about them and reflected in Sigyn's eyes which were themselves the color of sunset in jade. Setting her down to begin his task,
Loki looked into Sigyn's eyes and with a god's too-clear vision, saw
how in different moods they would be those of a beast who knew no
law but to feed, at others the reflection of the humanity in himself,
Volla, and the men creatures of Midgard. Wherein was she different
from them? Part hunger and part longing, ever caught between gods and
demons and bearing the stamp of both?

"Now your father will build for you."

And let those of Asgard, when they heard of this work, remember
that Loki, father of monsters, was human enough to create good as well.
If this was the curse of man, was it not Loki's too?

He knelt on the floor of the mere, the silence of the deep brooding
around him, and concentrated. Out of the power of his thoughts a force
went forth to the jagged stones of the lake floor, squared and smoothed
them until, like polished granite, they formed the floor of Sigyn's hall.
The very boundaries of Loki's spell began to harden, rising up in walls
and arches, forming chambers beyond and overhead. The labor told on
Loki, who had never attempted so noble a work before, nor any from
so great a love. He tired and faltered but would not desist; this was for
his child, his blood. For Sigyn he would draw the last beauty from his
vagrant soul as the blood from his veins. A passion of tenderness in

him raised her walls high, devotion sculpted the arches and carved from the dark waters the high roof of his daughter's enchanted hall.

From the purest fire of his mind Loki built for Sigyn. Just so, in a far and different reach of Midgard, men told of Mulciber, architect of another Asgard, yet loyal to Satan and cast out of that paradise with him, building Pandemonium for his exiled angel prince. Out of his own body Mulciber made a palace; out of a mercurial mind—while minded to love—Loki raised a hall for Sigyn and took up the sleepy infant in his arms, laying her to rest in her first bed.

Nine times Loki circled the bed back and forth, seeding the spells to protect her and this place. No human sword, be it forged by Wayland himself, would have power to injure Sigyn. No waters above might break through her walls, no creature of the mere touch her in her passage to and from the surface. Then, the charm completed, Loki paused over his sleeping daughter. What spell to guard Sigyn from eventual knowledge of herself or to dispel the loneliness she must come to know? But for those eyes with their aspect of dusky sunlight in emerald, hinting of all the beauty and ill to riot across the human soul, what man or god would find Sigyn anything but grotesque? Her limbs were dark as her mother's, their shape hinting of the impossible strength to come, her skin hard as cuttlebone or a warrior's mail. Where other infants gurgled or cried, Sigyn hissed and growled. She would feed on the mere creatures until she could rise above the turbulent waters to prowl the land for larger prey. When men saw her and lived to tell, she would become part of their nightmares.

Then let them be no more than hers as long as possible, Loki decided. Let their waking be as her sleep, and her true sleep untroubled. Let the mirrors in her hall show her only beauty. And for the beast sound of her that would only grow deeper and more terrifying with time, the sound of enchantment at least.

"Let it be so," Loki willed and stole away. If not the wisest provision of a father between heaven and earth, at least one made from love.

When Sigyn woke, she delighted in the splendor of the hall her father made for her. The high table shone with golden plate and goblets, each chair cunningly worked with intricate designs carved into the arms and back. She cried out for Loki to come and play with her—called again and again, then listened only to echoes and silence.

Until the hunger came over her like flame creeping through tinder, and Sigyn knew only that she must feed.

She grew slowly, with a child's sense of time that began when she opened her eyes each morning to the delights of her hall. She found each day clothes to wear, woven from the softest linen and wool, had only to think herself chilled and fire blazed up on the hearth to warm her. Sigyn ran and played all the day through the chambers of her hall, and if she was lonely now and then, Loki came sometimes to see her and to replenish the finite powers of his enchantment. Sometimes they would surge up through the calm, crystal waters of the mere, playing tag with the fish as they swam to break surface and make for the shore where spirited horses would bear them up and across Bi-frost to the gleaming rooftops of Asgard where Sigyn met grave Odin and stately Frigga and dined royally in Valaskjalf where all the gods payed tribute to her beauty.

Or so it seemed. Alone, her mirrors were always a source of fascination, for when Sigyn secretly yearned to resemble majestic Frigga, the polished glass would render a hint of the goddess in this or that attitude. But Sigyn decided she was far fairer than Frigga, her features stronger and more even, skin whiter and without a blemish—browning nicely in summer like the bare legs of the Valkyries, and she loved to work through her thick golden hair with an ivory comb until it flowed in waves of gold to put Gimli to shame. She grew taller than any Valkyrie and better formed, she judged. Her arms could break a thick tree limb like a stick of pine kindling, but as she neared the time of passage from girl to woman, Sigyn wondered where in the several worlds would she find a husband to claim her.

In this regard, her prospects appeared limited. Loki must have overlooked such a time, but in all, Sigyn was happy enough. Only in her sleep as she matured did she writhe and turn in the great bed with the same recurring nightmare. Her fingers grew long and black with nails hard as spear iron; her reflection in the mirror, when in the dream she passed it, was a dark horror from her deepest child fears. And always in dreams the gnawing hunger. Ravening, she would course up through the mere waters with the force of the earth tearing open to bleed fire into the deep trenches of the ocean, and swim with powerful arms and legs to reach a gray, sere bank and then hunt for food. Whatever she snared, goat or hare or hind, she slashed open and gorged upon. Her dreams were ever of hunger—then the satiate drowse after feeding as she sank homeward through the mere to a cave forbidding as the unclean form she hunted in, a twilit grotto where water dripped from lichened walls and crabs scuttled underfoot. Certain images carried over from sleep to sleep: picked bones littering the lake shore. In the dreams, food grew scarcer as animals shunned the place, and Sigyn had to range farther to appease her appetite.

As childhood passed toward the first signs of womanhood, other hungers grew in her. Solitude became loneliness sharp as her hunger. She began to yearn for something she could not name. The palace Loki reared for her out of his love and magic surely wanted for nothing, but night-ranging over Sjaelland, she had seen among the Spear-Danes one face that would not leave her thoughts, day or night, replacing at last some of the darkness of her dreams.

In time, Sigyn learned his name: Shild, the young king of the Scyldings; so much for his title. His beauty she marked for herself. No human king in Midgard carried himself with such pride. He must be god-born like herself. In her mirrors now, Sigyn imagined him beside her, placing the crown of the Scyldings on her brow as his consort. So it would be. None but Sigyn would be the queen of Shild.

2

NOT AT ALL WITTING that he was loved by Sigyn, Shild Scefing yet had much in common with her, being god-born and of
mixed blood. His mother, like hers, was a giantess of Utgard;
his father, Freyr of the Vanir, who were rivals to the Aesir and far older.
Where the Aesir boasted their powers over war, the Vanir were bestow-
ers of fertility and husbanding. Among humans their rites were those
of joy and ecstasy. In the hot, dry places beyond the sea Midjardar Haf,
these rites were led by priests sometimes dressed as women, which
Odin and Thor considered shameful but could never deny the Vanir
were the first gods. Men had to plant, after all, increase and survive
before they could conquer.

Rivalry is a short road to conflict. When the two races clashed in
open war, neither could win a decisive victory. Eventually, a truce was
concluded and important hostages exchanged for its surety. From the
Vanir to Asgard went Njord, god of ships, master of tides and winds,
and his son, Freyr, bringer of sun and rain to men, blesser of the barley
in the earth. Being older, Njord more readily accepted his captive state,
but Freyr chafed and felt, as Loki had, a dull sameness about the gleaming precincts of Asgard, a monotony of splendors. If the pork to the
tables of Valhalla never ran out, it lacked the tang of flesh fattened on
beech mast by a farmer who depended on his swine for food himself.
Milk from the goat Heidrun flowed inexhaustibly but tasted thin and
chalky to Freyr. Worst of all, he could barely abide the Aesir goddesses,
all militantly virtuous and, to a god who delighted in the quickening
of seed in earth or womb, lacking that ineffable feminine quality so
inviting to a mate. He missed home and his sister, Freya, longed for the
simple lives of Midgard farmers and the songs men sang when they saw
the green shoots break through planted earth. He missed all gentle,
fertile things men and Vanir alike thought of as *female*. As with Loki,
his condition seeded in discontent, yearning for something other and
elsewhere, and naturally, he fell in love with the first woman who was
both.

One place in Asgard delighted and intrigued Freyr, the high seat of

Odin in the hall Valaskjalf. To speak nothing of its powers, the great chair was magnificence in itself. Screaming eagles jutted from the arm-rests, the high back so intricately carved that the most cunning eye could never trace where the pattern began or ended. From this seat all Creation could be viewed at once: the heavens beyond Asgard, and all the worlds. Seated so, Freyr could see the World Serpent shift its coils in the deep ocean and how that motion stirred the tides. Odin sternly forbade him the seat but was often from home, and Freyr reasoned that a hostage ought to have some rights. He looked out from Odin's seat over all the heavens and turning worlds, regretting so few were fertile —and one day beheld the maiden Gerda in Utgard.

Not all of the race of giants were ugly, and where Gerda walked, the shadows of Utgard lightened and warmed. Freyr gazed on her a long time, so rapt he did not hear his servant Skirner address him. When he answered, it was only to question.

"Who is she, Skirner?"

His servant took the chair and inspected the gratifying view. "That is Gerda, daughter of Gymir the giant."

"How can such perfection come from them?"

Skirner's wisdom, as his master's, dealt more with husbanding, but he knew the elements that comprised beauty and how these rewarded study. "How do the Aesir tolerate flaws like Loki among them? I do not think men or gods can bear perfection too long. Just so, giants will weary of thorns and bear a blossom now and again."

"I am hostage," Freyr fretted, "while you may come and go on my business. Take my sword and a swift horse. Tell Gerda that Freyr, for all his seeding, has never looked till now on the woman he wanted to bear for him. She is fairest of all and I cannot sleep until she comes, for all the bright image of her in my desire. Until she loves me, I waste away."

"Indeed, you do not look well," Skirner observed. "I will haste me."

With Freyr's sword and horse, he dashed across fiery Bi-frost to-ward the mist-shrouded marches of Utgard, brandishing Freyr's blade for the sentinel Heimdall to show he was on his lord's errand, and so to the hall of Gymir where he stated his errand and asked to see the maiden Gerda. When she appeared in a gray gown woven of shadow and light, spider web and promises, Skirner perceived she was as delicate in every line as her father was coarse. Perhaps it was her hair, the color of ripe wheat that had fetched Freyr's eye, or her sure step like that of a mortal woman walking her own hall and fields. She greeted Skirner courteously, and when he presented Freyr's earnest suit, asked of his semblance and how she might trust the sincerity of his love.

"If we of Utgard are a suspicious race, Skirner, recall how the Aesir inspire distrust. Odin is changeable and faithless as Loki, Thor as impulsive, Balder as vain. If we are the dark side of Creation, the stain on them is their own. What is Freyr like?"

Skirner considered carefully before making answer. "My lord is the murmuring rill of small but valued gifts, the river of great ones. It is our pride to be of the ancient Vanir, lady, gods men have worshiped since they first scratched a line in the earth and planted a seed. Freyr's smile is the sunlight on men's fields and lives, his tears are the rain, his countenance gentle and strong as all good, enduring things women prize as well as men. To see a farmer study the sky, weighing the weather's promise, you see the wisdom in Freyr's look. See that husbandman working the soil through his fingers, judging its readiness for seed: There you have Freyr's hands. He is tanned like men who work daily in their earth, and the browning of his skin only stands out against the green of his garments. Sometimes he has such an aspect as I have seen in women carrying child: of peace and fulfillment and promise of life to come; sometimes of the child come from that pledge, fine-haired, soul and skin still smooth before it roughens against a hard world. Of that child's eye seeing afresh all the wonders and none of the lies of that imperfect place. Freyr is peace where Odin is war," Skirner concluded. "He is only hostage in Asgard, but will not always be so. The glory of war is sometimes, but the land and seed are forever. And Freyr chooses you. What answer to his love?"

Moved by Skirner's eloquent praise of his lord, Gerda forgot to ask of dowry, but old Gymli considered it prudent to make sure.

"He gives his love alone," Skirner replied, "and promises her a harvest in the form of her son."

In nine nights' time Gerda rode across Bi-frost with Skirner. Whatever Freyr felt when he saw her was repaid in the lavish favor she bent on him. Theirs was a natural mating. Men in Midgard came to consider this the true marriage of Earth and Sky, and as Earth quickened in spring, Gerda gave to Freyr a son whom they named Shild.

Shild's male beauty was so evident even as a child that it promised to surpass Balder's. As a father, Odin was not discomfited by the comparison, but mothers are never reasonable about children. Frigga grew jealous of Shild and bade Freyr and his alien family dwell far from Valaskjalf on the outskirts of Asgard. Even then Gerda did not feel Shild safe, trusting none of the Aesir. With Freyr's consent, a ship was fitted out to carry the boy to Midgard. With spells to keep him from harm on the journey and Njord to guide the winds over the whale-road, the ship's prow slid safely through sky and sea to beach on the shores of Sjaelland, where it was discovered by Danish tribesmen.

The keel was laden with such treasure that surely this waif was come to men from the gods. In his hands Shild bore a cask containing a sheaf of barley by which men knew he came from Freyr, and afterward, he was known as Shild Scefing, child with the sheaf. In time he came to rule and increase the people who found him. They followed their custom of taking their tribal name from their first god-king, come to them from the sea with the gifts of peace and plenty. In Denmark, they were known as the Scyldings. Shild was the direct ancestor of Hrothgar the Wise, ally of the Geats and friend to Edgetho, who was the father of Beowulf.

While he wore the Scylding crown, Shild tried to husband and increase the gifts Freyr had sent with him. Sjaelland grew fertile, men fed on plenty and waxed strong but never wise or satisfied. They wanted more and a king who could get them more. Rival tribes envied the Scyldings and made war on them. At first to defend and then to extend, Shild led his Spear-Danes through Sjaelland in conquest, then wherever the sea road carried them. He took the halls, broke and burned their mead benches, until all their kings paid tribute to Shild and their gold weighted his treasure casks.

Shild grew to fame while still very young, but in that growing time felt always lonely and out of place as Sigyn, set down in a world of men but never entirely of them. One day when this otherness lay heavy as the autumn overcast on him, Shild had to forsake his hall and ride. Calling his closest counselors to join him, the king mounted and rode out to hunt. Though with friends, he shared little talk with them this day, feeling that he was drawn toward something other than the sport.

This was the time called Blood Month when husbandmen slaughtered and salted the winter pork, when deer were in rut, and the wild boar of the forest were plentiful. The hunting party rode eastward through the morning, finding no game, only blood trails here and there and once, the freshly picked bones of a great stag. The royal huntsmen deliberated over the remains and the lack of game at this time of year when heath and forest should be teeming.

Shild's oldest companion, Hundulf, mused over the fact. "Few trails and no spoor. You might think they hid in fear of something."

"If so, it is not us." Shild rested the boar spear on his stirrup. A cold mist was rising. He felt chilled despite the thickness of his cloak, strangely ill at ease since waking that morning. He looked about at his friends confounded as himself by the scarcity of game. The horses stamped and snorted, their breath ghosts of vapor in the cold air.

"Not us," he murmured to himself.

Hundulf studied the bones of the stag. The kill was less than a day old, the stag's rack huge. He counted twelve points. What beast could have brought it down? A wolf pack perhaps, but wolves would leave readable sign. He put the question to his king. "Who or *what*?"

"What indeed," Shild answered in a strange voice. He thought a moment past he'd heard someone call his name: a woman's voice on a sweet falling note . . . no. Only the sad cry of a bird or perhaps a gull ranging for food from the mere to their north. For no reason he could devine, Shild had already turned his horse in that direction when one of the trackers broke out of the trees to report a boar trail leading north. By the depth of the prints in the damp earth, the boar would be of unusual size even for a prime male, though the tracks were at least half a day old.

They followed trail and spoor through the dark afternoon and thickening mist across open heath into forest again, where the tracks ended in a torn carcass stretched over the loam and dried leaves of a clearing. The blood scent was strong enough to shy their horses, eyes showing white and ears laid back. Some of the men made warding signs in front of them.

Daylight waned already; the clearing was dim with fog. There before them lay the half-eaten carcass of their boar, its fierce, ugly snout twisted unnaturally so that one wicked tusk slashed deep into the earth. The carcass had been *ripped* open, its tough hide stripped away easily as a man might pull the skin from overcooked chicken. Hundulf marveled darkly.

"What beast could do this to a boar?"

No one volunteered conjecture; the sharpest blades known needed frequent honing in cutting through pigskin. Hundulf looked around at the gray, wet wood that encircled them. "This is not a natural doing, lord king, nor a natural place we have come to. Let us leave it, break off the hunt, and ride home."

Shild barely marked him, leading his mount to the far side of the clearing to inspect its foreleg; the horse had begun to favor it. A wave of confused emotion washed over him, of dread mixed with eerie anticipation and something unstoppable about to happen. His senses open to more than cold and fog, the king heard again, distinctly now, that distant, yearning cry—

Shi-ild . . .

His hunting companions were grouped about the carcass and absorbed in its enigma. Unnoticed, Shild mounted and slipped quietly away. Restless and somehow drawn toward the cry, he put heels to flanks and rode north.

Behind in the clearing, Hundulf and the others tried to piece out the boar's fate. The more they discovered, the deeper the mystery. The animal's thick neck had been broken, apparently with a single blow. Here in the center of the clearing, the boar had furrowed the ground in anger with its forehoofs. Here he slashed the earth with his tusks. Then—as the huntsmen traced the boar's blood-furied rush across the clearing—the charge might have hit a stone wall. The tracks ended in midstride as something lifted the animal bodily and hurled it to the ground with such vicious force that the huge body slid the distance of a man's pace before the victor disemboweled it cleanly.

Hundulf stared down at the carcass. The air was cold against his face, colder memories in his mind. "I have heard tales . . . my grandam told a story once of a night creature."

"And mine and others before her," another man confirmed. "Of one who hunts but cannot be hunted or even seen. We must leave this place."

They all agreed. Huntsmen and thanes alike were anxious to put foot to stirrup and be gone. Brave men and tried, but this wretched place and the disquiet among their own animals set their very souls on edge.

Hundulf muttered as he quieted his horse and searched about for Shild. "A cursed place. Where is the king?"

Nowhere to be seen, which disturbed Hundulf the more, being the kind of man who reverenced his gods duly but day to day looked to facts and answers he could see or hold. With an effort, he shrugged off the oppressive fear and spoke firmly. "No man or beast is beyond hunting, none that leaves no track."

"There *is* a track."

The youngest of them leaned against a gnarled beech trunk; not as a man would rest at ease, but limply, in shock and weakness. "Here."

They gathered about him. Clear and deep in the muddy loam was the impression of a bare foot, high-arched and narrow for all its length, the down-curled nail marks deep where they raked the soil like the boar's. The footprint was twice the size of a large man's and almost human.

For a time, Shild heard Hundulf hailing him from far behind as he rode over the heath toward the mere through the last sickly daylight. He should have answered, but something checked the will to respond with his horn. Now, as he neared the desolate lake with its fringe of sere trees leaning out over the black water, he knew he did not want to be with his men and had ridden out to be quit of them. He had come to these Danes as a wander-waif, their first king who won the crown on his own merit, though Shild paid for that in days like this when he awoke from dreams of his parents and Asgard and walked a stranger among his thanes. Never before had his otherness lain so heavily on Shild's spirit, and when he first heard the ghostly cry, it plucked a new chord in his heart.

Or perhaps an old one remembered, Shild mused. *Clapper strikes bell, sword meets sword, each quivering to the other's blow.*

Often of late Shild felt so, of yearning toward something near that watched and perhaps waited him, and felt an indefinable kinship. Grasping his boar spear, he dismounted to let the tired horse breathe. The fog swirled thick around him, the ground beneath his feet soggy and yielding. He could smell the rank mere close by.

"Shild."

He started at the musical feminine voice. "Who is it? Who calls me?"

A slight whisper of reeds brushed aside. The mist before him dimly defined shape and movement; then the woman came into view. As she did, Shild's horse screamed, tossed its head, and bolted away into the fog, as if it had caught sight and smell of that beyond Shild's senses— or not quite beyond.

The woman was beauty itself as she advanced to meet him. More than lovely, she moved in an ethereal glow that hovered about her from the wild golden hair to her small feet, the white of her kirtle shimmering with all the rainbow colors white contained but could not always restrain.

"Shild," she murmured in a sweet, melodious voice. "Shild Scefing."

Shild took a step toward the shining vision of her, then froze. He did not know what checked or chilled him. It might have been the peculiarity of her green eyes. Even in the dark they flashed with an inner light. Shild blinked and caught his breath. The thing before him loomed suddenly huge, a giant distortion of a female dressed not in gossamer white wool but filthy rags, her skin blackened as if scorched by all the fires between Midgard and Niflheim.

With a cry of fear, Shild flung his spear straight at the thing, yet even as he loosed, the grotesque illusion dissolved, passed like a dark thought from a happy mind, and again, the exquisite woman was there. Exquisite but not frail. Her jade-green eyes followed the brief arc of the spear; she glided easily to one side. One white hand flicked out negligently and caught the thick ash shaft.

"No, Shild. Not this, my love." She took the shaft in two delicately shaped hands and snapped it like a dry twig.

Still unsure, Shild's hand poised near his sword hilt. "Who are you?"

"I am even as yourself," that lulling, lilting voice sang to him, in him. "I am yours and you are mine."

She flowed toward him like light over polished bronze, closing the last distance between them. Once more for a mere eye blink, Shild saw or imagined he glimpsed that other thing darken the mist like a monstrous shadow behind the woman's loveliness. As a king, Shild knew terror lived in all men, especially under a crown. He drew his sword, the point leveled at her breast.

"Stay or I strike."

"You would wound one who would only give to you?" she reproved sadly. "Oh, if I did not love you . . ."

One slender white arm stretched out. The blade was lifted from Shild's grip as a mother might take a small but harmful object from her child. "If I did not love you . . ."

She gripped the hard-tempered blade well below the hilt where both edges were keen. Her hand squeezed tight; before Shild's eyes the blade twisted easily as thin-beaten copper and snapped in two. The woman—the girl, for she appeared no more than sixteen—dropped the pieces and in the same moment, reached to stroke his cheek. For all her strength, the caress was feather-light. The touch of her fingers tingled through Shild, fire and ice together.

"I have looked on you often, king of Scyldings. Looked and longed for you. Until I beheld you, I knew neither pain nor sweetness nor hunger beyond what filled my belly. Now I must sup at a higher table and drink from a purer spring. Look on me, Shild. I am Sigyn, a halfling like you. Alone as you have been until the blood of Asgard which flows in both of us called one to the other."

That much might be true, the calling. Shild had seen many royal daughters whose perfections were sung to him as superbly fitting to bear his children, but none like this, none who so filled him with such a pang of sweet longing for some lost thing. If the gods were only best aspects of men, or at least the most intense, so his father Freyr must have been struck through when he first saw Gerda and knew she was his, knew that nothing could keep them apart or stay what would be between them.

Sigyn came even closer. Shild's arms of themselves went around the slender warmth of her.

"Look on me, Shild."

"I will. I do."

"What woman of Midgard is so worthy to be your queen? Be with me, Shild. My husband, come lie with me."

He wanted to, he would—but again for a chill instant he gathered something not yielding but black and hard to him. Only an instant, but Shild shuddered and loosed her. A sound somewhere between a woman's cry and an animal growl escaped Sigyn. Her right hand passed across and down his chest, parting his tunic like cobweb. He felt a sharp pain as Sigyn clasped him to the whiteness of her again and bore him to the ground. He had strength beyond any man he knew, but nothing like Sigyn's. The stroke that rended his garment could have disemboweled him as easily.

But now as she straddled him, Shild found himself hardening to meet her desire with his own. Sigyn crouched, murmuring over him, her scented torrent of hair brushing his belly and loins. A little cry of pity escaped her. In sundering his tunic, one of her nails had sliced his chest in a long wound.

"Dear love, forgive me. I have wounded where I never wished to hurt."

She licked at the blood; the heat of her tongue only urged Shild to possess her now.

"You tremble," she whispered with her lips near his. "Are you cold?"

"No . . ." He gasped with pleasure as he pierced up into her, tingling as if the woman of Sigyn were lined with lightning.

"Now I warm you," she whispered, bending close. "Now we warm each other. Oh, you are fair, my husband."

The musk of her body excited Shild as she moved purposefully over him. Many women had come to him but none like Sigyn. The need rose to fever not unmixed with an inexplicable fear. In their cleaving they were godlings, halflings, cast away between Asgard and earth, and never again would he find any mortal woman who answered him so completely.

Sigyn groaned and whimpered. Her body twisted, jerked, and ground against him as she neared the sating she sought. The dark air about them was cold but in the maelstrom of their mating, there was more than human heat. Sigyn gasped. Her back arched. The forest of shining hair whipped back and forth and her ragged cry merged with the scream of rooks over the mere. Shild gripped her thighs, spent himself in her but still Sigyn drove ruthlessly on. Heat cooled for Shild, pleasure became punishment. Her light body thickened and grew in the gloom heavier and heavier, while the scent of Sigyn turned fetid and clammy. The voice deepened, roughened. The small, hungry hands were now predatory claws that raked cruelly at what she loved and needed. Shild was a helpless rabbit mauled by a ravaging fox, then smaller under her, a mouse torn by a maddened, ravening cat. Bruised and bleeding, he cried out in terror for help—to Hundulf, to anyone who might save him from the huge, misshapen thing that croaked its grotesque, slow descent from passion until it simply rolled off and away from Shild, huddling on its knees, weeping with the sound of some gross, wounded animal.

Battered and bleeding, Shild groped for the remains of his garments. As he struggled to his feet, keeping as far as possible from the mere-hag, still mortally afraid, Sigyn spoke. Her voice was human again, poignant, an absurd beauty issuing from that inhuman throat.

"I love you, Shild Scefing. I meant only to love you for what you gave me in return. I will never hurt you again, but will you remember me always?"

Dazed, Shild mumbled something. The blood still ran from where her nails trenched deep in his flesh.

"Claim me as your queen," Sigyn entreated, "as I for all time claim you now. Give me your pledge."

Frightened and confused, Shild hardly knew what to say. "Pledge?"

The obscene head raised as Sigyn fixed him with her gaze. "I will not release you without it."

She flowed to her feet, her ungainly bulk belied by agility, looming hugely over him as she wrapped her rags about her. "I stay for your promise."

Through the night's gloom the amber fire of her green eyes bent on Shild with Sigyn's need—then suddenly beyond him as human voices pierced the darkness.

"My lord!"

"Lord Shild! Are you there?"

At the first intrusive sound, Sigyn's whole body flexed in a noiseless leap toward the reeds. Relief stained with other emotions, Shild managed to find his voice. "Here, Hundulf! Here, it is I."

He heard a faint rustling in the reeds. Sigyn was gone. Shild caught the muffled wash of something large moving through the shallows, then blurred pinpoints of light became torches held high by his companions.

"Here!" Shild wrapped the cloak about him as he recognized the fire-lit face of Hundulf. He stumbled gratefully toward his friend.

"My lord, you are hurt."

"No, it is nothing."

"Nothing? Look at you! You bleed. And those marks—"

"Nothing." Shild blinked at his counselor like a man wakened too abruptly, his sight and mind still clouded with dream. "Help me to a horse. Let us go."

They saw his rent garments and broken sword, but as the torches ringed about Shild, his men read such in their king's countenance as would not be questioned, wonder as they might.

Shild never saw Sigyn again, nor ever spoke of the encounter. Through later years and increasing cares, he sometimes heard tales of the mere-hag who dwelt in the shunned lake. Travelers eventually told of a youngling monstrous as his dame, loping the night with her, though none could guess what father had sired one abomination on another. It was the more merciful path for Shild to forget what he cared not to remember, though in troubled dreams, something came out of fog and cried her claim on him. Until age and passing time wore the image too faint to read, Shild would wake beside his human wife and remember horror achingly haunted by love.

When his time of forthfaring came, all the thanes heard Shild cry to Odin, but only his son Beow, kneeling closest by the bed, heard his father whisper to Freyr as well. As Shild had come to his people a god-king from the sea, so he departed, his funeral ship piled with wealth and war gear in such profusion that harpers afterward could never recall a death hoard to rival that which went with Shild home to Asgard.

Odin welcomed him in Valhalla. Shild was feasted and honored at the board. The first cup was presented to him by Frigga herself as the king who had spread the fame and fear of the Scyldings, though there were warriors at that feast in the hall of the slain who noted that Shild made no boast of his conquests, manly modesty which they said became him. As soon as courtesy permitted, Shild took his leave of Odin and the immortals and went home to the quieter hall of Freyr and Gerda.

With the wise vision of their kind, his parents could still find what they loved in Shild: the shining son sent forth so long ago with so much promise for men, but as well the stooped age, tarnished hopes and tattered accomplishments of an old king who could only be, in the end, what his greedy people demanded of him.

His mother was embarrassed at the shabby truth of it all. Freyr could speak only with difficulty. "Wherefore, my son? Why, when we sent you forth with such gifts, do you return with no more than the chaff and leavings of war? In other lands, wise men have written of the folly of buried talents. Wherein have you reaped more?"

Unable to meet his father's questioning gaze, Shild mustered all the truth he could. "I did what was possible. Njord's tide bore me to them, but ever after I was borne on theirs. I became like them and gave birth to far less than I hoped. I tried, Father. I did mean well."

Shild started to speak more, to ask his parents' forgiveness or at least some understanding. With the muffling burden of too many years on his lips, he could find nothing to say. He turned and walked away, a shifting double image in his parents' sorrowing sight: their proud, immortal son and an old man in whose bent shoulders and faltering step ageless Freyr perceived the weary king too worn away among humans to retain the clear semblance of a god. They sat silent together. After a time, Gerda sought her husband's hand, because even gods could be confused, helpless, and frightened by children and what they had wrought.

Shild had always meant well, but it is the doom of kings that gifts and horrors spring alike from their best intentions—including one Shild never acknowledged, if he knew at all. He was the father of the *mearc-stapa*. Grendel the mere-stalker, whose mother was Sigyn.

3

THE SWAY OF THE SCYLDINGS widened through war and policy and with passing time, men heard less and less of Sigyn and her get, until both were quite forgotten. The Danes, battle-fierce but wise as well, held the greater dragon of Rome at bay. By raid and trade, a river of gold flowed to Sjaelland and its jingle woke the northern spirit. Danish smiths melted the hoards and traced new designs in it with their own vigor. Now harpers and even the children of thanes wore necklaces that dangled coins stamped with the likeness of Rome's last, feeble emperors beside Thor's hammer and the raven symbol of Odin.

After Shild, Beow reigned and then Healfdene, who left Spear-Danes rich in tribute and three princes to succeed him. His son Hergar ruled first and briefly, a lion without the lion's majesty. As bright spring follows dark winter, Hergar was followed on the throne by his brother Hrothgar, deservedly called the Wise while still young. Where he did not rule, he persuaded or held enemies in check with firm sword and firmer policy. A prodigal with gifts, less generous with trust, Hrothgar's ears were ever more open to hear than his lips to speak. He approved the betrothal of his young sister Yrse to Onela, a prince of the Swedes, while strengthening his friendship with the Geats. By this nimble stroke and parry, he kept the one bound to him and blunted, for the present, a potential enemy.

"The marriage of your sister was wisely placed," his counselors advised. "Let yours be as shrewd. We are strong to the north, but southward, our latch is out."

"Between Elbe and Oder," Hrothgar agreed. "The Heathobards and Wylfings."

From Roman and Arabic traders, Hrothgar had gleaned the value of maps; from Saxons, a suppleness of thought to bend ancient custom to the needs of the time; from Germans, the need to keep them occupied elsewhere. Heathobards were too busied in conflict with Frise and Saxon to pose a present threat to Danes, but eastward, the

Wylfings controlled the Baltic coast and could strangle shipping trade at will.

Hrothgar plied his chief men: "What house rules the Wylfings now?"

The Helmings, he was told. Of their line, the princess Weltheow was eligible—but would Hrothgar trust any compact with Wylfings?

Hrothgar returned to the high seat, arranging his white lamb's-wool cloak, long legs sprawled out in their cross-gartered trousers. Lounging so, a careless observer might think him indolent as he smoothed the silky brown mustaches framing a shrewd smile.

"Until we must draw sword, is it not more frugal to draw a contract; one with sureties of sea trade?"

So, where he might have sent a challenge, Hrothgar dispatched a dove. The day this was concluded, four of his raiding keels returned from a sweep of Frisian and Frankish coasts. Into the merry hall where Hrothgar feasted, the victorious sea rovers brought chests laden with treasure and set them proudly before the high seat.

"Hail, Hrothgar! See what your fishermen have netted! The Romans become old women who buy off their enemies now. They pay the Franks, and the Franks yield to us."

Hrothgar descended, plunging his hands deep into the overspilling wealth of coins, jewels, and gold ingots. He laughed aloud, feeling truly like a god-king of the line of Shild. Some of this would go to the Wylfings with his marriage dowry for Weltheow, along with a Roman cloak of finest linen, part of the raiders' booty and of a hue never known in Sjaelland before, saving in rainbows, and what skill could weave them?

"What *is* this?" Hrothgar held it up to the warriors drinking along his benches. None had seen its like before, except the wizened little harper who came forward to run the fabulous garment through sensitive fingers.

"Lord, it is the color Saxons call *purpuran.* The only natural blending of red and blue."

"Wondrous," Hrothgar breathed in admiration. "Weltheow will have what no other queen could dream of. Is it from a berry like woad?"

"As I have heard, from a small shellfish harvested near Tyre. So many are needed for one garment that only emperors and the richest Romans can afford them."

"I will have one myself," Hrothgar vowed in swelling pride. But heavier, woven from virgin wool and dyed so. Like the sword of his father, it would be handed down to Hrothgar's sons and theirs in turn. Though wise and well governed, there were still moments when Hrothgar's youth rose to shake out its own fierce banner.

"Rome is old, we are young. Look about at these thanes of mine, harper. Men like Esher there. What king ever commanded so picked a company or feasted them in such a hall? If Weltheow will be my queen, I will build a hall yet more splendid and roof it with beaten gold like this. Rome dies while we but wake to life. *Our* day has come, and the world will remember the Danes as greater."

The old scop only shrugged politely. "Perhaps."

Cold water on a cheery blaze. "Only *perhaps*?"

In his long life and travels to perfect his art, the harper had listened to the music and looked into the hearts of men from the rocky shores of Eire to Tyre and Egypt. All kings claimed to come of gods—though he would not remind a very young one of this—and all passed to the funeral ship, the burial mound, or the fire. Who saluted the god-kings of Egypt now but desert wind that only buried them deeper in sand?

"Even the Romans reminded their emperors of mortality," he said. "Not a reassuring fact, not bright as this gold or purple, but more enduring. Our flame burns a span, burns down, the hall grows cold and dark. Be it fine or worthless, all we have is what shall be remembered of us. Fate is the weaver; what wealth to call our own but how we wear it? Even the gods will lose before the end. Not so, great king?"

"True. True . . ." Sometimes, young Hrothgar felt his harper to be unnecessarily tedious, always looking beyond bright noon to the coming dark. "Take up your harp; sing us a tale of victory. Tomorrow, I will send gifts and greeting to Weltheow."

As the harper drew music from his strings, Hrothgar already envisioned how he would welcome his bride and the new hall he would someday build. Drinking the undiluted Roman wine new and pleasing to his taste, he sighed with contentment, thinking it splendid to be young with all of life spread before him, a waiting feast. Danish mead and Roman wine mixed no better than their philosophies. Hrothgar's head began to swim. He grew raucous and roared rough boat songs with his companions, but made his way to bed before suffering the indignity of being carried there. It was not good to let strong men see incapacity of any kind in their king.

Hrothgar and Esher were inseparable from boyhood; to find one, you need look only for the other. When Hrothgar became king, Esher slept with drawn sword in the outer chamber of the royal bower, first to hear the guards' alarm, nearest to counter any danger to his king.

The night the treasure ships returned, Esher found sleep elusive. Hearing low groans from the inner chamber, he went to the door and looked in. Hrothgar turned fitfully and moaned in his sleep. Esher returned to his couch, finally on the point of sleep himself when he heard the king cry out—

"Esher!"

—not sharply, the voice thickened with wine-sleep. Esher sprang out of bed. In the light of the candle by his couch, Hrothgar sat bolt upright, staring wildly. Esher shook him, but the young king, still limed in the dark visions of sleep, struck out at him in terror, fighting Esher or something more fearful beyond him.

"Hrothgar!"

"He follows me! Look where he comes—"

"Hrothgar, wake!"

"The lightning—"

"It is I, friend. Peace. Peace now, you only dreamed."

And what he dreamed must have been sheer horror. In the candle glow, Hrothgar's reddened eyes still reflected nightmare, though gradually they cleared to focus on Esher and know him. "Oh . . ."

"All is well."

At the king's cry, the guards had dashed into the bower to stand uncertain but ready in the doorway. With a sign Esher sent them back to duty. Hrothgar called for water. Esher dipped the drink from a ready leathern bucket.

"My mouth is a desert."

"Mine, too," Esher agreed. "We must be careful of Roman wine and mix it with water as they do." He drank after the king.

"Poison." Hrothgar gulped more water. "Poison dreams so real that when you shook me, I thought he had caught me."

"Who, my lord? None can touch you here. Your guards are picked men, and there is myself. That failing, there's your own blade by your bed."

"But I was not here," Hrothgar mumbled. "I rode with all of you to welcome Weltheow. Bright midday, every tree and blade of grass real in my sight and bending to a real wind. Then suddenly, it was dark and I rode alone. My horse Bounder? No horse better broken to manage, but he screamed and reared, tossing about. It grew darker as I rode, and a storm coming. Thor hurled his hammer across the sky; the thunder hurt my ears. I rode toward the brow of a hill, but on that hilltop there was a man . . . give me more water."

Hrothgar drank greedily and buried his face in his hands to scrub away the persistent images. "Huge. Twice, three times the height of a natural man. There in the lightning glare, with skin so hideous and hard, it looked like our armor when we burned the Angles' stronghold at Hjortspring and the smoke tarnished all our mail and faces. Bounder screamed and bolted. I could not hold him, and all the while this *thing* ran after and shouted to me."

Hrothgar put his hand on his thane's shoulder. Esher felt it tremble. "As I live, Esher, I am king of real men in a real world, but this was not of any world we know or should know. He followed me, one of his demon strides to three of poor Bounder's gaining on me, calling me by name. Calling me 'Brother!' The lightning seared the heath all about him as if Thor played at targets with the monster. Then one bolt, truer than the rest, struck him.

"I should have known it for a dream for the loss of will and motion. Bounder slowed and stopped, floated about like a rudderless keel until I was facing the giant. The lightning flamed him still, crawled over him in rivulets of light, and in the glare, there seemed to be two figures, one shimmering over the other, different but melding as one. I swear to you, Esher—what flickered about the horror of him looked like *myself*. Then he came for me. I knew he would kill me, and as I reached for my sword no longer at my side, the word *brother* turned bitter in his —its—mouth. He said only one other word."

Again Hrothgar rubbed hard at his eyes and cheeks. "One word."

Esher leaned closer. "What word?"

"I have heard that men will cry out in sleep the guilt they dare not whisper in daylight."

"There is none on my king," Esher maintained firmly.

That king did not seem assured. "Esher . . . has any king of Danes since Shild been questionable in his right to the throne?"

"Never!" his friend scoffed at the absurdity. All Danes were sure of that. The line of descent from Shild Scefing was direct. Even his older brother Hergar might have been doubted in his wisdom but never his claim.

Hrothgar bent a haggard glance on his old friend. "Was it an omen? Must I go to the sacred horses?"

"Come now; for a dream after too much wine?"

"That was the word," Hrothgar hissed at him. "That was the word the creature snarled at me as he raised his claw to strike.

"Usurper."

4

THE BIRTH OF GRENDEL BROUGHT JOY to replace Sigyn's loneliness, enduring love in place of her brief but treasured moment with Shild. Sigyn's love was its own reason. She adored her son and in that blessed blindness saw him beautiful as Shild, fearing only that time which must come as it had to her, when day and night turned round for him and forced Grendel to see as others did. Her dilemma burdened Sigyn, and if she masked truth for a time with the remains of Loki's magic, she did so not from weakness but love soaring as the gables of Asgard. Since she could not forestall that awareness in Grendel, neither would she haste the day. For a time, he would know childhood enchanted as her own, of high, safe palace walls that warded away all harm, mirrors to show him a kinder truth while he needed it. A thousand candles would light their hall, lending brightness to the merciful mirrors that threw it back again. Beyond the impervious walls the mere stretched up and away, refracting day's glow from a land which was her son's by right. Sigyn never doubted or dissembled in that: Grendel was Shild's firstborn, heir to a god-king. His name meant "storm" or "dweller at the water's bottom." In their combination, Sigyn might have been prophetic.

His first clear memories were of safety, unshadowed happiness, and vast wonder. Nothing he saw that was not fair or fascinating. His mother bending over him, the scent of her skin, so white that the slightest flush of happiness rosed her cheeks. Sometimes when they played, her hair would tumble about his face and Grendel would breathe deep of its clean musk, pretending the thick, golden forest was another house. The sound of Sigyn was safety as well. No note of her voice that did not caress him, and so he grasped her hand and faltered into his first steps.

Sigyn dressed him in garments light as shadow, rich as delight, then let him revel in his own resplendent image in the tall mirrors. Some days his raiment was all of gold; others, silver, but always princely and perfect. In the mirrors Grendel saw that his eyes were as his mother's, green with hints of pale amber, and his skin as fair.

As childhood receded, memories drawing together as objects diminishing with distance, Grendel recalled few things vividly, and those were without exception happy and full of novelty. There was the day Sigyn took him in her arms and surged up through the crystal waters of their lake, breaking surface with a shout, ecstatic herself with Grendel's dazzled wonder at this new world of Above. The sun shone on this place called Sjaelland, but as they raced swifter than horses across the heath toward the fjord, she told him the day was not a happy one.

"The king, your father, is dead. You must look on his face and see in its lines what you are and what will be yours to come."

Death had no meaning to Grendel; what was death? He only shrieked with boy exuberance and raced after his mother, light as cloud shadow down the cliff face and into the water, swimming after the funeral ship that carried Shild on his last journey.

"I will go to Asgard someday!" Grendel piped as they grasped the beam planks of the keel and hauled themselves up over the side.

"In time, my son. Now look on your father."

Grendel's most vivid memory of that day was the blood-red sunset that suffused the scene, turning the sea to an unreal hue, bathing the heaped treasure in its glow, touching the face of the dead king with a semblance of ruddy life.

"Why does he look so strange, Mother?"

"He was very old."

Age was alien to Grendel as death. "What is *old*?"

"What he became," Sigyn explained—no explanation at all to Grendel. "Husbands and wives who live long together, they say, come to look alike. So with gods too long among men."

Most terrible of all—Grendel had no trouble recalling it because the nightmare returned later—he reached to touch his father's silvered hair and beard, and screamed with shock, the first ugly sound he had ever heard. His hand was a claw, black as charred wood, the arm, a twisted rope of rough-hided muscle. And Sigyn had vanished, replaced by a leering, lipless impossibility in which only the eyes were recognizable—

Grendel blinked. No . . . gone in a flash, though remembered afterward with sick horror. As he grew, he and Sigyn made more journeys to witness the births and funeral pyres of Shild's descendants, usurper sons and grandsons. More and more Grendel grew accustomed to his own fantastic nightmare form on these dream-farings, but always woke to safety and the lulling assurance of Sigyn's voice calming him while he cried against her breast and blurted the terrors lurking in his sleep.

"Hush. You only dreamed of those false kings who stole your throne," Sigyn soothed.

"No, it was *me*. The shape of me, what I became."

"Hush you now. More like Shild will wester into the sun or the pyre while my dear boy grows. Peace and patience."

In time, Grendel's mother taught him of other princes like her own sire, Loki of Asgard, though as he grew old enough to remark such things, Grendel wondered why so often the music of her sweet voice turned sad or bitter when she spoke of his heritage. Of her own, Sigyn said little and that known only from Loki's few brief visits when she herself was a child.

"My mother, Volla, was a woman of character, I gather; of a quick temper and deep feeling, parted from me while I was too young to remember. Ah, but Loki? Recall the sunset light on Shild's face as the ship bore him west into its heart. Loki is as burnished with the energy and imperfections of all the worlds. Folly and malice light his eye no more than wisdom and love. His mind has wings as his feet, darting him here and there, messenger to the gods or in flight from them. Beautiful and bountiful as nature, creating without thought to consequence. I have heard the Romans carved a winged god in their palaces, so perhaps they too have a notion of my father."

Loki and Asgard—Odin, Freyr, Thor, and the glittering company of them. When Grendel's mother spoke of gods, her voice wove the shape of them like a song-spell into his mind. One bright morning when Grendel woke, he found his finest gold tunic and cloak laid out and the boots of softest doeskin.

"Today, my prince," Sigyn told him as she stroked the ivory comb through his hair. "Today, we ride to Asgard. Forget these spindling men of Midgard. Today, you shall meet kings worthy of the name."

Her eyes shone as she uttered the promise. "They, too, are your heritage. Come."

The horses they rode were magnificent, with saddles silver inlaid, bridles merry with tiny bells. On the rainbow bridge Bi-frost, Heimdall greeted them with a gallant compliment for Sigyn's beauty and a hearty word for Grendel before passing them on.

From the middle of the fiery rainbow, Grendel beheld what Sigyn had so many times painted for him: the gleaming roofs and turrets rising above tall ramparts. Asgard: all too much for Grendel, whose face and garments alike went mad with colors shimmering from the multi-hued Bi-frost. More dream than waking. Giddy, delirious, he was presented to his father, Shild, who lifted him high before Odin and the warriors of Valhalla and proclaimed him son and heir to the high seat of the Danes. Grendel was fascinated by the patch over Odin's blind eye, exactly as Sigyn had described, and somewhat in awe of stern Frigga. Balder made no impression beyond strutting vanity. Balder never passed a mirror without pausing to admire himself. Sigyn called him a peacock.

"What is a peacock, Mother?" Grendel asked at home in their mere-palace.

"A brainless bird with excessive beauty in its hindquarters and not much else. Frigga so dotes on her son that she swore all Creation to an oath never to harm a hair on his empty little head. Every beast and bird, thorn and flower. All but the mistletoe," Sigyn recalled with a note of purpose in her tone. "One wonders what might come of that oversight. Go to sleep now."

Grendel visited Asgard often while the boy gradually overgrew the child in him, and no day without some wonder. Grandsire Loki sometimes shattered and shimmered into pure light when he laughed, and always had a new adventure for Grendel to share. They might commandeer Odin's horse Sleipnir and for a lark, with Grendel in the saddle before his grandfather, be away at a gallop after Thor's chariot thundering across the northern sky. Great, lumbering Thor would curse at them through his bristling red beard. He had none of Loki's quick-silver grace or wit but a temper to contend with. At first in annoyance, then genuine anger, Thor hurled lightning bolts at his taunters. Though eight-legged Sleipnir could easily outstrip the chariot horses, Loki was careful to stay out of range.

Very much like Loki, being of his turbulent blood, Grendel came in time to chafe at the unrelieved valor of warriors and the ponderous, stoic propriety of Asgard in general. In the midst of feasting he would hope to discover a fly in Heidrun's unfailing milk or for the kitchens to undercook the pork just once. The rarer the better to Grendel's taste as he grew older. He wanted to savor the life of the meat before swallowing.

Drearier still, those nearest his own age, the young Valkyries, were pompous and grim as Frigga, always descending on the aftermath of battle and solemnly bearing dead heroes home to Valhalla. When one of their culling revealed himself to be an Assyrian rug dealer merely plying his trade when the enemy fell on his buyers, Odin reprimanded the war maidens severely for their negligence. They in turn denounced Loki; the deception smacked of his depravity. Loki handsomely shouldered the blame for Grendel's inventive prank.

"Flesh of my flesh," he beamed at Sigyn's boy. "Blood of my blood. And where shall we adventure today?"

Where indeed with such a grandfather? Not that Shild neglected him, but Grendel's father had too much of the weary king about him to be company for a growing boy, and—most odd—Grendel could never see his face clearly. Shape-shifting Loki was ideal, old as time yet young as Grendel himself. What to do? Ride the meteors hurtling white-hot into the World Ocean? Plunge after them to its depths to twist the tail of Loki's serpent-son, then shoot up through whale and shark and myriad schools of fish to breast the resulting tidal waves? What a grandfather, what a golden time. . . .

But tarnished gold as time passed. As Grendel grew older, the dark dreams came clearer and more frequently. Always hunting through the night with a hunger that gorging barely appeased. The dream repeated with predictable features. He surged up through the mere waters, fending off creatures predatory as himself and the female thing swimming with him. Their blood, as he tore at the mere-denizens, only whetted an appetite like fever. Striding across the heath always with the same destination, a ramparted hall where puny men laughed and feasted and thrilled to music somehow hateful to Grendel's soul. Then the she-beast would whisper to him in Sigyn's voice: *All yours, though stolen from you.*

Night after month after year, captive in the murky dream, Grendel lurked on the outskirts of the royal steading at Lejre, coming to know certain men by sight. He saw in Hrothgar, his own great-nephew, a family resemblance to himself and Shild. There was the warrior called Esher, always at the king's side, and Weltheow the new queen. After much time, children were born to the royal pair, and of late, more men had come with axes and shovels. In a great laboring they felled and dragged huge logs from the forest, leveled the ground anew, and a magnificent new hall rose near the old one.

And within those doors, the sons of Hrothgar. More of them to claim what Shild bequeathed to Grendel.

Each night this dream-watching as the years passed. Then, drawn away by hunger, Grendel hunted—a sheep or cow or even a farmer abroad too late, tearing at the warm flesh as he shambled homeward toward the mere and down into a fetid den where black water writhed back from foul air and bone-littered paving stones; where the she-creature unspeakable as his own form crooned in Sigyn's loved voice and welcomed him with arms hideous, hard, and black as his own.

Frightened now when he woke, the dream aura lingering much longer, sometimes he would ask Sigyn to bring him one of her hand mirrors of bronze and silver. Grendel would gaze long at his reflection: pale perfection like his mother's, the hair, finespun gold. Something of Shild in the set of his head, a hint of Loki in the eyes and the way his mouth curled upward at the corners as if amused at the vast joke of the world—but no trace of that monstrosity he became in sleep.

"You slept and slept." Sigyn bent over her waking son, putting the back of one small hand to his brow for fever signs. "You look drawn. Some humor has taken you. What is the matter?"

Searching the mirror fruitlessly for answers himself, Grendel could only whisper, "I cannot tell. Something is changing in me."

Perhaps it was coming manhood, as he had seen such change in ordinary men like Healfdene and Hrothgar, except that they grew and withered swiftly as spring flowers. In no more than a season of Grendel's time, proud Hrothgar's waist thickened and the spring in his walk slackened to a more sedate pace. Where once he and Esher rode ahead of the war companions, now they gave grave counsel to younger men who rode in their place. In moments of avuncular empathy, Grendel felt it must be a tragic burden to be so frail and transient.

In his waking hours now he avoided Asgard, pacing Sigyn's hall in a heavy, inexpressible gloom, not hearing when she spoke to him or noting her fearful concern for his distemper, guessing its cause. Just so had it come over her at his age.

Grendel darkened. No longer did he want to play or swim with his mother. From time to time in the hall, always fresh-scented before, his keen nostrils caught the stench that pervaded his dreams. Violent drives seized on him. He wanted to kill something in reality as he did in the bloodstained dreams, rending a limb at a time, pretending the prey was Hrothgar, so complacent on his stolen throne. *Kill the pig, kill his sow-queen and their puny princelings—*

Then what? Grendel turned the notion of *then?* in his mind as his sharpening sense of smell detected blood scent from the mere above where, as always, one creature preyed on another. He felt hungry.

There were calmer moments when Grendel saw no puzzle in the mirror. In periods of reason, he pondered what was happening to him and tried to ask Sigyn, though the question somehow always died in his throat unuttered. At other times now he sensed Sigyn herself about to speak as of something weighing on her own spirit. Their palace became more silent, and Grendel felt the chill of its shadows.

One day, Sigyn reached quite naturally to caress him. Grendel shoved her away roughly, startled at his gross action and more by the ugly snarl out of his own throat. "Leave me alone!"

For a moment, he had an urge to strike her. Sigyn recoiled as if he had. "It is almost gone," she breathed.

"What is almost gone?"

"My poor son."

"Leave me, I say. Why do you gape at me?"

"I tried so hard to keep . . ." Sigyn said no more but crept out of the hall, face in her hands. A few moments later, Grendel heard her soft weeping.

Torn between urges to cruelty and remorse, Grendel hated Sigyn for a stupid, *stupid* cow and himself the more for giving her pain. Nothing would reconcile the warring humors now but furious movement. He lunged at the hall doors, dove into the water, and flung himself upward like a killing missile toward the surface of the mere, breaching in a crash of spray, churning for the shore where their saddled horses always waited. Their eyes were red fire, coal black coats steaming. Today, Grendel chose the wilder of the two to match his mood, leaped the saddle, urging his command in a growl terrible as the demon horse he rode.

"Go. *Fly.*"

5

THE STALLION'S HOOFS, STRIKING SPARKS from air itself, lifted Grendel high until forest and heath became fading patches of color on the earth and then vanished below billowing clouds. Higher still into the cold, thinning air, driving not at Asgard but the sun. Grendel had no taste or time for gods today, not in pain like his. Like a child who needs to beat and scream at the nearest object or person, he reined and reared the snorting horse in furious, aimless circles, roaring at all Creation—

"I hate you! I hate you!"

—then slowed, trembling. Listening.

Thunder rolled across the sky—no, not true thunder but the sound of movement. Far off to the north over the lands of eternal ice, Grendel heard a great, bellowing voice. Small in the distance, a black insect against deep blue sky, something approached with spider-thin legs flashing out from side to side. The chariot took on form as it hurtled toward Grendel: two plunging horses fierce as the blood-eyed creature he rode, now screaming its shrill challenge at the beasts drawing Thor's chariot.

Sigyn said Thor carried lightning as mortal drivers' spears. The sight had always thrilled Grendel who worshiped the virile god even as he teased him, but darker drives impelled him now, turning reverence to murder. A madness coursed its venom through his veins. He needed to fight this great, gross dimwit of an alleged god.

Go, whispered the agony in Grendel's mind. *Defeat him, bring him down.* The same message quivered through the horse's back into Grendel's thighs. *Go. Destroy.*

His horse shot forward like a missile from a catapult, veering onto a collision course with the plunging chariot. Loki had once done the same in sport, passing close enough for Grendel to tweak the off horse's ear. Today, his dagger would mark that ear. But even as he streaked forward across cold sky, the chariot horses reared, screaming in terror as Thor fought to control them, turning the chariot to one side and tugging the team to a full halt. Grendel wheeled on him, capable of anything now.

"You great ox," he sneered. "You mindless boar. Drive horses? You could not drive a bargain for supper were it not given you free."

Without the thunder of the chariot wheels, the high air grew ominously still. Thor and Grendel faced each other. Grendel's horse made low, growling noises in its chest and pawed at the ether, lusting to attack. Thor's animals tossed their heads and showed the whites of their eyes. Some small atom of sense sent a warning to Grendel. The hammer Mjollnir was raised in Thor's mailed fist. That weapon had once sheared through a stone pillar, it was said, to kill an enemy. Threatening now, but Grendel saw an odd confusion and something very like fear in Thor where none had ever shown before.

More, Grendel felt a strangeness, something alien about the whole encounter.

"Whatever you are," Thor warned, "from whatever bottom pit of Hel or night, get back."

"Son of Odin, what ails you?" Grendel called, moving a little closer. "Do your eyes grow weak that you don't know the firstborn of Shild Scefing?"

"Shild?" Thor actually gasped. "Not of Shild, not you. Back, I say!" His muscled arm raised higher with the hammer. "Nothing like you has ever entered Asgard, All-Father Odin be thanked."

There *was* fear in the god's strong, open face, and beyond that, a kind of stunned revulsion. "What *are* you?"

"Now you jest in turn." Yet Grendel felt a chill of confirmation creep through his marrow. "Shild presented me and my mother to all Asgard. You were there, guzzling and stuffing as always. You know my grandsire Loki who is father to Sigyn."

"Loki I know," Thor conceded with something like a shudder; it seemed so incongruous to him. "That much I can believe. He was ever a breeder of monsters—"

"I am no monster!"

"—and you bear his sooty looks. He has dared much by way of mischief and dishonor but never brought his spawn into Asgard. You pollute the sky! Get away!"

Grendel hesitated, unsure. The rage had drained out of him, re-

placed by something more sickening, a malady of the mind that remembered dreams of pure hunger and darkness. And Thor's eyes
avoided him as if inflamed by something they could not bear to behold.

With wounded dignity, Grendel said, "Perhaps I have jested too
harshly myself, thinking you a man who could take a joke and laugh.
If not, I will leave you, and good riddance. What are you but a glorified
blacksmith unfit to shoe my horse?"

"Horse?" Incredulity colored Thor's revulsion. "That . . . that is
no horse but a *thing* like yourself. Back where you came from before I
send you there. You affront my sight."

Grendel began to feel afraid. Everything he saw—Thor, the chariot,
the horses that drew him, the bright illumination of day itself seemed
different somehow, not *quite* as remembered. With an effort, he reined
in his resentment. "Lord Thor, forgive my words. In all peace and
friendship, do not joke with me now. What is amiss? Have I not been
familiar in Asgard?"

"Familiar?" Thor's echo sounded feeble, revolted. "Do you think
a bad dream such as you could cross Bi-frost or walk among heroes?"

"Aye, and have often." Grendel urged his horse nearer. "Say you
know me and I will go in peace."

"Get back."

"No! You will deal honestly with me."

"So I will!"

The hammer Mjollnir flew at Grendel. At his mere thought of eva-
sion, the horse beneath him twitched and dodged aside. Grendel felt its
muscles coil and bunch to attack.

"I will show you what you are," Thor howled in his rage and naked
fear. His head with its red sunburst of flaming hair and beard snapped
back. Thor flung a pointed finger in command at the sun. An arrow of
fire lanced downward from the orb, glowing as a shaft of light in the
god's iron-gloved grip. The lethal bolt flew, piercing deep into the flank
of Grendel's horse. The animal convulsed with a shriek not at all the
sound of a stricken horse. Grendel had only an instant to see what
writhed in its death throes under him, but it was nothing like a horse.
An amorphous, twisted, ropy thing formed of no flesh, from no world
he knew. No time at all to understand the horror before a second bolt
struck him full in the chest.

The spear of light pierced and dissolved to running fire through

Grendel's body. The fires of change traced his being to its last particle, shattering the fair illusion, revealing a hide black-scorched as burned pork or a ravaged field. For the shapely hands Sigyn was wont to admire and kiss—travesties like the talons of a beast, flailing for a futile hold on sky itself as Grendel fell forever out of dream toward a hard, real earth. Out of boyhood and magic to what he was and would always be. Out of love and safety to bewilderment and rage at answers forever denied, out of blindness into cruel sight.

Below him, disintegrating as it tumbled, he saw a black, shapeless thing absurdly girdled with a jeweled saddle. Plummeting in its wake, Grendel screamed with terrible knowledge: where it came from and how and its reason for existence in his blindness. His own nightmare form burned through the thickening air, glowing red, then white as meteor iron until he plunged deep into the mere that hissed with the heat of him. Yet the fire was not so hot as that searing Grendel's brain.

His lipless jaws gaped open, breath and hate exploding out of him into the murky waters. His outsized hulk of a body flexed in a deeper dive. Thor had wounded him; his hide was lacerated and bleeding. Other hungers in the mere, their senses keen as his own, detected the blood trail and turned in pursuit. Grendel tore at the nearest of them, forced its maw open and back, plunged a claw deep into the throat and plucked the living heart from the creature, stuffing it into his own mouth. The unappeasable hunger for flesh was real, no part of dreams. Only the beauty had been a lie.

He tumbled through the water barrier surrounding their palace onto hard stone, crouching, listening to his own breath sawing deep in his barrel chest. Grendel rose, fisting one claw to batter in the doors. They gave before him, his rage carried him through in lunging strides—

The she-thing waited him in the reeking den. No candles burned —why should they? Grendel allowed in the cold part of his suffering. They were part of the illusion stripped from his new sight. No gold plate or jeweled goblets, noble furnishings and tapestries no more than lichened stone and seaweed, the high table at which they had supped delicacies only a damp-rotted plank. Mirrors that once showed beauty to Grendel—now only what reflection water surface gave back to feeble light.

His mother saw the terrible wound of knowledge in his eyes and flinched away from it. Her obscenity of a mouth opened over large, serrated teeth. Unbelievable: She was trying to smile at him. In one blood-smeared claw she gripped the carcass of a freshly killed goat. Sigyn held it out to her son.

"You have been gone for hours. Have you eaten?"

Hours! Yes, Grendel realized numbly. He must think in the time of men now, measuring the horror of his existence in their creeping hours like acid falling drop by drop on his flesh. And yet Sigyn's voice was still a lulling song; that much had been no illusion. What else of beauty remained to him against the unspeakable rest?

"I have been with Thor, Mother. Really been with him."

The misshapen head drooped. "I thought as much. Now or later."

"Not asleep, not dreaming of Asgard or riding a black stallion. Oh, I *saw* what I rode. Thor didn't know me, nor I him. Does that surprise you, Mother?"

"No." Her tone was flat, dead. "I am sorry." To escape the accusation in his stare, she held out the food again. Fury exploded in Grendel. He lunged at Sigyn, striking the pathetic offering from her grip. "Who was my father? What was he?"

"Shild. I told you, Shild. I did not lie."

"By everything sane and good, what *part* of Shild?" But for the sick horror in him, Grendel would have battered at that parody of a face. He grabbed Sigyn's wrist viciously and forced her down on her knees. "And the rest? All the rest of it all these years? We have never been to Asgard, have we? *Have* we?"

"No . . ."

"Never rode across Bi-frost or bathed in the colors of the rainbow. Never save in the dreams crooned into my stupid, trusting little ear in your sweet, lying voice. We never met Loki—"

"I only wanted—"

"Never feasted in Valaskjalf, never met Shild," he lashed at her, rage a rising snarl in his throat. "Never heard him recognize me as heir to anything. Except this . . . grave. Isn't that true, Mother? Tell me."

"Grendel, let me go. I am as helpless as you, cursed as you."

Grendel flung her across the body of the goat. Sigyn was weeping. Then, womanlike, she did the simple, needful things, peeling the skin from her kill, unable to look at her son. "When the magic faded for me, my only wish was to preserve a little for you. I know your pain. It has been mine for so long. With what enchantment remained, I turned waking into sleep for you."

"Yes." Grendel quivered over her. "To make me believe."

He should have known long before this. The recurrent nightmare of hunting and unrelenting hunger, shambling over the heath for prey, feeding unutterably with the she-thing at his side. "Thor could not look at me. But he struck me with his lightning."

The fatal bolt seared through memory now as it had pierced his flesh. "He enlightened me."

"You bleed. You are hurt."

"Not from that."

"No matter. Knowing would have come in time, now or later."

Did all parents in their blundering fondness build such lies for children? Gilded fairy houses for them to enter only to find sharp knife-truths to cut them? Which was the worser wound, Sigyn's lie or Thor's bolt? With a low snarl Grendel dragged Sigyn to her feet and pulled her toward the water mirror. He would put cauterizing fire to the wound and close it now. "No more lies, Mother. No more believ—"

Grendel saw their reflection and screamed with truth that tortured sight. An insane distortion of a human face with predatory, grinding jaws, marred midway between prognathous ape and primordial fish— all that, and yet the eyes and brow further mocked humanity in their intelligence.

And the rest of him . . . not a dream but truth. The towering body, beetle-black in its tough near-carapace of a hide rippling over long, ropy muscles like to human but infinitely more powerful. Arms that ended in five-fingered claws. Elongated feet with toes prehensile as the hands, each with curled, horny nails that could gut a horse or boar with ease, and had done so often, he knew now. Between him and his mother, only Sigyn's ugly paps and his male organs set them apart.

"All true." Grendel's wail trailed off into a moan. Claws lifted to cover what only madness could describe as a visage. He sank to his knees, sobbing uncontrollably. "Mother—"

"My baby."

"Help me."

Sigyn knelt over her son slumped on his knees in the shape of misery. "My poor baby boy."

"Why?" The animal sound of him heaved with human anguish. "How? If—if I am a beast, where did I learn of beauty? If I am human, why am I so, why is it all taken from me like this?"

"How many times have I thrown that question at the gods? Once Loki told me how, in other lands, men prayed to more merciful gods than ours; at least more responsible." Sigyn stroked his head. "I would find that mercy for you if I could."

"Mercy? All my life you gave me nothing but lies."

"I called it love."

Grendel raised his face to her. *How ridiculous*, he thought clearly. Hideous as she was, to read so vast a pity there. "What ran in Shild's blood or yours to make me so?"

"The same as in all men and gods," Sigyn answered out of a scarred knowledge of her world. "Men carve their gods from the best of themselves. What is left must define their fears. They can't help it."

She rocked him in her arms. Shuddering, Grendel wiped a claw across his face to blot the tears. That was true, he recalled. So often, lurking in the night outside Hrothgar's hall, he had heard the scops, those poetic liars, sing of heroes, honor, and courage, then as counterpoint always the wretched betrayal of these virtues. They had so little of any value but could always count on the treacheries.

"I was so alone before Shild came," Sigyn murmured over him. "I tore at myself and the world, killed for killing's sake to stop my pain. I howled at the gods as you do: *Why? How?* We are more like men than not. Like them, we tire of our pain and it numbs. When the pain faded, I had time to think. We are their nightmares. If there were more of us than them, I suppose they would be ours. Surely they have been mine," Sigyn added with an edgeless bitterness. "But I loved Shild, and he did see the beauty in me for a moment. You are his son."

Grendel felt wearier and more battered than ever before in his life. And now, how long and heavy the weight of all those years since he looked on the dead face of his father. Ages. He pushed himself up, avoiding the mirror surface. "I must sleep now."

With the need for that rest, Grendel felt the first stirrings of the hunger that was no dream but would always be with him.

"Eat," Sigyn urged.

"Later I will hunt. As always."

"As always," his mother echoed. Her muscled shoulders rippled in a shrug. "Loki was not unkind. He gave me a little beauty for a little time. Shild gave me you. I did try. I would try now. Oh, Grendel"—her claws reached for him—"I would be beautiful for you if I could. I would have all women and all worlds fair for you—and for me, while the wishing. But I am a god's get in the body of a beast. Pity, but can Hrothgar or his kind say more? I am sorry the colors faded. Deal with what you are, my son. Eat the goat."

His dreams were only mundane continuation of waking, of the blood scent calling him to feed. As Grendel woke, his preternatural sense of smell caught the rank odor of their den, more familiar and less offensive than before. He opened his eyes in gray twilight and turned over on the pile of rags and weed that had been his bed since birth.

He called Sigyn. No answer. Wisely, she left him alone tonight. He was in no vein for her now, no drive in Grendel but hunger and revenge for the foulness meted out to his innocent life. By whom? Shild? The weaving Fates? Who and where were the guilty?

Who stood in direct descent and profit from the primal wrong?

"Hrothgar," Grendel breathed. Hrothgar and his blood.

His glowing green eyes swerved upward. Far above their den his acute hearing caught the muffled rush of the mere creatures in their own feverish search for food, and beyond them, the fainter sound of rain. Cattle, sheep, and swine would be byred tonight. No matter; this night Grendel craved more delicate flesh, as much as he could gorge. Only a little time past he had seen the torchlit procession at Lejre as Hrothgar led his family and thanes into the new hall. So many of them and so prime, like pigs in Blood Month, ready for slaughter. Rage still seethed beneath appetite. Beast he was, but one who thought, loved, and sorrowed even as he hungered, much like Hrothgar's kind. Then bend the beast rage to purpose, elevate mere instinct to human viciousness. Go and feed.

He thought to arm himself with the sword that hung over their bone-littered table. The blade, forged by giants, had been an early gift from Loki to Sigyn. A toy in her hands or Grendel's, the sword would task the strongest man in Denmark to wield. Grendel drew the weapon from its scabbard, spun it, balanced the point whirling on his hard palm—

No. How frail to need a sword against such feeble prey as men. He thrust the blade back into the scabbard and ran down the hall, burst through the doors, and dove into the water wall. His body flexed and shot toward the mere's surface, broke it with a roar, and swam with powerful strokes for the shore.

The rain stung at his skin, driven by a demon gale even as he was propelled by fury toward Heorot. Grendel broke into a trot on a course well known by now.

"Hungry . . ."

He did not think to voice the word; the sound escaped like a saw drawn through hard ash, part of the thunder above as he loped over hills and heath. For a while, Grendel fancied a cadence in that booming, and in the flicker of sheet lightning, he delighted in his shadow as it capered and leaped high, arms flung out, head back and maw gaping to bite at heaven, drink the rain, suck the very marrow from the stars. Beyond pain there was a cold joy. All lost, what more left to lose? From now on, he would only win.

The lightning that eccentrically lit his dance was punctuated suddenly by a forked bolt. The spear of flame lanced into the ground near his foot, smoldering through wet grass and bracken.

Grendel jumped aside, pausing to listen.

Now he heard that other rumbling behind the thunder. His head lifted, searching. The lightning seemed to emanate from a central but moving point above him; its flickering glare silhouetted the chariot careening wildly across the clouded night sky.

Thor again: Old Red Beard making free with his power over wind and storm. Grendel's green eyes narrowed to calculating slits. The horses were barely managed, the chariot swerving and teetering. From the flat, tuneless sound of Thor whose voice was never meant to sing, Grendel knew he was drunk.

Scant time to think it before Thor, with a great tugging at the reins, veered the team into a circling path over Grendel and slung another bolt far wide of the mark.

"What do I see down there? Are you not that unmentionable thing I met this morning?" Thor jeered, his roar filling the night sky. "Night is the time for such as you, not the light of day. How do you like this for a storm, animal?"

The lightning flew straight at Grendel's head. He sidestepped the fire-spear which struck and flamed an oak tree nearby. "Your aim has been better," he bellowed back.

Thor's raucous voice was slurred with drink. "The farmers asked for a gentle rain, but then you rose from the mere like corruption from a wound and I had to do more, even to flattening every stalk of grain on the island. Things like you cannot be allowed to live."

"Blaze away, I care not!" Grendel howled back. "You old guzzler, you've drunk away what little wit or skill you had. Try harder."

"You impossibility. You cannot *exist*."

The god's arm flexed and hurled bolt after bolt at dodging, dancing Grendel. The heath about him smoked and smoldered, soaked though it was. Trees split and burned. Grendel grew tired of the poor sport.

"Thor," he taunted in a blandly reasonable tone. "This is boring. Put more effort into it. Take better aim. Will it help if I stand still?"

"Then stand!" Thor pulled the chariot to a stop again, the two horses snorting and pawing at inky air. The sky flickered ominously as Thor's arm shot up in command. The whole vast dome of heaven seemed to wrinkle; all the power of all the lightning in the north glowed and shaped to a missile in the god's hand. The bolt pierced through Grendel with a *crack!* that might have rended Creation itself.

Drunken Thor blinked in amazement. The giant figure of Grendel went incandescent as the lightning became part of him, exploding him in a myriad of sentient sparks, each with a mocking voice of its own that jeered at Thor's impotence and lit Grendel's mind with savage triumph.

"I cannot exist?" he challenged as the sparks drew together again, forming the outline and then the substance of him. "I live, I am. I *am* the lightning and the storm. I am the chaos behind Hrothgar's illusion of order and behind yours, clown-son of Odin. I am the cold that chills the embers of their fires, the darkness to snuff their little light as you have killed beauty in me. Wherefore impossible? If poets can dream of monsters, can I not dream poetry? While I haunt their night, do they not haunt me with what I can never touch or hold? So be it. I am their boundary, their limit, necessary to them. If I defy, do I not define them as well? But must I love them or their world for this?"

Grendel stood erect on the scorched, smoking heath and roared his laughter by way of farewell to the inept son of Odin. "What, shall I curse myself, shrivel, and die? I think not. I will be part of men when you and Asgard are forgotten. Pardon my lack of humility; it doesn't seem to suit. And take my love to my dear father, Shild."

Under the driving rain, Grendel turned and ran away to the southwest, hunger-driven, fate-drawn to Heorot.

6

ROM BEYOND THE OUTER BANK and ditch, Grendel surveyed Heorot through darkness and rain. If he had constructed Asgard from Sigyn's and his own imaginings, this hall was truly known to him. Night after night he had seen men come and go about their watches, heard their low voices passing the night hours in muffled talk, and music and laughter from the hall. Grendel had seen new Heorot rise day by week in reality only thought to be a dream. As far as news of Hrothgar's hall ran, no man had seen its equal, and the tales traveled far.

Yes, Grendel thought over the hunger rumbling in his belly and not much longer to be denied: Thor woke him well enough. He knew this place, the artful use of the nearby lake to water the inner and outer ditches for defense. The line of outbuildings between ditches and those ringed by the inner bank. Heorot rose in the center, commanding all: high-gabled and iron-fastened, carved with the loops and scallopings in relief that these Danes worked into wood with awl and chisel, as if in fastening over the doors those great antlers from which Heorot took its name, they had absorbed the noble sweep of the stag horns into their own imagination and made it part of them.

Grendel had counted the strides of guards pacing the outer length of the great hall: forty for a tall man, half that or less for himself from the doors to the high seat Shild's descendants stole from him. As the wind-driven rain sheeted down, he measured now the distance to the nearest guard huddled in his cloak on the rampart over the outer ditch. He moved toward the figure, sliding soundlessly into the water, across it, gliding up into the shadows of the bank. The sentinel, his vision limited by the hood of his cloak, moved away now into the wind and pelting rain. He would not persist long in that before turning. Grendel bellied upward toward the rampart. Now the guard paused, flinching against the rain needling into his face, gave his back to it and paced again toward waiting Grendel. Past him.

The shadows at the guard's back rose up massively and struck.

The wind veered suddenly, wafting music from Heorot. Crouched over his kill just below the outer rampart, Grendel winced at the painful sound, the thin pinging of the harp, the monotonous rise and fall of the quavering yet compelling voice of the scop. An old man. They lived such brief lives.

Grendel would feast in Heorot tonight. The bit of liver he nibbled now only whetted appetite. He finished it and licked the warm blood from his claws. When the beer feasting was done, Hrothgar and his family would leave the hall, but many would sleep within as always. Grendel searched out the nearest guards, then crept down the rampart, slipping between the outbuildings toward the inner ditch. He would cross the ditch submerged beneath the guarded bridge, and wait. Justice, not vengeance. What cruelty did he inflict that had not been dealt out to him? In the shining gloss of youth he had been stripped of that wealth forever, made to *know* what he was, where puny men like Hrothgar could go to the grave thinking themselves invincible. Admirable. Beautiful. In the unweathered newness of Heorot, Hrothgar would know the same loss and how impotent he was.

Grendel flowed forward silently, part of the dark.

Hrothgar's heart was full this night. Chief of Scyldings, overlord of Danes and more tributary bands than he could count at any one time, he sat in his high seat, drank, and set the gold-filigreed horn in its stand. Enough of feasting tonight. Time for rest—and yet for this one satisfied moment, he could not exchange the usual glance with Weltheow nor signal Esher to call an end to the festivity. At the mead benches, his older thanes drowsed over their drinking horns, and even the new younger companions had left off their raucous jesting, ready to lay out their beds for sleep. The old scop's harp couched in its soft goatskin pouch, the harper himself wearied with sagas sung, eased his stiff limbs in a place of honor near the high seat.

On Hrothgar's left, his young sons Hrethric and Hrothmund compared their lavishly decorated new toy swords; on his right, Weltheow sat erect and serene, the silver threading through her plaited hair the only contrast to the beauty that would not leave her yet.

Attended by servants carefully chosen for the task, the Heathobard ambassador and his party had no cause to complain of stinted welcome. The choicest cuts of meat were theirs, and gifts of jewelry and war gear from the Danish king. There had been polite exchanges when they arrived and more to come tomorrow, as courteous but more subtly designed to draw them out. The intentions of any nearby foreign power were of vital interest to Hrothgar.

Still, this evening he had a full heart; of late, he had begun to regard his as a full life. Not that he was old by any measure of the term—

Liar. Forty-five was old enough, and every sunset added to the weight bowing his scarred shoulders. He married young enough. His youthful pride once thought that Wylfing alliance shrewd, whereas it brought more value to his own life than safety to Danes. Weltheow was a jewel in his house, though Hrothgar had long abandoned hope of lasting peace with her royal kin.

And the growing, central problem here at home. Weltheow's first two sons died as infants, the third, their daughter Freaw, now gone to Ingeld of the Heathobards. The queen had been ill for years after Freaw's birth with a malady that wrenched her courses askew so that she did not conceive. Some believed it witches' work and certain suspect women were examined, though the runes indicated no such mischief. Still Weltheow continued barren. Hrothgar was gone much of that time from Lejre, fighting or attending to the trebling cares of an expanding overlordship. Then, before her courses ceased altogether, his queen conceived twice again. Sons, but born dangerously late. Hrethric was now only five, Hrothmund, barely four. If Hrothgar were called to Odin before they grew, the crown must be protected by his nephew Hrothulf, the son of his late brother Halga.

Hrothgar studied his nephew covertly now, as he had so often of late: Hrothulf lounging in his place at the head of the nearest table, fastidiously wiping the meat grease from his Frankish dagger. Handsome and amiable, quick to make friends, matching cup for cup in drinking contests but no more open in drink than when sober.

Halga was a fine man, one who might have stood before all the north as a model for kings, just as Hergar stood for all crowned folly. Who are you, Nephew? Will you guide my sons to power or steal it from them?

Despite the noble dynasties sung by scops, there was that recurrent dissonance in so many of the songs. Never could greatness, however true the ring of its currency, be trusted to beget its like. Edgetho of the Geats was of unquestioned honor, but in that quality and others, his son, Beowulf, was one over whom men of judgment hesitated to wager.

Hrothgar remembered the clumsy, brooding boy prone to accidents and crippling headaches.

Perhaps his own nephew was beyond reproach, but would that were beyond doubt. Transferring his attention to Esher down the hall, Hrothgar did not see Hrothulf's eyes flick toward the royal sons. Queen Weltheow marked it, though. She loved her sons fiercely with an instinct for the smallest seedling danger to them. Her mind reviewed the long distrust of this smiling nephew. Hrothulf was afforded every honor and worth them perhaps, but closest to power after her sons. Now he noted her glance, and smiled. Weltheow nodded graciously, raised her Roman drinking glass to the young man and privately wished him an even shorter life than his honored father.

From long years at Hrothgar's side, Esher read in the king's attitude that he was ready to end the evening. Esher signed to Wulfgar the royal herald who came to stand before the high seat, facing the mead benches.

"Let there be silence! Silence there for Esher, the king's first counselor."

The tables took some time to quiet. Some of the men were near to being drunk, all ready for sleep, but the moment was meet for a last cheer. All turned expectantly to Esher, who stood with his horn raised in salutation to the high seat. Not a large man but of a bearing that commanded respect. A measured man, others said, who never, on the eve of battle, boasted what deeds he would perform, nor afterward of those he had. Measured in speech, a guarded vault of counsel. Secrets shared with Esher vanished into silence or were unlocked to Hrothgar alone.

Esher gave the cheer to his king. "Hail Hrothgar! Hail to the king who promised this new Heorot, greatest and strongest of halls. Hail to the king who hoards no treasure but pours it out like water among his thanes."

From all the tables to the rafters that threw the cry back again. *"Hail!"*

"Hail to the ring-giver who never broke a promise to his men."
"Hail!"

Esher's salute rang again to the roof beam. He hoped the Heathobards would see the honor in which his king and queen were held. "And to Weltheow, best of wives, who kept her bridal promise of sons. All has endured in proof as this hall against the night and elements. Ever hail!"

As the company drank his health, Hrothgar stood up in his place. "May it well become you. Now the queen is weary, and my sons"—as he descended to gather each under an arm—"your future guardians bid you a drowsy good-night. This is a new hall meet to house so many new thanes. Well have you warmed it with this night's feasting."

Hrothgar gave his squirming boys into the charge of Weltheow's women and turned to find Esher at his elbow. They spoke in low tones.

"Our Heathobard guests were impressed?" Hrothgar hoped. "They spoke of wanting a lasting peace. Do you believe them?"

"The ambassador's eyes did not shift away when he gave his reasons for a treaty," Esher judged.

"You believe they are sincere?"

"I mean we are safe to believe them so far," Esher qualified.

"You do not look convinced."

"No, it is not that."

"They have worn themselves out in war with the Franks. They want no difficulty with us." Hrothgar studied his friend's frowning countenance. "What troubles you? The Heathobards' bower is well guarded. There are no blood feuds between any of our men and them."

"I know." Esher glanced down the hall where the younger thanes were tipping up trestle tables and laying out their beds. "New men and new swords, nor one yet used in battle. I will stay in the hall tonight, my lord."

"But why? It's not needed."

"Oh—" Esher shrugged. "Give me leave. Indulge me. Good rest."

"And to you. Wake me early."

The royal family departed for their bower, protected from the rain by cloths held over them by servants, the Heathobard guests suitably escorted to those quarters prepared for them. Esher claimed a place midway down the hall near the fire pit, making sure that each warrior knew exactly where his weapons were, to be grasped instantly in the dark. As the last taper was extinguished, Esher lay down with his sword to hand.

Something kept him alert. Call it womanish apprehension. He reverenced Odin sincerely, but intuition and common sense as well. In emergency these untried companions would fare better under a more experienced sword. Moreover, when Esher raised his toast to king and queen—for no good reason, as a man's mind will hold more thought than he speaks in any moment—Esher recalled a night years gone when Hrothgar woke out of nightmare, his eyes still terrible with the vision, and asked . . . what was it he said?

But the thought had passed with his salute to Hrothgar, though its shadow lingered over Esher. He stared up into the darkness, in the same wish summoning sleep and staving it off.

GRENDEL STAYED HIS HUNGER while Hrothgar, his family, and guests scurried through the downpour to shelter. He watched from the shadows the last faint torchlight darken through the casements of Heorot, heard the last good-nights muffled under rain. No movement now, no sound. From his hiding place, Grendel glided forth in a sweeping curve, faster and faster until he ran straight at the broad barred doors of Heorot at the speed of a galloping horse. Hunger chewed at his belly, rising as a growl in his throat. Grendel raised his hard arms like battering rams and burst through the doors, his hurtling passage carrying him well within the darkened hall.

"Wake, you Danes!" he bellowed at the dim forms stirring from sleep. "Your king comes for tribute!"

Ravenous, Grendel's scything claws snatched up a squirming body. He sank his teeth into the man's neck. The blood tang drove him mad. He tore a huge bite from the body as someone came screaming at him, then hurled the lifeless carcass at his attacker. They were all awake now, crying out in fear or bravado. He heard the scrape of metal on metal. Young, most of them, from the sound of their shocked voices, but then there came the deeper timbre of an older man.

"Get clear of him! Circle him! Spears!"

These pitiful boys moved so slowly compared to himself or Sigyn. In a flicker of lightning, Grendel saw the spear launched at him. He fended the cast aside with one arm; with the other, he struck the heads from two of the nearest Danes and swept them up under his arms. The second spear flew too swiftly, striking him full in the chest with a dull *clung*, then simply rebounded from his tough hide to clatter on the floor.

"Stay back! I have him."

Grendel crouched in their shadowed midst, far abler than they to see without light, clearer still with intermittent lightning. He knew the one called Esher who came at him now, sword ready and shield raised. Grendel's free arm swooped to strike the shield aside, but miscalculated the man's agility. Esher faded aside and came in again with a sword slash that glanced off Grendel's forearm. If the weapon could not wound, it could smart. Raging in his war fury, Grendel caught Esher's wrist, lifted him like a straw doll, and flung him half the length of the hall, then turned and leaped toward the broken doors, snatching up a hapless man trying to bolt for freedom. Racing for the ditch, he saw figures running, doors opening, torches thrust out to sputter in the rain. Faster he ran, plowing across the first ditch, across the outer court, and up the second rampart. One leap took him into the icy ditch water. He churned toward the outer bank and up it toward the heath. The cries from the steading faded behind him. Munching as he ran, Grendel turned his head to see feeble lights like frightened fireflies darting back and forth along the ramparts.

The right thing was begun at last, he exulted as he ran with the limp forms stowed under his arms. He would share the feast and honors with Sigyn, whose right surely it was. His mark was known in Heorot and would be seen again. Tomorrow night, if Danes were dim enough to risk their rest in the hall, he would oblige them once more. He laughed aloud to the heavens as the lightning lit his way.

"Are you there, drunken charioteer? Do you see me? Do you mark how little power any of you have over me? Where I plundered tonight, look for me henceforth as true king of Danes!"

Sweet vengeance pouring hot through him, Grendel dove into the turbulent waters of his mere, tearing bits from his prizes to delay the predators surging after as they stayed to fight over them. He shot through the water wall, kicked in the doors of Sigyn's den, and strode into the reeking lair he had once seen as beautiful through illusion. No part of illusion or glamor now, but still home.

"Mother!"

Grendel hurled the bodies onto the table and tore the clothing from them as he would skin a fish.

"Mother, come!"

She appeared as he expected: not fair nor clad in a gown that reflected different hues of a rainbow as she moved, but foul rags that clung damply to her hulking frame over which nothing shimmered or rippled but the play of brutal muscles under iron-tough hide.

"Come, Mother," Grendel invited with cold pride. "Sit by me and forgive the cruelty that came from my pain."

Sigyn surveyed the waiting feast. She was hungry. Her tongue flicked out between jagged teeth. "Then you understand at last? You accept?"

"Oh, I do. I have claimed my own in Heorot."

"And you have no regret?" Sigyn urged. "When I could no longer dream—when waking and dream turned round for me, I was bitter, too. I begged the Fates to let me die. Were it not for finding Shild, I would have given myself to the mere drift and any creature with an appetite."

"No regret, Sigyn." Grendel guided her to the ready table. "When Danes drink too much, they ease the misery with another draft of the same. One pain numbs another, the stronger suffuses the lesser hate. I will walk in my hall again tomorrow night, and at your pleasure, so shall you."

Grendel busied himself with carving and serving her. "As you said, let us deal with what we are and eat."

In the morning, joyless in the hall so joyfully conceived, Hrothgar and Weltheow watched in silence as the broken bodies were taken up and servants worked to eradicate the stains from the night's horror. Hrothgar escorted his pale queen to her place before turning to his counselor. But for sheer chance, Esher would not have survived, his left arm useless and bound tight in a sling. Every thane who had witnessed and survived the fury stammered out the same story. Esher's eyes were dull with pain, sleeplessness, and the residue of shock.

"Some four are gone," he reported. "The creature carried them off."

"What manner of creature?"

"Like a man somewhat but taller than three together, with a hide like mail. No spear could harm it, nor any sword. The thing caught my arm . . . flung me like a stick. The young ones tried to fight. . . ."

Esher faltered into silence. Hrothgar decided to spare him further effort and looked to his ashen queen, then the men waiting for the king's word when he had none. What could he say, save he was thankful that Esher at least had been spared? If so attacked by men, Hrothgar would have no hesitation. Esher would summon the older thanes to council, and there would be war on the enemy or restitution demanded.

Such was the custom, but this was elemental, the mindless fury of the night's storm that had raged over Sjaelland. As a king, Hrothgar had long known what Grendel but recently learned: that man's control of his fate was laughably limited. Only vanity enlarged it by reflection. Raise pride to any height, the Fates at their whim could lay it low with one swoop.

Always that. And yet we must go on as if we are at the tiller.

"Wulfgar," he ordered his herald. "See the hall set aright. Wash out all trace of this outrage. Prepare another feast. This is Heorot and will be lighted again. Esher, please attend me."

The king and his thane walked alone through the mud of the inner court, mindful of the shaken men who watched and depended on their decisions.

"I know not why the gods have done this, why we should be so afflicted, but you were brave to stand against that thing."

Beyond valor and pain, Hrothgar could read in Esher's drawn face the bald truth. What defense against such a demon if it returned?

"I will watch again in the hall," Esher said reluctantly.

Hrothgar refused out of hand. "No, not you."

"Someone must," Esher insisted. "Hrothgar, if the women and younger men see us helpless with fear—"

"No, I say. You have done enough. Some men I will not lose. Those who watch tonight must be the most tried, I agree." Hrothgar grinned sourly at his old friend to lighten their gloom. "Fine fight you'd make of it with one arm. Come, help me choose the best men."

That night's gathering in the hall was loud with angry boasts of vengeance. This man would avenge his fallen friend, that one would set his bed nearest the door and show courage equal to Esher's. As the feast commenced, Grendel woke in his cave with an appetite. When Weltheow gave forth the strained but gracious cheer, Grendel rose out of the mere and swam shoreward, not in haste, but deliberately. The skies were clear and a new moon rode the scattered clouds as he made for Heorot.

When the moon set and the sun rose on Hrothgar's hall again, no Danes volunteered to rest another night in the hall. Some went to the longhouses beyond the inner ditch, others henceforth to the outlying farms, as far as possible from Heorot. The hall stood empty and dark each night, barred at first until morning presented doors splintered and sundered, then ripped from their hinges easily as well-cooked meat from a bone.

Breached and lost, conquered by a beast no man could describe clearly nor any two alike, but which returned with each night's dark, an obscene shadow stalking across the inner court into the lightless, empty hall. As time went by, the frightened night guards formed their own opinions.

"Strange how it claims the hall alone."

"If you ask me, I think it is the ghost of old Hergar."

"*Nej!* That's foolish."

"Oh? This thing has the shape of his nature. He never gave anything away. He wants his place back."

"But *I* heard—wait, did you hear that?"

"Hear what?"

"That's him. It."

"Of course it is. The thing's in the hall, where it is every night, what did you expect? We're just lucky if it doesn't come for us before the sun rises."

"No, I thought—sometimes it roars out words I understand, or almost. Its voice is like thunder beyond a hill."

"A giant, you think? One of the Utgard folk?"

"So it seems in man shape, but I have seen the lightning *pour* into it. Listen, I am no liar. From my post on the bridge I saw, and so might you on nights when Thor brings storms. Lightning—not just random, but *aimed*—as if Thor would kill the thing. Bolt after bolt which this thing swallowed and seemed to take strength from it as men nourish on meat."

"What did it cry out?"

"Hrothgar's name, that much I heard for certain. And it called to great Shild as well. What do you make of that?"

"Do I look like a priest to read omens? Do I know the tongue of the white horses?"

"The king tried all these but still it comes."

"Well, Hrothgar is descended from Shild. Shild was a god—they say; I don't know, but the plain man in Hrothgar must be scared as I am."

Whatever snarl in the Fates' skein had shaped the beast, they alone must undo in their weaving. The tracks leading to and from Heorot were traced northeast to the dismal lake and ended there, worn deeper with each month and then the years, a long scar of shame pointing to Hrothgar and his folk.

Hrothgar did all humanly possible. Sacrifices were made in all the temples of Sjaelland, runes thrown, rethrown, and their portent debated. With each waxing moon Hrothgar purified himself in the sweat house and went to the sacred grove where the four white horses, never ridden or defiled with common work, were yolked by priests to the chariot employed only in such divination. Hrothgar drove them about a circular course, listening carefully to their neighings and snortings, then he and the priests consulted, since the horses alone were the messengers of Odin, king and priests merely interpreters.

"What have you learned?" Weltheow asked anxiously of her husband after these efforts. "Do they tell anything? Is it some crime or wrong in us? Some shadow on my sons?"

"No," Hrothgar told her with bleak honesty. "Nothing. The runes and horses will not speak."

Or nothing that made sense. At a loss himself, he was increasingly sceptical of his priests. They expounded at great length on the various rune readings and what they might mean, but their words were only fustian to him, fog raised to obscure their own ignorance and impotence.

At first, there were visiting groups from tributary kings who stayed the night in the hall against the beast as a matter of prestige. Younger sons of chiefs, eager to make a name for themselves, but in time, as Hrothgar admitted bitterly to his wife, even fools' courage faltered.

"Wife, I'm at the rope's end," he despaired in Weltheow's arms when they were alone. "I have done all I can. If the gods want my life, let some sign tell me so clearly, and I will give it. What more can I do? What *more*?"

Plowings, plantings, and harvests came and went. No valiant-foolish boys dared the hall's darkness now. Hrothgar grew grayer and then white-headed with the contradiction of honor abroad and unrelieved shame at home where, from sundown to moonset, the heart of his kingdom and that in his breast were conquered and ravaged. Weltheow aged as swiftly with the same dangerous knowledge while Hrethric neared manhood. As for their nephew Hrothulf, if he harbored kingly ambitions, he was no readier than other sane men to brave Heorot after sunset.

For twelve winters, while boys became men and men grew older, Grendel commanded Heorot in his kingdom of night. For most of those years he rejoiced in his dogged occupation of the hall, though as time went on, he often came more from habit than pride.

This night he was not hungry, having gobbled three of the wolves that tried in vain to bring him down. He passed insolently in plain sight of Hrothgar's sentinels. Grendel never touched the guards, nor any member of Hrothgar's family or steading. More in malice than mercy, he preferred to shame the usurper, feeding on Hrothgar's withering fame rather than his flesh. Let him sit on Shild's throne while day lighted it; with the dark, he must slink away, afeared to tarry overlong. Grendel knew ongoing victory in this.

Somehow there was no savor to conquest this night. When he stamped into the deserted hall, the emptiness descended like a weight on his soul. Cold moonlight, moted with fine snow, drifted through the open windows and gaping doors. No shields hung in pride along the wall, no tables stacked with their trestles. These winter afternoons when the dark came early, the evening meal was eaten in one of the longhouses. Only the two high seats remained. Hrothgar would not relinquish that last rag-end of pride.

Grendel stalked down the hall and, as always, knelt to the king's chair in homage to Shild. He never took that place himself. Sigyn had made him promise out of respect to his father and her wish never to do so until she herself gave him leave.

"Royal father, once more I come," Grendel addressed the empty chair ghostly in halflight. "Once more the usurper flies from me. If I only dreamed of you, were they not at least noble visions? Will you not recognize me? Send me your sign."

The wind moaned across the inner courtyard, hollow as Grendel's hopeless plea, empty as this hall, his barren domain. Conqueror and true king—but what subjects or court beyond the fine-driven snow and dry leaves drifted through broken doors? They did not bother to repair the doors anymore. More than once in a red rage, Grendel had torn them from their hinges as he would, despairing, tear his life from its own cursed foundations. Some nights when the wind went mad, he would dissolve into light and float on moonbeam, let the air send him whirling with the snow about the deserted walls of his kingdom.

Not so in the beginning when Grendel was a boy himself and curious, before Hrothgar's men stripped the hall. Grendel would examine the benches and how they were made, admiring how cunningly wood was joined to wood or iron, how firmly each beam supported the gabled roof. Inquisitive and even courteous in the first fancy of those early days, he played the king in Heorot, standing before the high seat, one talon fisted on his hip, the other open in generosity or pointed in imperious command.

Several times he was invaded. Rash outsiders impudently dared to take their rest in his domain. Grendel left little of them to burn or bury but the now-ineradicable stains on floor and walls. Where Danes once hung shields, these were *his* marks of honor and accomplishment. He issued decrees to his silent court, the first that Sigyn be recognized as Queen Mother of royal Danes. On nights when she came with him to Heorot, he led her to Weltheow's place with all ceremony while dream-Danes knelt to pay her homage, though Grendel always denied himself the king's place.

But tonight, Grendel questioned Sigyn's wisdom. Wherefore should he *not* assume the throne clearly won and so long unchallenged?

The wind was from the east tonight; in it Grendel felt some prompting. He moved to stand in the pale light streaming through a window. Sometimes, when he melted into lightning or moonbeam or whirled as dust in the air, he could hear, like different instruments bent to music, disparate voices on the wind. He opened himself to the light now and let that unintended gift from Thor dissolve him. He became one with air and light. Flowing so, the voices came more clearly—deep and low, part of windsong, surging like ocean tide, murmurous as the Norn-Fates talking among themselves, counting stitches as their fingers knitted each day into men's lives.

Different voices with tidings and . . . a name? The wind whispered it; the name crackled in the shore ice, roared distortedly across the water, crunched with men's plodding footsteps through distant snow just below the threshold of clarity. Swimming on the breast of light, Grendel strained to hear the name sung by the elements.

When he combined again, he moved to the high seat, heart and mind resolved. He turned to face his phantom court.

"My people! The gods to whom I am kin send tidings on the wind. Once more strangers come to try against your rightful lord. As I am king in Sjaelland, I will meet hate with hate."

As I am king.

Impulse became command and movement. Grendel bounded up onto the dais and wedged his broad hips into Hrothgar's throne chair that protested beneath the weight of him. His claw shot out in imperative command: His chimera-thanes stood to attention—

"As *we* are king!"

The vision could not hold. His court faded. Nothing answered Grendel but the wind and the little snow-ghosts whirling through the ruined doors. He had spoken, but so had the voices from the east, the name blurred but the message clear. Someone of name was coming to Heorot.

BOOK II

TOWARD HEOROT

8

THE SNOW THAT DRIFTED OVER HEOROT that week had packed earlier around the palisaded hall of Hygelac in Helsingborg. The light came late these winter mornings and left sooner. The royal hall of the Geats was shadowed and gloomy shortly past noon, needing tapers and both fire pits blazing for cheer and warmth.

The morning audiences were done, petitioners and counselors dismissed. Only two men remained in the great timber hall, Hygelac standing by one fire pit, warming his back. His old steward Garmund had delivered his news and waited the king's word. Hygelac hefted a heavy log and dropped it onto the fire in a blaze of sparks before responding to the steward's tidings.

"Beowulf will go to aid Heorot?"

"And no sooner said than half a hundred volunteered to sail with him, but your nephew would ask your leave first."

"As if I could spare him that many." Hygelac raked callused fingers through his graying brown beard. "Not now, surely. Not a winter voyage?"

"He would wait on the first spring thaw and good portent from the runes," Garmund said.

"Is he outside?"

The steward nodded but hovered yet with something unsaid.

"What matter else?"

"My lord, Beowulf draws young men to him easily. Prince Herdred is all afire to go with him."

"No. Absolutely not." Hygelac rejected that out of hand. His only son and heir could hardly be exposed to such risk. "Herdred will be no part of it. For the rest, tell Beowulf I will send for him later."

As the fire built up, Hygelac paced alone about the pit. Four servants entered to wash down the tables for the evening meal, but he sent them away, weighing considerations of debt and diplomacy. A king could do nothing impulsively, not even with the best intentions. The Danes had sheltered Beowulf's father; some like favor was owed in return. Hrothgar held sway over Danes on Hygelac's southern border and was always more of a friend to Geats than Swedes. Hygelac and his fathers had ever to be mindful of that delicate balance. Beowulf's proposed venture, not a royal mission but a voyage of independent warriors, repaid the debt while neatly leaving Hygelac out of it, whatever befell.

Beowulf might go, Herdred would stay. Hygelac's famed nephew was only second in line and considered a poor second for most of his youth. After the hare-brained Frisian raid, so costly in promising lives, men weighed the surviving boy's account in silence the more eloquent since Edgetho never spoke of the matter. Beowulf's arms had borne no mark of battle . . . what had really happened?

A pity Hygelac had only one son. So all men thought until Beowulf's nineteenth year. If anything happened to Herdred, who would swear allegiance to the clumsy, unsure ox of a boy so blinded at times by headache he could bear no light at all but lay for hours in a darkened chamber? A feeble choice, they all thought then, barren soil for the seed of courage. All the more miraculous when that soil quickened and Beowulf's name grew to exceed his father's in fame.

When did it change? Hygelac thought back. When the Bronding prince Brecca visited Helsingborg nine years past—*that* was the clear if inexplicable turning point. Brecca and Beowulf were of an age, nineteen, but there the likeness ended. Undersized Brecca made up for lack of stature with the aggression of a wild boar, asserting himself in everything. None could ride better, he boasted, no horse he could not break to manage, no shield defense withstand his sword . . . and so on, the usual bravado of a visiting prince from a smaller court, constrained to courtesy while showing that Brondings were every jot the equal of Geats and probably more.

That "friendly" sword match with Beowulf . . .

Hygelac's bark of laughter echoed in the empty hall. Awkward Geat bear against the Bronding gamecock. Hygelac was surprised and impressed. While Brecca was swift and skilled, wherever his blunted sword cut or thrust, Beowulf's shield blocked him. The wagers in the snow-packed field above the beach shifted from Brecca's favor to even, but no bets were collected that day. The end of the match was indecisive and comic.

Once Brecca lost his balance on the ice-slicked snow, recovering quickly but for an instant unprotected. Beowulf stepped back and waited his readiness rather than press advantage. Hygelac's queen Hygd applauded the sporting gesture, and the Geats cheered. Once more, the opponents circled each other; then in Brecca's rush, Beowulf slipped on the ice himself. Not as coordinated as the Bronding, he fell heavily. Short of temper as well as breath now, Brecca darted in with sword raised to slam the flat across Beowulf's chest in victory. Beowulf blocked with his shield and tripped Brecca neatly off his feet. The Bronding went down solidly on his rump.

The Geats roared with amusement. When Beowulf rose, he had Brecca tucked helplessly under one arm like a piglet, spanking him soundly. Hygelac chuckled over the memory—Brecca sputtering and incoherent when Beowulf set him charitably on his feet, glaring about at the grinning Geats.

"Foul!" he screeched. "Foul! You *can't* say you won."

"Oh, have it your way," Beowulf conceded lightly, adding to injury a more stinging solicitude. "You seemed about to hurt yourself."

A more mature man would have laughed and taken the hand Beowulf offered along with the questionable victory. Brecca struck it away, glowering at his opponent. "You have dared cold iron. Will you dare cold water?"

He pointed away to the boreal waters whipping up onto the beach. The watching circle of men knew he must be bluffing. Mad, impossible. No one could last half an hour in such a sea at this time of year.

"To swim as long and as far as I?" Brecca challenged. "How long can you last out there?"

Beowulf looked out over the icy gray water. Since his father's death, there had been a sadness about him—for want of a keener definition—which some like his friend Hondshew opined only partly due to filial grief, if at all.

"You're a difficult man, Brecca," Beowulf said. "When?"

Brecca unsheathed his own sword. "Now."

Mad in truth, but if they would—but wait. The wager was still unresolved. What hazard and new odds?

Beowulf handed Hygelac the large golden horsehead brooch that had clasped his mantle and a golden snake ring from his finger. Against these Brecca pledged the equivalent, ten øre of gold weight, then stalked away toward the shore, sword in hand.

The handicap was even more lunatic: to swim in full mail, each with a sword. The blade would be proof against sea beasts or each other, Brecca maintained, *if* Beowulf dared fight him in the water with an unblunted weapon. Hygelac and the court followed them down to the sea, the king already regretting a matter gone too far. He had thought at first to forbid the contest and name Brecca winner. Beowulf would not have cared.

On the other hand, whatever Beowulf lacked in repute, he had physical endurance, and subtler values were now in the balance. The Brondings, tributaries of Hygelac on his northern border, might report withdrawal as weakness to the more dangerous Swedes. Out of hard political sense, Hygelac would rather lose his nephew than his buffer tribe's respect.

Hygelac stood with Queen Hygd and Garmund and watched the two wade out past the frothing surf into swimming depth, then struggle gradually away, farther and farther out until their heads and sword points were mere dots against the choppy waters in growing dusk. The company returned to the hall, expecting the swimmers to return in an hour at most. The hour passed, then two. When they had not returned by morning, Hygelac gave both up for dead.

"Mad indeed," Hygd expressed to her husband privately. "Yes, yes, a wager of honor, no blame to us, and no one will miss that little loudmouth, I suppose. But Beowulf was second in line to the throne. If Herdred dies young, what of the succession?"

"In truth?" Hygelac looked up from his breakfast oatmeal. "The loss of Beowulf hits closer to me than Geats at large. Garmund is already searching the lineage and abilities of several other kinsmen."

A week later to the day, almost the hour, since Beowulf and Brecca walked into the water, as the court sat at dinner, Garmund hurried into the hall distractedly and pounded his staff on the floor for silence.

"My lord king—Beowulf, prince of Geats."

Exchanging incredulous glances with his wife and son, Hygelac beckoned the steward close. "Beowulf? We were just discussing funeral honors."

Garmund answered in a mixture of pride and his own astonishment. "No need, sir. I know not, nor could any short of the gods tell how, but it is he. And claiming the wager you hold for him."

Claiming more than the gold, Hygelac reflected now as his boots echoed softly in the empty hall. For the first time in memory, Beowulf had himself announced as prince. Men gaped as the huge figure, closer in height to seven feet than six, limped painfully into the hall on frozen legs to stand midway between the doors and the high seat. Water puddled about his feet, ice clung to his clothes and mustaches. His blond braids were dark and stiff with salt, the ring mail smeared with wet rust and stuck about here and there with ragged ends of green seaweed, but the sword was still in his grip and he stood straight and defiant. Men at the tables whispered among themselves and made warding signs against evil. The son of Edgetho towered in their midst like a frost giant or some grisly revenant come from the sea to claim its due, resting the point of the ice-sheathed sword on the hall floor.

"Now I am Beowulf again."

"See, Father, see?" Little Herdred, ten years old and a worshiper of his cousin, itched and jiggled to go to his hero. "I told you there were none like him. *We* showed those Brondings."

So they did, and yet afterward, Hygelac was not the only one to notice a new and alien bearing in his nephew. Dismiss it as a joke, call it a sea change, a *cold* suffused Beowulf, wrapped him about as it had standing there that evening in a puddle of sea water. He was more distant and more finely balanced. Where before he had shambled and stooped, some correction had drawn him together and up to full height, measured and tempered the essence of Beowulf. He never afterward suffered headaches nor ever appeared hesitant in anything. Boys idolized him at a distance, but men found him hard to hold cheer with.

As for Brecca, he reached home safely, they heard. Report was sketchy, but the Brondings remained loyal. Brecca never acknowledged Beowulf the victor; on the other hand, he never sent to collect his wager. Meanwhile, the highborn Geatish youth flocked to Hygelac's new-famed nephew, sought and followed his counsel in all things. He became their touchstone and standard. When talk of establishing a Geatish colony in Britain occupied the counsel, Beowulf was nominated to lead it.

He refused laconically. "I was not born for such."

To Hygelac, Beowulf seemed singularly unambitious in any practical regard. "What *was* he made for then?" the king once asked Hondshew, Beowulf's one close friend. "I ask you. No man has his size or strength, no man questions his honor but holds it up as a model, and yet what man knows him at all? Who *is* he?"

"Say rather *where*," Hondshew answered question with question. To the king, Hondshew was admirable himself, respected and liked as well, warm and open, a man whose emotions were easily read in his swarthy face at all times. "He is like this Heorot we go to help, built high behind defenses. 'No courage without fear. . . .' "

Hygelac raised a quizzical eyebrow at the warrior thane. "What?"

"Something he said once. Strange as the man himself. I have seen him helpless as a sick child with the pains in his head, and like a fortress in battle. When we last fought the Swedes, Beowulf led us on that last charge into their thickest ranks."

The decisive charge, the king recalled. "Yes."

"Who could forget? I looked for us all to die. I saw Beowulf disappear in a knot of enemies. As I fought my way toward him, it was a knot of fallen men and himself rising unhurt over them. As a boy, he had many fears. After that madness with Brecca, he had none, but that was when I ceased to know him really."

"Distant."

"More, my lord. Something beyond death."

"Come, Hondshew." Capable of subtlety himself, Hygelac often foundered on the more complex shades of Hondshew's reasoning. Beowulf's companion was not pure Geat. His mother was taken in a foreign raid, the king forgot just where. Hondshew had her swarthy looks and canny, un-Geatish turn of thought.

"My lord king has fought many battles and knows fear is never absent, no mind what poets sing. Beowulf said, 'No courage without fear.' In most men, the conquest of fear is their greatest victory. So it was for me, but in Beowulf, it is a two-sided coin. Am I being clear?"

"No," Hygelac grumbled, wishing he hadn't asked.

Hondshew made a new effort at precise meaning. "In confidence?"

"Of course."

"I feel in Beowulf a contempt for his life, a different thing from being unafraid to die. I honestly don't think he cares to live."

Herdred was denied the voyage, protesting bitterly. From the rest, Hygelac culled out his most experienced thanes as needed at home. Beowulf accepted his uncle's decision, aware of the king's layered motives and agreeing with them. Fifteen would sail with him to Sjaelland, though only he and Hondshew were seasoned battle veterans.

Since Edgetho's death, Beowulf headed his own house and servants, unmarried and solitary in possession. Consultation of runes in this venture was his responsibility. He whittled a number of flat slivers from fruitwood, marking each with the runes of divination. After purifying himself in the sweat house, Beowulf sacrificed properly to Odin, discoverer of runes as man's link to the gods, and cast the sacred sticks out onto a marked white cloth.

Nothing in the signs boded ill for his undertaking. Next morning, he noted the first flight of birds over his house. They flew west toward Sjaelland and Heorot. Beowulf followed the line of their passage to the shore of Eyrarsund, the narrow neck of water that separated Geats from Hrothgar's island by no more than a day's rowing. Gulls hovered and cried on the frigid wind as Beowulf gazed out over the sound. The wind whipped at his unbraided hair as he studied thicknesses of shore ice and judged the time remaining before they broke in the coming spring thaw.

His face was bleak as the air that stung at it. Over the years, the periwinkle shading of his eyes had faded gradually to the color of shadow on snow, clouded now with memories that would never leave him. Nine years since that foolish, fateful wager with Brecca, twelve since the Frisian dishonor and the gentle old priest who looked through and through Beowulf to the mortifying wound of his shame and saw but did not judge the truth of a terrified, miserable boy.

That was kindness, Eligius, even strength. Would I could send to tell you I have gone beyond fear and even courage, but never far enough. Repute has come and even fame, but no peace, not that serenity I sensed in you. That recedes like the rainbow while I stumble after. I am not unhappy, that's for the living. I died for the first time when my father found out.

Saxon traders put in at Helsingborg two summers after the Frisian affair, when Edgetho had been recalled by Hygelac. Beowulf's father stormed into his house, dispatched the servants with kicks and curses. Seething, he gripped his callow son by the arms and threw him into a chair. Edgetho trembled with a rage he could barely contain, a strong man known more for berserk courage in battle than sagacity in counsel, whose pride was all in his sword that he now declared he would shatter before bequeathing it to such a despicable son.

"Thank all the gods those sailors didn't know you were my son;

didn't know any of the names. I paid them—*paid* them not to spread the story. Told them the families of foolish boys, dead or not, would be grateful for their silence. Not *my* son, of course, he was better raised. You worthless cur, I feel sick when—you should not have gone, but I hoped it would—no matter now what I hoped. You have covered yourself with the deepest dishonor. Deserted in battle, don't deny it. Everyone knows the story in Frisia. Nothing a scop would tarnish himself by singing. Such are beneath them, but *comic* rhymes sung in taverns by nobodies about those with even less honor."

Miserable, cringing, white-faced in the chair, Beowulf tried to answer his father's contempt with bald truth. "I wasn't the only one."

"You turned and ran!"

"They all would. Most never had the chance."

"Ran! My own son a coward." Edgetho lunged back and forth before his hang-dog boy. "It is only mercy your mother, the king's own sister, did not live to see this day."

Beowulf could not speak further. In the unreachable person of his father, all men and honor spat on him and cast him out. *I died in that moment and you never noticed.*

"You are my only son," Edgetho trembled. "My house goes to you, but nothing else. You are second in line to Hygelac's throne. He will never know. I cannot disown you save to wish I had another son or even a lame girl to pass on my blood."

His father hauled the boy out of the chair slapping him hard back and forth across the face, then hurled him toward the door. "Get out of my sight. For now I want to drink this shame away."

His father drank much away in those last months of his life; drank until he became sodden and maudlin, falling down and needing to be helped to bed, or rutting his favorite fat scullion. Until he died in a border skirmish with the Swedes, Edgetho showed his son public courtesy and private contempt. At home, they barely spoke.

Died in a meaningless fray, more private feud than war, but you must have welcomed that dark summoner. I knew him long before he called you, Father.

The sea wind lashed Beowulf's hair across his eyes and he wondered if the stinging tears were from the cold. He shook his head to banish the thoughts and forced his attention back to present concerns. The ice would break up soon. Another ten days, fifteen at most, and they could take ship. His younger boat companions talked of nothing else, preparing their war gear, eager to sail into the heart of this venture, grapple with the demon in Hrothgar's hall, ignite with valor and be known for it ever after. Beowulf's lips twisted. He knew how the stories would go afterward—

"I was with him, at his side when we dared beyond the limits of lesser men. . . ."

Is that all?

"There were Beowulf and Hondshew to lead and I was with them. The scop isn't born, the harp not yet carved or strung that can sing what we did. Listen and I'll tell you. . . ."

Oh yes, tell them. Heroism is easy when nothing else hangs on your heart. All of them save Hondshew speak of nothing else. In their eyes, the deeds are already done, the honor stored and accruing more. Hondshew prepares quietly. He is the only one of us married. He comes because I asked; the thing is to be done.

Ina is a good wife to him and I know she sees more of men's hearts than they would suspect. I admire Hondshew for persisting in his suit for her, ignoring the taint on her family and blood. Admire him and perhaps envy a little. He at least has someone to miss. I think I'll be a secret thief and miss her a little myself and never tell.

For the rest of Beowulf's band, they were boys who had yet to die even once.

9

THE SHORE ICE WAS THIN and brittle when they carried their gear and provisions down to the beached keel. Hygelac clasped his nephew's hand. Hygd and her women waved from the cliff above as Beowulf and Hondshew jolted down the steep path past the line of their boat companions toiling with stores.

Hondshew had chosen a smaller craft for their reduced company, only thirteen paces from prow to stern. Some of the men thought the boat too small, others too frail.

"She's solid and well caulked," Hondshew attested, pounding a fist against the upswept prow. "I looked at every seam. She'll carry any men strong enough to pull her oars."

And yet only sixteen out of all those so eager to go? The king *might* have left them a few more. Some of them entertained private second thoughts, but none wanted the shame of begging off.

"Sixteen: That is our number," Beowulf cheered them from the high prow. "Sixteen Geats can do what countless Danes could not. Two reliefs of six rowers, two extra to relieve when needed. Hondshew and I will take turns at the steer board."

Each man labored up the gangplank with a heavy stone. These were set amidships in a solid ring about a circular iron plate the size of a man's shield. On this plate they set a wide, shallow iron pot full of peat turves which were lighted and fanned to heat before the keel swung out into the current of the sound. No shelter was rigged, since they would spend only one night at sea and raise the Danish coast near midday tomorrow, barring mishap. The stones would ballast the keel, the fire cook their food and warm the off watch through the night.

Beowulf held a southwesterly course by pale sunlight. When the brief day darkened, he marked the North Star and passed the tiller to Hondshew. In the deep night with the stars tilting back and forth overhead and the monotonous drone of Ulf, their first rower, calling the stroke, Beowulf sat on the fire-warmed stones with his off watch. Their prow lifted and spanked down, slicing the swift Eyrarsund current.

Closest to the stern in the circle of light, Beowulf noted the North Star and called to Hondshew at his tiller.

"Bring her up west. She's falling off too far south."

The sea air was biting cold. Some of the off watch rolled in blankets, others swaddled in thick cloaks and huddled close to the fire, woolen caps pulled low about their ears. One or two like Gorm sat bareheaded, ostentatiously contemptuous of the cruel wind, honing spear points and swords, hoping Beowulf noticed their hardiness even at the expense of cracked lips and frozen ears. In the fire's glow their attention did not long stray from the figure of Beowulf, as wolves and wild dogs stayed alert for the moods of the dominant pack member. Wind and the sluicing of their prow through the sea punctuated their talk.

"Twelve years . . ."

"Um? What? Sorry, I was nodding off."

"Twelve years this thing has claimed Heorot."

"Only at night, they say. Sporting of him."

"What kind of hall where war thanes are afraid to sleep?"

"Many have challenged him."

"And Hrothgar's folk had a mess to clean up next day. None lately, of course."

"None but us," Beowulf reminded them.

A short but eloquent silence fell among the young men about the fire, ended by one youth who spoke out defiantly if only to sweep away silence and his own thoughts. "Won't have to trouble themselves where we're concerned."

"This creature has never dealt with Storm-Geats," said Beowulf.

They nodded, eager for reassurance. "Think of the reputation we'll have when we get home," one dreamed.

"And gifts," Gorm anticipated, the *zang-zang* of his honing stone cold counterpoint to the night wind. "Hrothgar has as much gold as troubles."

"Oh, his generosity is fabled," Hondshew put in, a dim form at the tiller aft. "Along with his wisdom. Such kings make an art of the possible. Part of his royal craft."

"But we Geats," young Gorm asserted boldly, "we sail for the *im-possible*." He covertly watched Beowulf for approval. Gorm worshiped

Beowulf, but in moments of candor wished his chief a little easier to approach, like Hondshew.

"Well said and true," Beowulf answered. "Gorm goes to the heart of it. That's the spirit that led me to choose you. Most men, ordinary men, would answer: If it's impossible, why do we try? Because voyages like ours, against the unknown, against the impossible, are what men remember. I'm told there was a warrior among the Russ who adventured so until nothing mortal remained to come against him, so he challenged the gods themselves."

Gorm leaned forward over the sword across his knees. "And what happened?"

"Don't you know the tale?" Beowulf poked up the peat embers with his knife point. "The gods killed him for his pride, but it is for that trying that men sing of him. Ilya his name was."

Their keel rolled with a swell. The wind blew over the night-bound men.

"The impossible," Beowulf mused into the fire. "The fabulous. Our kind has drunk in such deeds with mothers' milk, yet I think the world comes to a time when thanes like ourselves will mean less."

"No!"

"Never!"

"Who has measured never, my friends? Who thought Rome would grow feeble and die? What man ever thinks he will? I once met a priest of the White Christ. Strange religion; I don't understand it at all, yet he was a wise man and I think a strong one. His kind are venturing farther north, I hear, to try their magic against Odin. The gods themselves will go down, so the harpers sing. Nothing lasts but honor, so let's try the impossible while some remains. Hondshew! What say you? Next year, shall we pull oar to the edge of the Outer Sea and find what really lies beyond?"

No answer from the steersman but ready opinions and volunteers around the fire. Edge of the world—*there* was voyaging for a man to dream on. They all believed, when they actually thought of it, in a flat and finite world, but other notions had left traces on imagination. There *was* no end, some had maintained, only more land beyond, a fierce island crowned with ice sooty with fire belched out of mountaintops. Tried and truthful men from the northern fjords said this and speculated that more land lay beyond that, no edge at all but a *roundness*.

Some of the boat companions scoffed openly. A round world? Get away! That made no sense when one could see it was flat as a table.

"I think a round world would be dull," Beowulf opined. "What? Sail from Helsingborg, sooner or later only to find Helsingborg again? Only land and sea and land again? No wonders, no fabulous beasts, nothing to let a man feel he's sailed close to the gods and reached for them? No. I *will* go to the edge of the world someday—of all known worlds," he improved on the thought. "Past all the tedious known and possible, past reason itself if my oars will take me, to see if I really tumble over into limbo or if my keel will carry me beyond the void to the moon. Such a voyage takes men like us."

They were all impressed and flattered, except perhaps Hondshew, whose wry laugh came out of the dark aft. "Who else would be so mad?"

The remark told on the young men. Beowulf rose from the fire and joined his friend at the tiller. "Hondshew, there's a time to be sparing with honesty. You are the wisest of us, but as you would not leave untended fire in a dry barn, don't leave such thoughts among young men whose courage yet stands in a delicate balance with fear. Do you think this voyage is mad?"

In the gloom, Hondshew's expression was hard to discern. "Say I admire the art of the possible."

Beowulf gripped the man's wiry shoulder. "What is it, Hondshew? Truly? You never kept anything from me."

A freshet of wind drenched them in icy spray. Hondshew wiped at his face before answering. "It's only that I don't know you anymore or what you want."

What he wanted. He had what he once thought he wanted. A man should always want something, else like pure water he ceased to run and became stagnant. He could want what Hondshew had so effortlessly, could want Ina or a woman like her. Could want simple things. More truthfully Beowulf could yearn for a way to such things, some way out of himself. But not even to Hondshew could he speak of this, so he answered lightly.

"Who was the first to stand when I proposed to sail?"

Hondshew said with that odd, skewed humor of his, "What's a born leader without born followers? There is the doom of greatness on you. Indeed, my mother says lives like yours never give the gods a moment's rest. I have smaller ambitions but they must account for more than myself. I am poor, and you know what Hygelac and others think of Ina's family. Honor is lovely, but I hope that Hrothgar's gratitude will ease a number of our wants. The first to stand up? I was the first you looked to, and perhaps just then, too afraid to say no. But you are right. Such things should not be said in front of fire eaters who have yet to taste their first flame. Forgive me, friend."

Beowulf set his hand to the tiller. "Go get some rest by the fire."

But Hondshew kept his grip on the steer board. "In a little. This mere-beast interests me as much as he scares me. You heard the tales. Comes at night, only at night, never enters any other longhouse, never harms any who do not come against him."

"In the hall," Beowulf finished, the thought intriguing him as well. "He forbids nothing else, walks nowhere else. You'd think he would."

"That might tell us something," Hondshew allowed, handing the tiller to Beowulf. "That he perhaps has an appetite for more than flesh."

The light was a hard sheen on the sea at midday. Holger, the Scylding guard on coast watch, had to shield his eyes against the cruel glare. Against that brilliance he saw the keel, a minute shimmering speck against light on the horizon, making straight for the anchorage below his cliff perch.

Holger cursed under his breath. He was not young anymore, but dependable in the charge inherited from his father long before the curse fell on Heorot. Through the past twelve years, forty-eight turning seasons of shame, their night-conquered hall was the true symbol of the helpless Danes, an empty shell. In the first years of their affliction, visiting thanes made good their vow to stay the night in Heorot, but none after the first year. Some called the place Blood Hall now, for the dark stains that would not scrub out of walls and floor.

Holger rubbed his eyes and narrowed them on the approaching vessel. Pirates? Swedes or Geats? His wide lips grimaced in disgust, baring strong yellow teeth. More trouble? Their plight was that widely known by now. The demon still walked Heorot by night for its own obsessed reasons. How long before outsiders thought to rout beast, king, and Danes alike from the most splendid but most dishonored hall in the north?

His companion guards were warming themselves by a fire in the protection of a boulder farther down the hill. No, Holger decided: Raiders would avoid smoke, not come on like these. He laid his spear against a rock and whistled to the small, shaggy-maned horse, making sure the saddle was securely cinched. Spear in hand, he forked the animal's broad back and set shield to his left arm, watching the keel as the rowers pulled for the beach. Holger counted the crew as they became more distinct. Sixteen: not much for raiding or anything but some kind of envoy.

The keel grounded. The plank was shoved out and men began to pass forward mail, shields, and bundled spears. Young men all, from the way they jumped to their tasks, but of what origin Holger couldn't tell. Now one of them noticed him and alerted the others, pointing his way.

Holger walked his horse down the lee side of the cliff toward his two young relief guards squatting about their fire. "A strange boat just landed. I'm going down to see who they are. Don't look like pirates, but you two get up to the lookout and stay mounted. If there's trouble, ride for Lejre."

They put on their helmets. "We should go with you," one said with no great conviction, visibly happier to remain above.

Holger had already considered and rejected that. If the sixteen meant trouble, three were little better than one against them. "Watch close. If you have to ride, ride fast."

He swung the horse toward the path leading down to the shore. When he broke out onto the narrow beach no more than fifty paces from the strangers, Holger could judge more accurately of them. By now, they had armed themselves and grouped behind one helmed warrior who stood head and shoulders above the rest. As Holger bore down on them at a deliberate walk, spear at the ready, they made no hostile move he could detect. The wind cut at the watchman's face. He was relieved when the towering leader jammed his spearhead into the sand and stepped forward to meet him. A smaller, dark man made a sign to the rest and moved up beside his leader, bearing a filled wooden cup. Holger reined to a halt within easy spear cast of the two.

The wind blew; the water whispered up onto the sand.

Holger addressed the dark man with the cup. "If you drink to a victory, you can just wait until I know who you are. I am Holger of the Scyldings, thane to Hrothgar. My father watched this coast for him and so will my sons after me. Who are you? Speak."

For answer, the dark one lifted his cup to the sky and poured its contents onto the sand. The tall man spoke for all of them. "I am Beowulf. This is Hondshew. The offering is to Njord, who gave us safe crossing from Helsingborg."

"Geats? Has my king given you the password? Has yours sent messengers? Be careful, I warn you. If it's plunder or mischief you come for, there's battle first and you start with me."

Beowulf removed his helmet, scratching his scalp. He regarded Holger calmly, then signed his men to sit down. Holger could read much in their dress and gear. Their braided hair was clasped in gold or silver wire, all weapons of fine hiltwork, mail new and well oiled. He relaxed a little, lowering his spear point.

"You are not common pirates."

Hondshew saluted him with the empty cup. "Thank you; we are not."

"Nor have I ever seen a man who threw a longer shadow than that one by you. Geats you say?"

"From Hygelac," Beowulf confirmed. "He greets your king."

Holger nodded. "We hold peace with the Geats but heard of none coming. No message was sent."

"Does your king remember Edgetho?"

"Ja. In the court I saw him many times."

"Now you see his son," Beowulf said. "Guest sometime myself to Hrothgar. This is Hondshew, my first companion. These others have come with me to aid your king, every one a volunteer of high house and name. When Edgetho could not return home, Hrothgar befriended him. My house stands in debt to his for that. We heard of Heorot's curse, how it is yours only until sunset, but from set to rise otherwise occupied."

"A man-beast!" Holger raised his voice to all of the listening Geats, waving the guards above to join him. "Bigger than any mortal man; even you, son of Edgetho. Do you think that Danes have not tried against it for all that?"

"We know."

Holger could read nothing in the big man's acknowledgment, neither compassion nor contempt. The watchman turned his horse, ready to lead these strangers to Lejre and their fate. "Listen, all of you! I know Geats can fight, surely as I know the difference between brave words and deed. But—welcome. My men will guard your ship for those who have the good luck to need it again. Follow me."

Hondshew snickered ruefully as he rose, brushing the sand from salt-stiff trousers. "He could be more encouraging."

"Could I?" Holger caught him up. "I tell you, Geat: Only one man has grappled with the beast and lived. Esher. His shield arm is nigh useless to this day. Come with me."

Most of the Geats remained seated, waiting for Beowulf's word. Their chief's gaze remained on Holger in that cryptic contemplation. Under that scrutiny Holger felt compelled to say more against the dishonor of twelve years. "You think Scyldings did not try? And others, they came and died. You can mark them by the bloodstains that don't wash out. The road to Heorot begins at the top of that cliff. Come, I'll guide you."

Beowulf signed to his men. "Up! Hondshew, form ranks."

Three hours the Geats marched as the sun poised high overhead and then slid westward. Riding ahead, Holger marked every degree of its descent more closely than the visitors. Not a night since the affliction lighted on them that the demon had not come. Tonight would be no different except for a scrubbing detail in the morning.

Beowulf's men trudged sturdily on with Hondshew calling the pace: thirteen miles from beach to royal steading, baldricked swords swinging on their hips, no straggling or calls for rest until they came to a place where the beaten dirt track became a cobbled road rising over a low hill. At the crest, Holger called a halt and reined aside, pointing ahead.

"There. Heorot. From here, three miles."

The Geats saw, set in greening heath and spring-budding patches of forest, the gold-gleaming roofs of their destination. The younger ones were duly awed. They would not say as much before a Dane, but compared to Heorot, their own hall at Helsingborg was a cattle byre. They admired the opulence and cleverly ditched ring-fort plan and felt decidedly rustic.

"We heard of a new hall," Beowulf said, squinting at Heorot's splendor against the declining sun.

Holger gazed at his king's stronghold with a sorrowed pride. "Like an outwardly healthy man who wastes in his vitals." Then, feeling he

had said more than was wise to outlanders, he turned the horse eastward again. "I must return to my watch. Not all ships will bring
friends."

"Pirates have tried?" Beowulf asked.

"Now and again. And others more royally plumed, but scavenger
birds the same. Such always know their time. Let them come. They'll
find more fight than they bargained for."

Beowulf offered his hand to the grizzled watchman. "And that
starts with you."

"So it does, Geat."

"Our thanks to you."

"Njord guided you safely here. May he grant you the like return.
Farvel!"

The Geats shouted good-byes as Holger galloped away, then took
their first rest since the beach, passing waterskins about while Beowulf
and Hondshew admired the looming royal hall.

"By all I've seen in a traveled life," Hondshew avowed, "there's
majesty."

Beowulf inspected the salt stains and dust on his own clothes. "But
we're not."

He gave orders to burnish the copper and gold of their helmets,
beat the dust from their clothing and boots, and to sling shields to the
back that the guards at Lejre could see they came in good order and
peace. His youths rubbed a shine to their shield bosses, splashed water
over their stubbled faces, straightened cloaks over their mail, mindful
that their conduct and appearance would reflect on Hygelac. Report of
good or lax discipline would weigh for or against them in future
venturings.

"Two files," Beowulf ordered, slinging the oxhide shield at his
back. "Follow me."

They stepped out after their leader and Hondshew, who shaded his
eyes to estimate the daylight left to them. "I give us three hours until
dark."

Beowulf increased the pace. "The day goes! You'll all want to eat
before you're heroes."

Walking backward, Hondshew surveyed the files. They pounded
along obediently at the accelerated pace but swayed this way and that,
hungry and tired by now, smartness worn away by hours of trekking

with only the one brief rest. The prospect of setting his rump to a bench at a generous board invited Hondshew as well, but on no account would they droop like wilted flowers before Danes. "You, Ulf! Straighten up. And you, Gorm. All of you."

From the rear of the column: "We're tired. They won't see us for another mile or more."

"He said STRAIGHT!" Beowulf barked in a voice that might have carried to the guards around Heorot. "I hear they sup early in Hrothgar's hall. If you weary little women will step out, we might be in time."

Beowulf swung about with a wink at Hondshew and set the brisk pace with his own long legs.

10

WULFGAR TOOK PRACTICED MEASURE of the men arranging shields and spears by the longhouse wall as he approached them. Herald and keeper of keys to Hrothgar, it was his place to welcome, sort out, or reject such visitors. Over the years he had developed a keen ability for quick assessment of such men. He knew the motley bands of border scum who would sell themselves to a lord and just as quickly turn on him. Men from the Rhine tribes, once federates of Rome, were wandering mercenaries now. Wulfgar knew the look of those: rough homespun wool tunics and loose, frayed trousers, ring mail, if any, rusty and tattered. These men were well dressed and looked well-enough fed, their arms clean and polished. The long ring shirt of the giant man who led them was washed in silver.

"I am Wulfgar, herald to Hrothgar." No small man himself, the officer had to look up at Beowulf. "Who are you?"

Beowulf inspected him up and down with a flick of his eyes, noting the tow-colored hair. "You're not a Dane, I think."

Wulfgar drew himself up. "A Swede of the Wendles."

"We are Geats. And you are a long way from home."

A brief silence between them, not hostile but reminiscent of ancient enmities.

"Not in loyalty," Wulfgar maintained. "I have laid my head on Hrothgar's knee and called him lord. Not where a man is born but where sworn, there his heart should be."

"True. I am Beowulf of Hygelac's hall and blood. My errand is to Hrothgar who knows me and my father. We ask that he receive us if he will."

"I seem to remember. Beowulf . . . not the son of Edgetho who—?"

"Was your king's grateful guest," Beowulf finished, putting a firm period to the credential.

"Yes." Wulfgar told them to wait and returned to the longhouse entrance. He well recalled the gangling, outsized boy who had somehow grown into this formidable mountain; nor had Wulfgar forgotten Edgetho, much too ready with his sword, which had dropped him into the Wylfing trouble Hrothgar mended for complex political reasons. An honorable man, perhaps, but always there seemed about Hygelac's thunderous brother-in-law more of outward force than inner strength, which might explain why Edgetho never held an important post in Helsingborg.

When Beowulf first came to Lejre, so eager in every word and deed to please his father, Edgetho treated the stumbling boy as a dog at heel, and so Beowulf followed him, like a hound hungry for a pat from his master's hand.

That boy is gone, Wulfgar concluded as he paused at the longhouse doors. *This one wants nothing from anyone.* Desired nothing but could see like anyone else the veneer of Danish pride thin-painted over their enduring shame. The broken doors of empty Heorot, the court at supper in a meaner house. Wulfgar looked at the sun sinking down the western sky and his shoulders sagged.

Two hours until dark, no more.

When the Geats were summoned into the supper hall, men put down their knives and drinking horns to stare at the strangers who ranged themselves in good order behind their captain at a respectful distance from Hrothgar and Weltheow.

Beowulf saluted the king. "Hail, protector of Danes."

"Prince Beowulf, hail. You come from Hygelac?"

"My uncle and lord, sir, but not on his embassy. You housed my father in his exile. The debt is mine."

Amid quizzical murmurs from the tables, Weltheow commented behind a napkin to her husband, "To say the least, he's grown."

"In more than height." Down the years Hrothgar had received fabulous report of this warrior; of his sudden transformation from a pathetic boy of slight regard to a prince whose battles against the Swedes had been sung by poets in Lejre. Now Hrothgar saw for himself. The callow youth once so painfully unsure of himself, stooping as if in apology for his size, stood erect in perfect composure, his slightest movement in balance. For all his mass, he gave the impression of supple lightness, like a thin rod of tempered steel. Yet, to Hrothgar, there was something in the prince's countenance indefinably chill, even alien. Fixed on the king, Beowulf's eyes never wavered, did not even seem to blink. The men behind him, though very young, were nigh as still.

Below the royal high table, lounging on the lip of the dais with Hro-thulf, young Unferth whispered to the king's nephew—

"That's the great swimmer, is it?"

"In the flesh, and such a great deal of it."

Unferth wiped the beer foam from his mustaches. "Well. Fancy that."

Beowulf spoke for all to hear. "From miles away we saw the roofs of Heorot throw back the sun to its source. And we have heard how the best and most famous of mead halls stands empty because of this curse which no sacrifice or men's striving can drive out."

Beowulf turned about to address all the Danes. "Not a man here who does not know my name, house, and deeds. I come to ask Hrothgar grant me one request. Let us—we sixteen—stay alone in Heorot tonight and we will contend with this thing you call the *mearc-stapa*. For this we have come."

"Ready the lye and ashes," Unferth muttered to Hrothulf. "More scrubbing tomorrow."

"But a valiant pledge," Hrothulf granted, adding pointedly, "I've not heard the same from you since you came to Lejre."

Unferth was stung but made a bluff answer. "I would not usurp the honor from you, were you ever so inclined."

"Thank you. I am not."

"Ah, then."

"Prince Beowulf," Hrothgar addressed him. "I am grateful that you see fit to repay hospitality with such extravagant interest, but men— good men, my own and others—have tried. For the love I bear your uncle and his house, I bid you share our feast but not our sorrow."

One thane far down the hall stood up in his place, respectful but serious in warning. "Beowulf, fighting Swedes is not the same as facing the demon of Heorot."

"And so soon, dark as it grows," Unferth sniggered into his beer.

"We mark the time, fellow," Hondshew answered him stiffly. Then to the hall at large: "I am Hondshew of the Geats, and I have fought Saxons, Swedes, and Finns. If *they* aren't monsters, they're monstrous near enough."

Over the laughter that leavened the mood in the hall where shadows deepened in contrast to the torch lights, Hrothgar beckoned Beowulf forward. "Does your father still live?"

"No, my lord."

"I settled his feud out of policy, you know. It is better to use gold where more blood is useless. But now I think we need much more than policy."

"A miracle." Seventeen-year-old Hrethric finished his father's thought. "Can you do this for us?"

"Once more, let us try."

"They all tried," Hrothmund, the king's youngest, burst out. "Haven't you heard? No sword or spear can *scratch* the thing."

"My boys speak truth," Hrothgar cautioned. "No weapon avails against the mere-stalker. Snares, ropes, iron-springed traps, they've all been tried. He snaps them like dry sticks."

"Not this sword." Young Gorm advanced three pride-stiffened paces. "Lord Hrothgar, my spear and sword were handed down from my great-great-grandfather, who had them from Wayland, god of forges, and proof against any spell."

Unferth smirked behind his drinking horn. This became ridiculous. These rustic Geats needed humbling and no tongue readier to that than his own.

"Gorm, these good Danes know their enemy," Beowulf said. "If blades are useless, then I will use none but try its strength against my own."

The old king shook his head soberly. "A worthy pledge but futile."

"Will Hrothgar deny me the chance to repay him? I and my men will stay this night alone in Heorot. If the demon takes me, send my sword to Hygelac, since it came from his royal father. If we prevail, you have your hall again, the dark will be no more than a time for tapers, and in the morning, Danes can once again walk gaily to mead in Heorot."

"Report of you is more than justified," Hrothgar acknowledged warmly. "But it would be a heavy leave and no favor I gave. So many young men have made the same promise. We buried or burned what was left of them. Their blood still marks my wretched hall. Think, son of Edgetho: Will you still make this vow? Neither I nor any of my thanes, so schooled in sorrow, will think the less of Geats for avoiding what no man can do."

"Then to what no man has done so far we are committed," Beowulf swore. "I speak for all of us."

"So be it then." Hrothgar beckoned him forward. "Come and greet my wife and sons. You at the tables, give place to our guests. Mead bearers, pour for them, and servers carve! They are welcome in Lejre."

That keen man Hrothulf noted wryly that his uncle did not say, "Welcome in Heorot," as perhaps presuming on the Fates who had been consistently unforgiving in that regard. As Beowulf and his men sat down among the Scyldings, Hrothulf conferred privately with his uncle.

"Valiant men, these, but victorious or not, shall I see to the usual arrangements?"

Hrothgar nodded reluctantly. That some of the Geats would die was virtual certainty; that all would breakfast unscathed was beyond hope. "Let the wood be put aside for a pyre. But discreetly, Hrothulf. We must make every show of confidence."

Show indeed. A mask of hope over naked despair. Hrothulf bowed away from his uncle. He would have the servants choose out hardwoods and aromatic seasoned pine for the funeral fires. Others would put aside ashes and lye to scrub the new marks of carnage from Heorot come morning. Hrothulf left the hall unobtrusively on his errand and with genuine regret. That he must likely remove his young cousins in a few years time in order to rule would never be more to Halga's son than a necessity of power. No more of a beast than Grendel and quite as human, he could sincerely decry the waste of lives to no purpose.

The sun was down, dark come quick and full as the supper neared its end. Unferth always drank more than he ate and had reached that corrosive stage of mind that unlocked his tongue and questionable wit. Hrothulf and others thought it more blunted than barbed, but the jocund custom held among Scyldings to jest with visitors within certain limits, the more honored the more enjoyable the roasting. In this pastime young Unferth was, if not most deft, at least most dogged. A man with shadows over his own soul, he resented Beowulf for pledging what for years neither he nor any Dane had dared, and he had long heard of the scop-sung swimming match with Brecca. Unferth gave his drinking horn to a servant and rose, weaving only a little as he raised his voice to the hall at large. "Beowulf!"

He saw the massive Geat turn from his place at table.

"Beowulf the swimming man!"

Gradually the hubbub subsided as thanes understood what Unferth was up to.

"So you're the prince of Geats we've heard so much about."

"So my father told me."

"I am Unferth, the son of Ecglaf."

"Then I have heard of you as well."

The tables went even more silent. Something in the tone of both men suggested more than mead wit. Weltheow whispered to her husband: The time had come to break up the supper before Unferth did it for them and brought trouble where they had strife enough.

Seated beside Hondshew, Gorm nudged the older warrior. "Who is that rude son of a fishwife?"

"You wouldn't recall Unferth," Hondshew told him. "A brewer of large storms in small cups. Years ago, he came to Helsingborg with his father. Not much of a head for drink. Challenged two or three men before being downed by his own mead horn."

Hondshew took in Unferth's spoiled good looks and his unsteadiness as he advanced toward Beowulf. "But for being carried to bed, he would have been a hero, no doubt of that. He said so more than once next day."

"We've all heard of your famous contest with Brecca," Unferth declared. "He wagered to outlast you in the winter sea and did, I hear."

Beowulf looked him up and down, a hint of amusement playing about the corners of his mouth. "He lost."

"Not as *I* received it, but then the tale is hard to swallow no matter who tells it. Seven nights without rest or warmth, contending with sea beasts and deathly cold? Swimming with a sword in one hand? Brecca reached his Bronding home as the story goes, and claimed the victory. How say you to that?"

Beowulf shifted about on the bench to face Unferth. He yawned with elaborate disregard. "I say that would be news in Helsingborg yet, since Brecca never claimed the prize. He was strong, but he couldn't outlast me in the water."

"Seven days and nights?" Unferth challenged in a tone acrid with disbelief. "Come, Geat. We tell the truth here."

Beowulf stretched and got up—not a lifting of his bulk from the bench but the effortless swell of an ocean wave. "Some say we did. Some say we didn't. But in the water, Brecca turned his sword on me—"

So he did and so we contended, Brecca wasting his strength in fury while I fought him off and tried to keep from sinking or freezing, until at last it was all either of us could do to stay afloat. I could hear my own breath like a file on iron—

"The stir of our battle brought creatures from the deep who attacked us. There, now, was Brecca fierce as reputed. We left our own battle feast to serve theirs. Pity it was not to their liking, for we fed them full on iron, so punctual in service to their table that we found no time or taste to our own."

—frozen numb, we could have died, both of us regretting the mad boast that would surely kill us soon. Then that other huge shape loomed nearer. We thought it was a breaching whale. A capsized boat, shattered and about to break in two. We clung to it, Brecca at one end, I at the other. Even then, the futile man cursed and challenged me while the feeling went out and cold crept up and up my limbs. Sanity fled, leaving open that door where my father came, and Eligius. Freezing to death is a merciful way to die. Did I pass from this world for all the right reasons or all the worst?

"Brecca won only in that he lived to reach home," Beowulf concluded. "For myself, Unferth, I died striving against him and the sea."

A swell of muffled astonishment ran around the tables at the matter-of-fact statement.

"Frozen, my hands lost their grip on the wreck. I slipped down into the water and died."

Unferth guffawed. "You are saying—?"

"That I died, Dane. Went down into death, knowing the place well for having been there before."

Beowulf moved toward his taunter and looked down into the younger man's eyes that wavered with drink and now uncertainty. "There was emptiness and the cold of the underworld. I take no offense at your mock, drunk as you are, but you're not the man to laugh at me."

Near whispering now; none heard him but Unferth. "If you were sharp in deeds as in words, this beast would be dead as the brother you slew by accident, son of Ecglaf. As any tale will vary with the teller, some say it was not accident."

"It *was*," Unferth hissed under his breath, glad none could hear them.

"I can't deny you; I wasn't there. You did not die with me. Trust my word and I'll trust yours."

Unferth retreated an unsteady step from the larger man, not afraid of him, but disconcerted by the unnatural stillness of one who spoke of cold that indeed seemed yet to hover about him. "You have been lucky, Beowulf. You will not fare so well in Heorot."

"Unferth, enough," the king commanded. "It grows late and the queen would honor our guests before they take their rest."

Weltheow descended from the high table bearing a large pitcher. To show that their court revered the young volunteers no less than their veterans, she served young Gorm first, making much of filling his horn, and with a smile Gorm might have taken as invitation from a woman younger or less royal.

"Be so good, warrior. Drink this slowly and savor it, a perfect square of the brewer's art. Pure water, honey, malt, and yeast. Every so often, the four blend to perfection. No art can achieve this; it is a sometime gift of the gods. *Velbekommen.*"

The queen poured out the cheer to each of the Geats, who avowed they had never quaffed better or more potent. When she came to Beowulf, Weltheow whispered as she bent over his horn. "Take no note of Unferth. When he drinks, his own demons speak. We have prayed for such as you and some end to this."

Beowulf raised the horn to her in pledge. "I will do this thing, lady, or you may put me on the pyre tomorrow."

"There's my good friend," Hondshew sighed to his leader as the queen moved on. "Ever a ray of sunlight in my gloom. Must you be so negative while I'm drinking?"

Beowulf chucked him in the ribs. "Are you warrior or worrier? You fret like your old mother."

"Did she grow old by being suicidal? Peace, now: I think Hrothgar comes to say good night—or good-bye, depending on your point of view."

With his wife and sons, Hrothgar passed down the hall as his thanes rose in respect. Bidding his family go on, he paused to draw Beowulf aside.

"This is a worthy pledge, Prince. You give heart to my people."

"No more than I owe, sir."

"As custom reckons debt, perhaps; but this?" Hrothgar looked through the open doors to the dark outside. "No man owes that much. I have seen so much young blood try against this curse, and all wasted. It is late. This is the time when *he* comes. Listen to me: In the first years, he came like a storm; now, sometimes so silently, the guards never see him. Be on guard."

"Isn't it true he kills only those who venture into Heorot after dark?"

"So it has been. Sometimes there are two of them," Hrothgar told him. "Night guards have seen a female with him from time to time."

"And heard him cry out your name as well, Holger said."

Hrothgar frowned with the chilled memory of a dream and a word within that dream. *Usurper.* "No. I don't know. So many stories . . . the old folk say the female is its mother."

"This is no dumb brute, my lord, nor does he come for prey."

The years of shame without reason or resolve flared deep in old Hrothgar. *Him or her or they, why don't you ask when you meet?* The surge of temper died within him, quelled by kingly reserve. Hrothgar beckoned to Esher, who waited his command. "My first thane will prepare the hall for you. Heed him, Beowulf. Esher is the only man who grappled with the beast and lived. Good rest and better fortune to you. Every door is barred down but my poor Heorot—and it is late."

11

IN HEOROT, THE SERVANTS' TAPERS flickered eerily over the dusty surfaces of gold and silver inlay. In the smoky, trembling light of the torches, the stains on floor and walls showed black and ominous. Beowulf asked for fires to be laid in both pits while other servitors hurried back and forth across the inner court with bedding and pillows for the Geats.

Gorm watched them come and go. "Never saw servants move so fast without being helped by a boot."

Burly Ulf wrapped the baldric about his scabbard and set it aside, warming his hands at the growing fire. "They want to be done and gone. Can't blame them. Gloomy place. Smells dirty and cold. Must be a ton of cobwebs up in those rafters."

Gorm indicated Esher by Beowulf's side on the dais. "That old fellow up there with the prince? Did you see his left arm? They say the beast did that."

Esher held a taper close while Beowulf made a minute inspection of the two throne chairs. He retrieved several small objects like dried leaf from the king's chair of state and grunted in satisfaction. "We could just be right. Thane Esher, before the servants leave, we will need a dozen fresh resin torches."

The torches were rapidly procured by servants clearly not inclined to tarry any longer.

"The creature will know there are men here," Esher said.

"I want him to."

Esher looked around at the Geats sorting out their bedding. "Weapons are useless, true, but to fight it barehanded . . ."

"My men will be armed. They'll feel safer with something in their hands."

"As you will." Esher's shoulders heaved reluctantly. "Don't let him get you off your feet. You're finished then." He lifted his deformed left arm. "Or like this. May the Fates be kind to brave men. Good night."

Esher had barely departed when Gorm planted himself solemnly before Beowulf, requesting the honor of the bed nearest the door that he be the first to fight. "Do not refuse me, Prince."

"I must," Beowulf denied him gently. "You have other work. Take one of the torches. All of you, lay one by your bed, ready to hand."

The men gathered about their leader, the glow of the fire pit washing light and shadow over their anxious young faces.

"I'll take the first bed, Hondshew across from me, Gorm on my right. Everyone remember: When I call for light, let it be quick. Don't leave me in the dark. Now to bed. Rest, but don't fall asleep. Ulf, put some more wood on the fires."

Before stretching out on their blankets, Beowulf and Hondshew closed the broken doors part way, leaving a narrow gap. If the beast tried stealth, the rusted hinges still intact would betray it noisily.

"How is it with you, Hondshew? Ready?"

"Some of the other lads are asking that of each other: Are you ready? Are you scared? If you take their word for it, there's not a man here won't front the beast with a fruit knife when it comes."

Beowulf grinned at his friend, realizing how seldom he smiled these last years, and how much his own chilly spirit relied on the warmth of Hondshew. "And you?"

"Much too nervous to fall asleep, if that's your meaning."

The others were abed now, the chink of mail muffled in blankets as they settled to rest and wait. Beowulf lay down opposite Hondshew. The shiftings and mutterings of his men gradually ceased.

They waited.

Hondshew turned over, mumbling. "Cursed uncomfortable bedding in iron. How did you ever swim—?"

"Wait." Beowulf sat up. "Hear something?"

"No." Hondshew's advice was tinged with amiable irritation. "Try to rest. If that thing's big as they say, it's not going to tiptoe in unnoticed."

Surely not. Beowulf grinned up into the dark overhead. Hondshew would say something like that. The bravest man in Helsingborg, yet so like him to admit fear casually as hunger. For himself, fear was no part of the undertaking, only atonement for the unatonable, on and on, the eternal debt for Frisia. If he died tonight, would that quiet Edgetho and the other ghosts? Or would he live long enough for honor to become more than the counterfeit men accepted so readily from him?

He lay alert, preparing himself, sensitive to any sound. Far away along the outer ramparts, one guard called to another.

Anytime now.

His fatigue betrayed him; not asleep, but close to it when the doors burst inward with a screech of wood and ruptured hinges. Beowulf's eyes snapped open. He saw, silhouetted massively in pale moonlight, the looming figure that lunged into Heorot with a low growl. Beowulf sprang to his feet.

"Torches! Light your torches!"

Gorm scrambling up, Hondshew already moving in the darkness, others stumbling toward the fire pit—and that other sound like the deep-throated feral purring of the god of all great cats. Closest to the beast, Beowulf leaped back out of its reach as the torches flared one by one into life. He might have gasped at what he saw, but there was no time.

"Gorm, no!"

Hondshew's desperate warning as the boy, sword and shield at guard, advanced on the ghastly thing. Too quick for Beowulf to intervene, Gorm too eager for the honor, going for his own kill—

"Get *back.*"

—and Hondshew springing between him and the night creature blinded by sudden light but lashing out with an arm thick as a tree limb at what moved across his dim vision. Hondshew pushed Gorm hard; the boy flew backward and went down in a clatter of mail and weapons. Someone screamed warning to Hondshew, but too late.

A horrible, torch-lit stillness then. Gorm got clumsily to his feet, numb at what Hondshew had saved him from and the price of that mercy.

In the growing light from a dozen torches, what had been Hondshew hung limp in the grip of something out of the worst of Gorm's childhood night fears. He was prepared for monstrous appearance and size. What forced a moan of revulsion from him was the grotesquely exaggerated likeness to a human face in its upper half, the great jaws smeared with blood, the green eyes half closed against painful glare.

Beowulf moved squarely into the creature's path. "Stay back, all of you. Forget sword; you're holding what he can't bear. Torches forward!"

On three sides of the crouching obscenity, they thrust out their lights. The beast flinched away from the glare, roaring—or a sound like a roar, except that it rose and fell with something like articulation.

One of the youths choked out: "Is it trying to talk?"

"Yes. It's not just a beast." Beowulf swung his torch toward the high seat at the dim end of the hall. "That's what you come for, isn't it? Every night, year after year. The king's chair. You've split the joints and left bits of seaweed."

"You." The creature took a step toward him, sinews flexing. The long, curled toenails scraped against the floor planks. A short, harsh bellow exploded from the fish mouth. *"Go."*

Gorm swallowed hard. "It *can* talk."

"You sailed for the impossible," Beowulf reminded him. "Here it is."

He darted his torch out at the mere-beast, who reacted, retreating a step with Hondshew's broken body draped over one thick arm. "No, you can't bear the light, can you? You can't see me well at all, but here I am, all that stands between you and what you came for. Get past me if you can."

The beast emitted a low, sibilant hiss like the rushing of water through a conduit. The great arm rose and chopped down. Hondshew's head fell heavily to the floor. His body was flung aside like a child's rag doll, landing at Ulf's feet. The boy gripped his torch and forced back the sickness rising in his throat. Part of his mind, white with horror and fear, refused to believe he was seeing this. They were all going to die. This was how it felt to die.

"Prince, please." His plea for Beowulf's safety emerged as a squeak. "Don't. It's just too big."

The thing struck with an adder's speed, reaching to pin Beowulf's arms, but the torch glare hindered its aim. Beowulf dropped the light and caught the mere-beast's wrists tight, kicking at the groin with all his strength.

The blow told. Pain and shock flared in the green fire of the eyes. Beowulf held on, whispering into that hideous visage so mockingly haunted with intelligence.

"Look at me. Look on the real face of death."

For an instant he imagined that a different expression flickered in the nightmare eyes. Then he was lifted off his feet as the creature thrashed to shake free of him. Beowulf was whipped about violently like a banner in a high wind. The other Geats fell back. Some dropped their torches and reached for swords to strike at the beast from behind. The air burst out of Beowulf's lungs as he was hammered against a post with a force that would have cracked his ribs but for the mail and padding over his tunic. Bit by bit as he flailed through the air, his fingers spidered over the thick wrists, seeking leverage.

Impervious to the futile swords that could no more than sting him, the beast made a fatal mistake, tore one talon free to strike at the nearest of its assailants—then, as the frightened youth fell back, raised that arm to break Beowulf's neck. Beowulf caught the wrist as it descended. The incredible force shuddered through his arm to the shoulder, but now he had the needed grip. Bone strained in the ebony wrist and then the elbow as he twisted outward. The beast's roar became a scream as the wrist, elbow, and then the huge shoulder dislocated and snapped. Badly battered now, Beowulf lost his grip on the other arm. It flashed up and down, a hammer fist crashing into the base of Beowulf's skull.

Red light exploded behind Beowulf's eyes. The world darkened.

Then voices swam back into his awareness. He was lying face down, his left hand gripping something hard and thick he must not relinquish.

". . . would have killed him."

"Almost did but he's breathing."

Someone tried to laugh: a nervous, silly sound. "I guess we're heroes."

Someone else said only, "I feel sick."

Beowulf opened his eyes, which refused to focus well at first. His body reacted instinctively, bunching him up onto his knees. He stared around with confused double vision at his companions, then at what was still vised in his left hand.

Gorm looked pasty white in the smoky torchlight, but gripped his sword firmly. "We cut it the rest of the way," he managed feebly. "It was near through. You would have torn it clear away if . . ."

Beowulf had ripped the arm completely away from the mere-beast's shoulder before the thing escaped. His head throbbed vilely from the blow to his skull. He could feel it swelling, dizzy but graced with unbelievable luck. The creature had struck while off balance and terribly wounded; otherwise, his skull would have been driven into the brain beneath.

He lurched to his feet, still dragging the massive arm. "Hond-shew—get a blanket. Wrap him up. All of him."

Beowulf staggered toward the sagging doors. He heard men outside. The sword dropped from Gorm's hand and he sat down heavily. "I want to go home."

No one disagreed with him. Gorm uttered it again in a ragged voice drained of everything but conviction. "I never wanted to be home so much in all my life."

The noise from Heorot had drawn guards from the inner ramparts, flinching in empathy from the sickening sounds of flesh colliding with more solid objects. Torches thrust out of nearby bowers. Hrothgar and Esher approached the hall cautiously where, through open windows, torchlight flickered eerily and walls shook as from a war in Asgard itself. The deep baying of the beast had risen to an unearthly scream that went on and on, then ceased abruptly.

"Back," Esher warned his king. "Everyone back."

The broken doors burst outward. Something huge stumbled forward, lurching, oddly unbalanced and incomplete in the poor light. Men fell back from the creature as it wove on its feet, hissing at them, then loped away from the hall. They waited through a terrible silence.

Hrothgar ventured toward the entrance where one door still hung from a single, twisted iron hinge. As he did, Beowulf appeared, moving heavily as one too quickly awakened. One hand rubbed clumsily at the back of his head; the other trailed something that might have been part of a tree. He staggered forward holding up the prize for Hrothgar to see before the knees buckled under him.

12

RAN THROUGH THE WANING NIGHT toward home, fighting shock and pain as his life bled away. The last miles to the mere were a gauntlet run through hunting wolves howling after him as they caught the blood scent. Grendel spent his failing strength on the snarling brutes that leaped to hang on him before he shook them off. He staggered into the lake shallows, lurched out into deeper water, then sank toward the bottom with a plea to faceless and indifferent gods. His blood trace woke hunger in the mere predators. Grendel fended them off weakly, tearing at the largest and leaving it sacrifice to the others. He burst through the water wall and lay moaning before the doors of his birthplace.

Returned earlier from hunting, Sigyn had expected her son as he always came, striding into their twilit grotto, triumphant for one more night's reign in his rightful hall. The smell of blood woke her maternal instinct for danger. Sigyn flung open the heavy doors to see the mutilated flesh of her flesh struggling to rise, his blood puddling on the damp stones. The shriek tore out of her.

"Son!"

The mother's instinct to protect wiped out all else. She yoked Grendel's one arm over her broad shoulders and dragged him to his bed. Crouched over him, whimpering with fear, Sigyn cast about distractedly for something to staunch the bleeding, then tore at her own garments, pressing the strips to the stump of his shoulder as her terror grew to a fury winding tight as the windlass of a giant catapult.

"Who has done this?"

Difficult to speak with his life ebbing away fast as the blood. Grendel wanted to cry out the last anguished *why?* of so many that summed to his existence. He was the firstborn of a king; all others since Shild usurped his right. Hrothgar must have known and understood that, for he abdicated with every sunset and lately, altogether. As true king of Scyldings, Grendel would harm no man who did not trespass in Heorot at night. Did Sigyn not see the foul injustice he suffered?

"I punished none who honored my truce," Grendel choked out in his mother's arms as she rocked him in her misery.

"Who did this? Tell me."

"They used torches. . . ."

Bright stabbings of light, more than he could bear after so many nocturnal years, and out of that glare came something in man shape. "But not a natural man. He bade me look on death. He was death. I looked into his eyes and saw nothing. Emptiness, a starless void."

That was the horror that betrayed Grendel's will to prevail. He had loved life, exulted in being even when he raged at fate. "Not a man but a thing. A monster."

"Even curs are named," Sigyn pressed him. "What did they call this beast?"

"Beowulf." Grendel could struggle for life no longer, felt the darkness coming down. That at least had always been a friend. "When my arm hung loose as a tatter, the others cheered him as they hacked at me. He hurt me . . . Hrothgar loosed his dog on me, the one called Beowulf—"

"Gods? Father? Do you hear this?" Sigyn sobbed. "Do you see?"

"Not our fault," Grendel whispered as his eyes closed. "Hrothgar is our kin. The hall is ours."

"It *is*."

"He owes us, Mother. . . ."

The great body shuddered and lay still in Sigyn's arms.

"They will make good," she vowed. "It is sworn."

Her hands were the only tender part of her as she straightened the long limbs and pillowed Grendel's head in her lap. The rest was a gathering storm. Hrothgar and all his client kings together had not gold enough for this wergild owed her. No, her rage reckoned as the vengeance blackened and rose in her. She would merely begin with Hrothgar's family and leave a long bloodstain from Heorot to the sea.

"Father Loki," she prayed, bowed over Grendel, "come to me now. Your child has need of you."

Come! her soul pleaded savagely as she rose from her dead and her insupportable loss. *Come!* Sigyn's great clawed talons flexed and beat at her hard thighs as she gathered and channeled the primal fury of her soul. Centuries of existence, as men measured time, and all the meager joy of her wasteland of a life had died in her arms, leaving her alone again. So died the innocence of childhood when Loki's magic could no longer hide the horror of herself from maturing eyes. So perished love with Shild and more when Grendel in his own agony dragged her to the mirror and faced what a loving lie could no longer conceal.

No, enough. *Loki, come!*

From the beginning, the Fates had discarded the snarl of her life in this black cesspool of a mere. Even then, she had been content to sit as queen in Heorot, empty and dark as it was, seeing her son in Shild's place—

Father, come to me!

—but now she would tear all, wreak such havoc as would send harpers yet unborn to their direst word-hoards to find a new color for ruin in the red wake of her purpose. When she had passed like pestilence through Hrothgar's blood and nothing moved in Lejre but ravens and moles fear-shivering in the blighted earth, Sigyn would build a funeral pyre for her son. For tinder, the splintered thrones of Hrothgar and Weltheow; for kindling, the fat and rent limbs of their sons, a blaze of wood and flesh wherefrom the smoke would rise thick and black to write Sigyn's deed across heaven, corrupt the air in Asgard, and choke the gods themselves.

The spasm of rage spent itself. Pain returned. Sigyn wilted over Grendel's body while fresh grief wrenched at her body and soul. She held him close, whimpering, crooning to him as when he was newborn and she could still veil them both in merciful love to hide truth behind the glamor of what should have been.

Dully, as she rocked back and forth, cradling his head, Sigyn became aware of new light invading the twilit cave. Points of brilliance here and there, as if some mercurial servant darted about to fire a thousand tapers. The light gathered into a small, intense sun, softened and became the umbered form of Loki.

"Your need must be great. I heard you clearly."

Sigyn would have run to the shelter of his arms but sorrow weighed her down. "Where have you been these many years when we needed you?"

"Where I must go," Loki said simply. "What I must be."

"You forgot us."

"Evidently." Her demigod sire gazed about the drab place he had long ago enchanted for her from some unexpected nobility of inspiration. The walls still held, but glamor was long worn away. "I fear I've never been very retentive."

"Look on him and remember. This was your grandson, killed by a man creature."

"Poor child." Never able to concentrate long, anomaly among gods and demons but never wholly of either, Loki forced himself now to terms with what he had begun and then largely forgotten. His restless attention could still pierce beneath surface to subtlety and find in the features of Grendel the likeness to himself and acknowledge the debt of that.

"An animal did this, Father. An empty, cursed thing named Beowulf. Grendel said he had the look and the cold of death about him."

"I have heard of that one. As deaths go, he knows some of them."

"Help me then!"

"My child, I—" Loki found himself suddenly incoherent with the alien emotion engulfing him at the pitiful sight of them. In flashing about the world of men to hide his child from Asgard, love and caring had ambushed and dealt him a glancing blow. A shock then, worse now. He had never been able to deal with honest feeling or its consequences at all.

"So this is remorse," he marveled softly. "Because of an idle whim on a day when I was bored with a wife and godly splendor. I had to tip something over, anything. You at least have lived, daughter."

Her head was bowed over her son. "They call it life."

"Let your tears teach me. I will try to understand. Who fathered him?"

"Shild."

Loki sighed: Freyr's godling. That much at least could not be laid to his charge, though his chief talent had always been for confusion and by no half measures. "To unbalance something . . . and so, this wreckage. I will aid if I can. What would you have me do?"

"Nothing beyond your powers."

Loki felt uncomfortable. He had devised too much through unbridled imagination and all to answer for. "Not too sweeping," he cautioned in prudence. "Contained within Sjaelland, I hope."

"Not a foot beyond, but that terrible."

"Done," Loki agreed.

"Nothing we loved so much as beauty, my son and I, nor anything so denied, save through the mercy of your magic. Weave my soul into vengeance itself. Make me a match for this creature who killed my only boy. Aye, and if they ask in Asgard, call it justice."

No more than that. If Thor called Grendel an impossibility, at least he was part of life; he thirsted to live. If men cleped him monster, he could still look into the eyes of true otherness and be humanly horrified at the desolation there.

Loki watched as the huge, grotesque chimera form of his child lunged this way and that in her fury, her lovely voice, the one beauty that never deserted her, breaking with agony as she besought his powers.

"Make me apt to this Beowulf. Not now, not in rage. No, I'll let that cool and harden until the sun goes down. Make cold murder my warmth and dark of the moon my sun. Go to Freyja; let her plead to Odin for that vantage seat from which Freyr first saw Gerda and, loving her, made my husband. Let her look out now and see my grief. Has she not wept tears of gold for a lost love? But let her see my son and my pain, and Freyja will weep acid and salt on the fields of Sjaelland and a blight to make plague seem pleasure."

"Done," Loki promised. *One way or another*, he amended mentally. Beside those malefactions for which he must answer already, this would be no more than trifling misdemeanor.

"Do these things for me." Sigyn lifted Grendel's body and carried it to the long table. "For if there was joy in my getting, there's been little in your get."

Sigyn laid Grendel on the damp, moldered boards. Above the table hung the giant-forged sword, Loki's long-ago gift. She drew the ponderous blade, feather-light in her broad fist. Sigyn regarded her own gross body, loathsome even to Shild without the glamor.

"One more boon, Father?" she implored. "One so simple for you?"

"Of course, child."

"I am no longer a child," she reminded him sadly. "Not for many, many years. Tonight, I go to Heorot to front the usurper and his little bitch queen in her finery. Do not make me face them like this."

Drawing on more courage than Loki would have suspected, Sigyn moved to one of the water mirrors. She avoided them out of habit, but now she had a purpose and gazed steadily on her reflection. "Weltheow was lovely once—a crow beside me at my best—but still comely in her age. Give me back for a little time the beauty Shild first loved."

"Memory is not my strongest asset," Loki admitted. "When I could recall, I loved you in any form because that form held you. But you were a child then."

He had no idea of her need. "Try."

"It will be difficult now. Children believe so easily and with all their hearts."

"Am I less of a woman than Hrothgar's wife, less a mother or a queen? I conjure you. *Try.*"

The form of Loki blurred and shimmered with brilliant color as he worked to Sigyn's desire. Second only to the building of her palace long ago, this was his finest moment, never to be known in Asgard or sung on earth. As he labored, the cave became again the hall Sigyn remembered from infancy, bright with blazing sconces that hurt Sigyn's eyes after so long. Beneath the great sword, the moldered ruin of the table became a noble catafalque on which Grendel lay like a prince, clad in samite, in the golden-haired likeness to his father, Shild—while, in the mirror gone clear and bright, Sigyn relished each minute transmutation, the talons that paled and shaped again to long, feminine fingers. The ghastly parody of a face that drew in from fantastic exaggeration to human proportion, refining at last to a striking harmony of color, line, and plane. Hrothgar might have died for her when young, Sigyn judged with pleasure, and to-night he would. Not vanity, this, nor too much to ask.

Sigyn turned from the mirror, radiant and grateful. "They slander you in Asgard. There are crueler gods by far."

"I have always thought so." Loki's mercurial, shining figure melted into light again and flowed toward the doors. Sigyn might have spoken truth; he was what he was. Frigga, that eternally dull goddess, always predicted a bad end for Loki, but he knew better than the complacent Aesir that all worlds and all heavens were mutable. Perhaps some future and lenient cosmos might mitigate his inevitable punishment.

The light of him faded, but the warm voice remained. "The least I could do. Fatherhood in the usual sense is alien to me. I grow old, Sigyn. Even Asgard becomes turgid and ridiculous."

Sigyn heard her father's soft, impish chuckle.

"I may have to unbalance something again. Farewell."

13

THE BEAST WAS DEAD. Before dawn, messengers had ridden to the outlying steadings, bidden their chieftains come and see the grisly remnant hung high from Heorot's roof pole, and to reaffirm their loyalty to Hrothgar's restored power. Before midmorning, they began to arrive by horse or in wagons to marvel at the arm turning slowly this way and that over the shattered doors. But where was the demon itself?

"Went to die in its own stinking lair," Prince Hrethric told them, pointing to the blood trail that led off along the now beaten path to the mere. "Our men are tracking it."

From early light a dozen well-mounted thanes had followed what a blind man could not miss, spatterings of dried blood that led straight to the shunned lake, thinning out as the creature weakened; until, at the mere's edge, men had to search for the last traces.

"Couldn't be alive, not after losing that much blood."

The oldest and most experienced boar tracker paused long over the larger stains on the heath. Now, kneeling by the last signs only yards from the water, he muttered thoughtfully, "Almost human."

Except for an unusual property in the stains that would not dull as they dried but shimmered in the morning sunlight.

"My grandsire's father told the tale," the old tracker said in a voice soft with memory. "And my grandfather told it to me. Our first king, great Shild, was so fine and human a ruler that men forgot he came from the gods. But once, wounded in the arm by an Angle's sword, the staunching bandage shone so with his blood. My great-grandfather saw with his own eyes the blood of the Vanir from whom Shild came. This is much the same."

The other men absorbed this uneasily as they gazed out over the dreary lake. If Beowulf had killed some godling unthinkably descended from the benevolent Vanir, then this night-demon's death might not be the end of their affliction.

"We will say the creature is dead," the old tracker decided, searching each man's eyes to find agreement there. He found it in all but the youngest, a thane's son named Frithmund, who only laughed and drew his sword. The boy was new to Hrothgar's service, laboring under the burden of an illustrious father and painfully eager to prove himself. He jammed the sword into the sand by the water.

"And if it be not dead," Frithmund declared in a loud voice, "*I* will watch here for when it comes forth. The big Geat took one arm. I will take the other and the head to lay at Hrothgar's feet."

The others overruled him firmly. No watch was needed; the beast was surely dead or dying. The boy relented without too much persuasion, feeling he'd made his mark on the issue, actually a far deeper impression than he guessed. Across the lake among the black rocks, her sight and hearing thrice keen as any hunting beast's, Sigyn heard Frithmund's boast and wrote it in memory.

She was calm now, composed, nothing to be done in haste. She had washed and combed through the tumbling golden hair and lay back to let it dry soft and gleaming in the sunlight, langorously smoothing long white hands over her stomach and slender thighs, admiring the gown woven from Loki's magic. Her slightest movement caused the garment to flash with different colors.

Loki was kind indeed. Her mirrors presented the same beauty Shild had first seen and desired, youthful and firm. Let wrinkled Weltheow see and envy that before she perished, the bitch.

When Hrothgar and Weltheow came from their bower, the crowd of Scyldings and visitors was already clustered before Heorot, gaping up at the huge arm that would tear no more lives from Dane bodies. His queen on his arm, old Hrothgar moved through the onlookers toward the doors of Heorot and the tall, aloof figure of Beowulf, noting how men marveled at the battle prize—"Look at the size of that thing! See the claws, the skin like a fire-blackened shield!"

Long in power and wise in its imperatives, Hrothgar and Weltheow did not have to speak their satisfaction. This would be the turning point as Yule marked the beginning of the sun's journey home to warm the earth. Battered and bloodstained though it be, tables and decorations, new spring flowers and old honored shields would be returned to Heorot this day, where as many as could crowd into the hall would hold holiday and feast the night through.

"A wise festival," Weltheow said to her husband. And a calculated one. Many of these minor chiefs and thanes in the courtyard must have weighed their oaths of loyalty against Hrothgar's helplessness in his own hall and come near to dangerous conclusions. This would bring them securely back into the fold.

"It will be expensive," Hrothgar said to his wife.

"As always, but worth it," the queen returned. "Every proper show must be made and even more." Weltheow inclined her silvered head in the direction of her meaning. "Beowulf."

Yes, a great expense. Before hailing the Geat prince who stood with his men beneath the dangling victory prize, Hrothgar called his steward to him and gave hurried instructions. "Let the kitchens prepare; we will feast as soon as the hall is fitted out. Spare nothing, Wulfgar. All we have. Now as to gifts . . ."

Not only a feast, but a show of power and policy. The protector of the Danes rewarded service lavishly and would punish defection in equal measure. Before all of them, even as grinning servants carried the tables back at last into reclaimed Heorot, Hrothgar embraced Beowulf and proclaimed:

"Henceforth, to make even stronger the ties between ourselves and the Geats, Prince Beowulf will be as a third son to me!"

On the fringes of the crowd, next to young Unferth, Hrothulf cheered enthusiastically for the heroic Geat with the others, while musing on what curb this might lay on his own future. On Hergar's death, his own father, Halga, had been passed over in favor of the more aggressive Hrothgar. A treasure of wisdom in council, Halga the Good plainly lacked ambition; but for that and Hrothgar's popularity and persuasiveness, Hrothulf would be king now.

He nudged Unferth, who was staring somberly up at the severed arm. "Gratifying sight."

"A miracle."

"If I were king, I would not have suffered twelve winters' shame to see it."

Unferth might not have heard him at all, so rapt he was. "And I mocked the man who did this."

Recalling his drunken jibes, he missed the quick, sidewise scrutiny of his companion. "They were strangers. You had only a bit of fun."

"He'll hear no more of that from me."

"Unferth, don't punish yourself." Hrothulf put a brotherly arm around his friend's shoulder. "There is a complacent falsehood that holds the Fates are skilled. They are so inept that not design but caprice and accident are the weave of men's lives. Whatever judgment was pronounced on you, accident alone cast you out from your father and family. Just so it may raise you up. You're a loyal man, Unferth. You can't drink well and shouldn't—but be as loyal to me when I must wear the crown."

That much Unferth heard clearly. "You mean *if*."

"Of course," Hrothulf shrugged lightly. "I hope you don't think I meant anything else. That would insult me."

In the early afternoon, following their king into Heorot, the Danes sat to feast in triumph. Barrel after barrel of beer was broached; the roasted pig and wine-sauced venison came on heaping, steaming platters. By royal request (and young Hrothmund's imploring), Beowulf took a place of honor at the first bench between Hrethric and his little brother. At the next table his young Geats laughed and gobbled and drank with the Danes, though Gorm seemed noticeably subdued. It seemed to Beowulf they all sat straighter now than yesterday, none of them cocky as they might be, passing through such danger and living to tell of it. He could hear them and observed from their gestures that they were recounting the battle, but Beowulf heard no boasts from them and was privately glad. Mead-bragging was expected, as much a part of his way of life as the code that bred Edgetho out of iron. A man should always do more than he promised, and thanes like Edgetho were the mail protecting a king's breast—and yet Beowulf recalled Holger the coast guard's sentiment toward Heorot: outwardly hail while decaying within.

That is me, Edgetho. You won. I have become what you desired, though it has been so costly. We will have pointed words in Valhalla, you and I.

If there had been feeling in him or a heart left to break, Beowulf would have wept, howled, for the loss of Hondshew, so much more of a man than Edgetho or himself. When his friend died, and thank all merciful gods he died quickly, Beowulf was as horrified as the others, but at such a *distance*. How gullibly men hailed as heroism what was merely a lack of life.

Young Hrothmund tugged at his elbow. "Prince?"

Beowulf sighed. The king's youngest would be asking more details of the battle and more after that, relishing the gore. What more could he tell? Ask of the others, boy. "What, then?"

"You do not hear? My father calls you."

Beowulf pushed himself away from the bench to face the high table where Hrothgar was on his feet, one hand raised. Wulfgar advanced down the noisy hall, pounding his staff for silence, while Weltheow waited before the dais holding a rich cloth in her hands.

"Silence for Hrothgar, protector of the Spear-Danes!"

The king's voice carried, reedy with age but still commanding. "Thanes, let us render what is due. For Hondshew who died in our aid, full measure of gold weight will go to Helsingborg for his family."

All the Geats stood up in honor of their friend's passing. Unferth himself, quiet and sober this evening, deposited the two heavy bags at Beowulf's feet with a respectful nod. Beowulf gave the gold into Ulf's charge.

"I thank my lord for Hondshew's kin. He wanted—"

Wanted so much, that man. Aye, Hondshew would with all that zest for life dancing in his eyes. To watch with Ina as their children grew and later bear the joyful weight of them clambering over him to hear Hondshew tell of his adventuring and perhaps exaggerate a little as if any enlargement were needed. Now the gold would go to his wife and the small, wizened widow who bore him. Geatish tongues stumbled over her Pictish name, which sounded like *Itharne*, and so she was known. Itharne, the woman with blue-black hair and leathery olive skin, who could never abide the sound of a Geatish harp but taught Hondshew instead songs from her Caledonian home: of Artos and Gwynhwyfar, Dorelei of the Faerie folk and her love for Padrec Raven, and how a man might gamble and lose all for a woman, which had once seemed trivial and unrealistic to Beowulf, though deep-dyed in the man he called friend. What could he say now for Hondshew who had far more music in him?

"He wanted to do his best," he finished shortly. "May we make a pyre for him this afternoon?"

Wulfgar assured him as to that. "The logs are laid and the body prepared. We will honor him in the morning."

"Now let us honor the living." Weltheow unfolded the rich cloth she held: a golden banner with fine embroidery inset with jewels in the outline of a boar. At the entrance of the hall where the ruined doors had been removed stood three of the queen's most honored women with gifts of war gear.

Four hours past noon, the sun going low. Manfred the sentry left Heorot, still chewing the last of his ample supper. With one appreciative glance at the great arm swinging high overhead, he swigged lightly at the battered tin cup of mead poured for Walsing, whom he was to relieve on the bridge between the inner and outer ramparts. He was punctual. Older Walsing would want to be at supper and see the goings-on.

"And they are something to behold!" Manfred told him, presenting the cup and taking Walsing's spear and signal horn. "The *gifts* to that man! To all of them! Eight horses with golden bridles, one with a jeweled saddle. Hrothgar's own, you know the one. Helmet and mail and one of the fine old heirloom swords from the armory, the one with the boar carved on the pommel. And a necklace and gold armbands from the queen. If those Geats weren't rich before, they are now."

"Um." Walsing's attention was not wholly on young Manfred as he studied the eastern sky. "And how did Beowulf take that?"

"In his stride, very cool. You'd think he did this all the time: another day, another demon."

"Heroes are well paid—when they work," Walsing allowed. "But it's all show, Manfred. There's chiefs in Heorot tonight who haven't seen Hrothgar for years, men who might have been inclined to take their people to some other lord's protection, but not now, I'm thinking."

Walsing gazed into the distance, leaning back against the bridge railing. "Very strange."

"What's strange?"

Walsing tilted his chin for pointer. "That."

"Where?"

"There. Dead northeast."

Manfred narrowed his eyes. "I don't see anything."

"The long cloud."

Manfred saw it then: a single cloud like a long dark stain against the late afternoon sky, just edging over the horizon. The cloud had an unnatural color.

"Dark green," Manfred decided. "Maybe it's the light, but it looks green. Like seaweed."

Walsing scowled at the nearing cloud. "Or poison."

As daylight faded, tapers were lit in festive Heorot. From time to time, beer-heavy revelers emerged from the hall to relieve themselves at the latrine pits. Before rejoining the feast, some of them noticed the single cloud drifting closer like a derelict keel.

For Hrothgar, the occasion fulfilled joy and purpose, since he shrewdly used the feast to reaffirm local loyalties. This consumed most of the waning afternoon, and when the last doughty old chief had bent a stiff knee and laid his gray head on the king's knee, Weltheow called for the great ceremonial measure to be filled with their cellar's rarest wine.

The elegant, handled silver cup, set with emeralds and rubies about the rim, was used only at solemn functions such as this. A relic of ancient Rome, it was decorated with bas-relief figures of Jupiter and Minerva instructing some long-dead Caesar. Before the waiting servants filled the vessel, Weltheow held it high for all to see.

"We have heard loyalties resworn today—and on such a day! I present the first cheer to my lord and king in this cup, which was brought from Rome in the days when their legions sent my people to Tiber from the Rhine as slaves, but not easily. They took our fine men and put them in chains. From our captive women they cut the flaxen hair to make wigs for their own weak, indolent wives, for they had never seen men so large nor women so fair. Nor any so unwilling to be enslaved that they ran away or took their own lives."

A murmur of approval ran through the men at the tables. Slavery was despicable to them. A man might wager his freedom on a throw of the dice and, losing, accept his fate without complaint, but to be forced into servitude was worse than death.

"Here in the north," Weltheow proclaimed proudly, "here where Roman eagles have never dared to fly, we have fought and bargained but never served. Rome is dead." She held forth the measure now to be filled. "And here are her jeweled bones, mere trinkets beside the honor we value above all. Health and life to Hrothgar Ring-Giver."

"Hail!"

"And to his royal sons."

"Hail Hrethric! Hail Hrothmund!"

The little imp Hrothmund jumped up from his place beside Beowulf and took a lavish bow before being squelched by Hrethric. "Down, idiot."

"To Beowulf of the Geats, now as near in our love."

"Hail!"

The cup was presented to Hrothgar and his sons in turn, finally to Beowulf before the queen reclaimed it.

"Hrothulf," she singled him out. "My nephew, son of Halga the Good."

The hall quieted even more, curious. The cheer for king and honored guests was customary, but this was something out of the ordinary. Beyond respect for his royal kinship, Hrothulf had never been so cited before. Weltheow spoke clearly for all to hear.

"Hrothulf, who was first to reswear his loyalty to our king this day."

Hrothulf did not miss the irony beneath the honor. Weltheow approached with the measure. "Swear now that which I know you will keep: your equal loyalty to my sons if their father is too soon lost to the Danes. I know you will take this oath as a debt, to father my orphaned boys even as Hrothgar sheltered you when Halga died."

Their eyes locked, held. Hrothulf took the silver measure. "With this pledge, I swear as much. Their fortunes will be mine to follow ever."

He drank amid cheers and the drumming of knife handles on the boards. Weltheow received the cup from his hands again.

"All men witness my nephew's pledge. I well know his kindness and gratitude that stand its security."

The queen passed the cup to a serving woman and was returning to the high table when she faltered unsteadily, one hand to her brow. Nearby, Unferth sprang up to support her.

"My queen, how do you?"

"It is so close in here . . . perhaps some air. My lord Hrothgar, pardon me. This thane will walk me out, but I will return."

Weltheow passed down the hall on Unferth's arm, staying Beowulf and her sons as they rose. "No need. I'll recover in a moment. I just need to breathe fresh air. The hall is so smoky."

"You should return quickly," Unferth advised. "Night air is not healthy."

"That inside could be as unhealthy."

Unferth led her outside, where Weltheow sank down on a bench in the dark, breathing deeply as she rested against the wall. "Unferth?"

"Better, lady?"

"Much. You heard Hrothulf's oath and know him well."

"Not well, but acquainted."

"Would you trust him?"

The young warrior hesitated, avoiding her searching question and eyes in the dusk. "That's difficult to say until tried, lady. He has always seemed—"

"Seemed?" Suddenly, Weltheow was anything but faint or in need of assistance. "Listen to me. I do not mean to be cruel but I must be plain. But for Hrothgar, you would be a lordless outcast now. Give me truth. Would you trust Hrothulf?"

Unferth felt distinctly uncomfortable in these dangerous waters. "In what circumstances?"

"If my son were in the balance against a crown?"

Still he hesitated, troubled as much by insights of his own. Hrothulf had shown him favor and friendship, but Unferth remembered the man's slip of the tongue that morning, if it was a slip. Unlike most men in casual converse, Hrothulf never said the wrong thing at the wrong time. To the contrary, he cultivated men carefully and patiently, and why that labor if not toward eventual harvest? For Unferth himself, honor was lost forever at home; whatever store he had or could anticipate derived from Hrothgar.

"No," he said finally. "I hope I do him no dishonor in an honest answer."

"Thank you. Neither would I," Weltheow said. Nor would Hrothgar for that matter. "He's sworn to follow Hrethric's fortunes. Wherever they lead, see that he does. After all," Weltheow favored the young man with a faint, hard smile. "It is no more than he promised."

"I swear it."

"Good. I am better now." Weltheow took his arm to rise, arching her back to uncramp aging muscles stiff from hours in the state chair. The natural movement brought her head back. She gasped.

"Look!"

Startled, Unferth cast about for the cause of her alarm. The queen pointed skyward. In the eastern sky, like a dark stain among already visible stars, one long cloud spread wide. To Unferth, the formation appeared to have a peculiarly thick texture but no more oddity than that. "Only a cloud, lady."

"No, it is nothing." Her hand fluttered to her brow. "But when I looked, I thought—it seemed to be a great bird hovering there."

"Let us go in," Unferth urged. "The king will be asking for you."

14

SIGYN STRODE TIRELESSLY OVER THE HEATH toward Heorot. She followed no star or path but that long stain, darker than the night it voyaged upon, deadly-coursed as herself for Lejre, where it would fall as mist on the fields to blacken and shrivel grain yet unsprouted. This was the dark side to Vanir fertility, but if Freyja could not bring herself to blight Sjaelland's fields, Loki would steal the power and do it himself. Such was her father's love. The giant sword Waster swung from the broad baldric over Sigyn's shoulder, forged ages ago against the coming Ragnarok. Well enough. Let gods, giants, and men—let all go down. Loki's gift was apt to this hour and Sigyn's need.

She was not conscious of time, but only her purpose as the miles passed. Now and again she broke into a run, sprinting lightly as a deer, reveling as much in her restored beauty as the payment she would exact this night. A lonely life with little love and that little gone now. Let men be struck with the woman she was before the sword came down.

Sigyn came onto the worn dirt track from the sea where it became cobbled road, and paused briefly on the same hill from which Beowulf first beheld Heorot. There before her like a beacon was the brightly lit hall. Sigyn counted the watch fires set against night attack beyond the outer ditch, then drew Waster and tossed it high. The great blade spun three times end over end. Sigyn caught it with negligent ease and slid it home in the broad scabbard.

She set forth down the slope, each long stride three of a man's.

In Heorot, the shattered doors had been stripped away and all windows braced wide, coursing more fresh air through the hall gone smoky from so many torches. Begun when the sun was still high, the triumphal feast would continue through the night until cockcrow. Beowulf reckoned his men must be exhausted as he. They had not slept since the boat. The bruises and lacerations on his own body ached and stung, and every fiber of him longed for sleep. The mead heavied his head, dulling a little the pain at the base of his skull. A bower well apart from Heorot had been readied for him and his Geats, and the need for rest invited him like a lover. He waited only the earliest moment when he could courteously say good night and close his eyes.

His companions caroused with the Scyldings and answered hail for hail, but fatigue and the death of Hondshew were a weight on cheer that none of them could entirely shake off. Across the broad table and three men down from Beowulf, Gorm drank morosely but ate little, hunched on his elbows, hands knotted into a single tight fist against his mouth. Earlier, young Canute, the most reticent of Beowulf's band, had mentioned the matter to his chief.

"We should look to him. Hasn't said much, but he blames himself alone for Hondshew."

Now, under the echoing roar of the feast, Beowulf studied the boy who had sailed so eagerly to beard the impossible for fame and a lark. Drawn close to the surface by drink, the tears glistened in Gorm's eyes. He blinked them away continually or wiped at them covertly—then sat straighter as Hrothgar's old harper carried his instrument and stool to the traditional place between tables and dais and began to tune the strings.

Beowulf dearly wanted to depart now and shepherd Gorm to bed as well. The boy looked terrible, but the harper performed in their honor tonight. To leave now would be plain discourtesy. He would stay for the first song at least.

The scop had chosen the lay of Finn and Hengest, known in every hall of the north, a tale of fruitless battle, uneasy truce, treachery, and revenge. For the first time in his life, perhaps abetted by the drink, Beowulf realized how much of futility and defeat ran through their most heroic legends.

So Hengest is sung and so will I be, most surely. I longed to be the fearless opposite of my fear, Eligius, and now I am. This is what I sacrificed life for. However rich or however quickly that rich turns to bile, such was the portion I asked and received. Fame sets me apart from other men, a high wall, a tower. They expect that, but who beside Hondshew ever scaled that wall to be my friend? What woman not so blinded by that polished surface that she could perceive myself, small and inadequate behind? Not even the stray curs worrying at Helsingborg midden heaps to wag a tail at me unless I threw them something. They say dogs and women have an unerring instinct for value in men. Trivial and commonplace for lovers and seekers to say, "Oh, I would

THE TOWER OF BEOWULF | 129

*die for him or her or this or that." I did. For this I perished and with
this, these dry bones of honor, I must be satisfied. A dark tower behind
a high wall. Hondshew wanted simple things. I wonder what such
desires feel like. How long since I wanted anything but an end?*

Oh, enough. Beowulf snorted in disgust. The mead cloyed on his
tongue and he was indulging in self-pity. The harper had dragged Hengest's tale to its doleful conclusion and now, amid cries of Sigemund!
Sigemund! struck the first chords and launched the first noble lines of
the well-known tale. Beowulf rose from the table to bid the royal family
good night. Gorm saw his chief rise and put down his cup.

"Prince, are you going?"

"I am."

"Me, too." Gorm passed a hand over his eyes. "Want t'sleep."

"It's time. You're far gone."

Gorm smiled muzzily, swaying on his feet. "Am I?"

"Best lean on something while I make our farewells."

"Sit down. . . ." Gorm collapsed like a sack on a bench to wait
him. Beowulf approached the high table, nodding to young Unferth as
the warrior stood up in pointed respect. "Lord Hrothgar, I must give
my thanks and say good night."

The young princes wouldn't hear of it: surely not so soon when
the first torches were barely burned through.

"We would have you remain," Hrothgar entreated warmly. "Do
not leave yet."

"Let him go, my lord." Weltheow knew the Geat's weariness. "I
helped my women in the salving of his wounds. They must trouble
him sorely. And I believe the young one yonder is feasted out," she
added, indicating Gorm with his head in his hands. "Good rest, Prince
Beowulf."

With the king's reluctant leave, Beowulf collected Gorm and bade
good night to those few of his band with yet the energy and inclination
to remain. Gorm needed guidance to find the entrance. The effort cost
Beowulf; every bruise, laceration, and pulled muscle protested as he
half-carried the boy along.

Gorm hung back at the entrance, wobbling about. "Listen. The
song of Sigemund."

"So it is, but you're for sleep. I won't have you looking green-gilled
when we honor Hondshew in the morning."

"But's my favorite story," Gorm protested. "Old Sigemund . . . searched the impossible just like us and found a treasure. He was luckier."

Nothing would do but Gorm would hear a few of the familiar lines—

Sigemund, son of Waels, hardened in war,
Heaved aside the great gray stone,
Killed the dragon jealous of its gold,
Drove his blade through the greed-guarder's heart
And took at will the ring-hoard there.

Suddenly, Beowulf felt he couldn't bear to hear one more heroic syllable. He led Gorm forcibly out into the dark courtyard. "Come on, we know the story. He wins, the dragon loses. Let's go to bed."

"Le' me go. I'm not drunk."

"Near enough you are."

The night air hit Gorm with the full force of all he'd imbibed. He peered wanly at Beowulf, then sank to his hands and knees and was sick on the ground. Beowulf waited patiently for the boy to be done.

At length, Gorm choked out, "I'm so sorry."

"It's nothing. Get up."

Gorm huddled on his knees. "Sorry I didn't—I should've followed orders."

"Gorm, enough. I'm tired."

"Should've been me . . ." Gorm mourned with a miserable shaking of his head, "not Hondshew, but me."

He began to weep, letting out all the grief held in check before.

No. The reaction surged up in Beowulf of its own volition. *No, not again, not with you.* Gorm had disobeyed orders, ran toward death rather than from it, but the same tragedy was seeding here before Beowulf's eyes. No, there would not be one more useless death.

"Up!" Beowulf yanked the suffering boy to his feet, dragged him to a longhouse wall, and slammed him hard against it. "Listen to me. Listen! You were wrong, you acted stupidly, but Hondshew took his chances. It's not your fault."

Beowulf shook the boy savagely, jolting the bitter lesson deep into him. "You will *not* blame yourself. You will *not* carry this until it rounds your shoulders and twists you into—do you understand? Do you? Because you will not *die* like this for the rest of your life."

Gorm wilted against the wall, shaken somewhat out of his drunken wallowing in misery. "What d'you mean, *die?*"

Beowulf put out a gentler hand to steady his friend and guide him the rest of the way home. "May you never have to learn. Going to be sick again?"

"No, it's out've me." Gorm snuffled and wiped his nose on the back of one hand, then meekly allowed himself to be led, stumbling, toward their bower, wanting only to close his eyes and sleep.

Unwearied by the miles from her mere, burning with the fire of her hate, Sigyn paused one last time beyond the light of Heorot's watch fires. She drew the sword and cast the baldric aside.

Now, Hrothgar.

She moved forward in long strides, breaking into a ground-devouring lope, then a sprint as the first firelight washed over her, hearing the cries of alarmed guards. There! Look there! What *is* it?

Spears flew at Sigyn. Swifter than a galloping horse, she dodged easily, bounding onto the first bridge over the outer ditch. One terrified sentinel stood in her way. As he raised the puny spear, Sigyn leaped clear over his head and landed without breaking stride. From all sides now, there came the bray of horns crying alarm, urgent two-note blasts like human throats cracking with fear.

The two guards on the inner bridge hurled their spears and then bounded into the ditch to escape the Leviathan charging down on them. Sigyn streaked between two longhouses, closing the last yards to Heorot. The doorless entrance gaped wide and bright: within, the usurpers who killed her son. Their very existence from moment to moment insulted her and Grendel, who had taken the womb-flawed lives allowed them and woven what joy they could from that blighted stuff.

A man dashed across Sigyn's path, whirling to loose a single arrow that flew wide before he scurried for the hall. Sigyn was on him in two strides, the great sword scything down. She snatched up the near-cloven body as men within Heorot, alerted by the horns, crowded to the entrance. Sigyn hurled the corpse into their midst like a battering ram. They fell back before her as she lunged into the hall, the pupils of her jade-and-amber eyes contracting against painful light, the giant sword

Waster lashing furiously like the tail of an enraged cat. Sweeping the blade in a wide circle, Sigyn cleared a path through panicked thanes toward her true targets.

"Hrothgar!"

Sigyn stalked forward, shearing through and kicking aside a table that blocked her way. "I am Sigyn, first wife of your god-king, Shild. My son Grendel is his firstborn. Where is this animal called Beowulf who killed that son? Where is he with the look of death about him? I come for him, Hrothgar, though payment but begins with his life."

Hrethric moved to shield his parents. In numbed fear, old Hrothgar gripped Weltheow's hand. True, then. The horror in his sleep had not been diseased dream but omen. But this giantess could not have sired that monstrosity. Every line of her, though towering to twice the height of the Geat prince she demanded, was fair and womanly.

Except the eyes that flicked from him to Weltheow. The eyes were not human at all.

"Back, all of you," Sigyn menaced, sword ready. She turned to Weltheow with icy calm. "Yes, I am Shild's wife and his widow, and my son Grendel true heir to that seat your husband and all since Shild have dared to assume. I remember you as a bride. My youth has well outworn yours; still, as a woman, have you not sometimes guessed at reasons these dull sword rattlers never fathomed? Where is Beo—?"

The name splintered on Sigyn's lips as the spear flew from young Frithmund's cast, striking her in the center of the back. Like softer, futile bronze struck against an iron door, the missile simply rebounded and fell to the floor. Sigyn whirled on the boy as he froze there slack-jawed and incredulous.

"I know you," she purred with a terrible smile. "The little hero who would crouch and wait to take my son's head."

With a movement too quick for human eyes to follow, Sigyn snatched up Frithmund by his neck—and faltered. For an instant, the hand that grasped the struggling boy became a brutal black claw. Sigyn blinked—no, only her hand, white and feminine. She held the kicking, strangling boy at arm's length like a curiosity to be inspected before disposal.

"Clever little fellow." Her grip shifted; now she held Frithmund about his skull. "I'd like to have your brains."

Sigyn squeezed. It was the sound of a walnut crushed in a vise.

She dashed the remains to the floor, stooped, and daintily cleaned her hand on Frithmund's tunic.

Close to the high table, Esher had noticed her aversion to light much like the other beast's. He gauged the distance to the nearest sconce as Sigyn turned on Hrothgar and his family; in the graceful movement, Esher saw the other image swirl darkly beneath the surface beauty like murky water flowing under ice.

"Mark me, Weltheow. My son died in my arms. Can you guess how much of a mother dies in that? Learn now."

Again her arm flashed out, catching Hrothmund so viciously that the breath was torn out of him. Sigyn raised him high overhead to break his bones.

Weltheow screamed—not only for her son's peril but at the changing image of the thing about to kill him. Sigyn, too, caught sight of her own arms gone suddenly black and ropy. And the *rest* of her—

"Loki!"

She dropped Hrothmund, crouching confused before them. Esher grabbed the torch from its sconce and lunged forward to divert her.

"Get the boy!"

Already in motion, Unferth charged at Sigyn, scooped up the dazed prince, and carried him beyond the creature's reach.

Pride alone, very human feminine pride, saved Hrothmund's life, saved all of them. For all her cause, Sigyn would not come to Heorot clad in any less than beauty. That stripped away, her first instinct was to hide, flee the cruel light and crueler sight of these Danes. She would return, oh yes, but something had miscarried, Loki's magic failed. Her light-dazzled vision caught a hint of movement, then someone hurled a blazing torchful in her face. Screaming, she snaked out a claw, raked, and caught at something solid. A man's body. Sigyn broke its back, tucked it under one thick arm, and bolted from the hall into kinder night.

15

THE DREAM HAD TORTURED BEOWULF many times through his life, but never with such an oppressive sense of isolation and terror, alone in the dark place where something inexorable glided closer and closer to destroy him. The exhaustion of his punished body sucked him down to a deeper level of sleep or up to clearer awareness. The place had form and definition now. The tower of his solitude, an ancient edifice of dry stone pervaded ever by cold fear of discovery and death.

Now a scuffling noise outside the tower. Something huge battered at the doorless stones, his hated prison whose walls must nonetheless stand against that death outside that struck and struck, the stones yielding, tumbling inward—

Beowulf woke. Someone had shaken him roughly. He was aware of movement around him and the rattle of gear in the darkened bower as his companions dressed hastily and armed themselves. Beowulf threw his legs over the side of the bed. "What's happening? An attack?"

Someone lurched past on his way to the door. "Don't know. Didn't you hear the horns?"

Beowulf groped for his tunic, jamming feet into boots. As he stumbled out into the courtyard, still bleary minded, he had for a few befuddled moments the feeling that he'd false-waked within sleep to another level of dream. Such visions could deceive with so much of the familiar about them: a real bed, known companions waking him.

Beowulf blinked and rubbed at his eyes. What met his sight outran comprehension. No hostile hoard pouring into Lejre, only running, shouting men and something oddly shapeless streaking over the outer bridge, now silhouetted against a watch fire as it slashed at tall guards dwarfed beside it, screaming at them in a woman's high voice before retreating beyond the light.

Gorm, Ulf, and the other Geats joined him, swords drawn. They'd all seen the monstrous figure but questioned their own senses. The beast was *dead*. Beowulf killed it, didn't he?

"Then what was that?" Gorm whispered.

Danger past for the moment, men hurried toward Heorot and their king. One of them paused at the entrance and pointed upward. Ulf found the focus of their attention. "Look. Where they hung the beast's arm. It's gone."

Yes, Beowulf recalled; that was what the apparition had clutched as it ran. "To the hall. Come on."

As they entered Heorot, Canute hurried to them from the crowd huddled by the dais. The boy was white as milk. Beowulf took him by the arm. "What happened?"

"It was all over. We thought it was all over." Canute stammered and swallowed hard. "The other one came. The mother. She killed Frithmund and old Esher. Went for Hrothmund. We thought it was all over. . . ."

Through a forest of legs, Beowulf caught sight of Weltheow kneeling over someone, Hrethric and Hrothgar close about her. A smaller group of men worked to take up something in a blanket while a serving man threw a bucket of water over stained floor planks. Beowulf elbowed his way to the queen, where she cradled Hrothmund in her arms. The boy was bruised and visibly shaken but not seriously injured.

Hrothgar told Beowulf what had transpired. The old king was unnerved by the demonic invasion and his son's close brush with death, close to the limits of his aged endurance. "She claimed to be Shild's wife."

"And that thing you killed she called her son," Weltheow added in a trembling voice. "I can well believe, they were alike. Her human shape was only a glamor. Underneath, we saw the other."

"She carried off Esher," Hrothgar said. "My oldest companion."

"It was vengeance," Weltheow declared. "A son for a son, she said, and then seized my boy. If not for Esher and Unferth . . ."

Beowulf looked around at the serving man scrubbing away the fresh stains. "Frithmund?"

"He tried to save us. Threw a spear," Hrethric said tightly. "You needn't look."

Hrothgar sagged down on the lip of the dais, looking older than his many years. "All this time while the beast walked my hall, I tried by every human means to learn what crime of ours or my own brought the affliction. Shild? Great Shild? Can it be possible?"

"Cried out to Loki," Wulfgar remembered. "When the magic deserted her, left her that horror we saw. Who does not know what discord Loki sows?"

"If she was Shild's woman, the years have been uncommon generous to her. Beautiful at first. If she came to Shild or any man in such a form . . ." Weltheow's eloquent look finished her thought.

"Oh, dazzling," Hrothulf agreed. "The fairest face, the sweetest voice I ever heard. To look would be to love if she weren't out to kill us all."

"Shild." Hrothgar struggled to believe or dismiss in the same breath. "The founder of my own line, my own blood, to couple with *that*? Impossible."

"No, my lord," Beowulf reasoned. "Else why the years of the beast? Why all this, the mother's vengeance?"

Hrothmund felt gingerly at the bump on his forehead where it struck the floor in his fall. The boy's eyes were dull with the fear and shock that had stormed through him. "And why call for you, Beowulf? She demanded your life first."

Beowulf turned Hrothmund about gently and held the boy in the safety of his arms as he spoke to all of them. "And she reclaimed the arm from where we hung it."

"Lord king." Unferth spoke, silent until now on the fringe of their fearful speculation. No man gainsaid him, knowing the son of Ecglaf and his doleful history. "If this Grendel is the son of Shild, then as you descend from the god, so this unthinkable mother claims her son a branch from that same root and his death a crime against your own blood. For what is left unfinished, she will return."

Hrothgar looked down at his hands. "My own blood?"

The probability hung over them all like a chill. They had rejoiced too soon. As Beowulf earlier thought himself trapped in false waking, they stumbled through nightmare yet.

"Yes. She will come for me and then my lord's family. But"— Beowulf gave Hrothmund a quick squeeze of reassurance—"we won't allow that, will we, Prince? Tomorrow morning, we take the battle to her."

At first light of a cheerless, gray morning, Hondshew's funeral pyre was lighted. Beowulf and his Geats stood in a circle about the fire, heads bowed over drawn swords as the flames rose, consumed their object, and gradually subsided. Hrothgar's chief shaman offered the proper invocations to Odin as lord of the dead, that Hondshew might be welcomed in Valhalla. A full hour they mourned as the smoke darkened the sky over Lejre. Then Hrothgar and a full company of thanes together with Beowulf and his men mounted to follow the shame-worn track to Sigyn's mere. Once more, Beowulf made it clear that he would front the she-beast alone.

"Me she wants and me she will get. If someone else tries now and fails, she will come yet again."

"And if you are vanquished, what then?" Unferth asked with concern. "There are human limits, sir."

"Then another man must try and more after him until she is dead."

"But where?" Unferth despaired. "On what ground? Down through that stinking mere?"

"Unferth, some men say water is only a symbol for the spirit," Beowulf told him as they rode behind Hrothgar. "Pass through water, pass through life to death. I know the way."

"Extraordinary man," Unferth confided later to Hrothulf as the company rode northeast through a chill drizzle blowing in from the sea. "Men have often told me how near to death they've come—aye, and told it so often, one could wish they'd gone all the way and be done—but none ever said they'd died more than once."

"A manner of speaking," Hrothulf dismissed the notion. "He's as incomprehensible as the creature he hunts. Heroes and their nemeses must be like that, I suppose. A match for each other. Part of their glamor."

"And even stranger," Unferth mused. "That frightened farmer who came to Wulfgar this morning? He said there was a peculiar mist over the fields they'd just seeded, with an evil smell to it. What's happening up there?"

Hrothulf stood up in the stirrups. "They've found something."

Found the grim signs of Sigyn's homeward passage where she'd fed as she went, leaving tatters of cloth stripped from her prey, recognized by all as the tunic worn by Esher the night before. At last, by the mere's edge, they found Esher's head in the sand, not carelessly discarded but set upright, the sightless eyes turned toward Heorot as if to give melancholy greeting to Hrothgar.

"Just there," one thane remembered, "where Frithmund vowed to watch."

"Vengeful bitch," Hrothgar vented through his teeth. "She defies and defies me. Is there no end to this?"

He stared down at the remains of his best friend with more sober consideration, wiser now than yesterday. "Or mayhap she cares no more for what fate weaves. If she had killed my Hrothmund, I would have as little heed."

The company dismounted, collecting about Hrothgar and Beowulf on the lake shore. The waters steamed where they met the colder air as if heated from below. From time to time, the turbid surface heaved and broke as primal struggles were joined just below and as quickly ended.

"Cursed place," Ulf muttered, pressing Beowulf with earnest advice. "Sigyn is one thing, but sea beasts something else. Did you set your sword edge?"

Beowulf had not. He drew the blade and tested it on his thumb: hacked and blunted. Gorm rolled his eyes upward. "Will I never learn? When you fought the beast, it was nearest to hand. I used it to cut through the arm. Should have reset it, should have told you at least, but with all that's happened—here, Prince. Take mine."

"No, mine!"

"Take mine, sir. Mine you could shave with."

The Geats and younger Danes crowded about Beowulf, a dozen swords offered. Then Unferth pushed firmly through them and led Beowulf aside to the water's edge. He spoke with a gruff reticence, holding out his own sword hilt to the man. "This one, Prince."

A magnificent blade, well balanced, with runes etched just below the hilt, proclaiming: I AM HRUNTING.

"Hrunting?" Beowulf received the sword with surprise and respect.

"Yes," Unferth affirmed with an echo of faded pride, "you know it?"

"All men know of Hrunting. I'd heard it was in your family, but . . ."

"But not in such questionable hands as mine." Unferth looked out over the mist curling up from the dark waters. "Whatever else great

Shild may or may not have done, he gave Hrunting to my ancestor Hundulf. When there was honor, I carried it well."

Beowulf twinged with compassion but said nothing, remembering Eligius and a boy who despised himself as beyond redemption, already dead. *When there was honor, I was Beowulf.*

"It's said Hrunting was tempered in a traitor's blood," Unferth declared. "Someone's, anyway. Best balance I've ever wielded. Better tempered than myself, in all events. Take it now and forgive my unworthy mock."

"Unferth—"

"No, hear me. Hrothulf said I don't drink well. I never could, nor my elder brother. I was jealous of his larger portion. We never got on. The night it happened, we were mad drunk and my tongue quicker than my wits as always. My words stung him and he struck me hard. I swung wild at him with my fist. Just drunken bad luck the aim was true. He went down and hit his head on the rim of the fire pit."

Unferth had always carried his brother's death and his own shame as wounds he would not show. "I know what men think, that I am a drunken filicide with a viper's tongue and temper, but I am too proud to sue for their respect, Beowulf. The tongue alone is turned on them; the viper's bite is sunk in me. There were witnesses to the quarrel. Some said I meant to kill, others held with mischance. They acquitted me, but Ecglaf cursed me, turned me out, and never spoke my name again, they say. He died of grief. That's been my portion. Always innocent, ever guilty. There are days when I sicken of life and wish it ended."

Beowulf inspected the buckles of his mail and set the helmet on his head. "I know something of this, Unferth. Fathers can be cruel and prodigal with curses, and sons can suffer what they may not speak. King Hrothgar!"

Poised to fill his promise, Beowulf spoke his last wish to the lord of the Scyldings. "If I do not return, my treasures to Hygelac, and receive my Geats in your service, those who choose to remain. You will find none better anywhere. Farewell."

Beowulf handed his own sword to Unferth with a whispered request. Concern for guilt-ridden Gorm had brought out something in himself earlier that did not stink of death. The same might in some part take Unferth out of himself. "Look after Gorm for me? He takes Hondshew's death on himself. Make him know what a waste of life that is."

"I will try," Unferth appeared to understand. "It is a promise."

Beowulf stepped into the water and waded out toward the turbulent depths.

16

THE WARM WATERS OF THE MERE closed over Beowulf's head, much warmer than the time of the mad, ice-ringed wager with Brecca. In his ears at first only the sound of blood in his own head—then a soft pulsing like the beating of a great heart, stronger and nearer as he sank toward the bottom. Giant shapes prowled about him, curious. Beowulf readied Hrunting but found no employment for its edge. The stillness, the muffled pulsing affected these creatures too as if their very existence danced now to its measure.

The water grew ever warmer as he descended, heated by the malevolent force of his quarry.

Not so when I contended with Brecca. I was freezing when I died, my mail coated to twice its weight with ice.

Long since he could feel his cracked, numb fingers clinging to the wreck, the wind shrieking and Brecca frozen as he but still defiant, rasping out curses and then encouragement as Beowulf's grip failed and, more in frozen hell-dream than waking, he felt himself sinking. The boreal water closed over his head that no longer felt cold or anything else. . . .

Then he was aware again, eyes still open, hands gripping surely at the wrecked section of keel that barely moved on a sea of smooth glass. No sound, no movement, no wind or cold. Brecca was gone. On one end of the capsized keel section, Eligius sat smiling at him; at the other, Edgetho perched cross-legged, a sword across his lap.

"Beowulf," Eligius urged, gentle and serious. "What was all this about?"

"Honor," he shot back without hesitation. Then Beowulf reached past that to truth. "No, about pride. Vanity. He will not give in. Neither will I."

"Oh? We've acquired things like honor and pride, have we?" Edgetho challenged scornfully. "Better late than never, eh? Where was pride when you ran from the Frisians?"

"I was afraid. I am afraid now."

"That I should live to hear a son of mine admit fear."

"Why not?" Eligius asked with the serenity that enrounded him like an invisible nimbus. "What meaning to courage without fear? It is no more shameful than hunger."

"Rot. Is it?" Edgetho prodded Beowulf's shoulder with the point of his sword. "Never, you hear? Never for an instant in all my life."

Eligius shook his head. "A dull life, that. So unexamined."

"No," Beowulf denied. "If not your truth, my father speaks what we know. Reach far enough back in our blood, we are god-born. Reach deep enough into our souls, we know that even gods rise and fall, go through life to death. It is inevitable, the way of things. Madness perhaps, but fear can be no part of us, Eligius."

"And I say rot to that. Absolute rubbish," Eligius scoffed in turn. "Courage is never the absence of fear but the conquest of it."

"That's slender hope in the midst of battle," Edgetho countered as the wreck floated still, still on a silent sea. "Our life is war, war is life. Hear me, spawn I am shamed to call my own. Born as we are, what we are, what choice of life do we have? Do we plan what the Fates weave?" He cackled derisively. "Do you think I never asked such questions and got slapped down time and again with the same unchanging answers? We are thanes and princes. We have less choice in our lives than farmers or fishermen. We give those lives for glory in return. Accept or chafe in that, it's your destiny. Be life long or short, wipe out that early stain and come spotless to Valhalla. Or be denied there by me. There is no life else for you."

"And you dare speak of running away?" Eligius queried from his end of the wreck. "That kind of courage is easy. Deny the value of life and what expense in losing it? How many brainless brutes have sacked a city who could not govern it in peace for a day?"

"By Odin's blood," Edgetho marveled coldly. "Is this the future, this gelded, self-pitying turn of mind? Your White Christ will corrupt men in their hearts' core, telling them their skins are as important as what they must do."

"Oh, I doubt that," Eligius denied casually. "Men are what they are and most will ever find your way easier. Whatever god or cause, they will find it simpler to die for something than to live with it. Fear, Edgetho? You lie to your son. You have feared life day to day. When the clash of swords fell silent and you had to listen to your own life, you drowned it out."

"Listen?" What Edgetho could make of that he despised. "What was there to hear but a whimpering wife and a worthless, sickly son? You make a comfort of cowardice."

"No, Father."

The grizzled thane looked down at Beowulf. "What's that?"

"I said no. Believe me. I'm dying, perhaps already dead. How you greet me or not in Valhalla does not concern me overmuch. I won't lie."

Freezing to death was supposed to feel like this, a drowsy and painless surrender to sleep. "You should have listened, for there was much to hear. My mother's voice when she tried to speak to you. Much to see: her tears when you pushed her away, and later, when she'd lost the habit of weeping, the unspoken loss in her eyes. My voice when I tried to find something in you beyond duty and iron. I hated you even as I feared you."

"And what of that?" Edgetho lowered the sword point to Beowulf's mailed chest. "Words, no more. You have nothing, there *is* nothing without honor. Glory or ignominy. Life? It's to be got through like a storm. Glory or shame, choose."

"Why not say life or death?" Eligius suggested reasonably. "For the choice is in what you mean by both."

Life or death. The choice echoed through Beowulf as the smooth sea heaved suddenly and went cold, the painted leaden sky darkened, father and friend vanished, and he found himself still clinging to his half of the broken derelict keel.

"*. . . in what you mean by both.*" Yes, he had thought then under the dull surprise at still breathing. *Now I am dead as you, Edgetho. I had not the strength to stand against your values or the expectations of others. I let you and them live for me, in me, stamped myself from the same mold. You won, Father. I took up your life like a fool finding dross with a feeble shine and calling it gold. How easy it is now that I have walked away from life, how easy to be dead.*

That he survived, that the drifting wreck carried him to shore, was incidental. But how quickly fame lapped him about afterward when he gave up and became what they all wanted. Hondshew alone sensed the disparity. Now and then, wearied beyond belief by what was asked and must ever be rendered, Beowulf might spend a secret hour beside the unmarked grave of his soul. Not often; such memories could be painful.

To blot them out there was always one more battle with the Swedes, another victory, and always some diligent harper eager to gild fact into legend.

What if he had lived? The bootless question bothered Beowulf less and less as time passed. For years, until the emotion withered in him, he hated Edgetho because the man had defeated him in his core, and sometimes as bitterly cursed Eligius for daring him to life—and pitied himself remotely now as, dimly below him, the bottom of the mere took on definition, because he could feel no fear or even life anymore, and only death went on like an idiot babbling—oh, matters of great import to fools, no doubt, but mere din in Beowulf's ear.

His feet touched bottom. His lungs and heart, starved for air, felt nigh to bursting. The needful blood beat through his veins as the water about him trembled with that deep, rhythmic throbbing; it shimmered, appeared to thicken as he fought forward and tumbled through to a place where he could breathe. On his knees, Beowulf sucked rank but reviving air into his body before a pair of massive doors. He took a gasping moment to fill his lungs before rising, Hrunting firm in his grip. Then the woman's voice lilted to him from within.

"Beowulf? Do you come? Hail him whom men call hero."

A lulling, musical greeting that mocked and promised at once. Beowulf pushed the doors open and entered Sigyn's den.

He blinked, dizzy at the trick of his eyes whose focus could not follow what they saw. He was in a vast, brightly lit hall—then a dim cave, visual treachery, each moment's message to his sight denying the one before. No light or line of structure in the opulent fittings that did not waver and dissolve only to re-form: now a hall whose rich appointments beggared Heorot, light blazing from gold and silver sconces to flash again in jewel or polished ornament, the aroma of spices in one moment giving way to drab gray stones and the stench of dead fish at low tide.

At the far end of the hall, huge and mercurial in form as all about her, the giantess slumped on her knees against the bier of her son. Distracted, doubting his senses, Beowulf moved cautiously toward her. Though she had called his name, Sigyn now barely heeded his presence. The body by which she kept vigil held its form no more firmly than the mourner. Nothing in this mad place captured reality for more than a passing moment before surrendering to new shape. Grendel's head:

now insane amalgam of ape and reptile, now the golden-haired likeness to the royal Scyldings, beauty and horror pursuing each other like swift storm clouds, vying for permanence neither could hold. As the son, so the mother, one corporal madness crouched by another, then a young girl whose every feature, from shimmering unbound hair to proportioned white limbs beneath her white kirtle would stir desire in any living man.

Her fine head moved slightly. Sigyn looked at Beowulf and he perceived with surprise and a pang of empathy the unmistakable grief in the eyes of amber-lit jade before all dissolved again to the inhumanly shaped skull and gaping shark's maw. Only the alluring feminine voice remained constant.

"Yes. Beowulf. It would be you. I heard you above. If your company had approached silently, I would have yet felt changes in the air."

The crouched obscenity lifted one claw, regarding with detached interest its progress toward tapering wrist and white fingers again. "My father's love is steadfast. Would his results were as reliable. Not that it matters. Now all illusion ends. Do you find me fair or are you not even that much of a man?"

Her image melted again: The shark maw parted to disclose wicked triangular teeth, then the godling child bathed him in a smile dazzling but cold as winter sun. The eyes blazed with alien enmity, shone with life and loss, seeing through and weighing Beowulf by values beyond him. Sigyn rose slowly from her mourning.

"Do you find me beautiful, little hero? Beside me was not Weltheow in her prime a drab goose girl?"

"No fairer anywhere when beauty rests there." Beowulf gripped the sword in both hands as Sigyn towered over him. Her green eyes followed his movements, flicked up to capture his own again. "But by all the gods—woman, thing, what *are* you that shift like shadow in moving light and melt like wax, one form to another? Where is the truth of you?"

Sigyn spread her arms. "Perhaps truth incarnate. Now one thing, now another. My son knew you for what you are. That blade will not prevail against me."

Beowulf lifted the sword to guard. "I must try."

"As I must and will come to Heorot tonight," Sigyn promised. Her head tilted slightly to one side as she caught a too-familiar voice.

"Hrothgar is talking again, promising to lavish yet more gifts when you remove the inconvenience of me. He talks to excess, that old man. What need of an ox like you? The fool could bore me to death."

Sigyn returned her lethal attention to Beowulf as he crouched, ready. "It is time."

She flowed toward him smoothly as water hurtling over a cataract as Beowulf struck with Hrunting only to hear the blade shriek in protest and shatter against the unearthly substance of her flesh. As he raised the broken sword in futile defense, Sigyn caught him up like a dry twig and hurled him against a wall. The brutal force of her might have crushed him against firmer resistance, but the walls, charmed as Sigyn by Loki's magic, were only yielding water. Beowulf hit and sank into it before dropping heavily to the flagstones.

Sigyn was on him in an instant, biting at his helmeted head, trying to tear open the mail that covered his breast. The war-proof held. The giantess snatched the dagger from Beowulf's belt, stabbing again and again at his heart. She could not pierce the mail, but each blunted blow punished his body.

Sigyn dropped the dagger; white hands/black claws reached for his throat. Beowulf snaked his left leg across her chest; the wrestling trick caught Sigyn off guard. His strong leg levered her off him. He rolled away, gaining his feet only to be clubbed down again by Sigyn's lashing, stone-hard fist. The blow tumbled Beowulf under the huge table on which Grendel's body lay. Dazed, trying to clear his head, Beowulf scrabbled away from the claws that groped for him, rolling out of Sigyn's reach to put the table and the corpse between them. Hrunting lay broken and useless on the paving stones, but Sigyn's own immense sword hung sheathed on the wall nearby. Beowulf dragged it free, amazed at the massive weight he could barely lift in both arms. Yet he must; whatever he did must be done quickly. He had time and strength for one blow, two at most.

"Sigyn!"

His voice froze her as he lifted the great sword and brought it down, severing Grendel's head.

Sigyn's horror burst out of her in an eerie wail. Instinctively, she lunged to hold what she most loved even in death. Too late she tried to guard against the one blade in Midgard to which her kind was vulnerable. The sword was already descending, driven by the last of Beowulf's strength, shearing deep into her shoulder. She staggered back and fell with the mortal wound. Still near-stunned from the blow she dealt him, Beowulf dragged the sword from her great, convulsing body. In the wavering light about him the huge blade, forged in Utgard, was still lit from within by the fires that formed it, poisoned now with the blood it was charged never to drink. Perverted, dishonored in purpose, the very iron shrank away, ate at itself. A hundred unearthly voices keened in the corrosive hissing as the blade remnant dropped from the hilt and fell, a shrinking lump, to the floor by Sigyn's body.

Beowulf faltered on his feet over the giantess, clearing his head as, around and above him, the illumination and magnificence of her hall dissolved for the last time to the dismal gray-lit cave. All illusion ended as she foretold, but as Beowulf turned to retrieve Grendel's head for Hrothgar, he saw that not all died in grotesqueness. Neither the head nor the body he had routed from Heorot but the finely resolved features of a young man who might well, for pure likeness, have claimed Shild Scefing for his father. A little distance away rested a young woman whose conception, in Loki's inconstant but tender mercy, might have been Beauty itself and her name no less than Love.

Beowulf thought, oddly enough, of Eligius in that moment: so strong and secure in his sane, kindly cosmos. *How when your kind comes north? How when your Christian vision is stained and darkened with ours? You will create a god more than a little mad.*

He became aware of a new, liquid sound. As Beowulf lifted Grendel's head by the blond curls, the water walls sagged and bulged inward. Long restrained by magic, the mere now recalled and reverted to its nature. Rising water swirled about Beowulf's ankles. The head and sword hilt gripped in his hands, he pushed through the melting hall doors that yielded as soft mud before him, sucked air deep into his lungs, and dove head first through the dissolving barriers, propelling himself toward the surface.

The water had gone much colder. Light filtered toward him as he rose. He thought of Sigyn and the centuried weariness with which she had discerned and dismissed Hrothgar waiting above. Yes, the old man would be generous with gifts for miracles promised and done. Afterward, he and the graybeards and above all the poets would talk and talk. After the bellowings of heroism, Beowulf would still have to stand before Ina and Itharne and tell them and read their judgment in that woman language spoken more through the eye than the lips, and by that sorrowing light so much more truthful. Not all of truth in that tongue but a *different* truth that somehow Hondshew had known.

Beowulf's head broke surface. Through water-filled ears he heard the distorted, muffled shouting of the Scyldings and his own men. As his feet touched firm bottom and dozens of hands stretched out to pull him ashore, once more to him came the image of Eligius, calm and wise in a hut on a far and fateful island.

BOOK III

THE

STRANGEST

SHORE

17

AMID THE UNENDING STREAM of garrulous boasters whom Hygelac and Hygd must suffer in their mead hall, Beowulf's return was curiously laconic. He and his companions dutifully received the toasts and tributes of the king's thanes but recounted their deeds baldly, with no more embellishment than a steward might add to his report of a harvest. Yes, Grendel and his dame were dead. Yes, Hrothgar and Weltheow were generous in their gratitude, and Beowulf rendered much of that treasure to his king. Yes, the bond between Danes and Geats was stronger than ever—

"Yet they don't brag like young warriors will, most of them home from their first venturing," Hygelac wondered privately to his queen. "The young ones like Gorm and Ulf: no foolish speeches, hoping some harper will set their words and deeds to music, and as for Beowulf—"

Modesty became a warrior but not to the point of utter self-effacement. Beowulf did not relish the feasts in his honor but merely tolerated them.

"He was nothing when young," Hygelac recalled. "Edgetho never spoke of him, gave him no more regard than he would a kitchen churl. Look at him now. Is there a scop in a hundred leagues who would not sing of him? Fame, wealth, a man who reached beyond this world and dared the next to beard giants and defeat them—what more could he want, I ask you? Is he distracted, you think?"

Hygd considered her nephew from more subtle feminine approaches. "He seems more . . . baffled."

"I'd like to know by what. He's far exceeded anything Edgetho achieved."

"Who knows? The apple may not fall far from the branch, yet I think Beowulf is more thoughtful than his father was."

There was truth at least. "My horse thinks more than Edgetho did."

"Stupid brute. Your sister never knew a happy hour with him."

"Hygd, what has that got to do with anything?"

His wife made a strategic retreat without yielding up her point. "Just a thought. But you are right. It was untoward."

Not entirely. The mention of Edgetho brought to the fore their own problem of Prince Herdred, twenty this year and so far clearly demonstrating Edgetho's immense courage and meager common sense. The boy idolized Beowulf. This past week, he and his close companions had been infected with the idea of a prestige raid on the Swedes, like Beowulf's against the Frise, for no more than the excitement and honor. Hygelac put his foot down. No raid was to be undertaken by any Geat without royal authority, nor sole and inexperienced heirs wasted.

Spring was still far from warm in Helsingborg when Hygelac summoned his son to a private meeting in the council chamber. Two nights earlier, he had asked Beowulf to sup with the family and sent one of his nephew's venture companions with the invitation. Canute found the prince not at home. Next day and again the next, Hygelac requested Beowulf's company, first through Gorm and then by Herdred himself who carried the message couched in courtesy but plain enough to take it as royal command. The king desired his chief men to confer with him on the growing menace of the Swedes to their north and would appreciate Beowulf's counsel in the matter. Herdred returned without having seen his cousin. The prince entered the royal hall where his father and old Garmund conferred, shook the chill rain from his cloak hood, and stumped forward to his father.

"Not there, sir. His people say he's hardly been home at all."

Hygelac felt himself increasingly irritated. "Doesn't he know he has obligations to my council? What's he doing?"

Herdred could supply no particulars, but the shaman Arn thought he had seen Beowulf strolling yesterday with a little girl near the sacred grove. They appeared to be gathering early flowers. "Arn wasn't sure, but the child may be Hondshew's daughter."

Herdred remained mystified as his father at his hero's inexplicable behavior. "Shall I go to the steading and command his presence, Father?"

"Command?" Garmund the steward shook his head. That was far too peremptory toward someone of Beowulf's station and reputation. "Rather, urgently request. The widow's name is Ina Gundarsdattir."

"Don't go yet." Hygelac hesitated, turning over second thoughts.

He rose from his chair and walked thoughtfully away from his son and steward. Gundar's family had always been shunned, never honored. Was Beowulf merely consoling the widow or considering her for a consort? Entirely unsuitable. Ridiculous. Politically worthless to a man who might well wear the crown some day. Kindness, sentiment? Perhaps a casual dalliance? No, far too soon for that. The woman must remain in decent mourning for some time. She was presentable enough, Hygelac recalled, but hardly the beauty to turn a man's head; the sort of plain and honorable lady toward whom men would always offer more respect than intent. Then there was the indelible memory of her father and grandfather. . . .

"No, Herdred. Not yet."

He deferred the summons and opened the subject with Hygd when they retired that night. His queen was carefully peeling a length of rush before replacing it in the wrought-iron holder by the bed in their bower.

"Ina Gundarsdattir?" Hygd combed out her long hair slowly, even as she drew her thoughts through the prospect. "Well, it is fitting up to a point."

"Yes, yes. Beowulf was closest to Hondshew, that's all well and good." Hygelac loosed the trouser thongs at his ankles and pulled off his boots. "But you know the talk about her family. And Beowulf traipsing about the woods with her child? He never *liked* children."

"He never had much time to be one with that father," Hygd remembered. "His mother was a gentle woman. She could never stand up to Edgetho. He raised his hand to her more than once."

"No!" Hygelac was shocked; he'd never heard a whisper. "My sister?"

"Oh, she hid it well always. When I found out, she begged me not to say a word. I'm sure Beowulf despised him and I would agree. Beowulf has always been alone in that house. He's had no one, really. I would leave him be for the time."

Hygd had pitied the mother and the son within the silence of propriety. Beyond that, Beowulf's life interested her only insofar as his actions might affect his image among Geats or put Hygelac in an awkward position. Whatever humor took her nephew now, it might be something so simple that the brusque, hurrying mind of her husband would never note it. So often for her and Hygelac, with one danger so close on the heels of the one before, it seemed the dearest luxury in the world was the leisure to do something of absolutely no consequence for just an hour. Beowulf might yearn now for much the same.

"When one thinks on what he saw there in Heorot, in that filthy mere. What he was called on to do . . ."

"Whatever, he ought to tell me at least," Hygelac grumbled.

"Perhaps he has nothing to say. Let be."

Her husband heeded Hygd's gentle advice, liking the state of affairs not at all. Strange behavior in a warrior prince and *most* peculiar company to keep.

Hondshew's holding lay a few miles beyond the northern limits of Helsingborg, most of it reclaimed from the shaggy forest of beech and oak through which Beowulf rode now toward the steading gate. Before marriage to Ina, Hondshew and his mother, Itharne, had lived on a much smaller place, no inconvenience, since Hondshew spent most nights with other thanes in the king's hall. Their house was too small for a familied man. Old Gundar, his only male heir dead in some luckless raid, left a larger property to Ina. The couple took their residence there.

Gundar's blood had never prospered, through widespread dislike and slow-fading prejudice among the Geats, who prized loyalty above all else save battle courage. When King Offa was murdered, his younger brother, Swerting, Hygelac's grandfather, assumed the crown. Geats suspected but never proved that Gundar's own grandsire was part of the plot, paid by Swedes to assassinate vigorous Offa, whose policy was unrelenting war against his northern neighbors. The grandfather lived and died under a cloud that lingered yet over his line.

Such treachery was not uncommon, but an older charge tainted the clan, a rumored marriage link between one of their dim ancestors and the cursed family of Hama, Teutons who had lived for some generations in these parts before dying out. Gundar's father and he himself certainly evinced that greed which had doomed the Teutons, driving the sharpest bargains for everything in matters great or small. It was said of Gundar that he was readier to part with an eye than an *øre* of gold.

This was the brood into which Beowulf's dearest friend had married for no more profit than love—not a motive to further fortunes but one Hondshew maintained firmly, though he found it difficult to serve a king and his property alike. There was a loving husband in Hondshew but little of husbandry, and a streak of negligent ease that would far rather sing than sow. He never got the most out of his people or the land. In the matter of mating, however, he and Ina proved a fine match. Marriage gave Hondshew a center. In Ina, the seriousness which might have set into stolidity mellowed to a glow by which Beowulf, for one, had always warmed himself and come away secretly envious of his friend. Hondshew bathed Ina in his spirit of wry fun, and the birth of Minna imparted to her a quiet radiance.

Ina might have known Beowulf was coming today. She waited him at the gate to let out the latch in welcome, a square-faced young woman near his own age, with a cast of features Beowulf thought at first placid, later, serene. Against the still-sharp March air she wore an old blue woolen cloak over a faded red kirtle trimmed in frayed gold piping. About the hall and outbuildings, neglect was clear as a rune sign: roof thatching long in need of beating out, a blackened patch by the hall's chimney hole, seared by lightning and not replaced. One whole section of the wattle fence about the steading had collapsed inward.

"One of the char burners saw you riding this way," Ina told him in greeting. "We knew you would come. Welcome, Prince. May we grain and water your horse in the stable?"

Beowulf walked the animal through the open gate. He'd chosen one of his older horses with a plain sheepskin saddle, since the magnificent mounts and gear presented him by Hrothgar would only remind Ina of her own loss, though that could not be entirely avoided today. Beowulf drew the heavy sacks from his saddle wallet. "These are from Hrothgar."

"Yes."

He admired her quiet propriety; in the single word, Ina acknowledged what was right and due her. When she had seen to his horse, she led him toward the hall. "A costly venturing, Prince."

He noticed she did not add the word *honorable* and wondered with a pang if Ina laid Hondshew's death in any part to him, as well she might.

"Young Gorm came yesterday," she said. "So sad."

Gorm? No need for the boy to come, though Beowulf quickly guessed why.

"He was in such terrible anguish," Ina said softly as they walked. "Swore he alone was at fault for Hondshew."

"I know."

Her voice retained all the pity Gorm's self-lacerating guilt had left with her as too heavy to carry alone. "He would have knelt before me if I let him. So ashamed of himself and shamed all the more by his tears, but he would let no one else bring the news, as if that would only heap more dishonor on him."

"He will make a fine man."

"If he lives."

Ina pointedly changed the subject then, casting her eyes about the delapidated steading yard. "The place wants so much work. Our servants are few and old; no one wants to work for Gundar's blood. I could better use Gorm's arm than his guilt, but he is a thane's son and would consider that beneath him. Such fools."

Inside the hall where dried rushes crumbled under his feet, Beowulf set the bags of gold on a trestle table as a small, swarthy woman joined them. One could recognize Hondshew's mother from a considerable distance. The plain, dull Geat colors in dress were never for her. Life was a fantastic and gracefully intricate pattern to Itharne of the Pictish Vacomagi, and these checked or whorled conceits she wove into her garments in red, green, blue, and whatever bright contrasts she could dye. She acknowledged Beowulf with a slight bow.

"Y'air weelcome."

Itharne never spoke Geatish well, and the Pictish fall of her speech with its ancient forms was difficult to catch. Ina had to translate.

"Mother would have you speak of Hondshew and what befell him."

He did so in careful courtesy, saying nothing of his own actions, only of her son's valor in saving Gorm from Grendel.

"Gren-del?" Itharne repeated, appealing to Ina. *"Nothur-sgathoch?"*

"Mother asks was this a dragon?"

"A mere-stalker." But the Geatish words meant nothing to Itharne. Beowulf had to paint for her a hybrid of dragon and troll. The old woman's dark, lined features were calm as she listened, but her smokey gray eyes gleamed. She pushed back the white-streaked, silky black hair that strayed forward over her brow and spoke again in her sibilant half-whisper.

"She says it was so with her own father when the Scoti came against their people. You will take dinner with us?"

Beowulf was on the point of excusing himself rather than intrude when Hondshew's daughter Minna, five years old and in high dudgeon, charged into the hall, yowling like a singed cat.

"Mama! I want to go look for flowers in the wood but no one will take me, not even Inge."

"Now, Inge has other things to do," Ina soothed. "But here's your father's oldest friend to pay his respects."

Minna looked up at Beowulf in shyness and suspicion. He didn't know why he smiled suddenly, the urge was simply there and felt good. "Good day, Minna. Do you remember me?"

She didn't and was not to be swerved from purpose. "Mama, can I go to the woods?"

"I've just come from the woods and it's too early for flowers," Beowulf told her.

"Isn't."

"Well, I could be wrong. With your mother's permission, let's go see what we can find. And Minna, such flowers as we find will decorate the table."

He held out his hand. Minna's curved inside, small and warm.

That afternoon brought chilly rain blown in from Eyrarsund. Beowulf was invited to stay and sleep in the hall. He woke several times before morning to the monotonous drip of water through the neglected roof. Someone really should see to repairs. He went back to sleep thinking of Minna. They hadn't found a single flower, so nothing would do but Beowulf had to climb an oak and cut her some mistletoe. The effort punished the still-tender bruises from his encounters with Grendel and Sigyn, but Minna was satisfied. It was the sort of thing Hondshew would have considered important. Beowulf smiled up into the darkness at the thought.

Before returning to Helsingborg next morning, Beowulf walked out into the fields with Ina. Taking advantage of the dampened earth, farmers were leading a team of four oxen dragging a brush hurdle, harrowing the soil before sowing the spring barley. Beowulf noticed bolts of willow rods stacked here and there for seasoning in the drainage ditches.

"Hondshew cut them last year," Ina said as they walked. "He

meant to repair the wattling this spring, but then he followed you to Heorot."

Beowulf stole a sidewise glance at the woman. He'd heard no accusation in the observation and read none in her face.

"It must be difficult to be a king's thane," she said. "For my husband, even contradictory. He liked his ease, but when the humor was on him he took great pleasure in working with his hands. He said it helped him to piece things out. So many questions he had."

"I saw where the fence has collapsed."

"Ach, ill done from the beginning. My father got more delight from finding the cheapest than the best. The timber slottings are narrow and weak."

"That never holds."

"Gundar hated spending money." Ina supposed that understandable in a way. When a man was denied honor, he would hoard something else. "You remember that tale about King Offa? You needn't be tactful, it's all true. Certain men were approached to remove the king. Gundar's father may have been one of them. Certainly Gundar knew much of the circumstances. At any event, the blood money was paid." Ina paused to look away after the oxen dragging the hurdle toward the far end of the field. "But it was not paid by Swedes."

"Not—? Then by whom?"

Beowulf realized the tactless question only after he'd uttered it. Ina gave him only a neutral shrug. "Gundar never said. Only in one bitter moment did he tell me that much. Not the Swedes. Gundar went through life a kicked dog. Snarling became a habit: Bite me and I'll bite back. Later, he learned to bite first. Men denied him honor, so he took their substance whenever he could. As you can imagine, arguing innocence would be profitless, then or now. He hoped my marriage to Hondshew would give us back some dignity at length."

When his horse was saddled and waiting, Beowulf asked Ina if he might come again. She answered with a long, appraising glance. "I am still in mourning, Prince."

She had misread his meaning. Beowulf flushed with embarrassment that she should think these overtures so soon after— "No, please. Just that Hondshew was my friend."

"Yes, he was." Her gaze did not move from his face.

"You said he had many questions. I have as many, so many, I feel smaller and more helpless than little Minna these days. I needed to go somewhere quiet. To be simple."

"Simple, Prince?"

Under Ina's level scrutiny, in which he imagined a kind of pity, Beowulf felt he was not making himself clear and felt ridiculous. "Thanes like Hondshew and myself have little room for ourselves, yet Hondshew found something. I would learn that. May I come again?"

"What can our poor house teach the son of Edgetho?"

Not to be like him. Not to be forever what I have become. Are only gods capable of resurrection?

He struggled for meaning, more inarticulate for trying not to betray the immense effort. "Not—not words. Not a thing words can hold. Something I felt walking with Minna. I will remember that always. I would like to do that again."

Ina held out both hands to take his. "Whenever you will, Baywoof."

"What?"

"What Minna calls you," she laughed. "Now she wants to know when she'll grow big as you so she can hunt trolls. Come tomorrow if you will."

The rush of happiness overwhelmed him. "I will."

Strange man; strange, imprisoned man, Ina thought as Beowulf rode away. As Minna couldn't yet shape her baby tongue about his name, simplicity still eluded Beowulf. As the child learned better to speak, so perhaps would he. A closed-in and buried man, Hondshew had said of him. Yet Hondshew loved and bonded with Beowulf. There must be much there to bond with.

She regretted misunderstanding him for an instant, because that made him visibly more awkward in explaining his purposes which now seemed very touching. Hondshew had been a lovable, ordinary man with a duty to a king and certain ideals. Beowulf *was* an ideal who thirsted after the ordinary in himself.

If such was there. He might never find it, Ina concluded. That didn't seem a natural part of him, but he was so grateful when she asked him to return.

18

HYGELAC WAS GROWING IMPATIENT with his absence and where he spent his time, yet Beowulf continued to draw heavily on his uncle's indulgence. He visited the delapidated steading day after day as spring grew warmer, the fields were plowed, and the barley sown. At first, like Itharne's difficulty with his language, the newness of what he thirsted to learn was a barrier until, as sunlight gradually warmed his senses, he ceased to sift fresh thought through old patterns and began to hear the music of it all as Hondshew must have.

For music was the key. All his life Beowulf had listened to the plucked notes under the spoken lyrics of harpers. Each line's cadences drew together into a striding whole, clipped or drawn out as the measure demanded. Now he watched as the sowers walked the fresh-plowed furrows, each man counting his deliberate steps to determine how many casts of grain to so many paces for an even sowing. He had never considered that there must be an exact cast to a given distance, just as so many beats to the poet's line, but once realized Beowulf could admire the precision of their dance and perceive how it fit into the whole.

It is all music, all of it.

Hygelac had ceded him several large royal estates on his return from Heorot. They required attention, particularly in spring. Beowulf grudged the time needed to confer with and direct his stewards, sorely missing Ina and the child who had become warm sun to his chilled life. When he was able to visit again, Ina greeted him worriedly. Minna was ill. Nothing more than a child's fever, but it ran high.

Beowulf waited with her in the child's bedchamber and saw, in the eloquent curve of Ina's form bent over that treasure made from Hondshew and herself, the image of Sigyn crouched and mourning over Grendel. All was madness except that truth.

Minna broke her fever and recovered lustily, drawing Ina and Beowulf after her as the flowers bloomed in the meadow near a rill, skipping ahead of them to find one more trove of bursting color.

"So much life," Beowulf breathed.

Content that the child was well again, Ina said, "Yes. The flowers."

"No, in Minna. In children. Look. See there: She doesn't just move; she dances and jigs with what won't be still in her, like turbulent water teetering its small jug this way and that. Why is it . . . ?"

Ina sat down in the meadow grass, one practiced eye on Minna playing among the willows that drooped out over the pattering rill. "Why is what?"

He sat down beside her, hands clasped about his knees. "This sunlight. This peace. Why do our harpers sing only of battle and never of this?"

"To what ear? Their bread is earned from battles and heroes. Besides, they're far too lofty. On days when Hondshew and I came here, times when we were very happy together, he often asked the same."

"Well he might." Beowulf lay back as a cloud shadow drifted over them. "Our scops teach nothing. They take our own thoughts and sing them back to us. Kings like Hygelac and Hrothgar strive so for order because there's more war than peace anywhere you look, and our priests go asking solemn questions of gods so witless and willful."

"True," Ina agreed thoughtfully. "Most men never think of such things."

"I'm beginning to. Like drifting with a river just to see where it leads. Sailing to Heorot, we talked of a venture to the edge of the world. Now I feel as if I'm on that voyage, but there's no edge nor end, only a new shore."

And perhaps voices alluring as those who sang to Greek sailors in old tales. Venturing forth from himself, as he did now, would he not be surely changed on his return? If the world was round after all, and the voyager only returned to his starting point, would he not still, by all that learned on the journey, see the whole so much more clearly?

If the world was round, he thought, it was still a fearsome big ball, and such a thought could be as hard to reach around. He groped at it until Ina spoke.

"I don't think you have ever talked so much with women before, have you?"

Not really; never marked what they said. Until Sigyn. Until now.

"I'll tell you, Ina. The thought's been with me these last days that we don't make sense. We don't honor adulterers, yet Odin is one. We despise useless boys with little promise as warriors, but what else is pretty Balder? We think of Loki as a malicious clown always tripping over his own treachery, but was his daughter so when she wept for her son? By all we hold good, sound reason, we would not for one moment—"

Beowulf rolled over and heaved up onto his knees before Ina with the urgent new thought. "Not for one moment would we endure such flaws in a king; why then do we suffer them in gods? I think this says more of what we are than what we say we honor."

"It says much." Ina looked down at her hands and a dear memory. "Hondshew thought it all mad, what a thane must believe and do. He had a clear mind, my husband. Between the madness and the must-be, he said, one can only laugh and try to find a little life of one's own."

"He knew much, that man."

"And questioned much. As you do now, Prince."

"Please don't call me that."

"It is your place."

"It's what I wouldn't be just now. Things I must do and dearly want to put off for the time. That's a great bore on a day like this."

"Well, then." Ina ran one of his braids through her fingers. "So careless. Don't you ever comb it out?"

"Sometimes. It's a bother."

Ina took a comb from the small pouch at her girdle. "I'll do it. Take it down."

"Now?"

She laughed. "No, next Wednesday, lump."

"It's not needed."

But she insisted gently. "Come. It will please me."

He fumbled at the gold wire binding the braids. He always did them carelessly because his fingers were too large and thick to work the strands deftly. Amused at the clumsiness, Ina undid the wire and strands.

"Now, turn about."

He felt the closeness of her body, her breasts pillowed against his back as she reached over his shoulder to gather the long hair. Beowulf sat very still as she worked the comb through the tangled strands, recalling later that year and still vividly in his age the loveliness of the moment, all of it. Ina close behind him, the scent of her in his nostrils, sea birds gliding westward overhead toward Eyrarsund—and Minna running toward them with her discovery.

"Mama! Bay-woof! There by the big rock." She churned to a stop before Beowulf, gesticulating dramatically. "Under the rock, there's a troll cave, and I swear I saw one of them."

Beowulf drew her close. "A troll? That takes a keen eye and a cool head. You did not disturb him?"

"Oh, no." Minna was too shrewd for that. Trolls were her latest pursuit. Wherever she led Beowulf in flower or berry hunts, every hollow and fox's den was suspected of housing trolls, or bears at least. "Will you fight them?"

"Can't you see Beowulf is busy?" Ina said, working at his hair.

"And alas, Minna. I don't have my sword."

Ina tugged at the snarls. "If I ever get this tangle straight, I'll have to give it a good wash. Don't plague our guest, Minna. He is resting."

Minna sat down by Beowulf's knee, obviously settling herself for a definite stay. "Then tell me about the troll queen and her son."

"What queen is that, Minna?"

"In Denmark," Ina reminded him. "She must have heard from old Inge. The tale is all over Helsingborg."

Working the comb through his hair, Ina leaned close to Beowulf's ear. "Don't speak of her father. She won't understand yet."

"No." He didn't want to say anything about any of that. His throat constricted oddly; there was a peculiar sensation in the pit of his stomach. "They weren't trolls, dear."

"Dragons?"

"Nor that." Beowulf looked away, hoping the child would lose interest quickly, but she only stared up expectantly at him.

"What was the queen's name?"

"She said her name was Sigyn."

Minna's eyes widened. "She said? She talked to you?"

"Yes." Beowulf needed a deep breath, then another. Breathing was difficult. His throat tightened.

"Perhaps truth incarnate, now one thing, now another. My son knew you for what you are."

"Not trolls but people . . . people. Not really in our world or out of it."

A gasp escaped him. The bottom dropped out of his insides; a wave of panic and then unreasoning anger washed over Beowulf. How could Minna understand where he could not, and why must she ask? He passionately wanted her to go away, not just sit there making him tell, throwing stupid questions like hurtful stones, making him see it all again. The words came by themselves, unwilled by him. He couldn't stop them.

"They were like fish in a reed trap, that's all, fish in a trap. Still in water, but caught. They would swim away to sea again if they could."

His breathing had gone shallow. Not only panic now but sharp terror. He gulped for air. "If they could . . ."

Sweat broke out over his face and body. Ina leaned forward to him, concerned. "Beowulf, how is it? Are you ill?"

He shook his head to clear it, his voice a frail squeak. "No. No. Minna, please. Go play now."

"But you started to tell me—"

"Child, you heard the prince. Run and play."

"But he *promised*."

"I can't, Minna. I—" Because he could not, because he was drowning now in what he dared not feel then, Beowulf began to weep. He hadn't wept for many years, never in front of women. He pushed Minna away almost roughly, head ducked to one side that she not see the foolish, unstoppable tears, because behind them was a grief so vast, its shadow darkened the world. No child in his sight but her father dead in shattered Heorot and a nightmare on legs who roared at him to go with as much pleading as command. And the mother as well: if not all of this world, yet enough for human grieving.

"I did what I had to. *Had* to, understand? Ask me why, why, why I had to, why your father—child, I don't know why, any of it. Go. . . ."

"Minna, you mind," Ina commanded. "Go down by the rill. Now."

Minna backed away silently. Something was terribly wrong, something frighteningly grown-up and beyond her ken. She stared at Beowulf, abashed, unable to speak.

"Yes, please go, Minna," Beowulf urged in a muffled voice. "I'll be better soon."

The child turned and ran away, disturbed but blessedly to forget before the hour was much older, because time was an endless road lying before her still, and no one ever died.

"Even Sigyn. Even she was less cursed."

Beowulf turned his face to Ina, hair falling loose about his tear-streamed cheeks. "What *is* it, Ina? When I was there, I never felt it so terribly. I'm sweating cold, sick with it, all my guts in one cold lump."

He huddled on his knees, his head bowed low. Ina took him in her arms as she would Minna. "It is all right; it is natural. Hondshew was often taken like this."

She knew clearly what afflicted Beowulf and thanes like him, as her husband had come to know it. The thing they could mask from each other but not from wives when they woke sweating at night. The fear of death always hidden but erupting inevitably sometime in some form because it must.

"Madness," Beowulf panted against her breast. "You should have seen it, Ina. Madness. Mother, son, the walls, light and shadow shifting, now one thing and then the other, as if they and everything about them blew like leaves in the wind between the worlds. Nothing constant except her pain. In the moment before she came at me, she spoke. That mere-creature, that woman knew more of life than I ever will."

Beowulf wrenched away from Ina, no longer caring what she saw of his anguish. In that nakedness, he was so homely and human that her heart went out to him.

"They wonder why I spoke so little of it, why the lot of us never boasted at the board? Boast of what? It's only now, this minute that I *feel* any of what happened. When . . . when it was over and she lay dead, she looked like a girl, just a young girl, all gold and white, while all around her the magic and the madness surrendered and the mere poured in. That's all I can think of."

He wiped at his eyes with a sleeve, tore up a handful of grass, and hurled it in barren disgust after the thought. "The Scyldings hailed me, and Hrothgar gave me gifts."

Beowulf seized Ina's hands with clumsy force. "Tell me. I need to know. What was in Hondshew that you loved? That cried out to you to be loved. Please, I must learn."

Ina was startled at the new intensity. "Don't grip so hard, you're hurting me. Learn what?"

He lessened his hold but still clutched at her. "To be alive. Again. Really alive. Just now I feel I'm almost there. Tell me about him."

Wind rustled through the willows where Minna played, and the sun was warm overhead. They hovered on their knees, facing each other, and Ina tried to tell him about the man who was her lover and his friend; how he listened to her always, as if what she said, serious or trifling, was of great importance. How he seemed ever to delight in her, though Ina never knew why, plain as she was and sometimes downright homely. How the man could laugh and be sometimes as much of a child as Minna, or let Ina be one and delight in her all the more.

Through it all, Beowulf held her hands tight and listened intently as Minna had to him when he tried to tell of darker wonders confronted and killed, only to rise and mock him now.

19

PRINCE HERDRED WAS MISSING and thirty youths with him. Evidently, they had commandeered a royal keel in the small hours before full light. By now, midmorning, they would be well north along the coast, as young Wexstan hazarded, in their honor raid against King Ohther's Swedes.

The hare-brained venture might easily give the Swedes a pretext for war which Geats could ill afford now. Hygelac must summon his council, the first call issued to Beowulf and carried by young Canute. As a father, Hygelac would sacrifice to his gods for Herdred's safe return. As a husband, he flinched from what he must tell the boy's mother and added that price to the severe lesson he would administer to Herdred on his return.

If he returned.

In his council chamber, Garmund at his side, Hygelac spoke to the thickset young man hulking before him and waiting orders. At nineteen, Wexstan already had the heavy, choleric countenance of a much older man, and close-set, belligerent eyes that reminded Hygelac of a dangerous boar. While the king waited word from Canute, Wexstan would post to call in the other members of his council, and there was one other unpleasant task the king could avoid no longer.

"Garmund, ask the queen to attend me here. Canute should be back by now. If you see him, send him to me."

"I will, my lord. I do believe I heard a horse in the courtyard just now."

Garmund was barely gone on his errand when the door opened again. Canute stood on the threshold, sweaty from an hour's fruitless ride in the hot sun.

"My lord said to come immediately."

"Beowulf?"

"Not at home, sir, but—"

Hygelac controlled the urge to scream at the youth. "Where is he?"

"At Hondshew's steading, his people said."

"Did you find him there?"

Canute did not. He dutifully followed but missed Beowulf again, only able to leave word of the king's urgent summons. "They said he was off somewhere with Hondshew's daughter."

Hygelac bit back his impatience. Again? What had taken the man? What was he doing? Wits softened, senile before his time?

Perplexed himself at his hero's uncharacteristic behavior, Canute struggled to flesh out the intelligence in so far as possible. "The servants at the hall mentioned something about willow rods, sir. Mending fences."

"Fences," Hygelac mumbled, noting Wexstan's smirk of contempt. A prince of Geats laboring in the hot sun like any slave. No need to prolong this; Hygelac made a quick decision. "Thanks for your pains, Canute. Ride now to the rest of my council; say I need them with all speed. Divide the task with Ulf or Gorm that the message is more swiftly delivered."

Canute did not relish more riding in this heat. He was never as hardy or physically resilient as the other companions on Beowulf's venture to Heorot. He could still conceal the shortcoming but would never be really fit as a warrior. He could not put on weight. Now and then this year there was blood in his sputum. Canute would not show one jot of this before his king or Wexstan. He bowed in obedience and hurried out on his mission.

No more time for understanding or notions of family. Beowulf would be brought and quickly by someone who would convey the command in no uncertain terms. "Wexstan, your father has never failed me. Would you be as trusted?"

The young man braced to attention, one hand on his sword hilt. "Sir."

"Ride to Hondshew's steading and find Beowulf if it takes all day. No nice courtesies, just bring him now. Clear?"

Wexstan's head chopped up and down. He stumped away on his errand.

Hygelac reprimanded himself for the wasted time. He should have sent Wexstan to begin with. Canute was too close in friendship, too soft to insist. Wexstan, on the other hand, had all the softness of an ax blade, and for his own reasons, always resisted the widespread worship of Beowulf.

Alone in his chair, Hygelac let out his breath in a groan of frustration. Tension drove him to move and act, but nothing more could be done until Beowulf and the council met with him. After that, they could only wait. Herdred's brainless folly and Beowulf's unfathomable behavior were now tangled in the knot of a common problem. One he could ascribe to thoughtless youth, the other—?

By all human reasoning, what worked in Beowulf's mind or on his spirit since returning that he lay aside home, duties, and the greatest honor in generations lightly as discarded garments? Did he court Hondshew's widow? His birth and responsibilities would plainly rule that out. Perhaps he had been the idol of younger Geats so long that he saw himself above the law and people's need. If so, Hygelac would disabuse him.

As for Herdred, if the Fates were kind enough to bring him safe home, he must be punished only that he learn. Where was the boy now? Soon he would be in Swedish waters, then beaching, wading ashore—

The door opened behind him. Hygelac raised his head to see Hygd in the entrance, haggard as himself.

"Is it true? Where is he? Will he be all right?"

Because he had no answer, Hygelac could only rise and wrap her in the helpless comfort of his arms.

From that day in the meadow, they grew closer without conscious effort, seeing each other in new light. From Hondshew's widow to Ina as herself; from Hondshew's friend to human and reachable Beowulf. For Ina, the surprise of her delight in his sudden smile, the attitude of his head or frown of concentration when a new thought burst upon him. For him, her exasperation when Minna brought a frog into the hall, and the child's subversive glee at Itharne's black fear of reptiles. The lift of Ina's chin, the swing of Beowulf's shoulders, the accidental brushing of their hands as they walked together. The gentleness of her spirit, the same discovered in him, waking from long sleep in his soul, a man who was so much but so passionately wished to be something else. Neither of them thought of tomorrow, only what was good now.

Standing over Beowulf at the rain barrel to scrub out his hair, Ina saw beyond the scars and indentations of bones broken and imperfectly set to the masculine grace of him. Beowulf watched her walking or sometimes breaking into a comic jig with Minna when the whim took them both, and he was fascinated by the different dance of her fingers at familiar tasks. Beowulf studied her intently as one whose growing knowledge of a new tongue only opened longer vistas of so much yet unlearned.

All his life Beowulf had lived among men and warriors. Women were a thing apart. Men made sour jokes and vowed it true that in ages past, females spoke a secret language among themselves, perhaps still did, which warped their thinking awry, when they thought at all, and made them enigmas to men.

Not so, Beowulf was discovering now. Words were no more than the door. Once past that portal, he found the same words used with different values by women. Men would discuss a battle in terms of who was killed and what gained and the honor of it. Women, using the same terms, would speak of how it felt to winners, losers, and who suffered.

Through the summer days they grew closer in a contentment neither spoke, since the words, like ill-aimed missiles, might shatter something delicate and not fully understood between them.

Itharne observed them together, accepting much and questioning other things in silence. Ina was a young widow; so had she been before Hondshew was born. That was her lot, a husbandless woman with a child among an alien and stoic people. Itharne had always found Geats unsubtle, their spirits dim. Pray to or revile their crude gods as they might, they never really heard any voice but their own, never knew those gods close about them as her own ancient kind always could. She loved Ina and took it for granted the woman would marry again, but hesitated over Beowulf, sensing dark currents that surged over him like a poisonous current about a river stone.

Toward Harvest Month, she asked Ina outright. "Is it that the prince has intentions toward you?"

"Oh, I think not, Mother. He adores Minna and I enjoy his company."

No more than that? To Itharne, her daughter-in-law seemed to brush the question too quickly aside. "And your intentions?"

Ina dropped the sewing in her lap. "What *is* it, Mother? Don't you like him?"

"Did I say one word or another as to that? But there is that about him—"

"Please, not your old Sight again." Hondshew's mother put far too much store in her "kennings" and too little in what was plain before her eyes. In truth, Ina felt and thought more in regard to the man than she was ready to share. "He is a good man. He has put his hand to much that needed doing since Hondshew left."

"Should one ask how much?"

"Oh, enough!"

No more on the matter. Itharne held her peace, but she sensed in Beowulf, imperfectly as one whose fingertips brush an unfamiliar surface in the dark, something that once horrified Grendel in Heorot. Death hovered about the man, if not part of him, then always near, plucking one by one the days from the stem of his life like petals from a flower still opening.

"Hey! Ho! On we go! Hey! Ho! Fast we *go!*"

Spurring with her heels, switching Beowulf's broad back with a whip of straw, Minna rode his shoulders regally as they jogged homeward along the edge of the hay field. A few mowers waved to her. Minna squealed in conquering delight and saluted them as they moved through the hay. A bolt of willow rods under each arm, Beowulf trotted toward the steading and the collapsed section of wattle fence—

"Hold tight, Minna."

—and cleared it in a bound.

"More! On!" she commanded.

"No more now." Beowulf dropped the rods and lifted her off his shoulders. "It's hot and you have little mercy on horses. Tomorrow, we'll go for moss to pack the new wall."

"Min-na? Come."

Ina stood in the hall entrance, one hand raised in greeting to Beowulf. He grinned back, warmed by the sight of her there. *Now I am truly close to life.*

Minna whisked away in Ina's care, Beowulf went to work with relish, boring deep holes with an augur into the new timber posts. All the timbers were placed and the first layer of willow rods set in when he saw the horseman break out of the forest toward him. Wexstan trotted the black to a halt by Beowulf. He did not dismount. Hondshew never had any liking for Wexstan, considering him arrogant and dull. While Beowulf had no quarrel with his distant cousin, the man's truc-

ulent manner hardly inspired friendship. Wexstan descended from Offa;
but for that unfortunate demise the Geatish crown might well have
stood in his line rather than Hygelac's.

"How have you had it, Wexstan?"

"Better than the king, my lord. Come to fetch you on his orders.
Your uncle wants you at his council."

Beowulf swabbed the perspiration from his forehead and considered excusing himself once more. Too fine a day to sit inside and this
work far too pleasurable, hands at one task and mind drifting peacefully
over not much at all. But he'd sent too many excuses already this summer. "My thanks, Wexstan. I'll be along."

"The king is mindful you said that the last time and more than
once before that," Wexstan stated in a tone bordering on insolence.
"You are to come with me. Not in a while, sir, but now."

"Am I indeed? So great a matter?"

"Prince, there is trouble. I'll tell you as we go."

Beowulf blew wood shavings from the augur bit deliberately and
without haste to show Wexstan he would not be hurried by the man's
mission or manner. Then he opened the gate. "Be so good as to fetch
my gray from the stable. I'll take short leave of the family."

Herdred's folly was known to all by now, but there was more matter the king would discuss only within his family, at least for the time.
He was hale enough but not young, nor would he live forever even in
a prolonged state of peace, which now seemed unlikely. There would
be no leisure to this day's council, no easy talk over meat and mead by
which a king gauged the temper of his chief men before addressing
business at hand. They would need clear heads this day.

When Beowulf entered and bowed in respect, Hygelac was shocked
at the man's appearance. Unwashed and sunburned, the second largest
landowner among Geats had come in a sweat-stained old linen shirt
and baggy trousers out at both knees, without sword or shield.

"Is this a way to attend council? You look like a field slave."

"My lord said to come now. Wexstan was most diligent in his
charge."

"That's why I sent him," Hygelac grumbled. He motioned Beowulf
to sit and drew a second chair close. "He's told you then?"

"About Herdred. Yes."

"When that fool boy returns—" Hygelac slammed his fist hard on the chair arm. Beowulf read his uncle's anguish and tried to ease his mood. "I did the same once."

"So you did and just as mad and just blind luck you weren't killed with the rest. It was different then. The Frise are not a stronger force on our doorstep. Whatever damage Herdred does, we must make good and quickly, you understand? We must apologize, humble ourselves, and offer wergild for any Swedes killed or injured. Make no mistake, this will cost us."

Hygelac exuded the naked fear of a father for a heedless son, but he had clearly thought out his intent. "My counselors are prudent men, but there will be some who say honor is involved; others, that apology might be seen as weak and base, the work of fear. Some of Herdred's boat companions are their sons. If those sons die, they'll want blood. They will demand I seek Hrothgar's aid and go to war."

And regardless of his own policies, Hrothgar would most like feel honor bound to help in Beowulf's name. Beowulf said firmly, "No. We can't squander that goodwill on a pointless war."

"We're not prepared for this."

Not now, perhaps not for years, if then. The life of the Geats had always been precarious. They had carved out their place and survived against larger tribes through energy and aggressive raiding, but any thinking man could see the time for that was ending, that these very qualities could now doom them. They could not expand northward without sufficient men to hold new ground against sure retaliation, nor wrest land from the Danes to whom their friendship was bound by oath. Nothing for the moment but pay up and back off, despite the predictable dullards who would mutter that the king's courage had fled.

"Herdred is not ready to take my place. Even Hygd says as much," Hygelac admitted reluctantly. "She is ill over this, beside herself. Nothing will comfort her until she knows the boy is safe. It is my fault. I have been too easy with him for her sake."

The king of the Geats sat back, gripping the chair arms. "Indeed," he added, looking directly into his nephew's face, "I have been too fond with all my family."

Beowulf sighed inwardly. *Here it comes.*

"We know where you have been these months, but not why. Was Hondshew's steading in such poor repair? I thought Hrothgar's compensation very generous."

"I owed Hondshew that much. And . . ."

"And?"

"I needed the time."

"Gold is cheaper than time today."

"Yes, sir."

Hygelac rose and went to gaze out an open window into the stockade yard. Certain things must be said privately before the council arrived. "If you've anything to tell me . . ."

"My lord?"

"In confidence for the time being. You know the general regard of Gundar and the history of his house."

Beowulf let the gambit pass in tactful silence. Gundar's white-knuckled avarice was one thing, but ancestral treachery and royal murder he would not broach since a strong light on one family's dishonor might reveal Hygelac's own grandsire in the same unflattering glare.

The king spoke again. "Ina Gundarsdattir."

He turned to Beowulf. "Hondshew was a loyal thane, though his house was of no great holding. No one cared when his father brought home a Pict wife."

"Vacomagi, my lord," Beowulf prompted politely. "Itharne's tribe was the Vacomagi. They hate being called Picts."

"Well, whatever. Painted and tattooed . . . they're all Picts to me."

"Just as we would rather be called Geats than thieves despite our many sea ventures without invitation."

Hygelac smiled thinly at the deft comparison. "You grow keen. A king must have such an edge, but for now I must be blunt. War and raiding were once our greatest honor and our only way. Now, we must look elsewhere. We must emulate Hrothgar and kings like him. My son is no longer a boy, but still a reckless fool. If, after me, he cannot deal wisely with other tribes, you will have to, in his council or in his place. Therefore—"

A hurried knock interrupted him. Hygelac opened the door a few inches, spoke briefly with Garmund, then closed it again.

"The council is arriving. Go to my bower, wash, and make yourself presentable. Borrow a mantle and sword. You are their hero; do nothing to lessen that respect."

As Beowulf rose to go, Hygelac laid a hand on his shoulder. "There are many things a king may have and many he cannot afford." He searched the younger man's face. "That is all I will say for now. Take heed, Beowulf."

Take heed. Hygelac had been subtle, mentioned her name once and veered away without really altering course. Soon or late, Herdred would wear the crown. From that day on, Beowulf must hold himself in readiness if the boy died young or proved unfit. The Geats could waste no advantage, including royal marriage. To defy this reality would be worse folly than Herdred's raid. Six months past Beowulf would have readily agreed when the point meant little to him. Now, it meant all. For Ina and himself, nothing was possible. There was no more time.

20

BEOWULF REMAINED WITH HYGELAC through the crisis, sending his regrets to Ina and assuring her he would return as soon as possible. The king well anticipated the temper of his council. Some few admired Herdred's venture and vowed they were ready should Ohther retaliate. These were a minority, however; Hygelac set forth their policy with Beowulf in firm support, let sword-rattlers grumble as they might.

Five days after setting out, Herdred's messenger panted into the royal steading on foot, having run all the way from the beached keel. Hygelac heard the boy in the hall with Beowulf and Garmund in silent attendance. Victory! Plunder and prisoners, two villages harried, a glorious stroke for the Geats. And lest the king or any father be anxious, not a man lost or more than minor wounds taken. Victory it was, and would the king give proper greeting to a princely son and his band?

The boy, all of seventeen, came to the end of his message and stood flushed, elated, and running with sweat before Hygelac, shield gripped in a bandaged arm, waiting for reply. Were he older and more observant, he might have read much in the king's stillness and spare response.

"Tell my son he shall indeed have a fitting welcome."

The hero's greeting for Beowulf fresh in memory, young Herdred intended a triumphal entry into Helsingborg, strutting at the head of his war band, spears clashing on shields to mark their pace, two men carrying a chest of plunder, the weight of which was no great burden, two more bringing up the rear with a pair of middle-aged prisoners, thanes who had served through far grimmer confrontations under Ohther's father, Ongentho. Long past their fighting days, they had expected to die when Herdred's boy-fierce band charged howling into their village. Seeing the boys more intent on prestige than anything else, they prudently submitted to spare their people bloodshed, more bemused than shamed.

The procession swept in through the stockade gates to find their promised welcome rather sparsely attended. There were the king and queen, Beowulf, the council, and every father whose son had joined the raid in direct disobedience to orders. Their mien was neither proud nor joyous.

Herdred halted before his father, signaling for the treasure and two chained prisoners to be brought forward.

"Men of rank for ransom, Father. And treasure!"

No one moved in the courtyard, no one spoke. Herdred's cocky, expectant grin faltered. He glanced at his mother. Hygd's face was a blank wall. A rook cawed overhead, perhaps in wry comment. Hygelac followed its flight before speaking.

"Fathers, see to your sons. Treat with them as fits. Herdred, unchain these men."

When the prince in some confusion made to order it done, Hygelac overrode him and commanded Herdred free them with his own hands and then to clap the manacles about his own wrists and ankles. Astonished, Herdred flatly refused, beginning to heat. When he resisted, Beowulf simply upended the crown prince of Geats, deposited him flat on his back, and sat on him while Herdred was chained hand and foot.

Hygelac bent over his son. "This is the welcome meet for fools."

The boy's face was scarlet with fury and humiliation. "Father, this is—get *off* me, Beowulf. I can't breathe!"

"Be still," Hygelac hissed over him. "For my own fear, I will charge you little. For your mother's suffering, more, and for the Geats' peril which you have brought on them, much."

Hygd's eyes brimmed with tears when Herdred appealed silently to her. She said only, "You have shamed us," and turned her back on him. Beowulf saw the shock that dropped Herdred's mouth open, but his lesson had barely begun.

The Swedish thanes were shown every courtesy. The same keel was fitted out for their return with all plundered from their village—a few gold torcs and jeweled brooches, a handful of silver ingots, beside full payment for their discomfiture and Hygelac's apology to their jarl and King Ohther.

Before departing Helsingborg, the Swedes were treated to the edifying sight of Herdred under guard, his shame displayed atop the high speaker's platform for all to see.

"A little pup has snapped at our heels," one of them allowed to his companion. No more than that for the moment, but the incident served to remind them and other Swedes how quickly pups grew and how Geats never changed.

While Hygelac could only wait and guess at Ohther's reaction, the reckoning would be stamped deep into Herdred's memory. For three days and nights under guard by vigilant sentries, he stood in his chains on the platform in the stockade courtyard, dressed in a tanner's old, ragged trousers and shirt still reeking of that pungent trade. The drooping mustaches of his first manhood, so proudly grown and groomed, were shorn from his upper lip. He was allowed no food or water and only one brief trip to the latrine each morning when the guards changed. Through the first day and night, Herdred stood erect and defiant, staring fixedly at the horizon, ignoring the taunts of boys below, while his ill-advised companions suffered private discipline at home. As a king, Herdred would bear his honors and mistakes in the sight of all; so in that unpitying light would he endure his shame.

The first day brought sharp hunger which he had never known in his life, the second day, even worse. Then hunger dulled under the increasing torture of thirst. He swayed and slumped as exhaustion crept up his body like tide over a beach. He must lie down, couldn't hold himself up another moment. He told himself he would pretend to fall —yes, the guards would prod him up, but at least there would be that brief, blessed relief. No, that would only bring more suffering when he had to stand again. Then he would try to swallow around a swollen tongue like dry wool and stand a little longer with the remnant of pride.

On the third morning, he could barely stagger between his guards to the latrine and hardly needed to. The guards had to help him climb back onto the platform. The sun climbed steadily, the day even hotter than the one before. With no more moisture to sweat from his body, Herdred blistered and burned. Only a few more hours; they would let him down at evening. But *was* this the last day? He'd lost track of time, unable to grasp any thought before it faded unfinished from a parched mind. He prayed to Freyr for a drop of rain, one trickle of sweat to lick from cracked lips. His shoulders weighed a hundred stone apiece while the mocking sun hung overhead and barely moved, creeping at cruel snail's pace toward a night it would never attain. The world for Herdred tilted and slid sideways. . . .

He swayed, buckled, and crumpled in a heap of misery from which all pride had fled, his chains thudding heavily on the platform planks. From far away Herdred felt hands groping at him, the chains stripped from his leaden limbs. Then lifted, being carried before he slipped down into dim, red dreams.

The miracle of water on his lips, trickling over his parched tongue, and a cool wet cloth over his eyes. Herdred lifted the cloth and blinked up into near gloom in his own bower. A single rush light illuminated the massive figure seated beside him. Another trickle of water over his lips. Herdred sucked greedily.

"More."

"Not yet," Beowulf denied. "Only a little at first or you'll be sick."

Herdred groaned. "I'm sick now. Did I last until sundown?"

"No, but the sun was very hot."

"More water. Please."

"There. Just a sip. You've not suffered as your parents have."

Herdred shut his eyes against his own shame. "I know."

"It was ill conceived, Cousin. Mad."

"What if it was? Did I deserve this? You raided younger than me. No one punished you."

Beowulf wet the cloth and replaced it over Herdred's eyes. "Listen to me. I was punished. I went for the same reasons you did. I wanted to be accepted as a warrior. We found nothing, got nothing. They all died for nothing."

"You fought your way out."

"No." Beowulf held the waterskin to the boy's lips again. "Most of us ran like rabbits. I'm here giving you water because I ran faster and hid better than the rest. My father found out. He said I should have died there rather than survive a coward. He made sure I died a little each day after. Yes, I was punished."

Herdred raised himself on one elbow with enormous effort. For the same reasons? He wanted to be seen a warrior and a worthy successor to his father, but more than all, like every boy who sailed with him, he wanted to be like Beowulf.

"I don't believe it. Not you."

"Even me. And better men than me, who knows?"

"But what you did in Heorot—"

"That was later. That was another day. As *you* will have another."

Herdred could barely grasp what he was hearing. "There's not a Geat who—you never said a word."

"Only to you. Learn from it."

"I'll never tell, I swear."

Beowulf only patted the boy's hand, rising. "It doesn't really matter. Learn from this and from your father. Take some more water."

Herdred drank gratefully and lay back too exhausted to feel hunger, even though he hadn't eaten in three days. Something worse gnawed at his vitals. "It is hard to be shown for a fool and know it is deserved. And everyone . . ."

And everyone watching, Beowulf finished in silent sympathy. "Well, Cousin, it's hard, but not mortal. I'll tell the queen you're among the living. I think she's made you some broth."

Rain fell before the last hay was in. Ina sent word to Beowulf that they would be short of winter fodder, and that he was missed more than the hay. He was pleased she'd thought of him and sent hay from his own ample barns. He could not be with them now, fiercely as he wanted to. With Ina he could breathe, could feel the nearness of life like a sweet voice singing, whose words, were he only a little nearer, would be richly understood at last.

In Helsingborg, Hygelac and his chief men waited word from Ohther: war or peace? More rain fell in early August. Garmund submitted daily crop reports, chastened Herdred rode soberly on his father's errands. Coast watchers drew their hoods tighter against the downpour through anxious sentry tours along the western cliffs.

Time passed, the weather cleared, but only their own fishing boats slid along the horizon. From Ohther there was no response of any kind, the silence of contempt—

"Or preparation?" Hygelac suggested to Beowulf, idly tossing a set of ivory dice on the board between them. "Will he come before winter or wait until spring or not come at all? He lets us sweat."

"Meanwhile, my lord, do we ask help from Hrothgar?"

His uncle swept up the dice and rattled them absently in his fist. "No. We will not send to the Danes. I say Ohther won't come."

Beowulf said from his heart, "I wish I could be sure of that."

"So do I." The dice clattered across the table. Hygelac read them and smiled sourly at his nephew. He had thrown Loki, a losing cast. "Good job I didn't bet my life on the throw."

They had bet their lives anyway, Beowulf knew bleakly, watching the man he served who was as wise and strong as Eligius but for the sharp wolf-edge set to his life by necessity.

We are warriors, but Hygelac sees the trap in that as I do. Our very sword-honor will betray us. War was the ideal; the ideal equaled survival, but now I think we lag behind the day. Time outruns us, time and the world. Will we have time and the mercy to change before destruction?

We are proud to be called sea wolves, but wiser dogs with no less courage are kenneled and kept where wolves are hunted and killed. No, we can learn. We must. Our own blood has gone to Britain and made a beginning at something better.

In my first long-ago sight of you, Eligius, you stood in the middle of your garden, and your delight and peace in merely being was clear to see. I have joyed as much in the face of a child and a woman who is my friend. I have breathed in the scent of morning as you did, and become drunk on that which took me out of myself if only for a moment. You would no doubt smile and say I've only touched some aspect of your god, your truth, where I've blundered onto life and found it good.

And you, dear Ina, who see the world and men through the clearest eye, can you peer ahead far enough to see a time for us? Do that, spy it out, for I can't. It's still night and that wyrd spun by the Fates for me is the wyrd of the wolf.

21

ON A WARM MORNING IN AUGUST, Beowulf was free at last to ride to Ina's steading. He looked forward eagerly to seeing her and Minna, though what he must tell Ina was shadowed with reluctance.

On the same day, Hygelac's emissaries put out into Eyrarsund for Heorot. In mending his own fences, Hygelac's policies were deliberate and shrewd, his question to Hrothgar to be held in strict secrecy. Would the Scyldings support him against a possible attack by Ohther? There were usually Swedes passing through Heorot; Geats must assume that Herdred's folly and Hygelac's humiliating apology were now common knowledge. Hrothgar's response would be further complicated as his sister Yrse was married to Ohther's brother, Prince Onela.

Who was an ally? Beowulf pondered as he rode. And in what degree of trust?

Hrothgar's reply reflected his usual deliberation. He was bound by gratitude to aid *against* any aggression but in support of none. This would be his counsel to Ohther as well. The message was clear: Scyldings would incur no unnecessary enmities. Let Geats and Swedes do the same. Hygelac needed no urging in that regard. Thus, the second pillar of his policy and the unhappy reason Beowulf must speak his heart to Ina Gundarsdattir and know hers in turn.

Ina's face and widespread arms proclaimed that heart in seeing him after so long. Squealing with delight, Minna bolted so fast to embrace Beowulf that she tripped and fell flat and had to be dusted off and her bewildered whimpers stilled with a kiss by Beowulf. He set her on his horse for a ride to the barn; then, with Minna riding his shoulders and Ina by his side, he passed the hall with regret for the fence he would not have time to finish this year or the many other tasks from which he would have taken so much simple pleasure in accomplishing.

They walked through the stubbled hay field for what might be the last time and returned to the hall where Itharne took protesting Minna in charge, and Ina slipped her hand in Beowulf's as if it had always belonged there. They walked to the meadow by the willow-bordered rill and rested on the grass. Summer did not linger as long here as it might in Gaul. If the nights did not yet darken much before dawn, they were noticeably cooler now. Summer—their summer, as Beowulf came to remember it—was dying. Against what must be, he hoped little else would die with it.

"I must leave tomorrow, Ina."

She did not look at him. "I know. Mother told me. She has a sense for such things."

"I've come to hate endings."

"So do I," Ina said. "Will you tell me?"

"None of it was my doing, Ina. Before all merciful gods, if there are such, this was not my wish."

"Such a swearing? What is it?"

He gave her the flat truth of the matter. Hygelac had ordained a double defense of preparedness and diplomacy. In the morning, Beowulf would lead a mounted search north along the coast for early warning against any attack by sea. They would visit the border Brondings to assess their loyalty, then swing inland for signs of possible invasion by land.

"Ohther has sent no word. We don't know his intentions. I'm to take Herdred with me for seasoning."

Ina asked with concern, "How is the boy?"

"I think Herdred has learned from a hard lesson. He may grow into the king his father is, allowed the time."

"Will you be home for Blood Month? Our pigs did well this year. We must repay you for the fodder as we can."

He would not be back by then, though she need not worry a moment over payment. Ina searched his face with the question. Beowulf read her disappointment.

"So long away, then?"

"Late enough in the year, when attack is unlikely, Herdred will return to Helsingborg and I am to cross the border to Ohther's court as a royal emissary."

Ina looked at him steadily, perhaps taking less from his words than their reluctant tone. "And then?"

Beowulf hesitated, surprised that he hedged so, tearing angrily at the grass about his thigh. "Gorm, Ulf, and Canute, other men from the Heorot venture, they'll ride with me. My uncle wants the mission to carry the weight of renown."

He chuckled at the wry thought. "Ever try to impress a Swede? We will assure Ohther that Hygelac wants only peace and proposes marriage between Herdred and Ohther's daughter Ermingard."

Ina nodded soberly. "What chance has this?"

"What you might suppose. It will depend on how much the alliance is worth to Ohther. The Swedes have always wanted to extend their sway to border with the Danes. They consider us an unnatural breach in their destiny. If Ohther can win that in bed rather than battle, he may agree."

"I see."

No, she didn't see. That much was easy to say, so much merely acknowledged the greasy kitchen work behind the lives and legends of kings. The rest was much harder. "There is more, Ina. My orders were secret, but I want you to know."

"It will remain secret, Beowulf."

So it would. Such women gave their word to few and lightly to none.

"The proposal will have a hinge for their surety and ours. If through any chance at all the marriage likes them not, or if Ermingard becomes Herdred's widow, I must pledge to marry her as next in line to the throne.

"Or—" Beowulf looked away from Ina and blurted the rest in a rush of distaste. "Some other Swedish lady of significant rank."

He found the courage or desperation to say the rest because he had to. "Dear Ina, do you know what I want to say? I want no part of this, none. But Hygelac must have his peace. The Geats must have it."

A small, sad smile played about Ina's lips. "The king plays shrewdly. No woman in the north will refuse Beowulf."

"Would you if I asked?" He clasped her hands. "You are the woman I would choose. The one I would die for."

"I know." She said it as a fact settled and done between them. "And even brave enough to live for me, I think."

Ina shifted close to rest her head on his shoulder. "So I won't waste our time in maidenly confusion. This is a time for truth."

Now the words came easily and simply to Beowulf because they were true. "I can never be Hondshew—"

"Hush, love. I don't want you to be."

"Please listen. That day here in this meadow when I asked and you told me how and why you loved him, I thought it was something I could learn. Hondshew had a music; I only have the need. I can hold the harp, but how call the song with my clumsy fingers? I am selfish, Ina. I can offer you so little and still ask."

He lay back in the grass. Ina leaned close over him, stroking the hair she loved to plait with her own hands. "Don't be foolish, man."

She held him close, her face against his, to cushion his despair. For once, life had put a thing in his path on which he might break. Poor man: Whatever the hard mold of that life, he was much more human than he gave himself credit for, merely less suited than Hondshew to deal with the feelings awakened in him. Given time . . . but when was there ever time? The Fates wove a different skein for Beowulf.

"It amazes me how a man can walk thirty years on the earth and know so little of women. No, listen to me." She blocked Beowulf's mouth with a kiss. "Listen. I loved Hondshew and I have Minna from that love. That part of my life is filled and complete, a part of me forever. I need not mourn nor seek it again."

Even when Minna married, there would still be her memories, whole years, days, or vivid moments to lift from her hoard, turning them this way and that in her heart's warm light and without regret when they faded naturally as wood darkened with time and the touch of loving hands. To cling to the past beyond that was both timid and lazy. There would never be another laughing, tender Hondshew who in his dear treason had loved life more than honor, but sacrificed one only to have the other heaped on his funeral pyre—and how her beloved man no doubt smiled behind his hand at that as they lauded him in Valhalla.

"Why should one love be the same as another?" she whispered against Beowulf's cheek. "Different, but not less, nor any less true in its time, you foolish man. You speak of music and the harp; is the wood shaped or the strings tuned to one song alone? I love you. We love you, Minna and I."

Beowulf looked up into the calm wisdom and acceptance of her eyes. "That wasn't all of it. You don't understand."

"Trust me, I do."

"No. There's nothing I can give you I can swear will last. I can handfast you in law, but never marry you."

Ina sat up away from him, frowning. "You sound like a man arguing himself out of love, not in."

"No, it isn't like that; only to beg you, that if you choose, know what you choose. You and Minna will never want—"

"You need not say that."

"I want to say it, Ina. I need to say it. Now, here, this moment before I drown in duty. For a moment, I want to feel more than I think. You don't know all about men. You will always be first, you and Minna, and always the first dear ones that I must leave behind, and *still* I'm coward enough, selfish enough to ask."

"Such a man." Ina laughed and stood up, putting her arms around him. "Hondshew always said—forgive me, I'm not laughing at you— that you had a vast talent for making yourself miserable."

"So I do."

"But that's only the joy of you emptied out. Then let's have what we can, love, while we can. Summer hasn't died, the king is still hale. While that lasts, we'll find what we can and come together when we need."

"Yes. Let me look at you." He cupped her face in his hands, marveling at the gift of her. "Then I've won something worth having for once. Something of my own, and I am glad. By the gods, I am not miserable now."

Their future would not be perfect nor even assured, but as their world went, it must be enough. While they clung together in the westering sun, the first leaves fell from the beeches verging their meadow.

BOOK IV

THE
TOWER
OF
BEOWULF

22

THE OLD KING OF THE GEATS rode a horse slow and ruminant as himself this tranquil summer day, clip-clopping along the cliff path south from Helsingborg toward the house of Father Justin. A quarter mile from the priest's stone cell and chapel, Beowulf dismounted and let the shaggy horse rest and graze before going on.

He was fifty-five this year, twenty of them as king after Herdred died. Neither treaties nor strategy had availed his people. The Swedes would overrun them someday; only a matter of time, opportunity, and King Onela's enduring enmity.

All that and, of course, more lives.

Beowulf wished away the mordant thought. A beautiful day, the sea lying like glass before him, dotted to the horizon with fishing boats. Too peaceful to grime with the doubts of age, and yet because they bore the weight of all those years, they were not easily dislodged from his mind.

Pointless. Useless. While scops sang of honor and loyalty, the treacheries and the wars and the deaths went on and on. After great Hrothgar died, amid years of blighted crops for which Scyldings could find no natural cause, Hrothulf murdered his princely cousins to seize the throne but was himself dispatched to restore the proper line in the person of Herward. Beowulf mourned the boys, especially brave, earnest young Hrothmund. Some said Unferth did for Hrothulf personally. Only a rumor, but Unferth seemed to carry himself straighter when he subsequently offered his services to Hygelac. The man died happier than ever he lived, falling with Hygelac in an ill-starred expedition against the Frisians. Beowulf survived that battle too, privately wondering how and why, and came home to crown Herdred.

Even success worked against them. Hygelac's request for a treaty with Ohther, sealed with a marriage alliance, was welcomed by the Swede king for his own far-sighted reasons. Herdred and Ermingard were formally betrothed, but the following summer a brief, virulent plague raged through Ohther's people, taking the princess with many others and leaving Hygelac committed to Ohther with no strategic profit from the arrangement. Shortly afterward, Ohther himself forthfared. The Swedish crown, which should have lighted on his son Eanmund, was seized by Ohther's able but ruthless brother Onela. Eanmund fled to Herdred in Helsingborg, insisting he honor the treaty and help restore the crown.

Before Herdred could act at all, Onela swept south with his army. Herdred and Beowulf stalemated him with a brilliantly fought defensive campaign that cost Onela dearly, but Herdred and Eanmund himself lost their lives in the conflict. When Onela and Beowulf met to make peace, the Swedish king made a show of magnanimity: Eanmund the pretender was no more, his own crown secure. He pledged to withdraw and leave the Geats in peace.

So Beowulf became king, hardly fooled by Onela's "peace." The campaign had cost the Swedish war band casualties of four to one against the wily and more determined Geats; to pursue it further would amount to tribal suicide. The Swedes retired to lick their wounds and wait. Beowulf had no illusions of lasting security. The Swedes would come again.

On and on, he reflected sadly and often as he grew older. Until the sight of sunrise itself could pall in a sane mind, and that which men called good and beautiful no more than tedium.

Looking out to sea, Beowulf arched his back to relieve the saddle stiffness. He shouldn't let such thoughts weigh unduly on him. Age gathered enough shadows to itself, but there was light along the way. Ina proved a wonderful gift of life all these years. Beowulf handfasted her in all but name. Ina kept her own steading and life and, as she promised, they came together as they could and when needed, lovers for years but first and always friends. Beowulf tried to grasp the essence of life as Hondshew had known and lived it, but the attainment could not endure. The passing years schooled him to accept that. Hondshew had been one sort of man, he another. One fortunate enough to be a private man, but Beowulf cast in a different mold of fate and circumstance. He was king; while Ina's place in his life was accepted and approved by most Geats, royal marriage like royal policy touched all even now, though the likelihood of such alliance receded with time and his advancing age, for which he was secretly grateful. Swedish alliance was out of the question now, and the other great houses of the north were thinned to near extinction from war and the migrations to Britain. Beowulf no longer believed that anything he did would change events for the better anymore than Shild Scefing could, born of the gods but dying a tired old man with the scars and smell of the world on him.

No, it was enough for this serene, sunlit moment to stand on the cliff and be glad for the few treasures accrued to his life: Ina to love, a friend like Hondshew remembered, Minna to raise, later the coming of Father Justin, a fast but most unlikely friend.

And as well for nothing more than this day's sun warm on his face. The countryside drowsed through midsummer, the most disruptive occurrence that morning the report of young Wiglaf that a slave had run away from the steading of his father, Thane Wexstan. Beowulf spread the news to his chief men. Wexstan was a kinsman, however distant and no closer in love through the years, and some effort should be made to recover his property. Wexstan was always too free with the whip. The slave most likely bolted after one flogging too many.

Beowulf gazed a long time out to sea, then went to mount again but found he simply didn't want to make the effort, reasoning to the ancient horse, "It is a good day to walk."

He took the reins, ambling along the cliff top toward Father Justin's cell. The wind blew gently from the sea, mild as the day itself. Beowulf walked more heavily now. Time was, he recalled with the last shards of vanity, when he moved like a man half his weight. Now his feet thudded on the earth, the knees bent with protest, while too many wounds rankled in wet spring.

"My love," Ina assured him caressingly when he mentioned age, "old is what others get, not you. Not us."

"I must be," he fretted. "Everyone makes a point of telling me how *well* I look."

In the main, Beowulf had discovered that the fact and the face of age were not physical things, not his whitened beard or the crow's-feet around Ina's clear eyes or the wrinkling and mottling of skin. These Beowulf hardly noticed, so gradual was their onset. He couldn't name the month or day when age battened on him like an unwelcome guest, only became aware that he spent more time remembering than looking forward and with more regret than hope.

Come, I said enough of that.

Far more comforting on such a day to wile the afternoon with

Father Justin, whose mentor had been Eligius himself, and who had come to Helsingborg soon after Beowulf reluctantly assumed the crown. Ascetically thin in his black robe, sandaled feet punished with cold he would not acknowledge, Justin must have looked much like the Paul he quoted so often in those fervent early days, planting himself before the Geatish king, the letter in his hand.

My older thanes made warding signs against his magic, and Justin, so young he was then, gave me condescending courtesy as the heathen king of a benighted land, reading Eligius' letter to me.

> **My dear friend, you once asked a small kindness of me when one was sorely needed. I have since heard how you turned each fear into an opportunity for courage, so that no head in the north stands higher or more illustrious than your own. For myself, God has been so liberal with his gift of earthly years that now, at the close, I would be an ungrateful servant to complain of stinting. I ask that you receive Father Justin, who wishes a mission among your people. Beside his holy orders, he is skilled as a physician. I dreamed once of such a mission among you myself, but lacked the courage to dare. You see? We all have some fear. I say farewell, trusting your wisdom, generosity, and kingly spirit. ELIGIUS.**

Beowulf gave Justin his mission for Eligius' sake, but made no promises regarding conversion, either for himself or his people. He understood little of the new religion or its priests, though Eligius' pupil appeared of a very different cut from his teacher. Some of it was Justin's brash youth at the beginning. Among Geats and Danes, priests sacrificed and augured for the specific benefit of their tribe, which notion was alien to Justin, whose avowed purpose was to be alone with God.

"And to teach," he added—rather grandly, Beowulf thought at the time. Eligius had managed that benevolence without shutting out or exasperating the humanity around him.

Beowulf asked with sly humor, "Isn't your word *preach*?"

"They are same, my lord."

"I would have thought otherwise—but as you will."

Geat thanes grumbled at the contradiction of the young man who possessed obvious courage and independence, but what kind of shaman refused to cast runes for the future? Justin pronounced such a graver sin than treachery to a sworn lord. Nor would he accept the comfortable house and servant Beowulf offered but, with his first few volunteers, hauled the stones up from the beach, built a simple beehive cell and tiny chapel, laid out a garden and chicken coop, and lived season in and out atop his windswept cliff, spurning all comforts beyond bare necessity.

"They turn the mind from God," he declared loftily to Beowulf. Utterly ridiculous to any northerner whose life was so encumbered with cold and hardship that any ease was relished. To a Geat, bathing in icy water when warm was available demonstrated more perversity than virtue. In his first year, Justin washed and tonsured himself in cold water and went red-eyed with colds and chilblained much of the time.

With maturity and passing years, Justin's faith shed its ostentation. He came to accept warm clothes and boots and, with labor supplied by Beowulf's people, built a wicker-and-daub infirmary. He mellowed considerably, but if Eligius had been God's genial servant, Justin was more his warrior, one with a genuine facility for healing. King and priest might never understand the why of each other, but there grew between them a mutual respect and friendship.

The years had not much thickened Justin's hard-working frame and shot little gray through the coarse black hair which he now let grow through half the year. He had a direct, intelligent glance—less of a glare now than in former times—a strong acquiline nose and firm mouth. Imposing features perhaps for a bishop of civilized Gaul, but after two decades among the Geats, Justin looked less godly than plain unbreakable. With few converts, he felt that his religious mission was something of a failure. Geats came to the infirmary, but few to his chapel.

"It is discouraging," he admitted recently to Beowulf as they shared a boiled chicken and mead in his cell. "Only a few faithful and none among your nobles."

Beowulf refilled their cups, offering as much tact as truth. "They fear you will work magic on them."

"Oh, come."

"Many things are evil to them, especially closed-in places: your chapel, that ancient tower below this cliff."

Justin had always been curious about the stone pile. "No doorway, no opening of any kind."

"It is very old," Beowulf said. Difficult to tell an outlander like Justin that he'd built his mission in a place generally shunned by Geats. When he chose the site, Beowulf had tried to dissuade him, citing the constant exposure to sea wind and sure ruin to his garden from salt air.

The dry stone tower was perhaps forty feet high, bare and solitary on a narrow shelf midway between the beach and the cliff top. A long-disused footpath too steep for the most surefooted mule led from the tower to the beach, leveling out by the mouth of a tidal cave of rock and clay age-hollowed by the ocean. Its dark interior galleries were treacherous, fisherfolk said. The sea had dug its fingers deep into the cliff, carving random passageways that led nowhere except to the losing of one's way. Many had, never to be seen again and some folk said they had wandered into the very underworld of Loki's daughter, the goddess Hel.

The real story—as much as was remembered—was never recited by scops, considered fit only for the dark whisperings of peasants. Justin would call it mad in any case and so it was, all of that.

Staring down at the beach now, Beowulf caught sight of the small figure running along the water's edge. The man faltered and fell to his knees, head hanging; then with a fearful glance behind, he struggled up and staggered into the cave. Beowulf's eyes were not so keen as formerly, but he thought he saw a broad leather slave collar about the runner's neck.

Almost certainly Wexstan's runaway, a tawny-haired Wylfing named Yan who occasionally accompanied his master or young Wiglaf to the royal steading. Beowulf supposed he should report the fact, but he felt in no mood to go rooting after the fool now, who would have trouble enough in the cave with the tide coming in. Beside, Justin was hailing from the doorway of his infirmary.

Yan could be left to fate for the time. Beowulf returned Justin's hail and led his horse forward. The priest leaned his broom against the infirmary wall as the king approached.

"Welcome, my good lord! Only one poor soul sick today, so I was just sweeping out."

"Who is ill?"

"Just old Ashe, the crab fisher who lives down the beach. Stomach trouble he says. Old glutton eats too much and too fast and never chews anything properly. No need to lecture, the bellyache's doing that. Just needs a strong purgative. Come, take some tea with me?"

The sun was past meridian now, the day so lovely that they drank their herb tea sitting at the cliff's edge, watching the fishing boats bobbing far out and the tiny men on their decks moving back and forth.

Justin inquired politely, "And what of moment is happening today?"

"Nothing, I'm happy to say." Beowulf set his cup aside and lolled back on one elbow. "Slave gone from one of the steadings. I spied him down on the beach just now. If he comes here, tell him he's been seen and must return to his master at once. Tell him *I* said so."

"Yes, certainly." Justin sipped his tea. They lapsed into contented silence and let the afternoon drowse away. Justin's goat grazed on its tether. When Justin scattered corn for his chickens, they clucked and pecked furiously, the most active creatures within somnolent miles, or so it seemed to Beowulf luxuriating in the warmth of the sun on his bones.

They spoke a little of the new kingdom established by Ida in the northeast of Britain and how many war bands had left Denmark to join him. There was a swell of enthusiasm among Beowulf's younger men to try a raid or even to establish him there, but he declined as he had years before.

"Then I had no interest, now I'm too old. That's a young man's adventure, Justin. Such need a young king and perhaps new ways. Your White Christ . . ." Beowulf trailed off into silence.

Justin prompted him with gentle humor. "You were saying, my lord? Is even Beowulf harking to the Word at last?"

The old king grimaced good-naturedly. "No-o. Just shaping the thought to see how it suited. Fanciful, but I believe there have always been two worlds, each real as the other. The solid earth seen and felt"—he rapped it with the flat of one scarred hand—"and what we see with our hearts. And I think the Midgard I know began to fade when your Jesus spread north."

Justin's answer was much less militant than it would have been in youth. "Only His truth, my friend."

Beowulf smiled indulgently, remembering Sigyn and the mutability of perceived truth. "No, only a difference in how men regard it—wait!"

"What?"

"Someone shouted. Cried out."

They waited. Again the cry, no healthy shout but an outburst of raw human fear.

They peered from the cliff to see the slave Yan flounder out through the tidal water at the cave mouth, turn wildly this way and that as if unsure of safety anywhere, then flee down the narrow path toward the more accessible way to the cliff top.

Beowulf whistled his horse to him and gathered the reins. "He's coming up."

Father Justin tucked the robe up into his belt for striding room. "He sounds terrified. Let's go."

The footpath to the cliff top was only a hundred or so yards to the south. Justin running beside him, Beowulf trotted the horse toward that point where it emerged from the beach. Yan appeared before they arrived, panting, his abject terror apparent. At sight of the king, he started to run away. Beowulf's command froze him.

"Yan!"

They approached the fearful little man. Like most slaves in the north, Yan was nondescript and ageless, anywhere between twenty-five and forty, in rough gray homespun jacket, frayed trousers, and ruined shoes, all of him sopping wet with seawater. In one hand the bedraggled fugitive clutched a tarnished but rich-looking goblet.

"My lord—" Yan squeaked out that much only before going mute.

Beowulf dismounted and relieved him of the cup. "I know who you are and where from, so don't waste time lying. Did you steal this from your master?"

"No, no. I swear, lord. I—it—" Yan gestured vaguely.

"Where did you get it? Speak up!"

"There . . . in there." Yan fell to his knees. "We must *go*, my lord. Quick. All of us."

Beowulf passed the goblet to Justin and hauled Yan to his feet. Holding the thin shoulders, he felt the violent shaking that ran like palsy through the whole body. Fear of more than Wexstan, that was sure. "Easy, Yan. What's happened?"

"There is no time. We must *go*. The gods help us all. I didn't mean anything, just that I was afraid and had to hide. I didn't steal from the thane."

"No, he didn't." Justin turned the goblet in his hands. "This hasn't been used for ages. See the dust and tarnish? Very ancient. British work, I'd say from the way the bronze is decorated."

The goblet, with its intricate bas-relief designs, was set about the rim with several semiprecious stones and one unmistakable ruby worth a fortune by itself.

"Where did you find it?" Beowulf demanded.

Yan pointed again, more specifically this time. "Down there."

"In the cave?"

"I got lost, lord. No light and the tide washing in around me, all the tunnels leading down."

And all flooding rapidly. Yan had trapped himself where not even his bones would be found. Then a great surge of tide washed around him, sweeping him down, down until he was falling through utter darkness; only a few feet, but his heart nearly stopped. He felt upward and found he could stand. His groping hands discovered the rough face of a boulder. More accustomed to the dark now, he could see the faintest hints of light over its top. Terrified of drowning, he felt over the rock and discovered a narrow crawl space beyond it, a tight squeeze even for a small man, but there was no other way to go save forward. The light grew stronger as he bellied toward it. The passage widened until Yan could crawl on his knees, and then abruptly, he was in a vast chamber lit from several chinks through which light filtered from what must be the cliff face, because he could hear the sea close.

"Not a natural cave, my lord; mostly, it'd been dug out and shored with timbers. Just under where the old tower stands, must be. But what I *saw*! Treasure, my lord! Chests and loose piles of it all about. Old swords and mail, cups like this one, more than a man could begin to count. I've seen Roman coin; much of it was that, no mistake."

The cup was what started his trouble. Picking it up from a pile, he dislodged some other trinkets that rolled down and rattled noisily about.

"That's when it came."

From the deep shadows beyond the uncountable hoard, Yan heard a deep hissing, and then a great gout of blue flame shot upward. A scaled claw rose into the light and came down atop a pile of coins, illuminated by the fire of its own breath.

"On my life, sir," Yan swore with pathetic dignity. "It was a—a great snake. No, bigger. Much bigger and it had *wings.*"

"A dragon."

Something in Beowulf's tone arrested Justin. He started to speak but checked himself. The slave was lying to gain sympathy; such things simply did not exist.

The rest of Yan's tale was quickly told. No fear-turned to stone for him. He had more sense than that and hopped it out of there quick and was crawling around the big rock before he realized the cup was still in his hand. He descended as far as he could, then had to wait what seemed hours until the tide receded, groping his blind way toward what he hoped was the main cave, floundering at last out onto the beach, all the while sure that damned thing was coming after him.

His story blurted and trembled out, Yan huddled before his thane's own master. Dark wonders aside, he was a runaway caught and bound for another flogging sure.

Beowulf looked down at the miserable little man, who kept peering fearfully over the cliff toward the cave as if he expected the fiery creature to fly out any moment in vengeance, and equally frightened of the massive king before him.

Beowulf put the goblet in Yan's hand. "Mark me and obey, little Wylfing. You will return to Thane Wexstan and tell him all. Present him this cup as proof and beg his mercy. And give him this." The king slipped a ring from his own finger onto Yan's. "By this token say it is my wish that he spare you this time."

In gratitude and relief, Yan would have groveled to kiss the king's feet if Beowulf had not prevented him impatiently. "Go now. Directly, I say, to be home before nightfall. Bolt again and I care not if your master drowns you in a bog as you deserve."

No fear of that. In the late-slanting sunlight, Yan scurried away on a true course for Helsingborg and the steading of Wexstan.

Beowulf watched after him, then turned to gaze long and thoughtfully at the old tower. "Yes, there would be."

"Sir?"

"A way from the cave to the tower. No one ever found it, but there would have to be some way in."

Justin joined him at the cliff brink. "Surely, you don't credit this fellow's tale."

Beowulf turned to his friend, grave and still. "Believe what he says, Justin. And fear what that wretch may have begun."

Justin tried not to laugh; in the face of the king's gravity, that would have been bad manners. "My faith is Roman, but Greeks have been at my common sense, sir. It is impossible."

"Why? Your faith rests on certain miracles, while I have seen others much darker. Grant one, why not the other?"

That Greek strain in Justin's thinking rejected the proposition like inedible food. "Because Creation was made and moves ever by Divine logic and order."

"Does it?" Beowulf's bushy gray brow elevated slightly over an ironic smile. "Come, let's go back. I will tell you something."

He glanced westward at the sinking sun. "I am as afraid as Yan."

23

"I T IS A VERY ANCIENT TALE," Beowulf began as he and Father Justin walked toward the mission, the old horse ambling behind.

Old, but not a history honorable men or poets cared to remember, most especially Beowulf, who had seen more of chaos than Justin could conceive. As for madness, the old king had his own well-tried views on the sanity of Creation. The story of the tower had been handed down mostly by peasants who remembered the older ways and the elder fertility gods like Nerta, the Earth Mother.

"My old nurse told me the tale once to frighten me when I was bad. I believe it goes back—well, I can't say exactly to when." Beowulf found it difficult to measure time and events by the Roman calendar. "There was a Caesar called . . . August something?"

"Augustus," Justin recalled promptly. "Jesus was born in his reign."

"That sounds right. Toward the end of his reign, part of a legion set sail from northern Gaul to explore the Jutish peninsula."

"Yes, I've read of that in Tacitus. The idea was to extend Roman rule farther north."

Then Justin might recall the fate of those three cohorts and their ships. Roman craft were never seaworthy by northern standards and drew far more water than Jutish keels.

That stretch of coastline was held by the Teutons, a small but aggressive pirate tribe under a petty king named Hama. His tough, crafty people knew their treacherous beaches to the last submerged rock. At the approach of the Roman galleys, they collected all their own keels at a certain inviting beach to make it look like a well-used anchorage and much deeper than it actually was. The Roman ships ran aground or tore their hulls open on the rocks. Very few men got ashore, and most of those were slaughtered in the shallows by the waiting Teutons. In their retreat, the Romans had to abandon several foundered galleys. Justin might imagine the elation among Hama's men when one of the wrecks was found to contain a fortune in Roman coin. No one could imagine why they would be carrying so much.

"I can," Justin reasoned. "Probably the cohorts' regular pay in silver and gold to be disbursed when the landing was secured. Three cohorts . . ."

His own grandfather had been a camp prefect in Belgica. Somewhat familiar with legion pay scales, Justin reckoned the hoard between thirty-six and forty thousand gold *aurei*. He whistled softly. "Fabulous."

Which in one day rendered the Teutons the richest single tribe in the north, but with the wealth came the sickness of greed.

"You must understand, Justin. Our kings must be generous, even prodigal, to their warriors, for most have nothing but through their sworn lord."

"I know," Justin returned candidly. "And I've wondered how you can trust men so mercenary at heart."

"Not at heart. The heart is the warrior's oath. He is measured by how well he keeps it. If he must be ready to lay down his life for me, I must as readily lay out my treasures for him. That is why I keep so little for myself. Hrothgar was such a king, but Hama was not. The hoard *became* his honor and that of his kin, not to be given away. They guarded it night and day, chained their souls in a gold-and-silver prison as the sickness grew. They considered the hoard a sign that Odin favored them above all other families, even other gods."

In those old days, many ancient customs of worship were still observed. Nerta the Earth Mother was believed to dwell in a wagon on an island in the middle of a sacred lake, attended by her own priests and slaves. In the spring, when the priests divined the living presence of the goddess within her sanctuary, the wagon was drawn by white oxen about the countryside with great joy and feasting among the people after Nerta blessed their sown fields. When the festival concluded, the goddess's wagon was returned to her island where, after a ritual cleansing of the cart and the image of Nerta herself, the attendant slaves were always drowned.

"Yes," Justin remembered. "Tacitus described that, too. Monstrous."

"Great power means great fear," Beowulf reasoned. "People asked much of Earth Mother year after year. Much must be given in return.

In those days, Nerta was stronger in people's hearts than Odin. Even her priests could not approach her wagon erect but had to roll over the ground toward it."

But as Odin came to the fore, warriors began to hate Nerta as much as they feared her. King Hama and his sons despised her priests and worship as weak and decadent and speculated as to what else might lay behind the heavy curtains that hid Nerta from men's sight. So, one spring, they killed the priests and plundered the wagon. They found only a crude wooden carving of a woman wrapped in a scrap of wool, but nothing of value. Hama paraded the statue mockingly through his villages. *Look! This is what you feared and groveled before. To this you made offerings. A piece of wormy wood. Nerta is dead!*

"Reckless," Beowulf reflected soberly. "Sheer insanity, Justin. You cannot destroy a belief without replacing it with something else as enduring. Hama did not. The common people rebelled. Thanes and peasants alike, horrified by the desecration and fearing Nerta's retribution, renounced their loyalty to Hama and departed to offer their services to the neighboring Cimbri. The country of the Teutons became a wasteland."

Hama and his family were now in mortal danger: rich and defenseless. Only a matter of short time before both facts added up to clear advantage in the eyes of their enemies. They fitted out two good keels and sailed north, but their infamy had preceded them. No one would grant them a place to live, even for gold. Hama had violated the very person of the Earth Mother; every misfortune of nature, every ruinous storm or bad crop was laid to their blasphemy. They became like the Judas in Justin's Bible, beyond the pale of forgiveness or redemption. At last, with their gold and the curse of all men on them, they landed among the half-wild Skani and the early, kingless Geat bands who had never heard of Teutons.

"They bought this stretch of coast and paid the local chief in gold. Not much, I suppose, but then it wouldn't have to be."

The legend went that Hama built the tower to protect his hoard. Years passed, Hama died, and his sons and grandsons grew old, never venturing far from their gold except to raid for more. They took wives, but their women and female children did poorly. Nerta, unforgiving of the rape of her rites, had doomed Hama's family to slow extinction. One by one, they perished guarding the treasure that had become a weight of shackles about them like the cords used to bind and drown the foredoomed slaves of Nerta.

At last, only one old man remained of Hama's accursed line, feeble and sick but unable to part from that which most men had forgotten if they ever credited its existence at all. A doddering, snuffling, half-crazed old hermit in a ruin of a house above an ancient tower, throwing stones and cracked-voice threats at anyone who came too near. Shuffling amid piles of time-tarnished treasure, ancient helms, and rusted mail, muttering to himself of mostly forgotten days in a land he never saw—who carried this shield or struck with that sword when the Romans came. . . .

"Long ago and lost and gone." Beowulf gazed off toward the low evening sun over the water. "Even Rome has gone. Everything passes, Father Justin."

Justin had surrendered to the cadence of Beowulf's language in the melancholy tale, for in it, he seemed to hear the tread of ages. "Was that all?"

"Most of it."

"No forgiveness, no redemption?"

"Why should there be?"

"It is so dark. So futile and hopeless."

The old king smiled at his friend. "You are judging the whole house from the outside. Listen to our scops. It is the stand taken against the dark and in defiance of it that gives us meaning."

"And that last old man—any of them?—they never came to realize the crippling sin of avarice on their souls?"

Beowulf looked at him curiously but refrained from comment. Such "modern" men would never understand. Not the getting, not the stealing, if Justin wanted to call it that. Beowulf's own men had plundered much treasure from one tribe or another, and dutifully, he shared it out, gave it away. Ring-giver. Treasure-giver. The very root meaning of *lord* in the Geatish tongue meant one who provided. The denial of this was the sin that cursed Hama's brood.

"What happened when the last man died?"

"If he died. If one calls it death. No one found his body. Just gone."

"We are all mortal, my lord."

"As you say, in the flesh. But afterward, do not your souls take on their true form?"

"True, but I meant the tower; what of that?" Justin pressed. "Surely, someone investigated after all those stories."

"Of course. In the time of my great-grandfather King Swerting. They found nothing."

Not so much as a single coin or ingot, only a bare earthen floor and no entrance but that they made themselves in the tower stones. Some speculated on the tidal cave but were not as lucky or perhaps unlucky as Yan.

Justin struggled with the illogic. "But why? Why build a tower if not to use it?"

"Perhaps they intended that at first and then distrusted it. Why guard a hoard for centuries that may not be spent?" Beowulf countered. "Devious and more devious. The hoard became its own reason, and as it had once become their honor, unnatural in itself, the descendants of Hama became their own avarice."

Justin was not so easily satisfied. "You said *if* he died. What did you mean?"

Beowulf stared down at the cliff face below the tower, intently, as if his attention had been caught by some object or movement. "Didn't your Lucifer become the image of his own evil?"

Justin needed a moment to sum the implications. "You mean to tell me—"

"They say he's still here."

Justin passed a polite hand over his smile. "I hope my lord will pardon my skepticism?"

Beowulf's attention did not waver from the cliff face. "If you'll excuse mine regarding resurrection."

"That is altogether different."

"Is it, Justin? Why may not one more point of belief rest on a point of fact? Many lands and peoples tell of dragons. Among my Geats, they are believed to be in flesh what the dark spirit was in life. What the last of the Teutons would not share in one life, he cannot escape in this."

The sun sat on the western horizon, turning the gray-green water the color of forge-heated iron. At this time of year the sun never really set, but Justin was reminded of duty.

"If Ashe's bellyache has subsided, he'll want to get home. I must make up a purgative."

He started away toward the infirmary but Beowulf's sharp summons brought him back. "Quick. Come here."

Beowulf pointed down the beach toward the tower where Justin could see nothing unusual.

"There, just below. The face of the cliff."

For a moment as Justin stared, the spot indicated was no more than rough rock and dirt bathed in the sun's slanting fire. Then his stomach crawled before mind gave it a reason. A burst of dislodged rock and earth flew outward, scattering down the cliff face. Then more, faster, larger gouts of clay and dirt as something within battered and tore a widening hole as if hatching from some immense egg. The opening grew wider; other movement appeared behind the flying clods. With a stream of flaming breath, a flat, elongated head appeared, followed by leathery wings folded tight as the creature writhed free, teetered, and then plummeted down the cliff face.

Justin caught his breath involuntarily as the dragon fell heavily toward sure death on the rocks below, but with a sinuous grace the great wings opened and caught the wind. The drop leveled out into a long glide over the surf as the dragon's wings sought and found the updraft that lifted its long body. Justin might doubt a fantastic tale but not clear sight. By the side of the tall, impassive king, he saw the creature climb, incredulity for a moment suffusing fear. That anything so large could fly at all was wonder, but so *easily*, the wings sensitive fingers feeling for the wind's breast in the manner of a soaring raptor.

"Justin, run! To the cell!"

Beowulf pushed the priest ahead of him toward the small stone house as the dragon turned and spied them, fell off before the wind, and came down at the two men like a missile. Beowulf thrust Justin through the doorway ahead of him. They cleared the entrance just in time. A broad shadow flashed over them and they heard the roar of flame lick about the entrance arch, and the rush of great wings beating, passing over.

The two men stared at each other, shaken priest and winded old king.

Justin whispered in passionate gratitude, "The Lord is with us."

Beowulf nodded, trying to regain his breath. Violent exertion cost him much more now than formerly. "And the fact that stone won't burn."

"Burn?" Justin's eyes lifted anxiously. He heard another gushing roar of flame and furious crackling. "Listen. The infirmary. Ashe!"

Before Beowulf could stop him, Justin dove out the door to see his wooden infirmary with its dry thatched roof a broad swatch of flame that engulfed what had been the entrance. Beowulf emerged from the cell to see the priest dive through the fire into the burning building and his own panicked horse galloping away across the down. He swiveled his head about, searching the sky as the great shadow passed over him again. Beowulf had one heart-stopping glimpse of an ugly, flat head, glittering eyes, and extended claws before launching himself headfirst through the flaming doorway to land heavily in the smoke-filled interior. He labored up onto his knees, gasping and shaken.

"Justin!"

"Here. We have to get him out."

Another blast of flame seared the frail tinderbox structure. About them, all four walls and roof were an inferno, fiery thatch dropping from above. The fat fisherman Ashe huddled on his knees, frozen with fear, eyes starting out of his head. Justin struggled with the bulk of him.

"Help me! I can't budge the stupid—"

Sharp pain seared the back of Beowulf's neck. The shock broke from him in a bellow, paralyzed Ashe a target on which to spend it. He lunged at the peasant with a growl, hauled the man to his feet, and dragged him protesting toward the door.

"No—no, it's burning!"

"That's the notion." Aged but still powerful muscles lifted Ashe by his collar and rump and hurled him clear of the burning doorway. Beowulf plunged out, Justin close behind. The burn on Beowulf's neck stung fiercely and his hair was on fire. He slapped at it viciously. Justin was already dragging Ashe toward the stone house. Beowulf followed, alert for the dragon, found it climbing away into the evening sky northward toward Helsingborg.

He stumbled into the cell and collapsed on the hard-packed earthen floor. The burns on his neck rankled under the pungent smell of singed hair, and every muscle in his body quivered with violent strain. Ashe squatted on a stool, shuddering uncontrollably and muttering some mindless prayer-charm. Justin stood over him protectively. The priest's hands trembled on the man's shoulders.

"Well, Father Justin. What would your Greeks say about this?"

Beyond the stone walls that saved their lives, Justin heard the infirmary roof collapse in a crackling roar. He could only shake his head.

His mouth worked soundlessly. Finally he managed: "I have seen it. But it is . . . it is hard to . . ."

"Believe? Ashe has no such problem, do you, eh? You Christ-men will never believe a world that doesn't fit your Book. Oh, I can see it coming. You'll close ranks and say that miracles and prodigies ended when Jesus came from the tomb and all others since are lies and heresy."

The wound on his neck would blister; he'd need Justin to lance, salve, and dress it if any of the infirmary supplies survived. The pain and Beowulf's ingrained sense of doom focused acidly on the priest.

"You may be the future as you say, but it will never wholly fit our kind. We know what waits in the dark. Now you see it yourself. Look at Ashe: He knows the dark is always with us. Why have you never learned that?"

The terrified peasant huddled on his stool between priest and king, understanding none of what they said, only his own mortal fear.

24

THE DRAGON'S BROAD LEFT WING DIPPED; the right lifted and the long shape swooped homeward in a gliding turn toward its lair. In its wake, the long midsummer gloaming flared day-bright with the glare from a dozen fires, the royal dwelling at Helsingborg ablaze and any thane's steading or farm croft within half a day's travel staining the summer sky with smoke. In only a few hours, the dragon's fury had scorched a huge swath through the fear-stunned heart of Beowulf's people.

None were more afraid than the dragon itself, fear that kindled the primal rage to strike out in the single purpose of its malignant existence: to guard and keep.

Vast, unmeasured gulfs of time had passed since the creature's brain could generate much more than pure instinct. When the enemy disturbed its slumber, the dragon knew only fear that something precious was gone. The loss of one small part equaled the loss of all. It had forgotten the tunnel through which the enemy entered, or that its own form was too huge to pursue the fleeing thief. The great wings flexed and beat with the dragon's fear, thrusting it upward only to crash futilely against the cave roof. Down it tumbled, sprawling amid piles of jewel and coin in a jingling wash of wealth. Contact with the cold object of its existence brought some reassurance. The dragon paused, already unable to remember *what* had invaded its domain, only that something was gone and the whole diminished. Betrayed.

The glistening, scaly head rested on a pile of rusted mail. The eyes lit with murder and roved about, gradually fixing on the light filtering through a small chink in one wall.

There.

The evil head lifted; a drift of yellow smoke escaped the reptilian jaws.

Out.

The dragon surged with a roar upward toward the light, wings beating lustily as the claws tore at the wall, widening the hole until its long body could squeeze through to freedom and retribution.

Returning now, the wings kept the body hovering as it purchased a hold and slithered within to settle once more atop the piled hoard. The eyes closed. The dragon sank once more into its centuried torpor while the eternal fire, fed by hate and fear, glowed and replenished in its belly.

The dragon dreamed.

Red dreams that flickered within the small brain like reflections of flame washing over the face of a smooth wall, faint and without warmth.

As always, dimly and with no comprehension, it dreamed *he.*

He somehow had no uplifting wings or claws but tottered feebly over the ground on two slow stick legs. Images of others like himself came and went: a purposeful line of these little creatures, small and weak as himself, filing into a dark opening. . . .

More darkness; then crawling by wavering light through a twisting, turning hole in the earth that ended here in its cave.

Alone then.

Old.

In the dream already fading, he fell forward onto the great heap of treasure, spreading his absurd arms to hold it once more in a last embrace.

Dying.

Ending.

Then the long rebirth and transformation as, year by year, atom replaced atom in the manner of petrifying minerals supplanting tissue. The undead body grew and changed. Shoulder blades fanned, flattened, and spread, the skull warped and lengthened, the belly's volatile elements combined in undying fire.

When the dream dimmed in the rudimentary brain, the dragon remembered nothing. Pictures came, ephemeral as mist, and dissolved, meaningless. The great body shifted sometimes in fitful sleep, the wings flexed and settled, but the brain, the few vestigial crumbs of sentience within the elongated skull, sent its single, reflexive command to the rest as ever.

Guard. Keep.

From Beowulf to his meanest crofter, most of the coastal Geats were virtually homeless. The smoke spread for miles, reeking of dead

animals and funeral pyres. Of the royal steading, only two bowers remained habitable around the gutted hall. As soon as he could restore
some order to his terrified folk, Beowulf called for his fastest horse and
galloped north through the forest to find Ina. One small mercy: Minna
had married away among the Brondings; Ina need not fear for her daughter and grandchildren if the beast could be checked now.

Meager hope that she and the steading would be spared, and that
dashed as he dropped from the saddle at the gate. The barn was a blackened ruin, the hall roof gone, outbuildings still smoking—but he in-
haled none of that other sickly sweet smell that covered most of
Helsingborg now.

"Beowulf?"

She appeared around the corner of the hall with an aged manser-
vant, both carrying buckets of water to soak down the stubborn last of
smoldering fires. Beowulf sagged in relief, hurrying to her.

"Ina! Thank—is anyone dead?"

"Not here." She pushed back the loosened wisps of white hair with
a smoke-grimed hand. "Some at the crofts; I don't know how many."

They clung to each other in gratitude, saying very little, glad only
to be spared and together.

"I wish I could stay now, sweeting, but I can't. There's too much
to do. Anything you need, send to my steward. My northern holdings
weren't harmed. And bring your people to the council in Helsingborg
tomorrow morning early."

"Yes. At least none of this touched Minna. Not yet," Ina added
gravely. She touched his cheek. "You need sleep. You look terrible.
What will you do?"

"Do?" He sagged with his fatigue, smiling ruefully at her. "It's
good not to have to be strong in front of you at least. I don't know, Ina.
The beast must be stopped, that's all. Tomorrow, I may have an answer,
but none now."

Ina searched his eyes, knowing him so well by now. "Some will
say it anyway: It is Grendel all over again, and for that they will have
only one answer."

Beowulf had tried not to think of that at all, but true enough. As
if it were carved in stone, woven by the Fates into a pattern shaped
before they were born. "Tomorrow, my love. At Helsingborg."

———

When the doleful task of burning the dead was accomplished, Beowulf called his council in the courtyard of the ravaged royal steading. On the advice of his priests and the private urging of Father Justin, he included the common folk, who had suffered equal loss and stood now in as imminent a peril should the dragon return.

By early morning the people were trudging toward Helsingborg through the forests and over the down. They filed through the open gates to huddle in hushed, dispirited groups behind their lords. Father Justin's small knot of converts gathered about him for comfort which he labored to give despite the personal shock that had shaken his cosmos to the core. Some of his people now wore curious old talismans about their necks.

Ina rode in at midmorning at the head of a little train of servants and crofters. She greeted Beowulf and then stood to one side with her people. Beowulf hailed each thane as he arrived with the principal members of his family and following. By tradition, the thanes assembled in mail and carried shield and spear. Normally, they took much longer to gather, but before the sun poised high at noon, all were present. Every one of them had lost kin or friends, home or livestock to the dragon's wrath. Graver than famine, plague, or invasion, the choice before them was quick remedy or extinction.

Prominent among the leading thanes was sour, sharp-tongued Wexstan in old-fashioned scale armor, the ancestral sword on his hip. At his side stood his son Wiglaf, already marked to succeed on Beowulf's passing, which no doubt Wexstan considered only belated justice. Modeling his conduct on the image and exploits of the king, Wiglaf at twenty already enjoyed a reputation for reckless courage if little prudence. Beowulf hoped one quality would grow to balance the other in time, as it had been flowering in Herdred before his premature death. A brave king was a treasure to his tribe, a brave fool only a liability.

Wexstan had also fetched along Yan, in chains to emphasize his shame. The diminuitive slave dared not stir from his master's side, well aware he avoided the lash only through Beowulf's intercession. He reminded the king now of a dog thoroughly cowed to heel and obedience.

Present as well were Gorm, Ulf, and Canute, honored companions from the long-ago venture against Grendel, mature men now with holdings and families of their own. They had gone to Heorot fire eaters; they came back something else and later passed through more than enough flame fighting the Swedes. These late years their loyalty burned with a steady glow. Canute leaned heavily on the ash shaft of his spear. Weakened by sickness throughout his life, he had compensated by acquiring a shrewd knowledge of statecraft and men.

By custom at such meets, the chief priest Arn called the council to order by crying for silence, but only tense murmurs broke the stillness now as Beowulf stepped out to speak.

"We won't waste time crying out that something must be done. The question is what and how."

Wiglaf bounded forward so quickly that his mail and war gear rattled. "A venture, my lord! A band of volunteers to find the beast and destroy it."

"Good son!" Wexstan shouted for the benefit of other thanes, letting them perhaps regret they had not sons to equal his. "I would expect no less from you."

"There will be no lack of volunteers," Wiglaf asserted in a rush of pride. "Our homes were burned but not our hearts."

As his words died away, a quieter voice supplanted them. Canute stepped forward. "Lord Beowulf, my people have asked me to speak for them. They ask what use of the best and bravest against the anger of the gods? They believe something more must be done."

Wiglaf glared at the older warrior. "What use? Your people despair easily, sir. If the Fates send such evils, Geats breed heroes as remedy."

"So it is and we can be justly proud," Gorm agreed. "For twelve years Grendel held sway in Heorot, but in one night Beowulf slew him barehanded."

"And his demon mother the next," Ulf reminded them all. "None but Geats could do it."

"That is not my point," Canute tried to continue, but Wiglaf did not surrender the focus of attention so willingly.

"The odds are heavy but not impossible. And what if they were? Who would be sung by our scops tomorrow and ever after? Who will join me?"

"Wait." Beowulf signaled for silence. There were more considerations to weigh before action. Half a dozen hands were high in the air in response to Wiglaf's call: too-ready boys, most of them under twenty and untried, younger sons painfully eager for repute at his board. "The question is, who will follow me? *I* will lead, Wiglaf."

The thanes to a man cheered him while Father Justin bit back his feelings. *No, you're too old. Madness, all of this, and you compound it with more.*

Now Canute spoke again, carefully as always. "I say this. The dragon is only one enemy, our own fear another, and hesitation a third. To whatever solution we must add dispatch and above all, secrecy. The dragon may come again, but the Swedes for sure when they hear of our plight."

"*If* they hear. They shall not." Beowulf's tone brooked no further question. Every thane would therefore turn strangers back at his boundaries on pain of death. No boats would fish the banks farther north than Goteborg.

That presented more problems. The greater part of their crop was ruined, forest land still smoldered, boar, deer, and small game fled for miles around. The Geats must depend on fishing for the time, and the best banks lay to the north.

"Then avoid other boats," Beowulf warned. "Who allows one word of this beyond his boat's prow, I'll have his head."

One of Arn's subordinate priests broached the subject of proper sacrifice, but Wexstan cut him off. Never religious, he grumbled that sacrifice was sheer waste now when all would be on short rations.

Arn countered waspishly, "Proper sacrifice is never folly. One might question your common sense, Thane Wexstan."

"Then I'll put a common-sense question," Wexstan shot back. "Why didn't our chief priest foresee the dragon? How did *that* escape his notice?"

"I did foretell! At Yule feast, you will recall."

"Oh, surely. 'An evil close at hand that might become grave danger.' Trust Arn ever for the vital clue. When did we Geats not live with danger at our elbow and more often at our throat? Sacrifice . . ." Wexstan bestowed on the notion exactly what he thought of it. "Shit. Leave it to old women."

Bald, bent old Arn frowned at Wexstan, whose motives he distrusted. The father would likely give his own ambitions free rein once the immature son was crowned. Arn himself was a Dane, emigrated from Sjaelland on the death of Hrethric and Hrothmund and the resultant dynastic turmoil among the Scyldings. These Geats did not keep sacred white horses but read portents in rune, wands, and through the organs of sacrificial animals. Since the dragon fell on his folk, Arn had sought the gods' intent by every skill at his command and would try again, though in seeking one answer, another loomed clear as the giant figure of Beowulf before him—knowledge that Arn had not the heart to declare now among burdened, wounded folk nor even privately to their great king. He would far rather be thought incompetent. These evils, like the dragon, would uncoil soon enough.

"Thane Wexstan," he said evenly. "What the wise man cannot speak for truth, he leaves silent."

Once more, Canute raised his hand. "I had not finished, my lords. I ask you to hear me out."

As the lean thane stepped forward, Justin's attention was distracted by whisperings among the nearby peasants. He heard the word *sacrifice* and then a name. Their faces were blank with animal fear and Justin felt a danger in them. The name rustled darkly from group to group like a vengeful ghost.

Canute said, "My own crofters are already sacrificing to Nerta by the forest pools."

"Nerta?" Ulf repeated the name like something poisonous on his tongue.

"Yes, friend. They believe Earth Mother is angry because Geats have so long neglected her rites for those of Odin. They fear animal offerings will not satisfy her."

"Fear what?" Beowulf moved forward to confront his old companion. "That men themselves must go into the fire? Who says this, Canute? Who?"

"It is true," Arn confirmed reluctantly. "Not all the fires yesterday were caused by the dragon. Some folk are sacrificing secretly. I have warned them that they risk the just wrath of our own gods, but they are like dogs who grovel on their bellies at the sound of thunder."

"Aye, dogs indeed." Beowulf's disgust erupted into movement; he strode back and forth before his people with something of his old animal vigor. "Are we barbarians to bring back the old, savage ways out of fear? Restore rites of terror and those rutting orgies in the plowed fields? Drown a new batch of slaves every year?"

"Expensive as they are," Ulf considered.

Wexstan glowered at Yan. "Some are more trouble than they're worth. Here." He shoved the slave so hard that Yan sprawled at Beowulf's feet. "Give that to the bitch goddess if you must. Him we can spare."

An idle gesture of contempt, but Beowulf saw the vicious impulse surge physically through his peasants; a forward straining that might at a word bring them down on Yan. A few actually started forward toward the prostrate slave. Beowulf whipped his sword from the scabbard and leveled it at the crowd.

"Stay!"

They hesitated, but far back in the press someone cried: "Give the slave to Nerta!"

"He brought the trouble. Let him pay."

"He'll pay who next opens his mouth for blood." Beowulf raised the sword, meaning what he said. "Be silent."

Yan cowered at the king's feet, white with terror. His life had been lowly from birth and harder since he was sold into slavery, but always dear to him, bitterly as he cursed its cruel fortunes. When Yan thought of gods at all, he knew they had frowned on his very conception.

"Don't let them, lord. It wasn't my fault. I did as you commanded. I did go home again. Don't let them kill me."

"No, Yan." Beowulf lifted the abject man to his feet. "But in running away from your lawful master, you woke the dragon. You must guide us through the cave to find it."

"No, *please*. I don't think I can remember—"

Whatever Yan didn't think was cut off as Beowulf jerked him high off the ground with one yet-powerful arm. "Think again. Wexstan, what did you pay for him?"

Wexstan was not one to forget the price of anything. "Three øre in gold."

"I'll give you two for him here and now."

Wexstan spat on the ground by way of quick decision. "It's a loss, but so is he. Two and done, and a poor bargain you make."

Beowulf set Yan down and turned him about to face the crowd. "Hear me, all! I wouldn't sacrifice a sick hen out of fear, much less a man. We are a small people beset from our beginnings. That is why we've always been more than ordinary men. We're Geats. We meet the Fates head on; so will Yan. He will guide us through the tunnel into the dragon's lair. If he lives, he is free. Wiglaf! Gather your band quickly. We meet again tomorrow. Arn will take the auspices again at sunrise. If they yet favor us, we go forth."

The people shuffled about, beginning to disperse. Ina waited while Beowulf spoke with Arn, then caught his eye. In the silent exchange of meaning grown between them over the years, he'd know she wanted to speak and guessed the matter as well. He bade farewell to Arn and drew Ina aside before the speaker's platform.

She said, "So it *is* all over again."

"So it seems."

"Does it never end? Am I to be widowed twice? This is not needed."

"Yes, it is."

"There are other men, younger men. Even your Justin will say as much. I saw his face."

"Wiglaf must go because he is to be king after me. This will set the seal on his worthiness. No man will question his right."

"What man questions yours now? Why?"

She was not to be put off, and yet Beowulf could tell her nothing Ina would understand or accept. Since the appearance of the dragon, his presentiment was not all for the people. There was a doom on him, long and mercifully delayed in the years with this woman but always there—Beowulf knew that surely now—in his dreams of the tower and the sense that something converged with him soon or late, a design in destinies that now looped and tied off. He felt an empathy with the dragon, almost a kinship.

"Do you remember when you and Itharne taught Minna to weave, how she would start one pattern and then cross it for no reason with another? And she'd look at you and smile and say, 'It's wrong, but why change again?' "

He smiled down at the woman who had been so many years a mate to him and so tender in her charge that he never felt like a meaner choice. "I think the Norns started one pattern for me and lost the scheme or changed their minds in the middle. All my life, I've found myself brought again and again to that middle ground between men and gods where Grendel and Sigyn and this beast come from. No, don't speak, love. I know this is true. They stuffed me full to bursting with what men are supposed to be and want. For myself, you know what I wanted: what Hondshew was and had, and that's a rare thing. But for you, I would never have found it. Thank you, Ina."

Beowulf took Ina's arm and turned toward the ruined hall as the raven's wing shadow glided over the ground before him. He glanced up at the dark bird.

"But for you, my love, and that's enough. Let be."

25

ALL THROUGH THAT DAY and into the night that barely darkened before dawn, the anxious Geats watched the skies, but the dragon did not come. Perhaps, as Beowulf thought, the creature had vented its rage and now reverted to instinct, afraid to leave the hoard cursed as itself.

This second day's council excluded the common people, who were too terrified to be more than hindrance, and Beowulf had asked Ina to stay away herself. Arn and his priests went at sunrise to the sacred grove to confirm the good omens for the undertaking or to determine if that propitious balance had changed since yesterday.

As the sun climbed higher, the thanes began to gather in Beowulf's courtyard before the fire-gutted hall that still reeked of burned wood and fabric. One wall had collapsed and the hall lay exposed, the fine-carved ancient throne of the Geats a charred ruin from which servants and slaves read their own cheerless portents.

The speaker's platform had been scorched by the dragon but remained intact. This was assumed by the king and his priests only in the declaration of important decisions or omens such as they now waited. Yesterday, Beowulf moved among his nobles as one of them in debate, but this was a day of commitment. He mounted the platform steps and waited formally before his thanes.

Canute arrived with his men, the burliest of them bearing a broad shield of solid iron new-forged at Beowulf's command, since no fashioning of linden and oxhide, however strong, would protect a man from the dragon's withering fire breath. The shield was passed up to the king as Father Justin trotted into the courtyard alone and hurried to the foot of the platform.

"Then it is true?" The priest eyed the curved plate of black iron. "You will try yourself against the dragon?"

"First and alone."

"Why, when you will have a dozen younger men to aid?"

"Why?" Beowulf contemplated his friend, then descended to join him. Beyond them, thanes like Ulf and Gorm glowered at Justin and muttered with displeasure not lost on their king.

"They don't want you here today, and I agree. But listen and remember, Justin—above all, live to tell other Christ-men who come north. You have at least tried to understand our ways. Others may not be so wise."

Beowulf looked bleakly at his ruined hall. "How can a king ask anyone else to lead? A king is always a sacrifice for his people, Justin, no less than your Christ. And I have been granted certain signs myself."

A swell of voices among the thanes now. Gorm had climbed to the parapet, shouting to those below: "Wiglaf is coming with his men!"

Beowulf nodded. "You must go, friend. They took it ill that you were present yesterday and will not tolerate you now. You might bring evil fortune."

Through the open gate Father Justin saw Wiglaf's company turn sharply at a distance to make a straight ceremonial approach and entrance to the council: twelve men in all, Wiglaf himself strutting stiffly in the lead, the wrought silver on his helm ablaze with sunlight.

Justin couldn't resist the wry observation. "I must say, he seems impressed with himself."

"He has been honored," Beowulf said. "The people know he is chosen to succeed me. This day confirms him before everyone as worthy. He will have power, but that is only given to repute. Repute is earned only through deeds such as he hazards today."

Admirable, Justin agreed, but unreliable politics. "What if he dies today?"

Beowulf only shrugged. "As the Fates weave, but there's little chance of that."

"But—"

"Justin." Beowulf laid a stilling hand on his friend's shoulder. "How often have you read to me from your Book: *'Be still and know that I am God'*? Grant me as much in what I know, and draw wisdom from today's outcome as it falls. Say that the farmers are right, that Earth Mother herself demands a sacrifice."

Justin's whole, vibrant life rejected that. "That cannot *be*. True, I have seen things this week to shake my own faith, but—"

"Say that she does," Beowulf insisted, gentle but sure. "Better me than Wiglaf; better the old than the young. The people will remember me. The scops will tell my story. That is enough."

"You—" The stubborn Justin could not accept what he heard. "You blaspheme against God's gift of life in yourself. It is an insane waste of that gift to throw yourself away."

There were matters Beowulf would divulge to no one but Arn, truths the high priest would doubtless confirm. Fate walked with a man all his life and inevitably marked him soon or late for forthfaring. From the moment the dragon first rose up over the shore, Beowulf had felt that fate settle on his shoulder surely as he read the omen in his hall.

"Go home, Justin."

A passionate man with a deep affection for Beowulf, Justin was moved beyond tact by the man's serene, suicidal folly. "Damn it! You *want* to die."

"No more than your Jesus. For all the burden your god laid on him, he must have had some doubts at the end. Endings are never that neat or clear. Who can say? Perhaps I'll live to share many another supper argument with you. But leave us now."

Gorm hailed again from the parapet: "The priests are coming!"

"Good-bye, Justin."

"Then Christ be at your side and God in your arm." Justin took his friend's hand. "I will pray for you."

A loud clashing of spears on shields in salute as Wiglaf and his band marched through the gate in their youth and pride to range before Beowulf. Justin crossed the gate bridge, glimpsing the three shamans as he turned homeward. There would be his own folk to bolster and comfort, and wounds to be newly dressed. He hoped there would be enough clean bandage.

When the priests arrived, Arn went alone to mount the platform by Beowulf, raising his arms in proclamation.

"We have asked of the Seven Wands and been answered. There will be no better day than this for the king's venture."

Wiglaf's dozen broke out in cheers and a clattering of spears while more sedate approval murmured among the older men. Beowulf indulged a taste of irony. Portent and politics must often be one and the same. Every lapsed hour increased potential danger from the dragon and his own people's fear, and certain peril from the Swedes.

Arn continued in a strong voice. "Three times we asked: Will the

Geats be delivered from the beast? Three times the Wands said yes."

The old priest lowered his arms and fell silent, staring straight ahead. Beowulf heard no relief or joy in the good omens and sensed Arn might have revealed more. Nevertheless, he gave the order.

"Wiglaf, we are armed and ready. Fetch the slave Yan."

One of Wiglaf's men hurried away on the errand. The volunteers, solemn with their own fated image and relishing the novel glow of heroism, broke ranks to speak with fathers and friends before setting out. Beowulf picked up the iron shield to test it on his arm: a cruel weight but one the dragon could neither shred nor burn. He spoke softly to the high priest.

"Arn, a word. Was victory all you saw?"

"Of course." The old priest slid a hooded, canny glance at Beowulf. Their eyes met—then Arn dropped his. "Odin favors you."

"That's not what I asked. Be straight, Arn. I cast the runes for myself last night. They showed only endings."

Arn looked out over the men talking spiritedly in the courtyard below. "All signs augur well."

Beowulf flared with a surge of impatience. "You *know* it has to be today as time runs against us. What else? Speak, for I've already seen much myself. Yesterday, when I determined to spend no life but my own against the dragon if possible—I stood just there below us when a shadow crossed me suddenly. Looking up, I saw a raven circle the hall and then fly inside to light on the throne. Sign of Odin or of death, as Odin is lord of death, surely I am called to him."

In Arn's calling one had to know men as well as the will of gods. He thought he knew this paragon of kings, but could not look at Beowulf just then. "You have a great heart. Should I take that from you before battle?"

"You will not. Tell me."

"The raven spoke as the Wands. Three times they were thrown, once by each of us."

At each cast the long wands outnumbered the short in strong affirmative to Arn's second question, one he had never wanted to ask. Twice a majority of the sticks touched the Wise Wand itself. "Nothing could be clearer. The Geats will be delivered, but . . ."

Beowulf took a deep breath and let it out. Curious, but he felt a lightness, a kind of relief. "You will see all is done properly afterward."

Arn nodded, not trusting himself to speak more. Beowulf struck him lightly on the shoulder in reassurance. "Wiglaf is young, but he is the last of the royal line. He will need you, Arn. Come, it's not so bad. I have talked much with Justin about life and death. These Christ-men are obsessed with both."

"That one," Arn grimaced. "Do not heed his teachings. They are not for us."

"No, but you can learn much from him and he from you in time. Between us, Arn, I have been dead so long, I'm weary of the tomb. I want to live, to be out from under this grave mound."

Arn did not understand; so his expression showed, but that hardly mattered either now.

"Don't worry. Justin has not corrupted me. His god interferes far too much with what men must do from nature and duty. I shall go to Valhalla where my father will no doubt be astonished to see me. I expect he will even complain. Ah—they're bringing Yan."

Beowulf glanced up at the sun. "We must start."

26

THE NOONDAY SUN WAS WARM. Yan sweated under the weight of the king's iron shield as he tried to keep up with Wiglaf's long-striding boys marching in Beowulf's wake. The king rode his finest horse today, decked with a silver-mounted saddle and jeweled bridle. Yan had to keep changing arms with the great shield, finally balancing it atop his head, but then the fearsome weight made his head ache. The old man was much stronger than his new-bought slave would have guessed; picked him up easily with one arm. Still, Yan wouldn't give long odds on him against that thing in the cave.

He trudged along in the wake of Wiglaf's strutting heroes, honestly unsure he could find the right tunnel again and more afraid he might, even though the king promised freedom if he lived. The *if* bothered Yan terribly. In his hard-bitten but experienced view, all masters were the same and life reduced to fundamentals. One had to survive. For a master to command or slave to obey, both must be alive. To maintain that preferable state required a certain caution which the Geats, few and unlucky to begin with, seemed to regard with insane contempt. Wiglaf there: If you got it into his head—if you could get *any*thing under that helm but hair and solid bone—that honor called him to run headlong over this cliff, there he'd go and there he'd be, squashed but honorable at the bottom.

Rutting fine king he'd make when old Beowulf went west. Oh, very shrewd, that one. Said there was no need to find the tunnel; they'd just go down a rope and in through the hole the dragon made. Yan saw the flaw in that straight away. Easy in but a hard way out, dangling from a rope with a great flying lizard flaming your arse. The king saw it too and, heroes or not, the others looked grateful when he pointed it out.

The shield's weight bore down on Yan's skull. He shifted it to his left arm again. Sad but true, these Geats were unlucky enough under Beowulf; crown Wiglaf and they'd soon be no more than a memory among other tribes. Yan passionately wanted to be quit of this place and people.

If I get out, I'll go south, sail with fishermen, and maybe meet a Wylfing boat out of home.

No, too many *ifs* as usual. Better to go north among the Swedes, likely a slave again, but that might not be bad under a reasonable master who owned enough not to notice Yan nipping off a bit here and there. A slave learned how to go on living, and that included knowing winners from losers and how the wind blew.

Their procession passed Father Justin's chapel, where the priest was conducting an outdoor mass for some half dozen of his people. New timber and thatch were stacked to one side for rebuilding his infirmary. Beowulf raised a hand in salute. His friend returned the greeting before continuing his service.

Almost there. A hundred paces farther and Beowulf dismounted, looping the reins loosely about the silver pommel. He called for Yan to come forward with the shield as he peered down at the old tower and the narrow beach where the racing tide surged into the cave.

"You went through, Yan. How long before we can enter safely?"

"And return?" Yan amended hopefully. He gauged the incoming tide, calculation chilled with a memory of pitch dark and mortal fear. The tide had almost got him then. He shaded his eyes, squinting at the sun that shone through thin, muggy overcast like a vindictive eye. "Least an hour, my lord. And a half beyond that for surety. Tide, she'll be full flood soon."

"Wiglaf! Bring your men and follow me. We'll wait below."

Behind Beowulf and the slave trailing like a dog at his heel, Wiglaf led his band down the narrow footpath that leveled out near the cave mouth. They stacked arms and the resin torches each carried. Yan gathered driftwood which he kindled with clumps of dry sea grass. Slaves always carried flint and steel, and a good thing they did, Yan grumbled to himself as he blew the spark into flame. They all brought torches but not a one with the makings, as if they expected to borrow a taper from old dragon.

The young men ranged about the fire to wait. All of them could see, high above on the cliff as the sun moved westward, the faces of fathers and friends gathered from Helsingborg to wait with them in silent honor. Beowulf caught sight of old Arn standing by Wexstan and, to one side, the anxious face of Father Justin. He questioned Yan closely about his progress through the treacherous galleries and concentrated as the apprehensive little man tried to piece out clear memory from terror.

Conscious of his father's scrutiny and restive with waiting, Wiglaf rose before his volunteers, clashing spear loudly against shield.

"I say this. Wiglaf, Wexstan's son. Our king has chosen to go alone against the dragon, but we must be ready if he calls for aid."

"We will!"

"The greatest of Geats has lavished treasure and arms on us. For himself he will seek only fame as ever."

Beowulf glanced silently at the boy, knowing the treasure he truly sought.

"When Beowulf was of our years," Wiglaf began, "he heard of Hrothgar's plight. A great king of Danes helpless in his own hall. Beowulf gathered to him a band even as ours to rid Scyldings of the beast that held Heorot."

"Hail, Beowulf!"

"Noble thanes went with him, men we honor still. Ulf, Gorm, and Canute ventured with him as we do now."

In the propriety of silence, Beowulf pretended to listen as Wiglaf retold the great adventure in detail, but cast furtive glances at the sky. He could no longer see the sun but tried to estimate the time. The tidal flow hovered between flood and the beginning of ebb.

Wiglaf would deem it meet to laud him formally. As successor, the boy's every word and action this day would be judged and perhaps, if signally valorous, sung by scops in his lifetime and far beyond. Beowulf only half listened to the glowing words, the focus of his mind narrowed on the tunnel and what Yan told him. A tight squeeze until the very end. He would go first with his shield. When he entered the dragon's lair, the others would wait in the narrow tunnel where the creature could not get at them.

There was always a chance he could emerge alive one more time. Omens were not infallible—yet Beowulf could not shake off the brooding sense of fate and closure.

I will end the beast that will end me. Remarkable how clearly one can think at such moments. Say the dragon is no more than the warped spirit of that last Teuton who took on the shape of his avarice and, as Justin would have it, passed from life to death in life. Have I gnarled and twisted any less, becoming what Edgetho and the others wanted, that figure Wiglaf exalts who has no semblance to the me of me? No matter. Now is the end of it. Once more, the Fates draw the beast and me together like equal sums, owed and owing, to cancel each other out.

Beowulf became aware of silence around him. Wiglaf had finished speaking and the others looked expectantly to their king. High above on the cliff his people waited through the murmur of the ebbing tide and the scree of gulls overhead.

The old king rose. "It is time," he said.

He drew his sword to inspect the new-set edge, then the keen-honed dagger that might find subtler mortal entry where the heavier blade could not. Wiglaf chose among his youths, detailing those three most proficient with spear to arm with those and nothing beside but shields.

"Light the torches," Beowulf ordered. He searched the young faces about him as once he did in Heorot, reading the fear they would mask and the pride that choked it back. Wiglaf's tale had put heart into them for the time. Beowulf wondered what he could say to men so young whose faith was raw courage and carved now in his own image.

"To work, then. Let this day's task write itself on your hearts, and let you read often the lesson there."

They started into the cave, Beowulf and Yan in the van, Wiglaf next, the rest wading after them through the water that lapped calf-deep about their legs. The cave stank of stale brine, dead crabs, and the resinous smoke from their torches.

The outer cave ended in four or five dark galleries. Yan hesitated, then chose the rightmost, carefully setting his torch in the clay wall to mark the way. The men filed after him, already soaked to the knees as the gallery floor slanted ominously downward.

The tunnel twisted and turned. Yan slowed, feeling out each step forward before setting his weight down—then halted so suddenly that Beowulf's shield collided with his back. Yan's voice was muffled but wary. "Here, my lord. Another torch."

Wiglaf passed his forward, oppressed by the closeness of the tunnel and the dank air. "We must be deep under the cliff."

The men waited while Yan found by light what he had known first in darkness and terror. The cave floor dropped sharply away to a stagnant tidal pool below that dully reflected the light of their torches. Wiglaf's men felt disoriented, wrenched far out of natural time and place. None could tell how long they'd been groping along, only that each fumbling step brought them closer to the dragon or being lost forever if this fool of a slave took a wrong turn.

One hand locked in Beowulf's grip, Yan lowered himself into the pool, sinking until the water reached his waist. His teeth chattered and his voice echoed in the dark recess as he called for another light. With a new torch driven into the earthen wall, the men slid one by one into the water. They could no longer hear the sea without. The stale salt air, thickened with smoke, burned their throats. Far worse, for all Wiglaf could see, the worthless Yan had led them to a dead end.

"Little pig's got us lost."

"It was here. I was washed down with the tide. It *was* here."

"Then where does it lead?"

As Yan searched about, trying to remember which way he turned in the dark after the tide swept him into this pocket, one of the men jumped back with a cry of alarm.

"Over here. I fetched up against—it feels like—"

Ringed with the remaining torches, he reached into the black water and lifted part of the grisly remnant above the surface. The skeleton might have been there for centuries. Not a shred of flesh or clothing remained. Yan tried not to look at it.

"This is what you've brought us to," Wiglaf cursed him. "I *said* we should have gone in from the cliff." He rubbed at his smoke-stung eyes. "There are more bones about, I'll hazard. They came and drowned just like we will."

"No." Beowulf hooked several fingers about the skeletal ribs, lifting it higher into the light. The large bone of the upper left leg was clearly fractured. "He could have gotten out as Yan did if he had time and better luck. Must have happened when he fell."

He examined the roof and sides of the tidal pocket, which he estimated five or six paces across, the ceiling just beyond his reach, all the surfaces too smooth to be natural. Clearly, the small original recess had been excavated to raise the ceiling and deepen the basin. A trap set by old Hama's brood where even they must allow for tide in order to pass to and from their cursed hoard.

"Lord, look." Yan floundered to one corner, the water up to his chest but the torch thrust high and forward. "See, there! I told you."

In the wavering light, Beowulf detected the subtle obtrusion of rounded rock barely distinguishable from the earth around it, and over its top the narrow opening through which filtered a faint but different light. He took the torch from Yan and held it close to the opening. The flame bent in a new, inflowing current of air.

"We'll have to dig it out, make it wider. Quickly, you with spears."

THE SPEARS TORE AT THE EARTH, widening the hole and drawing the sulfurous dragon's breath into their nostrils. When the aperture was wide enough for Beowulf to pass through with the shield, the men jammed their remaining torches into the recess walls and waited the king's word.

"I will go first," he directed. "After me—"

"Myself," Wiglaf demanded.

"Of course." Beowulf expected that as did all of them. After Wiglaf, the three spear men, then the rest, Yan to bring up the rear. Yan had no cavil there. He might yet live to win his promised freedom.

Wiglaf and one other youth cradle-locked their hands to give Beowulf a leg up while he worked his weight over the rock and into the tunnel. He turned his head to call for the shield, stomach muscles already protesting unaccustomed strain, then heard the sound: an intermittent rasping sigh as from some great, congested bellows.

Inching forward on his side, the shield's inner concavity pressed to his body, Beowulf shut his eyes against the loose dirt falling in his face. The first yards were painfully slow, tugging the shield edges free when they wedged against tunnel wall or floor. Now he could hear Wiglaf worming along behind him. A little farther on the walls broadened; Beowulf hiked himself along faster. Wiglaf cursed sibilantly behind him while the light ahead grew steadily stronger.

A few more yards. Now Beowulf could progress on his knees. Just ahead the tunnel ceiling rose high enough for him to walk bent over. Fingers to his lips, he signaled Wiglaf to silence.

"Pass the word back. No noise."

Ahead, around a last bend in the passageway, light poured over the earthen walls. Beowulf heard, much closer now, the harsh bellows-breathing of the dragon.

"I think it's asleep. That gives us the advantage of surprise. I'm going out now," he told the others as they crouched behind him. "Make sure you're covered if the beast turns on you."

Beowulf stripped off his baldric and slid the sword free. As Wiglaf held the shield, he slipped his mailed left arm through the padded grips.

"From here, Wiglaf commands you. However I fare, take your orders from him."

Such was their king's farewell, brief and fitting. Beowulf stepped quietly toward the entrance to the hoard cave.

Light streamed through the gaping wound in the cliff face torn by the dragon in pursuit of its mindless vengeance, illuminating a scene to beggar the ravings of a lunatic. Madness itself, loosed to any excess, could not have carved such a likeness. The huge chimera-serpent, no less than fifteen paces from fangs to tail, sprawled stuporous atop a pile of rusted swords and armor, talons clutching even in sleep at the scattered wealth at once its comfort and enduring curse. The slack jaws hung open, through which fugitive gusts of yellow smoke escaped the infernal belly to float down the tunnel past Beowulf toward the tidal pool. Now and again, as a man might stir in bad dreams, the black claws scrabbled fitfully among tarnished silver and dulled gold. The broad, membranous wings quivered and twitched with a life of their own, and from the less armored underbelly, even as a man might sweat, faint ghosts of steam drifted upward in the rank air.

Justin, you should see this and remember. Your logic, your order are pale mockeries here where chaos and blind evil bring your hell to earth.

The rest of Beowulf's thought was as bleak but more tolerable to his world than to Justin's, whose mind would break against it. If his Christ was come to be with men always, so would this insanity lurk eternally just beyond his light.

Beowulf raised his sword and smote it, ringing, on the shield. Iron battered iron again and again, destiny's alarm, piercing the serpent's small, murderous brain and rousing it to peril that now charged out of the tunnel with a roared challenge.

As Beowulf strode forward, shield up, a torrent of flame met him. The fire struck and seared the shield, licking about the rims, and Beowulf felt the heat of that attack. Another blast scalded the metal. He would not have much time but must close now with the beast.

The dragon reared, coiled, and struck. Viper jaws unhinged, fangs propelled lethally forward only to meet unyielding iron. Beowulf rocked with the impact, caught his balance, and faded to one side, striking with all his strength where the neck and leathery wing met. The blade struck scale and bone harder than itself. Driven by and meeting hardness beyond its own temper, the blade shattered with a shriek of sundered metal. Beowulf could only fall back as another gout of flame covered his shield face. Blast after blast scorched the metal now glowing dull red in spots, nearly too hot to hold. Beowulf backed cautiously, aware of a long-forgotten sinking in his stomach, sick animal fear, and he realized with a shock that the animal in him very much wanted to live.

"Sword!" he cried to Wiglaf as another inferno washed over the shield. "Wiglaf, help!"

In the tunnel entrance, shriveled himself with a fear he had not thought possible until now, Wiglaf spun about to his men. "Follow me."

They didn't move. In their blanched faces Wiglaf saw the image of his own paralyzing fear.

"Come *on!*" He raised his shield through the worst moment of his life. With a snarl of contempt for his own cowardice more than theirs, Wiglaf tore the spear from one man's slack grip and hurled it at the dragon. He willed his legs to move but they refused. In another moment, he would stand frozen and useless as the rest. That could not be, *could* not. If he failed now, he failed forever. Who would trust or follow him? Wiglaf found his voice and the sharp sound tore him loose—

"To me, demon—to me!"

—with the will dredged from some unthinkable resource to charge as the dragon, freshly enraged by the spear's glancing but painful wound, swept aside the ineffectual shaft and turned on the new danger. They had come to take its treasure. With a high-pitched scream of rage and flame, the dragon met Wiglaf, who cast aside the burning linden shield to snatch up Beowulf's, wincing at the heat of it, and thrust it before him, felt it batter against the dragon's snout as he struck with his sword.

"Wiglaf, take care!" Burned and wounded, without protection of any kind, Beowulf knew their swords were futile unless they could pierce the vulnerable underbelly. As Wiglaf closed again, striking at the beast's shoulder, Beowulf drew his dagger and crouched, seeking opportunity.

Both underestimated the dragon's speed and an unforeseen

weapon. Lashing in pain, the long tail whipped around, sweeping both men off their feet. The serpentine head writhed back and forth, streaking a long line of flame across the cave and into the tunnel.

Sweating cold with terror but no less fascinated by what repelled him, Yan had crept forward among the others to stand in their front rank. He saw the king and Wiglaf knocked aside like frail reeds and the long daub of flame rush at *him*. Yan shrank back with a bleat of terror, but someone blocked his way. He was shoved roughly forward as the flames singed him. Stung, giddy with fright, Yan fled the only way he could, his brain blanked white of all but the need to save his life. He scooped up the fallen spear and charged screaming, point leveled. So they closed, killer and killer. The spear found the unarmed belly and drove home.

The stricken dragon rocked back on its haunches, great bat wings flaring. Beowulf rose and stumbled forward. The dragon slashed at Yan, who could only push harder on the spear, unable to let go. Now Wiglaf was on his feet again, moving in with sword raised. Beowulf hurled himself at the belly of the beast, stabbing with the dagger, rending a wound long as his arm. He felt a quick, sharp pain in his neck, then nothing at all.

Yan trembled violently with the aftershock of mortal fear, mind numb as his flesh. As the others laid old Beowulf to one side, Yan stared at the beast he had impossibly helped to kill. The spear was still in his grip, steaming with the dragon's fiery blood.

He felt nothing beyond the sudden, heavy need to lie down and sleep for a year. Then the owner of the spear—fine, stout hearts *they* turned out—came and took it from him, but Wiglaf wouldn't have that, grabbed the weapon away, broke the shaft across, and flung the pieces at the sorry boy's feet, weeping as if something inside him were broken with the ash shaft. He went to kneel by old Beowulf—painfully, with burned hands, his mail rent over ugly wounds that would become the first scars on a new king. Yan's lip curled in mute disgust. Scars were worth more to these Geats than common sense.

Anyone could see the old man wouldn't last long, torn as he was and that big wound in his neck. Not much blood; no, that was where the poison went in. As the numbness wore off, Yan's own wounds began to sting and he saw the stains soaking through his threadbare tunic.

Oh, no. I'm hurt bad as them. I'm going to die. Please don't let me die.

He opened the blood-sodden garment in a new fear, afraid to know how bad it was. A long slash from shoulder to hip, but maybe not that deep. Thank whatever gods were watching today, he wouldn't die. Yan dared to breathe easier and his sharp wits began to function again. Lying all about and ground under his worn shoes was more gold and silver than he could count in a year, even if he could reckon such numbers. Clear to Yan now why old Rome fell: All their money was right here. He shot a furtive glance at the others. They were grouped about the dying king. They wouldn't miss the little he could hide away. That was only fair. He would be free, and freedmen were paid for their work.

Beowulf rose slowly to consciousness to find Wiglaf kneeling beside him. He tried to move his head; the effort was far too much. His whole body burned and throbbed with the venom creeping through him toward his heart. He knew he was dying.

Done it this time. Well enough, but I feel sorry for the boys. They can't look at me. "Wiglaf?"

"Here, brave lord."

"I can't move at all. Is the serpent dead?"

"It is," Wiglaf choked. "You have killed it."

"And you." Beowulf weakly clasped the hand of the young man who must now rebuild and claim their raven-doomed throne. "And Yan. Who would have thought him capable of that?"

Wiglaf ducked his head away. "He shamed us. Warriors outfaced by a foreign slave. Disgrace . . ."

"Never mind, boy. Bring him here, let me speak to him."

When Yan was put before him, Beowulf asked to be raised a little so that his head could rest on the Wylfing's knees. Cradled so, he gave his last commands. "Keep my promise, Wiglaf. Be a king in small as well as great. Give Yan his freedom."

"From this moment, he has that."

"When the fire lifts my spirit to Odin, bring my ashes here and bury them where I fell. Seal the cave forever, the dragon and this blighted hoard with me. You hear? All of it. Bury the curse, Wiglaf. End it. And let fires ever be fueled for ships, blind in night and fog, to find their way by Beowulf's Tower. Swear it."

Strangled with grief, Wiglaf could only nod his obedience.

"My last venture and your first, king of Geats. We routed darkness and forever make this a place of light."

Beowulf struggled for breath, knowing he had little left. Too soon, so much undone, unexplained, unhelped. In the sick-white faces of the other young men—oh, he knew so well what festered in their souls, worse than the venom reaching to stop his heart: Already the self-loathing and self-exile to which he had condemned himself so long ago that would inevitably bend and warp these too into the agonized posture of heroes. No—he wanted to rise up and help them—no. Whatever fell out, give them the chance to find that men like marble mixed flaw with strength.

Drifting away from life, Beowulf heard weeping that Wiglaf could no longer control. The boy must feel even now the harsh weight of the crown descend on his head as a burden never to be laid aside, never eased until death, some treasure of youth flown and never to be found again. Someone had soiled his pure picture of life. Shamed by his tears, holding in his young heart the broken shards of a shattered faith, Wiglaf's grief burst forth in the guise of fury against the nearest target, his companions. He rose, speaking with as much cold dignity as he could manage.

"So our king fares forth and bids me end the curse. So I will, but not before he and you hear my own."

"Wiglaf." Beowulf's voice was faint. "Don't."

"It must be said." Wiglaf pointed to Yan. "This Wylfing slave, whom I called a worthless pig, this outlander took up the spear and, doing so, denied it to such as you forever."

In the storm of his emotion, Wiglaf wanted to move, to lunge at them, but he resisted the urge. From this hour, he would be what he must and look it.

"You were my companions. No more. You who sat in Beowulf's hall, sons of honored thanes, lapped in his gifts of armor, bright weapons, and rings; who boasted over mead of the deeds with which you would repay him at his need—how could you be so false or he so blind to mistake such hollow things for men?"

Beowulf tried to raise his head. It weighed too much. "Wiglaf, let them be."

"Let? How? How can you bear to look on them?"

No, Wiglaf had not yet come to that healing mercy. Among their kind, enemies were not forgiven but dragged into death if possible with one's last stroke and dying breath. Yet Justin's carpenter had spent that breath to forgive. The act had struck Beowulf as ridiculous and servile. Retribution and payment were the way of his kind, and only now could he dimly divine what Justin drove at and Eligius before him. Kind, wise Eligius who saw so much. There must be some hope against dragons in a world that bore such men.

But Wiglaf condemned them icily, pointing at one ashen face after another. "Never will you sit among warriors again. You fled honor, so honor flies from you now, and all who share your name and blood will carry it henceforth not as a banner, but a brand. Our life is iron, *must* be iron, pressed between enemies and the sea. The fewer the folk, the greater their spirit if they are to survive. Hope not for that here, any of you. From this day, you quit the land I call mine now more in sorrow than in pride, hide your faces and creep away. Were I as you," he finished, turning his back on them, "I would not suffer myself to darken the light of one more day."

"Lord Wiglaf, our king begs you to leave off."

The flat foreign voice eloquently undercut Wiglaf's righteous wrath. None of them would have expected it from little Yan. The Wylfing looked up at the seething king-to-be and spoke the one simple truth he knew.

"You make too much of it. It wasn't like that. I was too scared to know what I was doing. Weren't you?"

Wiglaf glared at him, then turned away. "No."

Yan knew he'd spoken more than he should but stood by the facts, humble as they might be. "Well, *I* was."

Beowulf rallied the last of his strength. "Wiglaf, come close. And you, Yan. Listen."

They had to bend close to hear the barely articulated words.

"They will live with it as they must. Believe me, Wiglaf: As surely as they will come to what you are, you will sometime stumble and fall to what they suffer today. You won't be able to help yourself—as once I could not."

"No," Wiglaf protested. "Not a king. How could I allow—?"

"Boy, don't waste what little time I have. Yan, you hear me?"

"I thank you for my freedom, lord."

"No more than my word, but do me one last errand. Tell Father Justin I know now what he meant. Can you remember that?"

"My word on it."

"And that . . . he must always watch for dragons among his own."

Yan promised. He understood none of this, but for the first time in his lowly life in a world where honor was a thing among masters, ever out of his reach, he had pledged his word to a king who accepted it without question. His life would go on or not, but the moment nourished Yan deeply somehow. He was almost tempted to confess the coins he pilfered, but practicality routed conscience. He was not *that* tempted.

"Beasts among his own," Beowulf labored. "Asgard will burn and all the gods pass—tell him I said all, Yan. But the dragons will always be with him."

Dragons and dearer things. Behind his eyelids he ran with Minna on his shoulders across the flower-strewn meadow to where Ina waited, holding out her arms to gather both of them to her.

Beowulf opened his eyes and smiled at Wiglaf. "Carry me out of here, son. Lay me in the light where the War Maidens can find me, and let me sleep."

Toward evening of the next day, under a sky turbid with wind-driven cloud, the funeral procession filed along the beach toward the readied pyre. Four honored thanes carried Beowulf. Wiglaf paced behind these. Just after him came Ina by herself, and then the noble Geat families in order of rank. Consigned to the rear of the solemn march with craftsmen and farmers, Justin trudged with his converts. By Wiglaf's stern order, any Christian prayers for the forthfared king must be silent.

By Beowulf's last wish, other workmen had labored through the evening before and all this day lowering stone from the cliff to build a beacon atop the tower that would henceforth bear his name. There a fire was laid with long-burning woods and, when all was prepared, the freedman Yan rode the sledge down to the new eyrie and stood by ready to light the beacon.

Not far down the beach, the Geats gathered in a wide ring about the funeral pyre. The four bearers of the pall—Canute, Ulf, Gorm, and Wexstan—laid Beowulf's body at its summit and reverently placed his arms about him. In the baldric, his richest sword; at his other hip, the broken blade to show Valhalla that though the iron failed in final proof, their king did not. They placed the iron shield at his feet, and over its fire-blackened face spread the torn ring mail from his last, mortal combat.

Wiglaf stood at the head of the pyre, Ina at its foot as the chief thanes formed a ring of mourning about them. The sea wind blew chill over the beach, colder in the hearts of Wiglaf and his people.

The shaman Arn fired a torch and passed it to Wiglaf, who thrust it deep into the tinder impregnated with resin and grease. As the flames licked upward, Ina lifted her arms in the funeral lament. Her heart was in the outpoured sound, as if sorrow itself, in a moment of mastery, gave her more than human voice. She sang not for her lover but those Geats around her, gave them the ritual of grief expected of their bereavement, but her soul rendered a gentler requiem.

No, I will not dirge for what is dead and lost. Nothing's taken from me, nothing gone. Your hand, as Hondshew's, is on me still, longer worn and shaping me to love day by year as sea will round a stone.

Snarls in the wool on the loom, we said. So we were: subversive hearts, my love. Though fools will come to harp a song for other fools, drone of dynasties and who-killed-whom, call you hero-king or demi-god, I'll mouth the sorrow they expect of me, but will not weep where I have been content.

This fire is not our flame; that's mine alone to warm me through the needless years to come when I wake smiling to another pointless day for lovely reasons far too secret and too small for bards to bother with. Be glad, sweet man. Give the Geats their Wiglaf and their fire and let them pass us by.

Head bowed over his sword, Wiglaf shivered in his soul, thinking less of today than heavy tomorrows, hoping he looked a king or at least the promise of one the like of him they sent to Odin. Already there was too much to do. He must always think ahead while the wounds and burns still rankled his flesh. He had been tempted to overlook Beowulf's wish about the treasure, use some at least for the people's need.

Canute counseled the same and even a more urgent purpose: to buy better relations with Frank and Frise, peace with Swedes, and to send Geat keels forth on the sea road in trade rather than war.

"We are the finest craftsmen and traders in the world, my lord. The best bargainers sailing the best keels on the ocean or up the shallowest river, from the Russ to the Middle Sea. What need to conquer the world when we can *shape* it?"

Possibly true. Sick as he was, Canute knew the world, and great Hrothgar thought such policy no dishonor, but Wiglaf's council in the main said no. That would seem weakness, they argued, an exhausted, womanish plea for mercy disgraceful to Geats. Wiglaf's will pressed its seal hard upon honor. A new king must be firm. The hoard would be buried. Evil it was and evil it brought. Geats would survive and prevail as they always had, through war courage.

Wiglaf dared not wince from his wounds nor show one hint of the secret worst of them, that moment in the cave when Yan's courage confessed so easily the natural fear that he himself could not own. His former companions, the wretched mirrors of his guilt, were already banished and gone by his decree and the tight-lipped assent of his thanes. That was hard; not their fate but their fathers' eyes when they had no choice but to accept. Each of them had laid his head on Wiglaf's knee in oath of loyalty, but already, Arn advised caution against the price of these banishments.

"Those who guard you while you sleep, let them be only those you trust."

And trust them only, the colder voice whispered in him.

So he must choose carefully, yet his conduct against the dragon was a known credit, the first earnest of his worthiness. He wished that pride were not already rotten with shame, that he could forget the dying king's prophecy.

His own courage had fled in that horrible instant like fragile glass falling and snatched back just before it shattered. But what if Beowulf spoke true? The old man was wise as he was brave. *What if I sometime fail as they did, a coward frozen, unable to act, breaking against fear like Beowulf's false sword when it means disaster as well as dishonor?*

Wiglaf felt only an emptiness where desperation huddled alone. That could happen next time or the next. The crown was cold on his brow, weighted with fears heavier than death or dragons.

I must follow the Geat way. Canute is wrong, my father and the others right. Offers and overtures will seem weakness to our enemies. I must take up every challenge upon the moment. No, more: I must not wait until Swedes know of our plight but take war to them now even as Beowulf flung himself at the dragon. One swift, daring stroke to end them all—warriors, women, children, steadings, all. Men are named for their chief renown. Beowulf the Great, Canute the Wise. To Hel then with soft policy. Wiglaf will study not to be loved but feared. Let Geats and all others clepe me Terrible, Death-Bringer, vengeance quick as my sword, resolve as tempered-hard.

And yet something natural in the young king, something born of woman, mourned keenly as did Beowulf's handfast woman now. Wiglaf clutched the sword hilt tighter, learning with bitter astonishment how ordinary a man was a king after all, and how little of that he might ever show.

Lowest of the low all his life, for this moment Yan could look down on all of them from the tower eyrie and take some pleasure in the inversion. The funeral blaze was high now, sending the old king up in black, greasy smoke to his gods or wherever. Kings got to go that way; at least that Christ-man, what *he* said gave a poor, honest man like Yan a place in the boat. He squeezed from his lean store enough charity to wish the old king good passing, but the woman down there was for sure making a sight of her sorrow. Look at the old bitch; you'd think no one close ever went west before.

Now the priest passed a new torch to Wiglaf, who thrust it into the pyre, then turned and walked stiffly through the people toward Beowulf's Tower, the fire held high.

Yan dropped a hemp line over the wall. It was time. The low sun was a feeble glow behind clouds. Yan waited while the young king secured the torch to the rope, then hauled it up.

Don't he look proud, now he's got it all! I caught some of what the old man told him. Lived a long time, that one did, and not the worst as kings go, but he died bloody like all the rest, and that fool Wiglaf will go on the fire just like him and my dinner, no difference, except they almost took me with them. No, thanks. When I die, I'll go full fed and warm in bed. Least I saw some gold for my trouble, hard earned as it was.

He couldn't see the body now for the enveloping flames. Yan thrust the torch into the laid tinder and logs, and the beacon fire rose up from the blood and heart of Beowulf, dedicated with Yan's sour sympathy.

Poor old bastard. No better off than me, were you?

In the background where now he must always remain, if Wiglaf allowed him a place at all, Justin silently mouthed the *Credo*. He dared not hope for friendship or support from Wiglaf, not yet, perhaps not ever. A civilized, educated man should always entertain more questions than answers. Today, both whirled in his mind and ground to incoherent rubble. Such mad worlds could not turn but did. Not long ago he swore such things could not be but were.

And he was troubled to his core by Beowulf's last message delivered by Yan. The Faith which, so short a while ago, *was* his breath and being, had gone numb and ceased to sustain him at all. Was this what Eligius passed through and foretold sometime for him, the crisis of belief? Feeling naked and fragmented, meaningless, random flesh in a place and time with no significance beyond the arbitrary impulse of the moment?

My God, I can't find you. Help, teach, explain to me why I feel nothing but chaos straining to rend blood from sense, all flying apart, Thor's brute hammer shattering Peter's Rock. As I cannot live without faith, these people live by madness grown to custom and called honor. Madness is the very mortar that binds them together, hardened to purpose and reason, and reason itself becomes counterfeit.

My own dragons? Perhaps in this chaos I sense them already, my old friend. Where are they and whence, crouched on what futile, worthless hoard? What shape and what voice? How will they be called?

Credo in unum Deum—

Help me against the dragons and the dark.

FOR HIS ULTIMATE CRIME, the murder of Odin's perfect son Balder, Loki lay bound in unbreakable chains deep in the underworld beneath the roots of the World Tree, Yggdrasil. Directly over his head on a twisted outcropping of one root, a serpent, prisoned to that purpose by Odin's command, spat venom into Loki's face and ever would until Ragnarok, the foretold destruction of Asgard and the gods.

Every creature and plant had sworn to Frigga not to harm her golden boy—all but the insignificant young mistletoe. Loki found this oversight admirably convenient and fashioned a dart from the mistletoe stem, then guided the blind god Hoder's hand in hurling it at Balder.

Neatly done, Loki thought. *Right through the heart.* He looked up but hastily shut his eyes against the next viscous gobbet of venom from the serpent's fangs.

True, he might have been somewhat excessive in disposing of bird-brained Balder, but so was this punishment for so trifling a loss. Perhaps in the next fumbling turn of Creation's wheel, he could be something innocuous like a patron saint. The novelty of the Christ-man was becoming fashionable in Midgard like all the miracle faiths before it and so many more to come. Yes, the very thing: a minor saint of low visibility but creative, invoked by children, thieves, and liars when they required authority to swear by.

But then this revolution hadn't been all bad; he did have fascinating loves and unusual children in general. Who else could have spawned the World Serpent and a wolf like Fenrir? And if Sigyn took after Volla's looks, who but himself gave her such inward beauty?

But his daughter Hel, who ruled and gave her name to this shadowed outback of an underworld—Hel who was tall, broad, and bleak, a desert for company, a rigid pillar of self-righteousness, eyes that saw nothing but fault and a downturned line of a mouth like a lid clamped hard over any impulse light or gay, barely woman in form and none in heart—how did *she* spring from his loins or the restless fire of his spirit? Loki could remember neither the moment nor the motives, but he must have been dismally sober when Hel was conceived.

A shadow stirred far down the vast hall, moved into the light toward him. Hel was coming, clad and hooded in gray, to stand over her incarcerated father, judgmental as always. Loki acknowledged her with an inward sigh. Hel's virtues were boreal. Like all Good Women, she had an undiluted passion for the reformation of errant men.

"Daughter, would it strain justice to move me beyond the range of our incontinent companion above? He drools unceasingly."

Hel's implacable mouth creased deeper in its grim line. "No. You deserve this and it is—"

"—'good for you,' " Loki finished wearily. "So be it. If my life has been reckless, clearly you are the reckoning."

"That is your nature, this is mine. I do not rule the happiest of kingdoms. But I bring news. You have a fellow inmate, my sister Sigyn." Hel clarified with audible disapproval: "My *half* sister."

Though the venom stung his face, Loki's spirits vaulted high as Asgard. "Sigyn? Wonderful! Haste her to me."

"Yes, you'll suit well together," Hel opined in parting. "Vanity, vanity."

Her meaning eluded Loki until Sigyn emerged from the shadows, hurrying down the limitless hall toward him. Loki's heart leaped. She was as he had last seen her: in white kirtle and cloak, her shining hair the color of new-struck gold falling over her shoulder in one thick braid bound with silver wire filigreed in small emeralds. Her father admired her lovingly.

"Changeable as I am, I must have been dreaming on love itself when I begat you." He stirred in his chains as the serpent spat again. "Welcome, child. Try to ignore the snake."

The radiant young woman knelt beside him, kissing his lips. "Dear Father, we'll be together always now."

"You've been judged then?"

Sigyn appeared not at all downcast. "By Odin and Frigga themselves. My first and last visit to Asgard. And you're right, it is so frightfully dull. However—" From the folds of her gossamer mantle, she produced an exquisite goblet. "I borrowed this from Valaskjalf. When they told me of the serpent, I thought it would help. Carved from a solid ruby. Vulgar, but useful."

"Frigga was always house-proud. Thank you, daughter."

Sigyn held the cup over Loki's face to catch the virulent stream. "Have you seen my son Grendel?"

"There's been no word. Perhaps he'll turn up one year or next, who can tell? Has Ragnarok begun?"

"Soon, I think," Sigyn estimated with cool satisfaction. "Asgard will burn and Beowulf with the rest, last and longest. He was at my trial, did you know? Actually presumed to forgive me. I wanted to bite his head off—but then I saw Shild."

Sigyn would have lingered with the memory, but the serpent spat again, outdoing its malevolent office. The ruby cup was almost full.

Loki tried to shift a little for ease, but the chains held him fast. "You would think that something in the cosmos might perpetuate itself beside malignance. Mind the cup, Sigyn."

"Yes, Father." She gazed around at the dreary hall vaulting over them. "That spiteful woman—I *don't* want to call her sister—said I must empty it beyond the hall. But we're a family again. Grendel *will* come, I know he will."

Sigyn glowed with the pure light of her dream. "And perhaps even Shild. He did remember me . . . I will hurry with the cup."

Loki tried to smile at her through a fresh anointment from above. "Please. If you would."

He waited then, eyes closed against the rain of judgment. The far end of Hel's hall was lost in an infinity of shadow. Sigyn must go a very long way again and again.

The venom dripped. And dripped.

Loki endured, waiting for Sigyn to return, waiting for Ragnarok and the whole ridiculous cycle to begin all over again. His sigh echoed through the underworld and rose, part of the night wind over doomed Helsingborg.

The serpent spat.

What a cosmic *bore.*

ACKNOWLEDGMENTS
AND AN AFTERWORD

AN ANONYMOUS POEM dating from the eighth century, *Beowulf* may be one of the least known classics of our culture outside academic circles, defined in a recent newspaper article as "a book *no* one has read." I hope the present effort will send interested readers to the original work in such fine translations as those of Burton Raffel (Mentor Books, 1963), Howell D. Chickering (Anchor Books, 1977), and the graceful prose version of David Wright (Penguin Books, 1957).

John Gardner's existential *Grendel* aside, rendering the poem per se into novel form presents pitfalls to writer and reader alike because it describes a remote culture to an audience within that culture and not far removed in time from the poem's setting, hearers as familiar with those values and events as Americans with the Civil War. Secondly, the *Beowulf* poet presented a pagan world to a Christianized audience and framed the whole in the moral sentiments of the new religion, though it would be unfair to call this a flaw. The poet in his century had no need for historical method or perspective since in universal Christian belief of the time, Christ held the transient world in his hand and his second coming was imminent. Thus the confusing double image of pagan drama crammed bag and baggage into the Procrustean bed of a newly dominant and very intolerant faith.

The internal digressions are also a problem: accounts of former wars, treacheries, and heroes familiar to the poet's audience but ruinous intrusion in a modern novel adaptation. Conversely, much of what a modern novel requires was unnecessary to the poet's original work. Of Beowulf's boat companions, only Hondshew is named, though hardly fleshed out. Grendel and his nameless mother are simply there, explained only as "children of Cain," though to the Anglo-Saxon audience, that was enough. Cain was the original outcast of Genesis, and the Norse mythos already had its giants and monsters for ready identification. For today's reader, however, such simplistic devices deprive the story of far too much dramatic meat. Consider our own enduring Grendels, like Frankenstein's creation or Dracula. Is it mindless rage and blood thirst alone or alienated need and longing in these figures that forever mingle pity with fascinated horror in our imagination?

Then the problem of Beowulf himself. As a peripheral character in Henry Treece's *The Green Man*, Beowulf works well as a grim brute, or as fateful nemesis in John Gardner's *Grendel*, where he is not the focal character. But where Beowulf must carry much of the story and reader identification, an indomitable destroyer strong as thirty men, who never knows fear, dishonor, or one fleeting thought unworthy of a superhero, he presents neither dimension nor relief and comes off as dramatically exciting as a dead whale, large but unmoving. No one can seriously present such a figure as human truth to our violent century, which has seen four major wars survived by so many men as badly wounded as those they buried.

This is why I depicted Grendel and Sigyn as near-humans who longed for beauty, however fleeting, and Beowulf as a kind of reverse Hamlet. Hamlet is burdened with a father's command that he cannot fulfill until his action is futile and too late. Beowulf succumbs early, not having that particular strength to resist, and so "dies" in life much as the dragon did. By this token, at the end, he can understand and forgive what young Wiglaf condemns as cowardice in the companions who failed their king in his last battle, and say with deep conviction when death is near, "I am weary of the tomb. I want to live."

The poet spoke to his own century. I have tried to make Beowulf speak to ours.

I must give considerable thanks to Dr. Susan Shwartz for keen scholarly insights and for passing on certain critical materials—and above all to Persia Woolley for critiquing these pages day by day with unfailing encouragement when it was sorely needed.

—P.G.

F
God   tow
GODWIN, PARKE.
  The tower of Beowulf.

28200